Dear Reader:

Remember Dillon Savich from *The Cove*? He's now the head of the FBI's Criminal Apprehension Unit (CAU), where he has developed predictive analogue programs to aid in the capture of serial killers.

Enter Lacey Sherlock, a very well-qualified new agent who seems bright and eager and on the up-and-up. But is she really?

When there's a vicious murder in Boston, she's off like a shot, lying to Savich.

When Savich finds out what's going on, he realizes they'll all be in deep trouble, maybe even victims themselves, if he and Sherlock don't find out who murdered her sister seven years before.

Are you ready to "walk the walk"? Are you ready to see who's waiting for you at the center of the maze? There are mysteries to solve and puzzles to sort through before you get to an ending that will have you bolting your front door, fast.

I hope you enjoy traveling through this bizarre maze to find out what happened both today and seven years ago.

Email me at readmoi@gmail.com and tell me what you think of *The Maze*. You can visit my website at catherinecoulter.com, and come talk to me daily on Facebook.com/catherinecoulterbooks.

Catherine Coulter

THE MAZE

An FBI Thriller

Catherine Coulter

JOVE BOOKS, NEW YORK

THE BERKLEY PUBLISHING GROUP
Published by the Penguin Group
Penguin Group (USA) LLC
375 Hudson Street, New York, New York 10014

USA • Canada • UK • Ireland • Australia • New Zealand • India • South Africa • China

penguin.com

A Penguin Random House Company

THE MAZE

A Jove Book / published by arrangement with the author

For information, address: The Berkley Publishing Group,
a division of Penguin Group (USA) LLC,
375 Hudson Street, New York, New York 10014.

ISBN: 978-0-515-12249-7

PUBLISHING HISTORY
G. P. Putnam's Sons hardcover edition / June 1997
Jove mass-market edition / April 1998

PRINTED IN THE UNITED STATES OF AMERICA

40 39 38 37 36 35 34

Cover art and design by Rob Wood/Wood Ronsaville Harlin, Inc.

THE MAZE

San Francisco, California
May 15

IT WOULDN'T STOP, EVER.

She couldn't breathe. She was dying. She sat upright in her bed wheezing, trying to control the terror. She turned on the lamp beside her bed. There was nothing there. No, just shadows that kept the corners dark and frightening. But the door was closed. She always closed her bedroom door at night and locked it, then tilted a chair against it so that its back was snug against the doorknob. Just for good measure.

She stared at that door. It didn't move. It didn't so much as rattle in its frame. The knob did not turn. No one was on the other side trying to get in.

No one this time.

She made herself look over toward the window. She'd wanted to put bars on all the windows when she moved in seven months before, but at the last minute she decided that if she did she would have made herself a prisoner forever. Instead she'd switched to the fourth-floor apartment. There were two floors above her and no balconies. No one could come in through the window. And no one would think she was crazy because she lived on the fourth floor. It was a good move. There was no way she could continue living at home, where Belinda had lived. Where Douglas had lived.

The images were in her mind, always faded, always blurred, but still there and still menacing: bloody, but just beyond her ability to put them in focus. She was in a large dark space, huge, she couldn't see the beginning or the end of it.

But there was a light, a narrow focused light, and she heard a voice. And the screams. Loud, right there on her. And there was Belinda, always Belinda.

She was still choking on the fear. She didn't want to get up, but she made herself. She had to go to the bathroom. Thank God the bathroom was off the bedroom. Thank God she didn't have to unlock the bedroom door, pull the chair back from beneath the knob, and open it onto the dark hallway.

She flipped the bathroom light on before she went into the room, then blinked rapidly at the harsh light. She saw movement from the corner of her eye. Her throat clogged with terror. She whirled around: It was only herself in the mirror.

She stared at her reflection. She didn't recognize the wild woman before her. All she saw was fear: the twitching eyes, the sheen of sweat on her forehead, her hair ratty, her sleep shirt damp with perspiration.

She leaned close to the mirror. She stared at the pathetic woman whose face was still tense with fear. She realized in that moment that if she didn't make some serious changes the woman in the mirror would die.

To the woman staring back at her, she said, "Seven months ago I was supposed to go study music at Berkeley. I was the best. I loved making music, all the way from Mozart to John Lennon. I wanted to win the Fletcher competition and go to Juilliard. But I didn't. Now I'm afraid of everything, including the dark."

She turned slowly away from the mirror and walked back into her bedroom. She walked to the window, turned the three locks that held it firmly in place, and pulled it up. It was difficult. The window hadn't been opened since she'd moved in.

She looked out into the night. There was a quarter moon. There were stars flooding the sky. The air was cool and fresh. She could see Alcatraz, Angel Island beyond it. She could see the few lights in Sausalito, just across the bay. The Transamerica building was brightly lit, a beacon in downtown San Francisco.

She turned away and walked to the bedroom door. She stood there a very long time. Finally she pulled the chair away and set it where it belonged, in the corner beside a reading light. She unlocked the door. No more, she thought, staring at that door, no more.

She flung it open. She stepped out into the hallway and stopped, every burgeoning whisper of courage in her freezing as she couldn't help but hear the sound of a creaking board not more than twenty feet away. The sound came again. No, it wasn't a creak; it was a lighter sound. It seemed to be coming from the small foyer by the front door. Who could be toying with her this way? Her own breath whooshed out. She was shaking, so frightened she could taste copper in her mouth. Copper? She'd bitten her lip, drawn blood.

How much longer could she live like this?

She dashed forward, turning on every light as she went. There was the sound again, this time like something lightly bumping against a piece of furniture—something that was a lot smaller than she was, something that was afraid of her. Then she saw it scurry into the kitchen. She burst out laughing, then slowly sank to the floor, her hands over her face as she sobbed.

2

SHE WOULD GET TO THE TOP of that rope if it killed her. And it just might. She could actually feel each individual muscle in her arms pulling, stretching, feel the burning pain, the rippling cramps that were very close to knotting up on her. If that happened, she'd go sprawling to the mat below. Her brain already felt numb, but that was okay. Her brain wasn't climbing. It had just gotten her into this fix. And this was only the second round. It seemed as if she'd been climbing this rope since she was born.

Just two more feet. She could do it. She heard MacDougal's steady, unhurried breathing beside her. From the corner of her eye she saw his huge fists cover that rope, methodically clamping down one fist over the other, not consuming that rope as he usually did. No, he was keeping pace with her. He wasn't going to leave her. She owed him. This was an important test. This one really mattered.

"I see that pathetic look, Sherlock. You're whining even though you're not saying anything. Get those twerpy arms working, pull!"

She grabbed that rope just three inches above her left hand and pulled with all her strength.

"Come on, Sherlock," MacDougal said, hanging beside her, grinning at her, the bastard. "Don't wimp out on me now. I've worked with you for two months. You're up to twelve-pound weights. All right, so you can only do ten reps on your biceps, but you can do twenty-five on your triceps. Come on now, do it, don't just hang there like a girl."

Whine? She didn't have enough breath to whine. He was goading her, doing a good job of it actually. She tried to get annoyed. There wasn't a pissed bone in her body, just pain, deep and burning. Eight more inches, no, more like nine inches. It would take her two years to get those nine inches. She saw her right hand pull free of the rope, grab the bar at the very top of the knotted rope that was surely too far for her to make in one haul, but her right hand closed over that bar and she knew she'd either do it or she wouldn't.

"You can do it, Sherlock. Remember last week in Hogan's Alley when that guy pissed you off? Tried to handcuff you and haul you off as a hostage? You nearly killed him. You wound up having to apologize to him. That took more strength than this. Think mean. Think dead-meat thoughts. Kill the rope. Pull!"

She didn't think of the guy in Hogan's Alley; no, she thought of that monster, focused on a face she'd never seen, focused on the soul-deep misery he'd heaped upon her for seven years. She wasn't even aware when she hauled herself up those final inches.

She hung there, breathing hard, clearing her mind of that horrible time. MacDougal was laughing beside her, not even out of breath. But he was all brute strength she'd told him many times; he'd been born in a gym, under a pile of free weights.

She'd done it.

Mr. Petterson, their instructor, was standing below them. He was at least two stories below them; she would have sworn to that. He yelled up, "Good going, you two. Come on down now. MacDougal, you could have made it a little faster, like half the time you took. You think you're on vacation?"

MacDougal shouted down to Petterson since she didn't have a breath in her lungs, "We're coming, sir!" He said to her, grinning so wide she could see the gold filling in a molar, "You did good, Sherlock. You have gotten stronger. Thinking mean thoughts helped, too. Let's get down and let two other mean dudes climb this sucker."

She needed no encouragement. She loved going down. The

pain disappeared when her body knew it was almost over. She was down nearly as fast as MacDougal. Mr. Petterson waved a pencil at them, then scribbled something on his pad. He looked up and nodded. "That was it, Sherlock. You made it within the time limit. As for you, Mac, you were way too slow, but the sheet says you pass so you pass. Next!"

"Piece of cake," MacDougal said, as he handed her a towel to wipe off her face. "Look at all that sweat on you."

If she'd had the energy, she would have slugged him.

She was in Hogan's Alley, the highest-crime-rate city in the United States. She knew just about every inch of every building in this town, certainly better than the actors who were paid eight dollars an hour to play bad guys, better than many of the Bureau employees who were witnesses and robbers alike. Hogan's Alley looked like a real town; it even had a mayor and a postmistress, but they didn't live here. Nobody really lived here or really worked here. It was the FBI's own American town, rife with criminals to be caught, situations to be resolved, preferably without killing anyone. Instructors didn't like innocent bystanders to be shot.

Today she and three other trainees were going to catch a bank robber. She hoped. They were told to keep their eyes open, nothing else. It was a parade day in Hogan's Alley. A festive occasion, and that made it all the more dangerous. There was a crowd of people, drinking sodas and eating hot dogs. It wasn't going to be easy. Chances were that the guy was going to be one of the people trying to blend in with the crowd, trying to look as innocent as an everyday guy; she'd stake a claim on that. She would have given anything if they'd gotten just a brief glance at the robber, but they hadn't. It was a critical situation, lots of innocent civilians milling about and a bank robber who would probably run out of the bank, a bank robber who was probably very dangerous.

She saw Buzz Alport, an all-night waiter at a truck stop off I-95. He was whistling, looking as if he didn't have a care in the world. No, Buzz wasn't the bad guy today. She knew him too well. His face flushed scarlet when he played the bad guy. She tried to memorize every face, so she'd be able to spot the robber if he suddenly appeared. She slowly worked the crowd, calm and unhurried, the way she'd been trained.

She saw some visitors from the Hill, standing on the sidelines, watching the agents' role-playing simulations. The trainees would have to be careful. It wouldn't look good for the Bureau if any of them killed a visiting congressman.

It began. She and Porter Forge, a southerner from Birmingham who spoke beautiful French without a hint of a drawl, saw a bank employee lurch out of the front doors, yelling at the top of his lungs, waving frantically at a man who had just fled through a side door. They got no more than a brief glimpse. They went after him. The perp dove into the crowd of people and disappeared. Because there were civilians around, they kept their guns holstered. If any one of them hurt a civilian, there'd be hell to pay.

Three minutes later they'd lost him.

It was then she saw Dillon Savich, an FBI agent and computer genius who taught occasional classes here at Quantico, standing next to a man she'd never seen before. Both were wearing sunglasses and blue suits and blue-gray ties.

She'd know Savich anywhere. She wondered what he was doing here at this particular time. Had he taught a class? She'd never heard about his being at Hogan's Alley. She stared hard at him. Was it possible that he was the suspect the bank employee had been waving at as he'd dashed into the crowd? Maybe. She tried to place him in that brief instant of memory. It was possible. Only thing was that he didn't look at all out of breath, and the bank robber had run out of the bank like Jesse James. Savich looked cool and disinterested.

Nah, it couldn't be Savich. Savich wouldn't join in the exercise, would he? Suddenly, she saw a man some distance away from her slowly slip his hand into his jacket. He was going for a gun. She yelled to Porter.

While the other trainees were distracted, Savich suddenly moved away from the man he'd been talking to and ducked behind three civilians. Three other civilians who were close to the other guy were yelling and shoving, trying to get out of the way.

What was going on here?

"Sherlock! Where'd he go?"

She began to smile even as other agents were pushing and shoving, trying desperately to sort out who was who. She never lost sight of Savich. She slipped into the crowd. It took her under a minute to come around him from behind.

There was a woman next to him. It was very possibly about to become a hostage situation. She saw Savich slowly reach out his hand toward the woman. She couldn't take the chance. She drew her gun, came right up behind him, and whispered in his ear as she pressed the nose of her 9mm SIG into the small of his back, "Freeze. FBI."

"Ms. Sherlock, I presume?"

She felt a moment of uncertainty, then quashed it. She had the robber. He was trying to rattle her. "Listen to me, buddy, that's not part of the script. You're not supposed to know me. Now, get your hands behind your back or you're going to be in big trouble."

"I don't think so," he said, and began to turn.

The woman next to them saw the gun, screamed, and yelled, "The robber's a woman! Here she is! She's going to kill a man. She's got a gun! Help!"

"Get your hands behind your back." But how was she going to get cuffs on him? The woman was still yelling. Other people were looking now, not knowing what to do. She didn't have much time.

"Do it or I'll shoot you."

He moved so quickly she didn't have a chance. He knocked her SIG out of her hand with a chop of his right hand, numbing her entire arm, bulled his head into her stomach and sent her flying backward, wheezing for breath, landing in a mass of petunias in the flower bed beside the Hogan's Alley Post Office.

He was laughing. The jerk was laughing at her. She was sucking in air as hard and fast as she could. Her stomach was on fire. He stuck out his hand to pull her up.

"You're under arrest," she said and slipped a small Lady Colt .38 from her ankle holster. She gave him a big grin. "Don't move or I guarantee you'll regret it. After I climbed that rope, I know I'm capable of anything."

His laughter died. He looked at the gun, then at her, up on

her elbows in the petunia bed. There were a half dozen men and women standing there watching, holding their breath. She yelled out, "Stay back, all of you. This man's dangerous. He robbed the bank. I didn't do it, he did. I'm FBI. Stay back!"

"That Colt isn't Bureau issue."

"Shut up. You so much as twitch and I'll shoot you."

He made a very small movement toward her, but she wasn't going to let him get her this time. He was into martial arts, was he? She knew she was smashing the petunias, but she didn't see any way around it. Mrs. Shaw would come after her because the flower beds were her pride and joy, but she was only doing her job. She couldn't let him get the better of her again.

She kept inching away from him, that Colt steady on his chest. She came up slowly, keeping her distance. "Turn around and put your hands behind you."

"I don't think so," he said again. She didn't even see his leg, but she did hear the rip of his pants. The Colt went flying onto the sidewalk.

She was caught off guard. Surely an escaping crook would turn tail and run, not stand there looking at her. He wasn't behaving the way he should. "How'd you do that?"

Where were her partners?

Where was Mrs. Shaw, the postmistress? She'd once caught the designated bank robber by threatening him with a frying pan.

Then he was on her. This time, she moved as quickly as he did. She knew he wouldn't hurt her, just disable her, jerk her onto her face and humiliate her in front of everyone, which would be infinitely worse than being actually hurt. She rolled to the side, came up, saw Porter Forge from the corner of her eye, caught the SIG from him, turned and fired. She got him in midleap.

The red paint spread all over the front of his white shirt, his conservative tie, and his dark blue suit.

He flailed about, managing to keep his balance. He straightened, stared down at her, stared down at his shirt, grunted, and fell onto his back into the flower bed, his arms flung out.

"Sherlock, you idiot, you just shot the new coach of Hogan's

Alley High School's football team!" It was the mayor of Hogan's Alley and he wasn't happy. He stood over her, yelling. "Didn't you read the paper? Didn't you see his picture? You live here and you don't know what's going on? Coach Savich was hired last week. You killed an innocent man."

"She also made me rip my pants," Savich said, coming up in a graceful motion. He shook himself, wiping dirt off his hands onto his filthy pants.

"He tried to kill me," she said, rising slowly, still pointing the SIG at him. "Also, he shouldn't be talking. He should be acting dead."

"She's right." Savich sprawled onto his back again, his arms flung out, his eyes closed.

"He was only defending himself," said the woman who'd yelled her head off. "He's the new coach and you killed him."

She knew she wasn't wrong.

"I don't know about that," Porter Forge said, that drawl of his so slow she could have said the same thing at least three times before he'd gotten it out. "Suh," he continued to the mayor who was standing at his elbow, "I believe I saw a wanted poster on this big fella. He's gone and robbed banks all over the South. Yep, that's where I saw his picture, on one of the Atlanta PD posters, suh. Sherlock here did well. She brought down a really bad guy."

It was an excellent lie, one to give her time to do something, anything, to save her hide.

She realized what had bothered her about him. His clothes didn't fit him right. She leaned over, reached her hands into Savich's pockets, and pulled out wads of fake one-hundred-dollar bills.

"I believe ya'll find the bank's serial numbers on the bills, suh. Don't you think so, Sherlock?"

"Oh yes, I surely do, Agent Forge."

"Take me away, Agent Sherlock," Savich said, came to his feet, and stuck out his hands.

She handed Porter back his SIG. She faced Savich with her hands on her hips, a grin on her face. "Why would I handcuff you now, sir? You're dead. I'll get a body bag."

Savich was laughing when she walked away to the waiting paramedic ambulance.

He said to the mayor of Hogan's Alley, "That was well done. She has a nose for crooks. She sniffed me out and came after me. She didn't try to second-guess herself. I wondered if she'd have guts. She does. Sorry I turned the exercise into a comedy at the end, but the look on her face, I couldn't help it."

"I don't blame you, but I doubt we can use you again. I have a feeling this story will pass through training classes for a good long while. No future trainees will believe you're both a new coach and a crook."

"It worked once and we saw an excellent result. I'll come up with another totally different exercise." Savich walked away, unaware that his royal blue boxer shorts were on display to a crowd of a good fifty people.

The mayor began to laugh, then the people around him joined in. Soon there was rolling laughter, people pointing. Even a crook who was holding a hostage around the throat, a gun to his ear, at the other end of town looked over at the sudden noise to see what was going on. It was his downfall. Agent Wallace thunked him over the head and laid him flat.

It was a good day for taking a bite out of crime in Hogan's Alley.

3

S HE MET WITH COLIN PETTY,
a supervisor in the Personnel Division, known in the Bureau
as the Bald Eagle. He was thin, sported a thick black mustache, and had a very shiny head. He told her up front that
she'd impressed some important people, but that was at Quantico. No one working here in Headquarters was impressed
yet. She was going to have to work her butt off. She nodded,
knowing where she'd been assigned. It was tough, but she
managed to pull out a bit of enthusiasm.

"I'm pleased to be going to the Los Angeles field office,"
she said, and thought, I don't want anything to do with any
bank robberies. She knew they dealt with more bank robberies than any field office in the Bureau. She guessed it was
better than Montana, but at least there she could go skiing.
How long was a usual tour of duty? She had to get back here,
somehow.

"L.A. is considered a plum assignment for a new agent
right out of the Academy," Mr. Petty said as he flipped through
her personnel file. "You originally requested Headquarters, I
see here, the Criminal Investigative Division, but they decided to send you to Los Angeles." He looked up at her over
his bifocals. "You have a B.S. in Forensic Science and a Master's degree in Criminal Psychology from Berkeley," he continued. "Seems you've got a real interest here. Why didn't you
request the Investigative Services Unit? With your background, you would probably have been escorted through the
door. I take it you changed your mind?"

She knew there were notes about that in her file. Why was

he acting as if he didn't know anything? Of course. He wanted her to talk, get her slant on things, get her innermost thoughts. Good luck to him on that. It was true it was her own fault that she was being assigned to Los Angeles and there was no secret as to why.

She forced a smile and shrugged. "The fact is I just don't have the guts to do what those people do every day of their lives and probably in their dreams as well. You're right that I prepared myself for this career, that I believed it was what I wanted to do with my life, but—" She shrugged again. And swallowed. She'd spent all these years preparing herself, and she'd failed. "It all boils down to no guts."

"You always wanted to be a profiler?"

"Yes. I read John Douglas's book *Mindhunter* and thought that's what I wanted to do. Actually I've been interested in law enforcement for a very long time, thus my major in college and graduate school." It was a lie, but that didn't matter. She told it easily, with no hesitation. She had practically come to believe it herself over the past several years. "I wanted to help get those monsters out of society. But after the lectures by people from ISU, after seeing what they see on a day-to-day basis for a week, I knew I wouldn't be able to deal with the horror of it. The profilers see unspeakable butchery. They live with the results of it. Every one of those monsters leaves a deep mark on them. And the victims, the victims—" She drew a deep breath. "I knew I couldn't do it." So now she'd go after bank robbers and he would remain free and she wanted to cry. All this time and commitment and incredibly hard work, and she was going to go after bank robbers. She should have quit, but the truth of the matter was that she didn't have the energy to redefine herself again, and that's what it would mean.

Mr. Petty said only, "I couldn't either. Most folks couldn't. The burnout rate is incredible in the unit. Marriages don't do well either. Now, you did excellently at the Academy. You handle firearms well, particularly in mid-distances, you excel at self-defense, you ran the two miles in under sixteen minutes, and your situation judgment was well above average. There's a little footnote here that says you managed to take down Dillon Savich in a Hogan's Alley exercise, something never before done by a trainee." He looked up, his eyebrows raised. "Is that true?"

She remembered her rage when he'd disarmed her twice. She remembered her laughter when he'd walked away, his boxer shorts showing through the big rip in his pants. "Yes," she said, "but it was my partner, Porter Forge, who threw me his SIG so I could shoot him. Otherwise I would have died in the line of duty."

"But it was Savich who bought the big one," Petty said. "I wish I could have seen it." He gave her the most gleeful grin she'd ever seen. Even that bushy mustache of his couldn't hide it. It was irresistible. It made him suddenly very human.

"It also says that you pulled a Lady Colt .38 on him after he'd knocked the SIG out of your hand. Do you still have this gun?"

"Yes, sir. I learned to use it when I was nineteen. I'm very comfortable with it."

"I suppose we can all live with that. Ah, I know everyone must comment on your name, Agent Sherlock."

"Oh yes, sir. No stone left unturned, so to speak, over the years. I'm used to it now."

"Then I won't say anything about offering you a pipe."

"Thank you, sir."

"Let me tell you about your new assignment, Agent Sherlock. The criminal you brought down in Hogan's Alley, namely, Dillon Savich, has asked that you be reassigned to his unit."

Her heart started pounding. "Here in Washington?"

"Yes."

In one of those sterile rooms filled with computers? Oh, no. She'd rather have bank robbers. She was competent with computer programming, but she was far from an intuitive genius like Savich. The stories about what he could do with a computer were told and retold at the Academy. He was a legend. She couldn't imagine working for a legend. On the other hand, wouldn't he have access to everything? Just maybe—"What is his unit?"

"It's the Criminal Apprehension Unit, or CAU for short. They work with the Investigative Services Unit for background and profiles, get their take on things, that sort of thing.

Then they deal directly with local authorities when a criminal takes his show on the road—in other words, when a criminal goes from one state to another. Agent Savich has developed a different approach for apprehending criminals. I'll let him tell you about it. You will be using your academic qualifications, Agent Sherlock. We do try to match up agents' interests and areas of expertise with their assignments. Although you might have seriously doubted that if you'd gotten sent to Los Angeles."

She wanted to leap over the desk and hug Mr. Petty. She couldn't speak for a moment. She thought she'd doomed herself after she'd realized she simply couldn't survive in the ISU as a profiler. The five days she'd spent there had left her so ill she'd endured the old nightmares in blazing, hideous color for well over a week, replete with all the terror, as fresh as it had been seven years before. She knew, deep down, that she could have never gotten used to it, and the ISU people did admit that many folks couldn't ever deal with it, no matter how hard they tried. No, she wouldn't have been able to survive it, not with the horror of the job combined with the horror of the nightmares.

But now, she felt an incredible surge of excitement. She hadn't known about Savich's unit, which was strange because there was always gossip about everything and everyone at the Academy. And this sort of unit would provide her with an ideal vantage point. At the very least, she would be able to access all the files, all the collected data impossible for her to see otherwise. And no one would wonder at her curiosity, not if she was careful. Oh yes, and she would have free time. She closed her eyes with relief.

She'd never felt as though anyone was looking after her before. It was frightening because she hadn't believed in much of anything since that long ago night seven years ago. She'd had a goal, nothing more, only that goal. And now she had a real chance at realizing it.

"Now, it's two-twenty," Mr. Petty said. "Agent Savich wants to see you in ten minutes. I hope you can deal with this work. It's not profiling, but I don't doubt that it will be difficult at times, depending on the case and how intimately involved you have to become in it. At least you won't be six floors down at Quantico working in a bomb shelter with no windows."

"The people in the ISU deserve a big raise."

"And lots more help as well, which is one of the reasons Agent Savich's unit was formed. Now, I'll let him tell you all about it. Then you can make a decision."

"May I ask, sir, why Agent Savich requested me?"

There was that unholy grin again. "I think he really can't believe you beat him, Agent Sherlock. Actually, you will have to ask him that."

He rose and walked her to the door of his small office. "I'm joking, of course. The unit is three turns down this hallway and to the right. Turn left after another four doors and two conference rooms. It's on the left. Are you getting used to the Puzzle Palace?"

"No, sir. This place is a maze."

"It's got more than two million square feet. It boggles a normal mind. I still get lost, and my wife tells me I'm not all that normal. Give yourself another ten years, Agent Sherlock."

Mr. Petty shook her hand. "Welcome to the Bureau. I hope you find your work rewarding. Ah, did anyone ever refer to a tweed hat?"

"Yes, sir."

"Sorry, Agent Sherlock."

It was hard not to run out the door of his office. She didn't even stop at the women's room.

Savich looked up. "You found me in ten minutes," he said, looking down at his Mickey Mouse wristwatch. "That's good, Sherlock. I understand from Colin Petty that you're wondering why I had you reassigned to my unit."

He was wearing a white shirt rolled up to his elbows, a navy blue tie, and navy slacks. A navy blazer was hanging on a coatrack in the corner of his office. He rose slowly from behind his desk as he spoke. He was big, at least six two, dark, and very muscular. In addition to the martial arts, he clearly worked out regularly. She'd heard some of the trainees call him a regular he-man, not a G-man. She knew how strong and fast he was, since he'd worked her over in that Hogan's Alley exercise. Her stomach had hurt for three days after that head butt. If she didn't know he was an agent, she would have been terrified of him. He looked hard as nails, including his dark, dark eyes. Pirate eyes, her mother would have called them. Her mother would have been right. There was nothing soft about this guy. He was patiently looking at her. What had he been talking about? Oh yes, why he'd wanted her reassigned to this unit.

She smiled and said, "Yes, sir."

Savich came around his desk and shook her hand. "Sit down and we can discuss it."

There were two chairs facing his desk, clearly FBI issue. On top of the desk was an FBI-issue computer. Beside it was a laptop that was open and humming, definitely not FBI issue. It was slightly slanted toward her, and she could see the green print on the black background, a graph of some kind. Was this little computer the one she'd heard everyone say that Savich made dance?

"Coffee?"

She shook her head.

"Do you know much about computers, Sherlock?" Sherlock, no agent in front of it. It sounded fine to her. He was looking at her expectantly. She hated to disappoint him, but there was no choice.

"Not all that much, sir. Enough so I can write reports and access the databases I need to do my job."

To her unspeakable relief, he smiled. "Good, I wouldn't want any real competition in my own unit. I hear you had wanted to be a profiler, but ultimately felt you couldn't deal with the atrocities that flood the unit every moment of every day and well into the night."

"That's right. How did you know that? I left Mr. Petty less than fifteen minutes ago."

"No telepathy." He pointed to the phone. "It comes in handy, though I much prefer email. I agree with you, actually. I couldn't do it either. The burnout rate for profilers is pretty high, as I'm sure you've heard. Since they spend so much time focusing on the worst in humanity, they wind up having a difficult time relating to regular folks. They lose perspective on normal life. They don't know their kids. Their marriages go under."

She sat forward a bit in her seat, smoothing her skirt as she said, "I know I saw only a small part of what they do. That's when I knew I didn't have what it took. I felt as if I'd failed."

"What any endeavor takes, Sherlock, is a whole lot of different talents. Because you don't end up profiling doesn't mean you've failed. Actually, I think what we do leaves us more on the normal side of things than not.

"Now, I asked to have you assigned to me because academically you appear to have what I need. Your credentials are impressive. I did wonder, though. Why did you take off a year between your sophomore and junior years of college?"

"I was sick. Mononucleosis."

"Okay, yes, here's an entry about that. I don't know why I missed it." She watched him flip through more pages. He hadn't missed it. She couldn't imagine that he'd ever miss a thing. She would have to be careful around him. He read quickly. He frowned once. He looked up at her. "I didn't think mono took a person out for a whole year."

"I don't know about that. I wasn't worth much for about nine or ten months, run-down, really tired."

He looked down at a page of paper that was faceup on his desktop. "You came directly to the Bureau after completing your Master's degree."

"Yes."

"This is your first job."

"Yes." She knew he wanted more from her in the way of answers, but she wasn't about to comply. Direct question, direct answer; that's all she'd give him. She'd heard about his reputation. He wasn't only smart; he was very good at reading people. She didn't want him reading anything about her that she didn't want read. She was very used to being careful. She wouldn't stop now. She couldn't afford to.

He frowned at her as he tossed her file onto the desktop. She was wearing a no-nonsense dark business suit with a white blouse. Her hair, a vivid sunset red, was pulled severely back, held at the base of her neck with a gold clamp. It was curly, he realized, seeing some curls ready to escape that clip. He saw her for a moment after he'd butted her into the bed of petunias in Hogan's Alley. Her hair had been ruthlessly drawn back then too. He wondered what all that curly hair would look like loose, wondered if he would ever see her wear it loose.

She was on the point of being too thin, her cheekbones too prominent, as if she was living on nerves, but why would that be true? But she'd taken him, not lost her composure, her training. He said, "Do you know what this unit does, Sherlock?"

"Mr. Petty said when a criminal took his show on the road, you're many times called in by the local police to help catch him."

"Yes. We don't deal in kidnappings. Other folk do that brilliantly. No, primarily we stick to the kinds of monsters who don't stop killing until we stop them. Also, like the ISU, we do deal with local agencies who think an outside eye might see something they missed on a local crime. Usually homicide." He paused and sat back, seeing her yet again on her back in the petunia bed. "Also, like the ISU, we only go in when we're asked. It's our job to be very mental, intuitive, objective. We don't do profiling like the ISU. We're computer-based. We use special programs to help us look at crimes from many different angles. The programs correlate all the data from two or more crimes that seem to have been committed by the same person in order to bring everything possibly relevant, possibly important, into focus. We call the main program PAP, the Predictive Analogue Program. I've also developed some very effective data mining programs that enable MAX here"—he gave the laptop an affectionate pat—"to chat with most every other computer in the world, even if they don't want to invite him in, something he really enjoys."

"You wrote the programs, didn't you, sir? And that's why you're the head of the unit?"

He grinned at her. "Yeah. I'd been working on prototypes a long time before the unit got started. I like catching the guys who prey on society and, truth be told, the computer, as far as I'm concerned, is the best tool to take them out. But that's all it is, Sherlock, a tool. It can turn up patterns, weird correlations, but we have to put the data in there in order to get the patterns. Then of course we have to see the patterns and read them correctly. It comes down to how we look at the possible outcomes and alternatives the computer gives us; it's how we decide what data we plug into it. You'll see that PAP has a good number of protocols. One of my people will teach you the program. With luck, your academic background in forensics and psychology will enable you to come up with more parameters, more protocols, more ways of sniffing out pertinent data and correlating information to look at crimes in different ways, all with the goal of catching the criminals."

She wanted to sign on the dotted line right that minute. She wanted to learn everything in the next five minutes. She wanted, most of all, to ask him when she could have access to everything he did. She managed to keep her mouth shut.

"We do a lot of traveling, Sherlock, often at a moment's notice. It's gotten heavier as more and more cop shops hear about us and want to see what our analysis has to offer. What kind of home life do you have? I see you're not married, but do you have a boyfriend? Someone you are used to spending time with?"

"No."

He felt as if he were trying to open a can with his fingernails. "Would you like to have your lawyer present?"

She blinked at that. "I don't understand, sir."

"You are short on words, Sherlock. I was being facetious."

"I'm sorry if you don't think I'm talking enough, sir."

He wanted to tell her she'd talk all he wanted her to soon enough. He was good. Actually, he was better with a computer, but he could also loosen a tongue with the best of them in the Bureau. But for now he'd play it her way. Nothing but the facts. He said, "You don't live with anyone?"

"No, sir."

"Where do you live, Agent Sherlock?"

"Nowhere at the moment, sir. I thought I was being assigned to Los Angeles. Since I'll be staying in Washington I'll have to find an apartment."

Three sentences. She was getting positively chatty.

"We'll be able to help you on that. Do you have stuff in storage?"

"Not much, sir."

There was a faint beep. "A moment," Savich said and looked at the computer screen on his laptop. He rubbed his jaw as he read. Then he typed quickly, looked at the screen, tapped his fingertips on the desktop, then nodded. He looked up at her. He was grinning like a maniac. "Email. Finally, finally, we're going to have a chance to catch the Toaster."

4

$\mathcal{S}$AVICH LOOKED AS IF HE
wanted to jump on his desk and dance. He couldn't stop grinning and rubbing his hands together.

"The Toaster, sir?"

"Oh yes. On this one, I had feelers out with everyone. Excuse me, Agent Sherlock." He lifted the receiver on his phone
and began to punch in numbers. He put it down and cursed
softly. "I forgot. Ellis's wife is having their baby; she went into
the hospital an hour ago and so he's not available. No, I won't
ask him. He'll insist on coming, but he needs to be with his
wife. It's their first kid. But he's going to be really bummed to
miss this. No, I can't. He's gotta be there." He looked down at
his hands a moment, then back up at her. He looked a bit worried. "What do you think of trial by fire?"

Her heartbeat speeded up. She was so new she still squeaked,
but he was going to take a chance on her. "I'm ready, sir."

She looked ready to leap out of her chair. He didn't remember being this eager on his first day. He rose. "Good. We're
leaving this afternoon for Chicago. Bottom line: We've got a
guy who killed a family of four in Des Moines. He did the
same thing in St. Louis three months later. After St. Louis,
the media dubbed him the Toaster. I'll tell you about it when
we're in the air. That was Captain Brady, Chicago Police Department, homicide, and he believes we might be able to
help him. Actually, he's praying we can do something. The
media wants a sideshow, and he can't even give them a dancing bear. But we can." He looked at his watch. "I'll meet you

at Dulles in two hours. We should be there no more than two days." He rolled down the sleeves of his white shirt and grabbed his jacket. "I really want this guy, Sherlock."

The Toaster. She knew about him as well. She scoured all the major newspapers for monsters like this one. Yes, she already knew the details, at least the ones that had made the papers.

He opened the office door for her. Her eyes were positively glistening, as if she were high on drugs. "You mean you know how to catch him?"

"Yes. We're going to get him this time. Captain Brady said he had some leads, but he needs us to come out. You go ahead and pack. I've got to update some people in the unit. Ollie Hamish is in charge when I'm unavailable."

They flew on United in Business Class. "I didn't think the Bureau let its agents fly anything other than tourist class."

Savich stowed his briefcase beneath the seat in front of him and sat down. "I upgraded us. You don't mind that I have the aisle?"

"You're the boss, sir."

"Yeah, but now you can call me Dillon or Savich. I answer to either one. What do most people call you?"

"Sherlock, sir, plain Sherlock."

"I met your daddy once about five years ago, right after he was appointed to the bench. Everyone in law enforcement was tickled to have him named because he rarely cut a convicted criminal any slack. I remember his selection didn't go over too well with liberals in your home state."

"No," she said looking out the window as the 767 began to taxi down the runway. "It didn't. There were two efforts to have him recalled. The first try was after he upheld the death penalty for a man who'd raped and tortured two little boys, then left their bodies in a Dumpster in Palo Alto. The second was when he wouldn't grant bail to an illegal Mexican alien who'd kidnapped and murdered a local businessman."

"Hard to believe there are people who'd want to rally behind those kinds of killers."

"Oh, there are. Their rationale in the first case was that my father showed no compassion. After all, the man's wife had died of cancer, his little boy had been killed by a drunk driver. He deserved another chance. He'd been pushed to torture those little boys. He had shown remorse, claimed grief had sent him out of his mind, but Dad didn't buy it and upheld the death penalty. As for the illegal Mexican, they claimed Dad was a racist, that there was no proof the man would flee the U.S. Also they claimed that the man had kidnapped the businessman because he had refused to give him a job, had threatened to call Immigration if the guy didn't leave the premises. They claimed the man hadn't been treated fairly, that he'd been discriminated against. It didn't matter that the businessman was an immigrant—a legal one. I also seriously doubt he made that threat."

"They didn't succeed in recalling him."

"No, but it was close. You could say that the Bay Area is a fascinating place to grow up. If there's any other possible take on something, some group of locals will latch onto it."

"What does your dad think of your joining the FBI?"

The flight attendant spoke over the PA system, telling them about their seat belts and the oxygen masks. He saw it in her eyes—the wariness, the relief that now she could concentrate on her flotation cushion instead of his questions. She was proving to be a puzzle. He appreciated puzzles. A good one fascinated him. He'd get her again with that question. Maybe when she was tired or distracted.

He sat back in his seat and said nothing more. Once in the air, he opened his briefcase and gave her a thick file. "I hope you read quickly. This is everything on the three different crimes. Absorb as much as you can. If you have questions, write them down and ask me later." He gently lifted his laptop onto the tray and got to work.

He waited until they were served dinner before he spoke again. "Have you finished reading everything?"

"Yes."

"You're fast. Questions? Ideas? Anything that doesn't seem kosher?"

"Yes."

This time he didn't say anything. He chewed and waited.

He watched her cut a small piece of lettuce from her salad. She didn't eat it, only played with it.

"I already knew about this man from the papers. But there's so much more here." She sounded elated, as if she'd made the insiders' club. He frowned at her. She suddenly cleared her throat, and her voice was nearly expressionless. "I can understand that he has low self-esteem, that he probably isn't very bright, that he probably works at a low-paying job, that he's a loner and doesn't relate well to people—"

He waited, something he was excellent at.

"I always wondered why it killed families. Families of four, exactly."

"You called him 'it.' That's interesting."

She hadn't meant to. She forked down her lettuce and took her time chewing. She had to be more careful. "It was a slip of the tongue."

"No, it wasn't, but we'll let that go for now, Sherlock. This family thing—the people in the ISU, as you've read in their profile, believe he lived on the same block as the first family he killed in Des Moines, knew them, hated them, wanted to obliterate them, which he did. However, they couldn't find anyone in the nearby area of the first murders in Des Moines to fit that description. Everyone figured the profile was wrong in this particular case. When he killed again in St. Louis, everyone was flummoxed. When I spoke to Captain Brady in Chicago, I asked him if the St. Louis police had canvassed the area for a possible suspect. They had, but they still didn't find anybody who looked promising."

"But you had already talked to the police in St. Louis, hadn't you?"

"Oh yes."

"You know a lot, don't you?"

"I've thought about this case, Sherlock, thought and re-created it as best I could. Unlike the cops, I firmly believe the profile is right on target."

"Even though they didn't find anyone in Des Moines or St. Louis to fit the profile?"

"Yeah, that's right."

"You're stringing me along, sir."

"Yes, but I'd like to see what you come up with. Let's see if you're as fast with your brain as with that Lady Colt of yours."

She splayed her fingers, long slender fingers, short buffed nails. "You still kicked it out of my hand. It didn't matter."

"But you're a good catch. I wasn't expecting that move from Porter."

She grinned at him then, momentarily disarmed. "We practiced it. In another exercise, he got taken as a hostage. I threw a gun to him, but he missed it. The robber was so angry, he shot Porter. As you can imagine, we got yelled at by the instructors for winging it." She said again, still grinning, "Practice."

He said slowly, shutting down his laptop, "I got creamed once when I was a trainee at the Academy. I wish I'd learned that move. My partner, James Quinlan, was playing a bank robber in a Hogan's Alley exercise, and the FBI got the drop on him. I had to stand there and watch him get taken away. If I'd thrown him a gun, he might have had a chance. Although I don't know what would have happened then." He sighed. "Quinlan turned me in under questioning. I think he expected me to break him out of lockup, and when I didn't, he sang. How he expected me to do it, I have no idea. Anyway, they caught me an hour later heading out of town in a stolen car, the mayor's blue Buick."

"Quinlan?"

"Yes." Nothing more. Let her chew on nothing for a bit.

"Who is this Quinlan?"

"An agent and longtime friend. Now, Sherlock, what do you think we're going to find in Chicago?"

"You said the Chicago police believed they were close. How close?"

"You read it. A witness said he saw a man running from the victims' house. They've got a description. We'll see how accurate it is."

"What do you know, sir, that's not in the reports?"

"Most of it's surmise," he said, "and some excellent stuff from my computer program." He nodded to the flight attendant to remove his cup of tea. He gently closed his laptop and slipped it into his briefcase. "We're nearly at O'Hare," he said, leaned back, and closed his eyes.

She leaned back as well. He hadn't shown her the computer analysis on the case. Maybe he'd thought she already had enough on her plate, and maybe she did. She hadn't wanted to look at the photos from the crime scenes, but she had. It had been difficult. There hadn't been any photos in the newspapers. The actual photos brought the horror of it right in her face. She couldn't help it; she spoke aloud: "In all three cases, the father and mother were in their late thirties, their two children—always a boy and a girl—were ten and twelve. In each case, the father had been shot through the chest, then in his stomach, the second shot delivered after he was dead, the autopsy reports read. The mother was tied down on the kitchen table, her face beaten, then she was strangled with the cord of the toaster, thus the name the Toaster. The children were tied up, knocked out, their heads stuck in the oven. Like Hansel and Gretel. It's more than creepy. This guy is incredibly sick. I've wondered what he would do if the family didn't have a toaster."

"I wondered about that too, at first," he said, not opening his eyes. "Makes you think he must have visited each of the homes to make sure there was one right there in the kitchen before the murders."

"That or he brought the toasters with him."

"That's possible, but I doubt it. Too conspicuous." He brought his seat back into its upright position. "Someone could have seen him carrying something. Another thing, in a lot of houses, kitchen ovens are set up high and built in. In a situation like that, how would he kill the children? In the photos, all of these are the big old-fashioned ovens."

"He had a lot of checking out to do when he visited the families, didn't he?"

She looked at his profile. He didn't say anything. She slowly slid all the photos back into the envelope, each of them marked. She slowly lined up all the pages and carefully placed them back into their folders. He'd given this a whole lot of thought. On the other hand, so had she. She still wanted to see the computer analysis. Then again, she hadn't demanded to see it either.

The flight attendant announced that they were beginning their descent into Chicago and for everyone to put away any electronic equipment. Savich fastened his seat belt. "Oh yes, our guy did a lot of checking."

"How did you even remember my question? It's been five minutes since I asked it."

"I'm FBI. I'm good." He closed his eyes again.

She wanted to kick him. She turned to look out the window. Lights were thick and bright below. Her heart speeded up. Her first assignment. She wanted to do things right.

"You're FBI now too, Sherlock."

It was a bone, not a meaty bone, but a bone nonetheless, and she smiled, accepting that bone gladly.

She fastened her own seat belt. She never once stopped looking down at the lights of Chicago. Hallelujah! She wasn't going after bank robbers.

5

CHICAGO WAS OVERCAST AND a cool fifty degrees on October eighteenth. Sherlock hadn't been to Chicago since she'd turned twenty-one, following a lead that hadn't gone anywhere, one of the many police departments she'd visited during her year of "mono."

As for Savich, he wasn't even particularly aware that he was in Chicago; he was thinking about the sick man who had brutally murdered three families. Officer Alfonso Ponce picked them up and ushered them to an unmarked light blue Ford Crown Victoria.

"Captain Brady didn't think you'd want to be escorted to the station in a squad car. This one belongs to the captain."

After a forty-five-minute ride weaving in and out of thick traffic, everyone in the radius of five miles honking his horn, he let them off at the Jefferson Park station house, the precinct for what was clearly a nice, middle-class neighborhood. The station house was a boxy, single-story building on West Gale, at the intersection of two major streets, Milwaukee and Higgins. It had a basement, Officer Ponce told them, and that was because it had been built in 1936 and was one of those WPA projects. When there'd been a twister seven years before, everyone had piled into the basement, prisoners and all. One nutcase had tried to escape. There had been little updating since the seventies. There was a small box out front holding a few wilted flowers and a naked flagpole.

Inside, it was as familiar as any station house Savich had ever been in—a beige linoleum floor that had been redone probably in the last ten years, but who knew? It still looked

forty years old. He smelled urine wearing an overcoat of flo-
ral room spray. There were a dozen or so people shuffling
around or sitting on the long bench against the wall, since it
was eight o'clock at night. At least half of them were teenage
boys. He wondered what they'd done. Drugs, probably.

Savich asked the sergeant on duty where he could find Captain Brady. They were escorted by an officer, turned wary
after he'd seen their FBI creds, to a squad room with several offices in the back with glass windows. The room was divided
off into modular units, a new addition that nobody liked, the
officer told them. There wasn't much noise this time of night,
just an occasional ring of the phone. There were about a
dozen people in the squad room, all plainclothes.

Captain Brady was a black man of about forty-five with a
thick southern drawl. Even though there wasn't a single white
hair on his head, he looked older than his years, tired, lines
scored deeply around his mouth. When he saw them, his
mouth split into a big smile. He came out from behind his
cluttered desk, his hand out.

"Agent Savich?"

"Yes, Captain." The two men shook hands.

"And this is Agent Sherlock."

Captain Brady shook her hand, gave her a lopsided grin
and said, "You're a long way from London, aren't you?"

She grinned back at him. "Yes, sir. I forgot my hat, but my
pipe's in my purse."

Savich was studying the computer on the captain's desk.

Captain Brady waved them into two chairs that sat opposite
a sofa. The chairs were surprisingly comfortable. Captain
Brady took the sofa. He sat forward, his hands clasped between his knees. "Bud Hollis in St. Louis said you had followed this case since the guy killed the first family in Des
Moines and the DMPD had asked the FBI to do a profile. He
said I should get you here, and that's why I emailed you. He,
ah, appreciated your ideas even though they didn't get him
anywhere. But you already know that. The guy's a mystery.
Nothing seems to nail him. It's like he's a ghost."

Captain Brady coughed into his hand, a hacking low cough.
"Sorry, I guess I'm getting run-down. My wife chewed me out
good this morning." He shrugged. "But what can we do?

We've been putting in long hours since the guy killed the family three and a half days ago. He did it at six o'clock, right at dinnertime, right at the same time he killed the other two families. Sorry, but you already know that. You got all the police reports I sent you yesterday?"

"Oh yes," Savich said. "I was hoping you'd contact me."

The captain nodded. "Bud Hollis also said you had a brain and weren't a glory hound and did your investigating with a computer. I don't understand that, but I'm willing to give it a try.

"I still wasn't sure bringing you here was such a good idea until five minutes before I emailed you. Thank you for coming so quickly. I thought I should talk to both of you for a few minutes before I introduce you to the detectives on the case. They're, ah, a bit unhappy that I called you in."

"No problem," Savich said and crossed his legs. "You're right, Captain. Neither Sherlock nor I am into glory. We only want this guy off the streets."

Actually, Sherlock wanted him really badly. She wanted him dead.

"Unfortunately we don't have anything more than we did when I emailed you this afternoon. The witness who claimed to see a man fleeing the house turned out to be a flake. The pressure from the mayor's office is pretty intense; everyone's hiding in the men's room because the media's been on a tear since the first night it happened. They haven't let up. Do you know one station got hold of the crime scene photos, and they splashed them all over the ten P.M. news? Bloody vultures. They know all about Des Moines and St. Louis and that the media there had called the guy the Toaster. Got everyone scared to death. The joke in the squad room is that everyone is throwing out their kitchen appliances. You've read all the files from all the murders, haven't you?"

"Yes. They were very complete."

"I guess it's time to cut to the chase, Agent Savich. Can you help us?"

"Both Agent Sherlock and I have a few questions. Perhaps we can meet with your people and get the answers. Yes, Captain, there's not a doubt in my mind we can help you."

Captain Brady gave Savich a dubious smile, but there was a

gleam of hope in his tired eyes. "Let's get to it," he said, grabbed a huge folder from his desk, and walked to the door of his office. He yelled out, "Dubrosky! Mason! Get in the conference room on the double." He turned back to them and said, "I hate these modular things. They put them in last year. You can't see a soul, and chances are the guy you want is in the john." He glanced at her. "Well, or the girl, er, female officer you want is in the women's room."

Evidently neither Dubrosky nor Mason had gone to the john. They were already in the conference room, standing stiff and hostile, waiting for the FBI agents. Captain Brady was right about one thing—they weren't happy campers. This was their turf, and the last thing they wanted was to have the Feds stick their noses into their business. Savich was polite and matter-of-fact. They looked at Sherlock, and she could see that they weren't holding out for much help from her. Dubrosky said, "You don't expect us to be your Watsons, do you, Sherlock?"

"Not at all, Detective Dubrosky, unless either of you is a physician."

That brought her a grudging smile.

She wanted to tell all of them, Savich included, that she now knew as much about this guy as they did, maybe even more than the Chicago cops, and she'd thought about him for as long as Savich had, but she kept her mouth closed. She wondered what Savich had up his sleeve. She'd only known him for seven hours, and she would have bet her last buck that he had a whole lot up that sleeve of his. It wouldn't have surprised her if he had the guy's name and address.

They sat in the small conference room, all the files and photos spread over the top of the table. There was a photo of the crime scene faceup at her elbow. It was of Mrs. Lansky, the toaster cord still around her neck. She turned it facedown and looked over at Savich.

He had what she already thought of as the FBI Look. He was studying Dubrosky in a still, thoughtful way. She wondered if he saw more than she did. Poor Dubrosky: He looked so tired he was beyond exhaustion, a man who wasn't smiling, a man who looked as if he'd lost his best friend. He was wired, probably on too much coffee. He couldn't sit still. His brown suit was rumpled, his brown tie looked like a hangman's noose. He had a thick five-o'clock shadow.

Savich put his elbows on the table, looked directly at the man, and said, "Detective, were there any repairmen in the Lansky household within the past two months?"

Dubrosky reared back, then rocked forward again, banging his fist on the table. "Do you think we're idiots? Of course we checked all that. There was a phone repair guy there three weeks ago, but we talked to him and it was legit. Anyway, the guy was at least fifty years old and had seven kids."

Savich continued in that same calm voice. "How do you know there weren't other repairmen?"

"There were no records of any expenditures for any repairs in the Lanskys' checkbook, no credit card expenditures, no receipts of any kind, and none of the neighbors knew of anything needing repairs. We spoke to the family members, even the ones who live out of town—none of them knew anything about the Lanskys' having any repairs on anything."

"And there were no strangers in the area the week before the murder? The day of the murder?"

"Oh sure. There were pizza deliveries, a couple of Seventh-Day Adventists, a guy canvassing for a local political campaign," said Mason, a younger man who was dressed in a very expensive blue suit and looked as tired as his partner. Savich imagined that when they took roles, Mason was the good cop and Dubrosky the bad cop. Mason looked guileless and naïve, which he probably hadn't been for a very long time.

Mason gave a defeated sigh, spreading his hands on the tabletop. "The witness was a dud and nobody saw anyone at the Lansky house except a woman and her daughter going door-to-door selling Girl Scout cookies, and that was one day before the murders. That doesn't mean that UPS guys didn't stop there a week ago, but no one will even admit that's possible. It's a small, close-knit neighborhood. You know, one of those neighborhoods where everybody minds everybody else's business. The old lady who lives across the street from the Lanskys could even describe the woman and the little girl selling the cookies. I can't imagine any stranger getting in there without that old gal noticing. I wanted to ask her if she kept a diary of all the comings and goings in the neighborhood, but

Dubrosky said she might not be so happy if I did and she might close right up on us."

Captain Brady said, "You know, Agent Savich, this whole business about the guy coming to the house, getting in under false pretenses, actually coming into the kitchen, checking before he whacked the families to make sure they had a toaster and a low-set big gas oven didn't really occur to anyone until you told Bud Hollis in St. Louis to check into it. He's the one who got us talking to every neighbor within a two-block radius. Like Mason said, there wasn't any stranger, even a florist delivery to the Lansky house. Everyone is positive. And none of the neighbors seem weird. And we did look for weird when we interviewed."

Savich knew this of course, and Captain Brady knew that he knew it, but he wanted the detectives to think along with him. He accepted a cup of coffee from Mason that was thicker than Saudi oil. "You are all familiar with the profile done by the FBI after the first murders in Des Moines. It said that the killer was a young man between the ages of twenty and thirty, a loner, and that he lived in the neighborhood or not too far away, probably with his parents or with a sibling. Also he had a long-standing hatred or grudge or both toward the family in Des Moines, very possibly unknown by the family or friends of the family. Unfortunately this didn't seem to pan out."

Dubrosky said as he tapped a pen on the wooden tabletop, "The Des Moines cops wasted hours and hours going off on that tangent. They dragged in every man in a three-block radius of the house, but there wasn't a single dweeb who could possibly fit the profile. Then it turned out that the Toaster wasn't a little-time killer, he's now a serial killer. Thank God we didn't waste our time going through that exercise. You people aren't infallible." Dubrosky liked that. He looked jovial now. "No, this time you were so far off track you couldn't even see the train. Like the captain said, we did talk to all the neighbors. Not a weirdo in the bunch."

"Actually, on this case, we're not off track at all," Savich said. "Believe me, it's astounding how often the profiles are right on the money." He was silent a moment, then said, "Now, everyone agrees the same guy murdered all three families. It makes sense that he had to visit each of the houses to ensure that there were both a toaster and a classic full-size stove/oven combo that sat on the kitchen floor. And not an electric stove, a gas one. There were delivery people all over the neighborhoods in both Des Moines and in St. Louis, but the truth is no one is really certain of anything. By the time they acted on the profile theory of the killer living in the neighborhood, there wasn't much certainty anymore about any repairs or deliveries. Nobody remembered seeing anybody."

"Good summary, Savich," said Dubrosky.

"Bear with me, Detective." He took another drink of coffee to be polite. "This stuff is so potent, I bet it breeds little cups of coffee."

There was one small smile, from Sherlock.

Savich said, "You guys have done hours of legwork here and you did it immediately. You've proven that there wasn't a repairperson or a salesman or even a guy whose car broke down and wanted to phone a garage near the Lansky house. So then we come back to the basic question. How then did he get into the Lansky house? Into the kitchen specifically so he could make certain they had all the props he needed?"

Dubrosky made a big show of looking at his watch. "Look, Agent Savich, we thought of all that. We found out that all the houses were older, here, and in Des Moines and St. Louis. To me it means that chances are excellent that you'd have a big low gas oven in the kitchens. And who wouldn't have a toaster? This is all nonsense. Our perp is a transient. He's nuts. None of the shrinks agree on why he did this. Maybe God told him to strangle every mother with the toaster cord. Maybe God told him that kids are evil, that he was the evil witch out of Hansel and Gretel. Who knows why he's whacking families? Like I said, the guy's crazy and he's traveling across the U.S., probably killing at whim, no rhyme or reason."

Mason said, "Buck's right. We don't know why no one saw him in the Lansky neighborhood, why a single dog didn't bark, but maybe he disguised himself as the postman or as that old woman who lives across the street from the Lanskys. In any case, he got lucky. But we'll find him, we've got to. Of course with our luck, he's long gone from Chicago. We'll hear about him again when he murders a family in Kansas."

And that was truly what they believed, Sherlock thought. It was clear on all their faces. They believed the monster was long gone from Chicago, that they didn't have a prayer of ever getting him.

"Let me tell you about the magic of computers, gentlemen," Savich said and smiled. "They do things a whole lot faster than we can. But what's important is what you put into them. It's a matter of picking the right data to go into the mixer before you turn it on to do its thing." He leaned down and picked up his laptop and turned it on. He hit buttons, made it bleep, all in all, ignored the rest of them.

"I've got to go home, Captain," Dubrosky said. "I've got gas, I need a shower or my wife won't even kiss me, and my kids have forgotten what I look like."

"We're all bushed, Buck. Be patient. Let's see what Agent Savich's got."

Sherlock realized then that Savich was putting on a little show for them. He had the pages he wanted to show them in his briefcase. But he was going to call up neat-looking stuff on the screen and make them all look at it before he gave them any hard copy. In the next minute, Savich turned the computer around and said, "Take a look at this, Detectives, Captain Brady."

6

THE THREE MEN CROWDED around the laptop. It was Detective Dubrosky who said suddenly, "Nah, I don't believe this. It doesn't make any sense."

"Yes, it does." Savich handed out a piece of paper to each of them. Sherlock didn't even glance at the paper. She knew what was on it. In that moment, Savich looked over at her. He grinned. He didn't know how she knew, but he knew she'd figured it out.

"You tell them, Sherlock."

They were all staring at her now. He'd put her on the spot. But he'd seen the knowledge in her eyes. How, she didn't know. He was giving her a chance to shine.

Sherlock cleared her throat. "The FBI profilers were right. It's a local neighborhood guy who hated the Lansky family. He killed the families in Des Moines and St. Louis because he wanted to practice before he killed the people he hated. He wanted to get it perfect when it most mattered to him. So, the families in Des Moines and St. Louis were random choices. He undoubtedly drove around until he found the family that met his requirements. Then he killed them."

Captain Brady whistled. "You think the profile is correct, but it was meant only for the Lanskys?"

"That's right," Savich said. "The other two families were his dress rehearsal." He turned to Dubrosky and Mason. "I wanted you to be completely certain that there was no stranger around the Lansky household before the killings. Are you both certain?"

"Yes," Mason said. "As certain as we can be."

"Then we go to the Lansky neighborhood and pick up the guy who will fit the profile. He screwed up and now we'll nail him. The computer hit on three possibles, all within walking distance of the Lanskys' house. My money's on Russell Bent. He fits the profile better than the others. Given how well the profile fits this guy and given no strangers, the chances are really good this wasn't another dress rehearsal. Also, Russell Bent lives with his sister and her husband. She is exactly two years older than he is."

"I don't understand, Agent Savich," Captain Brady said, sitting forward. "What do you mean she's two years older?"

"The boy and girl in all three families," Sherlock said. "The girl was twelve and the boy was ten."

"Why didn't you just tell us?" Dubrosky was mad, felt Savich had made him look like a fool.

"As I said," Savich said as he rose from his chair, "I wanted you to be certain no stranger had been near the Lansky home. It was always possible the guy was having a third dress rehearsal. But he wasn't. This time it was the real thing for him. I wasn't really holding out on you. I got everything in the computer this morning, once Captain Brady sent me all your reports. Without the reports I wouldn't have gotten a thing. You would have come back to this. It's just that I always believed the profile and I had the computer."

Russell Bent lived six houses away from the Lanskys' with his sister and her husband and one young son. Bent was twenty-seven years old, didn't date, didn't have many friends, but was pleasant to everyone. He worked as a maintenance man at a large office on Milwaukee Avenue. His only passion was coaching Little League.

The detectives had already spoken to Russell Bent, his sister, and her husband as part of their neighborhood canvassing. They'd never considered him a possible suspect. They were looking for a transient, not a local, certainly not a shy young guy who was really polite to them.

"One hundred dollars, Sherlock, says they'll break him in twenty minutes," Savich said, grinning down at her.

"It's for certain that none of them looks the least bit tired now," she said. "Do we watch them?"

"No, let's go to Captain Brady's office. I don't want to cramp their style. You know, I bet you Bent would have killed one more family, in another state to confuse everyone thoroughly. Then he wouldn't have killed again."

"You know, I've been wondering why he had to kill the kids like that."

"I've given it a lot of thought, talked to the profilers and a couple of shrinks. Why did Bent murder these families with two kids, specifically a boy and a girl, and in each case, the kids were two years apart, no more, no less? I guess he was killing himself and his sister."

She stared at him, shivering. "But why? No, don't tell me. You did some checking on Mr. Bent."

"Yep. I told Dubrosky and Mason all about it in the john. They're going to show off now in front of Captain Brady."

"I wish I could have been there."

"Well, probably not. Mason got so excited he puked. He hadn't eaten anything all day and he'd drunk a gallon of that atomic bomb coffee."

She raised her hand. "No, don't tell me. Let me think about this, sir."

She followed him down the hall and into Captain Brady's office. He lay down on the sofa. It was too short and hard as a rock, but he wouldn't have traded it for anything at the moment. He was coming down. He closed his eyes and saw that pathetic Russell Bent. They'd gotten him. They'd won this time. For the moment it made him forget about the monsters who were still out there killing, the monsters that he and his people had spent hours trying to find, and had failed. But this time they'd gotten the monster. They'd won.

"The mother must have done something."

He cocked open an eye. Sherlock was standing over him, a shock of curly red hair falling over to cover the side of her face. He watched her tuck the swatch of hair behind her ear. Nice hair and lots of it. Her eyes were blue, a pretty color, and soft. "Yes," he said, "Mrs. Bent definitely did something."

"I don't think Mr. Bent did anything. The three fathers Russell Bent shot were clean kills. No, wait, after they were dead, Bent shot them in the stomach."

"The quick death was probably because to Bent, the father

didn't count, he wasn't an object of the bone-deep hatred. The belly shot was probably because he thought the father was weak, he was ineffectual, he wasn't a man."

"What did Mrs. Bent do to Russell and his sister?"

"To punish Russell and his sister, or more likely, for the kicks it gave her, Mrs. Bent gagged them both, tied their arms behind them and locked them in the trunk of the car or in a closet or other terrifying closed-in places. Once they nearly died from carbon monoxide poisoning. The mother didn't take care of them, obviously, she left them to scrounge food for themselves. Social Services didn't get them away from her until they were ten and twelve years old. Some timing, huh?"

"How did you find out this stuff so quickly?"

"I got on the phone before we left to pick up Russell Bent. I even got Social Services down to check their files. It was all there."

"So the toaster cord is a sort of a payback for what she didn't do? Beating her face was retribution?"

"Yeah, maybe. A payback for all eternity."

"And he must have come to believe that even though his mother was a dreadful person, he and his sister still deserved death, only they hadn't died, they'd survived, so it had to be other children like them?"

"That doesn't make much sense, does it? But it's got to have something to do with Russell Bent feeling worthless, like he didn't deserve to live."

"But why did he pick the Lansky family?"

"I don't know. No one reported any gossip about the family, nothing about physical abuse, or the mother neglecting the children. No unexplained injuries with the kids winding up in the emergency room. But you can take it to the bank Russell Bent thought the two Lansky kids were enough like him and his sister to merit dying. He thought the mother was enough like his own mother to deserve death. Why exactly did he have to gas the children? Your explanation is as good as any. Brady will find out, with the help of the psychiatrists."

"Russell Bent coached Little League. The Lansky boy was in Little League. Maybe the Lansky boy got close to Bent, maybe the Lansky boy told Russell that his mother was horrible." She shrugged. "It really won't matter. You know what they'll do, sir. They'll dress it all up in psychobabble. Do you know what happened to the Bents' parents?"

"Yes," he said. "I know. Sherlock, call me anything but 'sir.' I'm only thirty-two. I just turned thirty-two last month, on the sixth. 'Sir' makes me feel ancient."

The three cops erupted into the office. Captain Brady was rubbing his hands together. There was a bounce to his step. There would be a press conference at midnight. Mason and Dubrosky kept giving each other high fives. Brady had to call the mayor, the police commissioner—the list went on and on. He had to get busy.

It took the CPD only two hours to prove that Bent had traveled to Des Moines and to St. Louis exactly a week before each of those murders had been committed there and back on the exact dates of the murders.

Unfortunately, at least in Sherlock's view, Bent was so crazy, he wouldn't even go to trial. He wouldn't get the death penalty. He would be committed. Would he ever be let out? The last thing she heard as they were leaving the Jefferson Park precinct station was his sobs and the soft, soothing voice of his sister, telling him over and over that it would be all right, that they were in this together. She would take care of him. She had been two years older and she hadn't protected him from their mother. She wondered if the sister was really lucky that her brother hadn't gassed her.

They took a late-morning flight back to Washington, D.C. It didn't occur to Savich until they were already in the air that Sherlock might not have a place to stay.

"I'm staying at the Watergate," she said. "I'm comfortable. I'll stay there until I find an apartment." She smiled at him. "You did very well. You got him. You didn't even need the police. Why didn't you call Captain Brady and tell him about Bent? Why did you want to go to Chicago?"

"I lied to Brady. I'm a glory hound—even if it's only a crumb, I'm happy. I love praise. Who doesn't?"

"But that's not even part of why you went."

"All right, Sherlock. I wanted to see this guy. If I hadn't seen him, then it would never be finished in my mind. Too, this was your first day. It was important for you to see how I work, how I deal with local cops. Okay, it was a bit of a show.

I think I deserved it. You're new. You haven't seen any disappointments yet, you haven't lived through the endless frustration, the wrong turns our unit has suffered since the first murders in Des Moines. You didn't hear all the crap we got about the profile being wrong. All you saw was the victory dance. This has been only the third real score I've gotten since the FBI started the unit up six months ago.

"But I can't ever forget that there was Des Moines and St. Louis and twelve people died because we didn't figure things out quickly enough. Of course Chicago was the key, since that was his focus. As soon as I realized the neighbors knew one another and watched out for one another, and there hadn't been any strangers at the Lansky house, then I knew our guy lived there. He had to. There wasn't any other answer."

He added on a smile, "You did fine, Sherlock."

For the first time in years, she felt something positive, something that made her feel really good wash through her. "Thanks," she said, and stretched out in her seat. "What if I hadn't known the answer when you asked me to explain it?"

"Oh, it was easy to see that you did know. You were about to burst out of your skin. You looked about ready to fly. Yeah, you really did fine."

"Will you tell me about your first big score sometime? Maybe even the second one?"

She thought he must be asleep. Then he said in a slow, slurred voice, "Her name was Joyce Hendricks. She was seventeen and I was fifteen. I'd never seen real live breasts before. She was something. All the guys thought I was the stud of the high school, for at least three days."

She laughed. "Where is Joyce now?"

"She's a big-time tax accountant in New York. We exchange Christmas cards," he said, and he drifted off to sleep.

7

$\mathcal{S}$HERLOCK MOVED A WEEK
later into a quite lovely two-bedroom town house in Georgetown on the corner of Cranford Street and Madison. She had
dishes, glasses, cups, a bed, one set of white sheets, towels, all
different, a microwave, and a dozen hangers. It was all she'd
brought with her from California. She'd given the rest of her
stuff to a homeless shelter in San Francisco. When she'd told
Savich she didn't have much in storage, she hadn't been exag-
gerating.

No matter.

The first thing she did was change the locks and install
dead bolts and chains. When she hung up her clothes on her
hangers, she was whistling, thinking about MacDougal and
how she'd miss him. He was on the fifth floor, working in the
National Security Division. He was big-time into counterter-
rorism. It had been his goal, he'd told her, since a close childhood friend of his had been blown out of the sky on the
doomed Pan Am Flight 103 that exploded over Lockerbie in
the late eighties. He'd gotten his first big assignment. He
would go to Saudi Arabia because a terrorist bombing had
killed at least fifteen American soldiers the previous week.

"I'm outta here, Sherlock," he'd said, grabbed her, and
given her a big hug. "They're giving me a chance. Like Savich
gave you. Hey, you really did well with that guy in Chicago."

"The Toaster."

"Yeah. What a moniker. Trust the media to trivialize murder by making it funny. Anything big since then?"

"No, but it's been less than a week. Savich made me take three days off to find an apartment. Listen, no impulsive stuff out of you, okay? You take care of yourself, Mac. Don't go off on a tear because you're FBI now and think you're invincible."

"This is training for me, Sherlock. Nothing more. Hey, you're good little-sister material."

"We're the same age."

"Nah, with those skinny little arms of yours, you're a little sister."

He was anxious to be gone. He was bouncing his foot and shifting from one leg to the other. She gave him one more hug. "Send me a postcard with lots of sand on it."

He gave her a salute and was off, whistling, as she was now, his footsteps fast and solid down the short drive in front of her town house. He turned suddenly and called back, "I hear that Savich is big into country-and-western music. I hear he loves to sing the stuff, that he knows all the words to every song ever written. It can't hurt to brownnose."

Goodness, she thought, country-and-western music? She knew what it was but that was about it. It was twangy stuff that was on radio stations she always turned off immediately. It hadn't ever been in her repertoire—not that she'd had much of a repertoire the past seven years. The last time she'd played the piano was in the bar at the Watergate a week and a half before. The drunks had loved her. She'd played some Gershwin, then quit when she forgot the next line.

She was standing in the middle of her empty living room, hands on hips, wondering where she was going to buy furniture when the doorbell rang.

No one knew she was here.

She froze, hating herself even as she felt her heart begin to pound. She had been safe at Quantico, but here, in Washington, D.C., where she was utterly alone? Her Lady Colt was in the bedroom. No, she wasn't about to dash in there and get it. She drew in a deep breath. It was the paperboy. It was someone selling subscriptions.

The only people she knew were the eight people in the Criminal Apprehension Unit and Savich, and she hadn't given them her address yet. Only Personnel. Would they tell anyone?

The doorbell rang again. She walked to her front door, immediately moving to stand beside it. No one would shoot through the front door and hit her. "Who is it?"

There was a pause, then, "It's me, Lacey. Douglas."

She closed her eyes a moment. Douglas Madigan. She hadn't seen him for four months, nearly five months. The last time had been at her father's house in Pacific Heights the night before she'd left for Quantico. He'd been cold and distant with her. Her mother had said little, and looked worried. Douglas had sat there on the plush leather couch in her father's library and sipped at very expensive brandy from a very old Waterford snifter, and frowned. It wasn't an evening she liked to remember.

"Lacey? Are you there, honey?"

She'd called her father the day before. Douglas must have found out where she was from him. She watched her hand unfasten the two chains. She slowly clicked off the dead bolt and opened the door.

"I've got a bottle of champagne." He waved it in her face.

"I don't have any champagne glasses."

"Who cares? You nervous to see me, Lacey? Come, honey, all you need is a glass or two."

"Sorry, my brain's a bit scattered. I wasn't expecting you, Douglas. Yes, I've got glasses. Come in."

He followed her to the empty kitchen. She pulled two glasses from the cupboard. He said as he gently twisted the champagne cork, "I read about you in the *Chronicle*. You graduated from the Academy and you already nailed a serial killer."

She thought about that pathetic scrap, Russell Bent, who'd murdered twelve people. She hoped the inmates would kill him. He had murdered six children and she knew that prisoners hated child abusers and child killers. She shrugged. "I was along for the ride, Douglas. It was my boss, Dillon Savich, who'd figured out who the guy was even before we went. It was amazing the way he handled everything—all low-key, not really saying anything to anybody. He wanted the local cops to buy in to everything he'd done, then give them the credit. He says it's the best P.R. for the unit. Actually, I'm surprised my name was even mentioned."

She smiled, remembering that the very next day Assistant Director Jimmy Maitland came around to congratulate everyone. It had been quite a party. "Savich told me I had arrived in time for the victory dance. Everyone else had done all the hard work. His main partner on the case was with his wife in the hospital, having a baby, the wife, that is. And so I went in his place. Savich was right. I didn't do a thing, watched, listened. I've never seen so many happy people."

"It was a Captain Brady of the Chicago police who thanked the FBI on TV, for all their valuable assistance. He mentioned both your names."

"Oh dear, I bet Savich wasn't very happy about that. I had the impression he'd asked Captain Brady not to say anything. Oh well, it's still very good press for the FBI. Now everyone knows about his unit."

"Why shouldn't the two of you get the credit? He caught a serial killer."

"You don't understand. The FBI is a group, not an individual. Loyalty is to the Bureau, not any single person."

"You're already brainwashed. Well, here's to you, Lacey. I hope this works out the way you want it to."

Douglas raised his glass and lightly clicked it against hers. She merely nodded, then took a sip. It was delicious. "Thank you for bringing the champagne."

"You're welcome."

"His wife had the baby at about midnight."

"Whose wife? Oh, the agent who'd done all the work."

"Yeah, I thought he'd cry that he'd missed it, but he was a good sport about it. Why are you here, Douglas? I only called my father yesterday with my new address."

He poured himself some more champagne, sipped it, then said with a shrug and a smile, "It was good timing. I had to come to Washington to see a client and decided to put you up front on my itinerary." He moved into the living room. "I like your living room. It'll have lots of afternoon sunlight. It's good-sized. Why don't you have any furniture?"

"It wasn't worth it to have all my old stuff trucked across the country. I'll get some new stuff."

They were standing facing each other in the empty living room. Douglas Madigan downed the rest of his champagne and set his empty glass on the oak floor. He straightened, took her glass, and set it next to his. "Lacey," he said, taking her upper arms in his hands, "I've missed you. I wish you had come home for a visit, but you didn't. You didn't write me or call. You left a hole in my life. You're beautiful, you know that? I'll bet all the guys are always telling you that, staring at you, even with those baggy jeans you're wearing and that ridiculous sweatshirt. What does it say across the back? *Dizzy Dan's Pizza?* What is that all about?"

"It's a local place. And no one seems to have noticed my soul-crushing beauty at all. But you're kind to say so." Actually, she'd gone out of her way at the Academy and now at Headquarters to dress very conservatively, even severely. As for her hair, she'd always worn it pulled back and clipped at the base of her neck. But this was Saturday. She was in jeans and a sweatshirt, her hair loose, curling wildly around her face.

"You're looking good, Douglas. But you never change. Maybe you get better." It was true. He was six feet tall, had a lean runner's body and a thin face with soulful brown eyes. Women loved him, always had. Even her mother had never said a word against Douglas. He charmed easily. He dominated just as easily.

"Thank you." He touched her hair, then sifted it through his fingers. "Beautiful. It's auburn, but not really. Perhaps more Titian. Ah, you know I didn't want you doing this silly FBI thing. Why? Why did you leave me and do this?"

Leave him? She said in her low, calm voice, the one she'd practiced and practiced at the Academy when she took courses in interviewing, "I always wanted to be in law enforcement, you know that. The FBI is the best, the very best. It's the heart of the whole system."

"The heart? I doubt it. As to your always wanting to be in law enforcement, I don't remember that. You started out as a music major. You play the piano beautifully. You were playing Beethoven sonatas since you were eleven years old. You wanted to go to Juilliard. I remember you dropped out of the Fletcher competition. I always believed you weren't quite of this world. You seemed to live for your music. Of course we all changed after Belinda. It's been a very long time now.

Seven long years. Your father didn't appreciate your talent, didn't understand it since he didn't have any at all, but everyone else did. Everyone was worried about you when you sold your Steinway years ago, when you stopped even playing at parties. You even stopped going to parties."

"That was a long time ago, Douglas. Dad isn't particularly disappointed in me now. He hoped I'd finally do something worthwhile. He hoped this was my first step to growing up. He only acted cold to me because I hadn't asked him to help me get in. He was dying to use his pull, and I didn't let him." Actually, she had blackmailed him. When the FBI agents interviewed him after she'd applied, he'd not said much of anything about Belinda or how his daughter changed. She'd told him straight out she'd never speak to him again if he did. He'd evidently glossed over everything, and very smoothly. She'd gotten into the FBI, after all.

She still missed her piano, but that missing was buried deep down, so deep she scarcely ever thought of it now. "Yes, I did sell it. It didn't seem important anymore." A piano was nothing compared to what Belinda had lost. Still, though, she would find herself playing a song on the arm of a chair, playing along with the music in a movie or on the car radio. She could remember when she was nineteen playing on the arm of a young man she was dating.

Douglas said, "I don't remember much from that time, to tell you the truth. It's blurred now, distant, and I'm grateful for it."

"Yes," she said. But she remembered; she had lived it and held it deep and raw inside her since that awful night. He moved closer to her and she knew he would kiss her. She wasn't sure she wanted him to. Douglas had always fascinated her. Seven years. A long time. But still it didn't seem quite right.

He did kiss her, a light touch of his mouth to hers, a brief remembrance, a coming back. His mouth was firm and dry. The kiss was so brief, she didn't get the taste of him, only the whisper of the tart champagne. He immediately dropped his hands and stepped back.

"I've missed you. I had to listen to your father yell and curse that you'd lost it and gone off the deep end when you told him you were changing your major to Forensic Science. 'She'll be wasting herself lifting some goon's fingerprints from a dead body.'"

"You know there's lots more to it than that. There are a good dozen specialties in forensics."

"Yes, I know. He wanted you to go to law school, of course. He still thought there was hope after you finished your Master's degree in criminal psychology. He said it would be helpful in nailing scum. Your dad, the judge, is always forgetting I'm a defense attorney."

"I changed my mind, that's all."

"That's what I told the FBI guy who came doing a background check on you. I figured if you wanted to go into the FBI, then I wasn't going to stand in your way."

What did Douglas mean by that? That he could have told the FBI that she was unstable, that she'd gone around the bend seven years ago? Yes, he could have said that. She wondered if anyone had told the FBI that. No, if they had, then she wouldn't have been accepted, would she?

"I know my father was positive when the agents came to interview him."

"Yes, he told me you'd given him no choice. I said good for you, it was your life and he should keep his mouth shut if he ever wanted to see you again. He was angry at me for a good month."

"Thank you for standing up for me, Douglas." She had assumed at the time that the people doing the check on her background hadn't considered it all that important. But they had, evidently, and they'd asked questions. "I had no idea, but I am grateful. No one dredged up anything about that time. Do you know you haven't changed? You really are looking good." He was thirty-eight now. There were a few white strands woven into his black hair. He was very probably more handsome now than he had been seven years ago. She remembered how Belinda had loved him more than anything. Anything. Sherlock felt the familiar hollowing pain and quickly picked up the champagne bottle. She poured each of them another glass.

"You've changed. You're a woman now, Lacey. You're no longer a silent kid. You still have a dozen locks on your door, but hey, this is D.C. I'd probably have a submachine gun sitting next to the front door. What does the FBI use?"

"A Heckler and Koch MP-5 submachine gun. It's powerful and reliable."

"I have trouble imagining you even near something like that, much less holding it and firing it. Ah, that sounded sexist, didn't it? You spoke of change. As for me, perhaps I haven't changed all that much on the outside, but well, life changes one, regardless, doesn't it?"

"Oh yes." She was the perfect example of what life could do to a person.

"You're on the thin side. Did they work you that hard at the Academy?"

"Yes, but it was a classmate of mine—MacDougal—who worked me the hardest. He swore he'd put some muscle on my skinny little arms."

"Let me see."

He was squeezing her upper arm. "Flex."

She did.

"Not bad."

"My boss works out. Don't picture him as a muscle-bound, no-neck bodybuilder. He's very strong and muscular, but he's also into karate, and he's very good. I was on the receiving end of his technique once at the Academy. The other day I saw him eyeing me. I don't think he liked what he saw. I'll bet he'll have me in the gym by next Tuesday."

"Boss? You mean this Savich character?"

"I suppose we're all characters in our own way. Savich is a genius with computers. One of his programs helped nail Russell Bent. He's the chief of the unit I'm in now. I was very lucky he asked for me. Otherwise I would have ended up in L.A. chasing bank robbers."

"So may I take you out to lunch to celebrate your first case? How about we have lunch at one of the excellent restaurants you've got in this neighborhood?"

She nodded. "How long will you be here, Douglas?"

"I'm not certain. Perhaps a week. Did you miss me, Lacey?"

"Yes. And I do miss Mom and Dad. How is Dad's health?"

"You write him every week, and I know for a fact that he

writes you back every week. He told me that you don't like the telephone. So he has to write letters. So you know he's fine."

Of course Douglas knew very well why she hated phones. That was how she'd been told about Belinda. "Soon I'll probably be into email full-time. My boss is really big on email, and so is everyone else in the unit. It's weird, you don't hear all that many phones ringing."

"I'll write my email address down for you before I leave. Let's go eat, Lacey."

"You look like a prince and I look like a peasant. Let me change. It'll take me a minute. Oh yeah, everybody calls me Sherlock."

"I don't like that, I never did. And everybody has to make a stupid remark when they meet you. It doesn't suit you. It's very masculine. Is that what the FBI is all about? Turning you into a man?"

"I hope not. If they did try, I'd flunk the muscle mass tests."

Actually, she thought, as she changed into a dress in her bedroom, she liked being called Sherlock, plain Sherlock. It moved her one step further from the woman she had been seven years ago.

It was at lunch that he told her about this woman who claimed he'd gotten her pregnant.

8

SAVICH STOPPED BY HER DESK
Monday morning and said, "Ollie told me you still didn't have
any stuff for your apartment. I thought you were going to take
care of it this weekend. What happened?"

She looked over at Ollie Hamish and cocked her elbow at
him, tapping it with her other hand. He waved back at her,
shrugging.

Why should Savich care if she slept in a tent? "A friend
from California came into town. I didn't have a chance."

"Okay, take off today and shop yourself to death." Then he
frowned. "You don't know where to shop, do you? Listen, I'll
call a friend of mine. She knows where to find anything you
could possibly invent. Her name's Sally Quinlan."

Sherlock had heard all about James Quinlan, presumably
this woman's husband. She'd heard about some of his cases,
but none of the real details. Maybe when she met Sally Quinlan, she'd find out all the good stuff.

It turned out Sally Quinlan wasn't free until the following
Saturday. They made a date. Sherlock spent the day learning the
Predictive Analogue Program, and all the procedures in the unit.

That Monday evening, she found two lovely, but small,
prints at Bentrells in Georgetown, which would probably look
insignificant against that long expanse of white wall in her
living room. She bought some clothes at another Georgetown
boutique. When she got back to her apartment, there was
Douglas waiting for her. He'd been busy Sunday, hadn't even
had time to phone her. She said, "I'm starving. Let's go eat."

He nodded and took her to Antonio's, a northern Italian restaurant that wasn't trendy. Over a glass of wine and medallions of veal, he said, "I guess you want to know about this woman, huh?"

"Yeah, you dropped that bomb and then took off." She fingered a bread stick. "If you don't want to tell me, Douglas, that's all right."

"No, you should know. Her name is Candice Addams. She's about your age, so beautiful that men stop in midstride to stare at her, smarter than anyone I know." He sighed and pushed away his plate. "She claims I got her pregnant and I suppose I could have, but I've always been so careful. Living in San Francisco, you're probably the most careful of any American."

"Do you want to marry her?" Odd how it hurt to say the words, but they had to be said. Although she didn't know what she wanted from Douglas, she did realize she valued him, he attracted her, he amused her, he stood up for her, at least most of the time. And he'd been there for her through it all. She'd been closer to him during those awful months than to her father. Of course no one was really close to her mother. That was impossible.

"No, of course not. She's a local TV reporter. I can't imagine she wants to have a baby now."

She felt suddenly impatient with him. "Haven't you spoken about all this with her? Does she want to have the baby? An abortion? Does she want to get married? What, Douglas?"

"Yeah, she says she wants to marry me."

"You said she's smart and beautiful. You said you always wanted to have kids. So marry her."

"Yeah, I guess maybe I'll have to. I wanted to tell you about it in person, Lacey. I don't want to marry her, I'm not lying about that. I'd hoped that someday you and I could, well, that would probably never have happened, would it?"

She set down her fork. The medallions of veal looked about as appetizing as buffalo chips. "There's been so much, Douglas, too much. I'm very grateful to you, you know that. I wish I could say that I wanted to be with you—"

"Yeah, I know."

"What will you do?"

"I'd turn her down flat if you'd have me, Lacey."

She wondered in that moment what he'd do if she said yes. She'd thought several times in the last few years that she was a habit to him, someone he was fond of, someone he would protect, but not as a woman, not as a wife. No, she was Belinda's little sister and she probably always would be in his mind. She dredged up a smile for him. "I hope she hasn't given you an ultimatum."

"Oh no, Candice is far too intelligent to do that. I'm hooked, but she isn't pulling at all on the line."

It was his life. He had to forget and move on. It had been seven years. And as for her, well, she would move on as well, toward the goal she'd always had, toward the goal she would pursue until the monster was caught and dead, or she was.

She'd heard Russell Bent had gotten himself a hotshot lawyer who was claiming police brutality and coercion. The press was speculating that the lawyer might get him off. She wouldn't let that happen to him. Never.

On Thursday, Savich said, "I don't want you to flab out on me, Sherlock. You don't live more than a mile from me. My gym is right in between. I'll see you there at six o'clock."

"Flab out? I've only been out of the Academy for two weeks. And I've walked every square inch of Georgetown since Monday, shopping until I dropped, as you ordered me to do. Flab out?"

"Yeah, you haven't been lying around, but your deltoids are losing tone. I'm an expert. I can tell these things. Six o'clock."

He strolled away, singing, *"Like a rock, I was strong as I could be. Like a rock, nothin' ever got to me . . ."* He walked into his glass-enclosed office. That wasn't country-and-western, that was a commercial. Was it Chevrolet? She couldn't remember. She watched him sit down at his desk and turn immediately to MAX, his laptop.

Flabby deltoids, ha. She grinned toward his office. He was being a good boss; that was it. She was new in town, and he didn't want her to get lonesome. She shook her head and went back to work. She jumped a good six inches when a woman's voice said from behind her, "Don't even consider going after him."

Sherlock blinked up at Hannah Paisley, an agent who'd started up with the Unit six months before. She'd been in the Bureau five years. She was very tall, beautifully shaped, and was very smart. Sherlock had seen her do her dumb blonde act on a witness at the Academy, on video. She'd made the guy feel like the stud of the universe. Then he'd spilled his guts. She was very good, which was why she was loaned out on sting operations. She also seemed to have a sixth sense about killers, which was why she'd joined this unit. Sherlock envied her this ability.

Hannah wanted Dillon Savich? She was jealous because Savich thought Sherlock was flabby? What was all this about? "I wasn't going after him, Hannah. Actually, I was thinking he was a jerk, criticizing my deltoids."

"I know. I was joking. Are you doing work on the Radnich case?"

Sherlock nodded. Was Hannah joking? She didn't think so. She didn't need this. Hannah gave her a small salute and went back to her desk and computer.

Sherlock was working with Ollie Hamish on the Radnich case. It had flummoxed everyone, including Savich. It wasn't the "who" of it that was driving everybody nuts; it was the "how." Sherlock was feeding in more data they'd gotten from the various local police reports and the autopsies and the forensic evidence, and in the back of her mind, she was also trying to figure out how this weirdo guy could have gotten into four nursing homes—the count as of today—and strangled old women with no one seeing a single thing. The first nursing home was in Richmond, Virginia, eight months ago. Then four months ago, it happened again in northern Florida, home of the nonagenarian. Norma Radnich was the old woman strangled at the South Banyon Nursing Home in St. Petersburg, Florida. They'd been called in by the SPPD only after this last murder. To date there were no leads, no clues, no guesses that were helpful. The profilers were working on it now as well. Ollie was committed to this one. He was the lead agent on it, and Sherlock wanted it that way.

She wanted to go digging. She'd figured out how to access everything she needed. Perhaps tonight after Dillon let her leave the gym she would come back here and work. If he didn't kill all her body parts, if she'd still be able to walk once he was through with her.

No one would know. She'd be very careful, do her work for the unit during the day and search at night. She felt her heart speed up at the thought. She'd get him. She had to get him. But he'd lain low for nearly seven years. It would be seven years in three days. An anniversary. As the past six years had each been an anniversary. Had he died? Had he simply stopped? She didn't think so. He was a classic psychopath. He would never stop until he was dead or locked away. Cycles, she'd thought many times. He was into cycles and so far it hadn't triggered yet for whatever reason.

The weekly update meeting was at two o'clock. There were nine agents in the conference room: six men, including Savich; three women; one secretary, Claudia, a gum-chewing grandmother with bright red hair and a brain like a razor; and one clerk, Edgar, who would bet on anything and won the pool on the birth weight of Ellis's baby.

Everyone presented what he was doing, the status, what he or she needed.

The status meeting went quickly, no wasted time. All the agents felt free to speak up when another agent wanted advice. Savich moderated.

When it was Ollie's turn, he said, "I'm working the Radnich case with Sherlock. She's up to speed on it now. We got the last pile of stuff today from the Florida cops. Sherlock, you finished inputting all the data a while ago, didn't you?" At her nod, he said, "We'll push the magic button this afternoon."

Savich turned to her. "Sherlock? You got anything to add?"

She sat forward, clasping her hands together. "It's like a locked-room murder mystery. How can this guy saunter into these three nursing homes in Florida and the one in Richmond at ten o'clock at night and kill these poor old women with nobody seeing or hearing a thing? Naturally, all the old women killed were in single rooms or suites, but that shouldn't matter. This whole thing is nuts. There has to be something we're missing."

"Obviously," said Hannah. "But we'll get there, we usually do."

Savich said, "Actually, Ollie and I are going to St. Petersburg tomorrow morning. I got another call from Captain Samuels. There's been another murder. That means our guy is going into overdrive. The profilers don't like it. It means he's losing control. Five murders in eight months, the last two in the past week and a half. Captain Samuels really wants us to go down there and poke around, look at everything with new eyes. So, that's where we'll be for the weekend."

Ollie nearly leaped out of his chair in excitement. "When, Chief?"

"Eight A.M. United flight from Dulles."

Ollie blanched and raised his eyes heavenward. "I won't get too up for this. No, I'm a fatalist. If I really want to go, then my future mother-in-law will tell Maria I'm a workaholic and lousy husband material and Maria will dump me. It's the way my life works."

"Don't worry, Ollie," Savich said, closing his folder. "It's no big deal. We'll go down there to see if there's anything they haven't seen. I think it's time to look the situation over firsthand."

"Do you already know who did it?" Sherlock asked, sitting forward, her hands clasped on the conference table.

Savich heard that utterly serious voice, looked at that too-intense face, at that thick curling red hair trying to break free of the gold clasp at the back of her neck. "Not this time— sorry. Now, Ollie, don't panic. Nothing to it."

Still, Ollie looked doubtful. Sherlock had heard he'd already wagered with at least a dozen other agents that his wedding wouldn't come off because either a terrorist would blow up the church or the preacher would be arrested for stealing out of the collection plates.

"I sure want to catch this creep," Ollie said.

"I do too," Savich said. "Like you and Sherlock and every cop in Florida, I want to know how he keeps pulling off this ghost act." He stood. "Okay. Everyone is cooking along fine. No big problems or breakthroughs. Cogan, see me for a minute. I've got an idea about those murders in Las Vegas."

At six o'clock, Lacey walked into the World Gym on Juniper Street, wearing shorts, a baggy top, and running shoes, her

hair pulled back and up high in a fat ponytail. She paid her ten
dollars and went into the huge mirror-lined room. There was
the usual complement of bodybuilders who watched every
move they made in the mirrors. She got a kick out of watching
them walk. They were overbulked and couldn't really get
around normally. They moved like hulks.

There were beautiful young women who were six feet tall,
professional women on the StairMasters, looking at their
watches every few minutes, probably thinking about their
kids and what they were going to cook for dinner and did they
have enough time if they did five more minutes.

And there were quite a few professional men, all ages, all
working hard. She didn't see a single slacker. Then she saw
Savich. He was wearing shorts, running shoes, and a sleeve-
less white cotton tank. He was doing lat pulldowns.

He was slick with sweat, his dark hair plastered to his head.
He looked good. Actually, he looked better than good; he
looked beautiful. She saw him glance over at a clock, do two
more slow pulldowns, then release the bar and slowly stand
up. He turned, saw her immediately, and waved. Seeing him
from the front made her realize that she hadn't seen any male
as a man in a very long time. She let herself appreciate the
clean definition of his muscles, the smooth contours of sinew,
then she set him away from her, back into his proper role.

He looked her over as he approached. "I've decided your
delts are okay. What you need is karate. I didn't like the fact
that despite the SIG and your Lady Colt, I still disarmed you
with no sweat. You need to know how to protect yourself, and
guns are dangerous. What do you say?"

What could she say? She'd begun karate and then had to
stop it because she'd broken her leg skiing. Two years before.
She'd gotten pretty good. But two years was a long time to be
away from an art like karate. He was offering her another
chance. She nodded. What followed was a warm-up, then
stretching, then the most grueling hour of her life. Savich realized quickly enough that she'd already had some training.
She did endless leg kicks against a kick pad he held against
his chest, fist punches, over and over until her arms and legs
died on her. "That's fine then. Okay, you need to practice your

falls," he said. She didn't have the energy to tell him she'd rather simply curl up beneath the chest machine. And so he threw her, hurled her, smashed her, and encouraged her endlessly, which seemed ridiculous since she could barely move. After a particularly bouncing toss, she lay on her back and stared up at him.

"I'm not getting up. I'm not that much of a masochist. You'll do it again. I'm tired of hearing how great I am at falling and rolling."

He grinned down at her. "You're doing very well. Don't whine. You took karate before, so it's not at all new to you. You know learning how to fall is very important."

"I'm still not going to get up. It's been two years."

He sighed, offered her his hand. "All right. It can be your turn now. But I didn't do all that to torture you. Now it's your turn. You get to toss me around."

With a spurt of energy she grabbed his hand, leaped to her feet, and took the position.

He grinned at her. Her look was intense, as grim as could be. She wanted to kill him. "Never stop thinking, Sherlock. Never stop looking at my eyes. Get your muscles ready, but don't tense. You know how to do it. Let's go."

He let her throw him, using his own momentum to help her. But she was hooting and shouting that she'd finally gotten him on the mat. "Not bad," he said as he got back to his feet. They went through that single routine for another half hour.

She finally stepped back, bent over, her chest heaving, so exhausted she could barely breathe. "Enough. I'm nearly dead. I've sweated off my eyebrows."

He tossed her a towel. It was perfectly dry. He wasn't even sweating. "Now that you've gotten a renewed taste, what do you think?"

She threw the towel at him. "I've never had so much fun in my life."

He laughed and tossed the towel back to her.

"I've never worked so hard in my life."

"Yeah, but on the other hand, it's you in control and not a gun."

"You can't smack someone from twenty feet, sir. Even I

could have blown you away if you hadn't been so close to me."

"True, but I was and if it had been the real thing, then you'd be dead. I don't want that to happen. I'll be spending a lot of time training you. I don't want you to go get yourself shot. Now, there's a class that would be great for you. It's both women and men, and the guy who teaches it is an old buddy of mine. His name's Chico and he's one tough buzzard. He might let you in even if you do have skinny little arms."

She laughed. It was impossible not to. They both showered and changed. He walked her home, gave her a salute, and said, "You get your apartment furnished this weekend, Sherlock. No more excuses. See you at headquarters Monday. Here's Chico's phone number. Oh, Sherlock. You might be kind of sore tomorrow, but nothing too bad. Be sure to take a long hot bath. Maybe a couple of aspirin, too. You might also consider some ice packs first."

He paused a moment, looking at her face, clean of any makeup, her hair ratty, thick strands curling wildly around her face. He cocked his head to one side, smiled at her. "You did fine, Sherlock. I plan to overlook all your whining."

She eyed the sidewalk, wondering if she could possibly throw him.

"I'm watching your eyes. I'm seeing right into your twisted mind. Nah, Sherlock, don't try to toss me into the flower bed, not tonight." He waved, and walked away.

She stood watching him a moment before she went into the town house. She watched him until he turned at the corner, east.

"Is that Savich?"

She was so startled she nearly fell over backward. As she was flailing for balance, he came out from behind a tree. "Oh my heavens, it's you, Douglas. You nearly stopped my heart. Is something the matter? Is everyone all right?"

"Oh yes. I've been waiting for you, Lacey. I came over hoping we could have dinner. But you weren't here."

"No, I was at the gym. Savich beat the stuffing out of me." At his stare, she added, "Karate. I don't know if you remember, but I began taking karate lessons two years ago, then stopped. I'm getting back into it."

"Why with him?"

"I'll be taking classes with a guy named Chico after tonight. Knowing Savich, he'll want me there every night."

"Is the guy coming on to you, Lacey?"

"Savich? Goodness, Douglas, he's my boss. He's the chief
of the unit. It's all business."

"Yeah, he's got the best way to get to you."

He was jealous. It was amazing to see this side of him. She
smiled up at him and lightly placed her hand on his arm.
"Savich is a professional. He has no interest in anybody in his
unit, not the kind you're worried about." She thought about
Hannah Paisley. Was there something between Savich and
Hannah?

Douglas saw the lie in her eyes. Why? He'd never known
her to lie, but on the other hand, he hadn't seen her in five
months. The FBI had had her in their clutches for sixteen
weeks. What more would they do to her? He breathed in
deeply. "Why don't we go inside? You can change, then I'll
take you to dinner. I've got to go back to San Francisco in the
morning."

"That would be nice, Douglas. When you get home, you'll
be speaking to Candice Addams, won't you?"

"Yes."

She nodded and preceded him into her empty town house.

9

SHE SMILED AT THE GUARD
and flipped open her black FBI wallet. Her beautiful gold
shield had a high shine.

"You're Agent Sherlock?" He checked the list in his hand.
"You're a new agent?"

"Yes, I would like to go to my office and do some more
work."

"Hey, you can't light your pipe here in the building, Sherlock."

"Thanks, I won't. But it's too bad, I've got a really nice
blend."

"Guess you hear that lots, huh?"

The guard was about her age, black, his head shaved, a real
hard jaw. "No," she said, grinning at him, "this was the very
first time."

"How about: Do you live on Baker Street?"

"Where's that?"

"All right. But I'll be thinking of a new one you really
haven't heard before. You're clean. Sign here. On your way
out, check with me again. Oh, my name's Nick."

She waved back at the guard. She walked to the elevators,
the low heels of her shoes loud on the marble floor. If anyone
asked, she planned to say that she wanted to do more study on
the Radnich case. She exited the elevator at the third floor,
walked down a long hall, turned right, then left, down another
hall. She unlocked the door to the CAU. It was dark. Unfortunately she had to light up the entire area. It was different
at night. The absence of people, laughing, talking, breathing,

.robbed her of even an illusion of safety. She was alone in this large room. She also had her SIG in her belt holster.

"Don't be a chicken." She laughed, a ghostly sound in the room. She hated the overhead fluorescent lights.

She brought up the menu on her computer and checked all the available databases. She found him after only twenty minutes. She would have found him in under two minutes if he'd killed any more in the past seven years. But he hadn't.

She read the profile, read it again, and had to laugh. She could have written it. She'd written profiles, dozens of them, during her graduate courses in criminal psychology. She'd even written her Master's thesis on *The Inclusive Psychometry of the Serial Criminal*. She supposedly knew all the ingredients that went into the psychotic mind, co-mingled in endless patterns to produce a monster. The "inclusive" had been her advisor's idea. She still thought it sounded obtuse and pretentious, but her advisor had patted her on the back and told her he knew what the professionals respected. She'd passed, so at least she must have sounded convincing in her defense. In fact, she'd gotten high grades on all the various protocols, tests, and measuring tools she'd developed to predict and judge the depths of contamination in the serial murderer's mind. None of it had helped. He'd gone underground.

But even the FBI profile hadn't provided a clue about where to find him. There was nothing at all that provided a different slant or perspective. Nothing new. Wait. She scrolled up again and reread two sentences. "The subject will never vary in his execution. His mind is locked into performing this single repetitive act again and again."

It made sense. As far as she knew, each of the seven murders had been utterly identical. She slowly went through all the police reports, including Belinda's, then printed them out.

She hated the autopsy reports, but through the courses she'd taken, she'd learned to remove herself from the gruesome details, most of which were couched in medicalese. But the photos were different, tougher. She didn't read Belinda's autopsy report. She knew she'd have to, but not now. No, not now, or tomorrow either. She printed out all of them, including Belinda's.

She had to stop. She'd barely be able to carry out all the papers she'd already printed out.

Nick was smiling, that jaw of his out there, when he saw her. "You got lots of stuff there, Agent Sherlock. You gonna take it all back to two twenty-one B Baker Street now? I remembered the two twenty-one B part."

"Yep. It's all on Moriarty, you know. I'll catch that villain yet."

"I don't know about this Moriarty. But I did see a Sherlock Holmes movie about that hound. Boy, that hound was butt-chew mean."

"It was a good one," she agreed as she signed out.

"You'll be working more overtime?"

"Probably. They're all real hardnoses here. They never let up."

When she reached her car, she clicked her security alarm before she reached her Ford Explorer. Everything worked. Lights went on inside. No one had broken in.

When she got to her town house, she checked all the entries, then fastened the dead bolts and the two chains. She turned on the security alarm. She left her bedroom door open.

She read over the reports far into the night. But not Belinda's, not yet.

"Feast your eyes on this, Sherlock."

She looked down at a map with dots on it. The computer had connected a number of lines. "It's the Star of David, Ollie. So what?"

Ollie was rubbing his hands together. "Nothing bad happened, Sherlock. Savich and I got there and we talked with everybody. You know Savich, he was cool and low-key and then he showed this to everyone. I thought Captain Samuels—she's with the St. Petersburg Police Department—was going to kiss him. These four dots are where the killer's already hit. Savich did some extrapolation and voilà."

"It could be anything, Ollie. A Star of David?" She studied the three dots that represented murder sites. They formed a nearly perfect right-side-up equilateral triangle. The other murder could very well be the beginning of an upside-down equilateral triangle, but who knew? "Well, sure, it could be, but it could also be random."

"We'll soon see," Ollie said. "If you go with Savich's reasoning, then the guy is going to kill right here next." He pointed to the next point.

"That's pretty neat," she said. "But no ideas on how the ghost gets into the nursing homes and out again without anyone noticing?"

"Not yet. But the surveillance on the next one Savich pinpointed is going to be intense. You know what? The media took up your word. All the papers and TV are screaming about The Ghost murdering their grandmothers."

"Surely not. How would they know about our saying that?"

Ollie looked down at his black wing tips. "Well, I kind of said it to a TV woman who was really pretty and wanted something so badly." Ollie looked up at her and grinned. "I thought Savich was going to deck me."

"Better you than me. He's already thrown me all over that gym of his. I'm still sore, but I don't dare say anything because he'll accuse me of whining."

"Ain't that the truth? He's got you into karate?"

She nodded.

"He told me I was one of the best basketball players in the Bureau. He said I should keep myself in shape playing games with all my nieces and nephews. He said kids kept you honest and in shape out of fear of humiliation."

"Ha. He said that because he realized he couldn't throw you around, the sexist jerk."

"Nah, he cleaned my clock but good when I asked him about karate. He really flatten you, Sherlock?"

"More times than I can count."

"What's this about a sexist jerk?"

Both she and Ollie turned to see Savich standing behind them, his laptop MAX in one hand, a modem in the other.

"I don't know about any sexist jerk, do you, Ollie?"

"Me? I never even heard the word except from Maria, and she didn't know what it meant."

Savich grunted at them. "What do you think of the Star of David angle, Sherlock?"

"It's so weird as to have a grain of truth in it. But you know, the murders started in Virginia, not Florida. That could put a monkey wrench in the works."

"Agreed. We'll see soon enough. The local cops are covering the next probable nursing home."

She frowned at him. "I do prefer comparing all the physical evidence, but truth be told there isn't all that much. Actually, this Star of David thing, well, I have this feeling you could be right. But I also have the feeling that it won't matter. He'll kill at the nursing home you picked out but no one will see him."

"She's said what I'm feeling," Ollie said. "It's weirding me out. I've asked the computer to compare and contrast all sorts of evidence, but we're coming up with nothing."

"We'll get him, Ollie."

"I sure hope so," Sherlock said. She turned to Ollie. "Did your future mother-in-law convince Maria that you're a workaholic since you were gone for the whole weekend?"

"No, I blamed it on the chief. I told her Agent Savich would kick me into the street if I didn't go with him. Then I'd be blackballed and permanently on unemployment. She backed off."

Savich laughed and walked back to his office. Sherlock saw Hannah Paisley rise quickly and follow him. To her surprise, Ollie was watching Hannah, a frown on his face.

"What's wrong?"

"Nothing really. I wish Hannah would be a little more cool about Savich."

Sherlock didn't say a word; she didn't want to know anything personal about anybody. It was safer that way. But Ollie didn't notice, said thoughtfully, "I heard Savich and Hannah dated before she came here. Then when she joined the Unit, word was that Savich called it off. I heard him say that no one in the Unit should dip his Bureau quill into Bureau ink."

"Now that was sexist, Ollie. You think Hannah's still interested, then?"

"Oh yeah, look at her. She can't keep her eyes off him. Why don't you talk to her, Sherlock? Maybe she'd listen to you. Savich isn't interested, or if he is, he still wouldn't go near a woman agent in his unit."

Sherlock shook her head as she punched up one of the

forensic reports. She didn't care what Savich did with his Bureau quill. Goodness, she thought, she'd made a joke to herself. It had been a long time. She saw Hannah come out of Savich's office, her face set. She wasn't about to say a word to that formidable woman. She sincerely doubted that Hannah Paisley would listen to Sherlock's opinion on the time of day. She went back to work on the ghost.

Sherlock unfolded the *Boston Globe*, the last large city newspaper in her pile. She was tired of scouring the ten largest city newspapers every day of the week, but she couldn't stop. She'd done it for nearly seven years. It cost a fortune for all the subscriptions, but she had enough money from her trust fund so she'd never have to worry about feeding herself and buying as many subscriptions as she wanted. She knew he was out there. She would never stop.

She couldn't believe it. She nearly dropped her coffee cup. It was on page three. Not a big article, but large enough to immediately catch her eye. She read:

"Yesterday evening at 6:30, Hillary Ramsgate, 28, a stockbroker with Hameson, Lyle & Obermeyer, was found brutally murdered in an abandoned warehouse on Pier Forty-one. Detective Ralph Budnack of the BPD said that she had apparently been led through a bizarre game that had resulted in her death from multiple stab wounds to her chest and abdomen. A note tied around her neck said that she had lost the game and had to pay the forfeit. At this point, police say they're following leads."

He was back. In Boston. He'd begun again. She prayed that this poor woman was his first victim of this new cycle, that she hadn't missed others, or that he hadn't murdered women in small towns where the AP wouldn't pick up the story.

Hillary Ramsgate. Poor woman. She reread the newspaper article, then rose from her kitchen table. She had died just as Belinda and six other women in San Francisco had seven years ago. They'd all lost the game.

What the newspaper article didn't say was that her tongue had also been cut out. The police were holding that back. But Sherlock knew all about that. She'd been brutally stabbed and her tongue had been sliced out.

She realized then that yesterday had been the seventh anniversary of the last murder.

Seven years. He'd struck seven years ago to the day. The monster was back.

Sherlock was pacing back and forth in front of Savich's office when he came around the corner. He watched her a moment. He said very quietly, so as not to startle her, "Sherlock, it's seven in the morning. What are you doing here? What's wrong?"

When she turned abruptly to face him, he saw more pain on her face than he'd seen in a long time. Then the hollow, despairing look was gone. She'd gotten a grip. She'd hidden the pain again. And left nothing at all.

What was going on here?

"Sherlock? What's wrong?"

She smoothed out her face. What had he seen? She even managed a smile. "I'm sorry to bother you so early, but I have a favor to ask. I need to take a few days off and go to Boston."

He unlocked his office door and waved her in. "Boston?"

"Yes. I have a sick aunt. It's an emergency. I know I've only been in the Unit a couple of weeks, but there's not anyone else to see to this situation."

"Your aunt is elderly?"

"Not really, well, she's got Alzheimer's. She's gotten suddenly worse."

"A relative called you?"

Why was he asking all these questions? Didn't he believe her? "Yes, my cousin called me. He, well, he's not well himself so there's no one but me here on the East Coast."

"I see," he said slowly, not looking at her directly now. She looked pale, scared, and excited—an odd combination, but that's what he saw in her face. Her hair was pulled severely back, held in the same gold clasp at the nape of her neck. It looked like she'd flattened it down with hair spray. She couldn't seem to be still, her fingers now flexing against her purse, one foot tapping. She'd forgotten to put on any makeup. She looked very young. He said slowly, "How long do you think you'll need to be away?"

"Not more than three days, long enough to see that her care is all locked into place."

"Go, Sherlock. Oh yes, I want you to call me from Boston tonight and tell me what's going on, all right?"

Why did he care what she was doing away from Washington? More lies. She hated lies. She wasn't particularly good at them, but she'd rehearsed this one all the way in. Surely he believed her, surely. "Yes, sir. I'll call you this evening."

He jotted down his phone number on a piece of paper. "My home phone." He handed her the folded paper. He said nothing until she was nearly at the outer door, then, "Good luck. Take care."

He turned back to his office only after she was out the door. He listened a moment to the sound of her quick footfalls.

Why was she lying to him?

It was 10:30 that night when the phone rang. Savich muted the baseball game between the Orioles and the Red Sox, Orioles leading 7 to 2 in the seventh inning. He kept looking at the screen as he answered the phone.

"Sir, it's Sherlock."

He grinned into the phone. "What's going on?"

"My aunt is fine. I have more details to tie up but I'll be back by Thursday, if that's all right."

He said easily, "I have a good friend at Boston Memorial, a doctor who specializes in geriatrics. Would you like his name so you can speak to him about your aunt?"

"Oh no, sir. Everything's under control."

"That's good, Sherlock. What's the weather like in Boston?"

"It's chilly and raining. Everything looks old and tired."

"About the same here. I'll see you on Thursday. Oh yes, call me again tomorrow night."

There was a pause, then, "Very well, sir, if that's what you want."

"It is. You sound tired, Sherlock. Sleep well. Good night."

"Thank you, sir. You too."

He watched her from his office. It was nearly one o'clock Thursday afternoon. He'd been in meetings all morning. This was the first time he'd seen her since she'd left for Boston. She looked tired beyond her years. No, it was more than that. She looked flattened, as if she'd lost her best friend, as if someone had pounded her, not physically, but emotionally. He wasn't at all surprised.

She was typing furiously on the keyboard, completely absorbed. He waited for a few more minutes, then strolled to her workstation. He'd spoken to her for the past two nights, both nights at 10:30, both nights mirroring the same conversation, except last night she hadn't quite been the same. She'd sounded beyond tired. He'd wished he could see her face. When he looked at her, her thoughts were clear as the shine Uncle Bob put on his wing tips.

"Sherlock."

She raised her face, her fingers stilling on the computer keyboard. "Good afternoon, sir. You just get here?"

"Yes. Call me Savich. Or Dillon."

"Yes, sir. Dillon."

"Would you please come in my office? In say ten minutes?"

She nodded, nothing more, a defeated nod she tried to hide from him.

When she walked into his office, he said immediately, "I don't like lies or liars."

She looked at him hopelessly.

"Your mother's sister lives in San Diego. You have three cousins, none of them older than thirty-five, all living on the West Coast. You don't even have a third cousin in Boston. Also, there's nary a trace of Alzheimer's in anyone in your family."

"No, I guess there isn't."

"Sit down, Sherlock."

She sat.

He watched her pull her skirt to her calves. She sat on the edge of her chair like a child ready to be chastised. Only she wasn't remotely a child.

"Don't you think it's about time you leveled with me?"

"Not until I call Chico and take a dozen or so lessons."

Humor from her. He appreciated it. At least she had her balance, if nothing else. "I could still wipe up the floor with you. I'm an old hand at karate and other things as well. Speaking of hands, I played right into yours when I requested you for my unit, didn't I? You must have thought God was looking out for you when Petty told you you didn't have to go to L.A."

It didn't matter now. He probably knew everything. At least she didn't have to lie anymore. "It's true I wasn't interested in bank robbers. I told you that the day you first interviewed me."

"Oh no, that's for sure. What you wanted was the chance to track down the serial killer who murdered your sister seven years ago. Her name was Belinda, wasn't it?"

10

SHE TOOK THE BLOW, BENDing slightly inward to absorb the pain of it, the unbearable nakedness of it spoken aloud. She knew she'd blown her chance. It was all over for her now. But maybe it wasn't. He was in Boston. She would simply resign from the FBI and move to Boston. She had no choice.

She didn't stir, looked at him and said, "They named him the String Killer. Isn't that a stupid name? String! Something hardly thicker than a thread, a piece of skinny hemp he used to torture the women, all seven of them—psychological torture—and the media reduced it to string, to make it sexy and clever."

"Yes, I remember the case well. And now he's struck again after seven years, in Boston this time. In fact, it's seven years to the day."

She sat there, looking at him, and said in that flattened voice of hers, that held no surprise at all, "How do you know?"

"I went into your computer, saw what you'd accessed, and downloaded. I saw that you'd used my password to get into a couple of specialized data banks. Odd, but I never thought one of my own people would steal my password. You looked over my shoulder one day?"

She nodded, didn't say anything, which was smart. He was very angry.

Savich drew a deep breath, tamped down on the anger. "I checked the security log. You spent three and a half hours here Monday night. You read the paper Tuesday morning and left for Boston the same day. I bought a *Boston Globe*. The story was on the third page."

She rose slowly, like an old woman. "I'll clean out my desk, sir, then go see Mr. Petty."

"And what will you tell Petty?"

"That I lied, that you discovered it, and I've been dismissed. I'm really sorry, sir, but I had no choice."

"I haven't canned you. If you think I intend to let you loose on the Boston Police Department, you're mistaken, Sherlock. But you've already spoken to them, haven't you? They kissed you off, right? No matter, don't tell me yet. I'll call Ralph Budnack."

She looked as if he'd struck her. Then she gave him the coldest smile he'd ever seen. Her chin went up. "I know how the killer got into the nursing homes in Florida to strangle those old ladies."

He realized in that instant that he admired her brain. Was she trying to bargain with him? Make a deal? Gain some kind of leverage? "I see," he said easily, sitting back in his chair, fiddling with a pen between his fingers. "I give you something and you give me something in return?"

"No. I guess I want to show you that I'm not a complete fool, that I do care about something other than the man who murdered my sister. I really don't want any more old ladies to die. I wanted to mention it before I forgot and left."

"You wouldn't have forgotten, just as you couldn't bring yourself to put your sister's death behind you and go on with your life. Now, I already told you. You're not leaving. Go back to your desk, Sherlock, and write out your ideas on the ghost. We'll talk later."

She didn't want to talk to him. She wasn't in his league. Her very first attempt at deception, and he'd nailed her but good. She hadn't realized she'd been so obvious. But she had been. He'd seen through everything. His anger was frightening, since he didn't yell. It was cold, so very cold, that anger of his. Why hadn't he just plain fired her? She'd betrayed him.

Why?

He would, soon enough; she was certain of that. She'd fire herself if she were in his shoes. She would pull everything else out of the database and then she would slip away. He would know what she'd done quickly enough, but who cared? She couldn't continue here. He wouldn't allow it; the breach had been too great, her conduct too far beyond the line. No, he wouldn't allow her to stay, no matter what game he was playing with her now.

She'd barely sat down at her desk before Hannah Paisley said from behind her, "You're stupid, Sherlock, or does he call you by your cute little first name, Lacey?"

"I'm not stupid, Hannah, I'm very tired. Well, maybe I am stupid."

"Why are you so tired? Did Savich keep you up all night? How many times did he screw you, Sherlock?"

Sherlock flinched at the harshness of Hannah's voice, not the naked word. That naked word conjured up some smutty, frankly silly photos in *Playboy*, showing contorting bodies. Now that she thought about it, they hardly ever showed the men completely naked, only the women. Really naked.

"Please, Hannah, there's nothing at all between us. Savich doesn't even like me. In fact—"

"In fact what?"

Sherlock shook her head. No, let Hannah hear it from Savich. It would happen soon enough.

"Look at me, Hannah. I'm skinny and very plain. You're beautiful—surely you must know that. I'm no threat to you, please believe me. Besides I don't like Savich any more than he likes me. Would you try to believe at least that?"

"No. I spotted what you were the minute you walked into the Unit."

"What am I?"

"You're a manipulative bitch. You saw Savich at the Academy and you got him interested so he'd bring you into the Unit. But you listen to me, you stay away from Savich or I'll take you apart. You know I can. Do you hear me?"

Ollie came walking over, nearly sauntering, whistling, if Sherlock wasn't mistaken, as if he didn't have a care in the world, but she saw his eyes. He recognized what he was seeing and he didn't like it. "Hey, Hannah, what's happening with the Lazarus case? What does the guy use all those Coke bottles for?"

She wasn't shaking because of what Hannah had said—no, Hannah and her ridiculous jealousy meant less than nothing to her. Sherlock had seen other women in Savich's office, young women, nice-looking women. Did Hannah go after all of them as well?

Who cared? Forget Hannah. She turned her back on both Hannah and Ollie and booted up her computer, tapped her fingers while she waited, then punched in Savich's password. Nothing happened.

Then suddenly, there appeared: *Not this time, Sherlock.*

The screen went black. The computer was her enemy. As long as Savich was still breathing, the computer would remain her enemy. She lifted her fingers from the keyboard and laid her hands in her lap.

"Your aunt all right?"

It was Ollie. He pulled up a chair and sat beside her. "You look like you haven't slept in a week, Sherlock."

"Thanks. Yes, my aunt is fine now."

"You look like you're ready to go over the edge."

She'd lived on the edge for seven years; no reason to go over now. She smiled at him. "Not really. I'm tired, and that's what I told Hannah. Thanks for drawing her fire, Ollie. I wish she'd open her eyes and realize that I'm about as much a threat to her as a duck in the sights of a hunter."

"That's an odd thing to say, Sherlock. Savich told me to tell you to come into the conference room. What's it all about?"

"Tell the agents how the ghost gets into the nursing homes, Sherlock."

She sat forward, her hands clasped together. "The ghost is disguised as an old woman, a nursing home resident. Ollie showed me how to mix and match report data and plug it into two overlapping protocols. I did it with data from what the witnesses had said after each of the murders. No one found anything unusual in any of these reports—not the witnesses, not the cops, not us. But the computer did." She handed out a piece of paper. "These are direct quotes from the witnesses, the pertinent parts, naturally, just the parts that, once tied together, pull the killer out of the bag."

Savich read aloud: "'No one around, Lieutenant. Not a

single soul. Oh, some patients, of course. They were scared, some of them disoriented. Perfectly natural.'" He raised his head. "This is from a night floor nurse." He read down the page. "This one is from a janitor: 'There wasn't anybody around. Just old folks and they're everywhere. Scared, they were. I helped several of them back to their rooms.'"

Romero nearly squeaked when he read: "'There was this one old lady who felt faint. I carried her into the nearest room, the recreation parlor. Poor old doll. She didn't want me to leave her, but I had to.'" Romero had a long narrow face, rather like Prince Charles's. He had thick, black brows that nearly met between his eyes, eyes that were black and mirrored a formidable intelligence. He shook the paper toward Sherlock. "Good going, Sherlock. That last quote was from a cop. A cop! It was there all the time."

Savich was sitting back in his chair, looking at each of the agents, one by one. "So," he said finally, once all of them were looking at him, "do you think this is the answer? Our killer is disguised as an old woman, a patient?"

"Looks good to me," said Ruth Warnecki, a former Metro detective.

Savich turned to Ollie. "You're the lead on this case. What do you think?"

Ollie was staring at Sherlock. He looked wounded, his mouth pinched. "I didn't know anything about what Sherlock was going to do. It seems fairly straightforward, put like this. Like it's so out there that we were all fools not to catch it. Of course they did already check this once, and we mulled it over too, but I guess none of us went deep enough. The first thing to do is call that cop and ask him who that old lady he carried into the recreation room was."

"Good idea," Savich replied. "That could pretty well clinch it if the cop remembers." He turned to Sherlock. "I don't suppose you know if the killer is Jewish, Sherlock? Or hates Jews? Not necessarily the residents, since only two of the five old ladies who were killed were Jews. The owners, you think? Or have you dismissed the Star of David idea?"

"I don't know, sir, about either. Listen, this idea came to me, that's all. It was blind luck."

"Yes, I rather suppose it was," Hannah said as she rose, "since you're so new at this."

Ollie was dogging Sherlock's heels out of the conference room. "Why?" he said, lightly touching her arm.

"There honestly wasn't time, Ollie. No, of course there was time. This sounds ridiculous, but I really wasn't even thinking about it until it popped right into my head. Surely you've done the same thing."

"Yeah, sure, but then when I find something, the first thing I do is tell my partner. You didn't say a word. You waltzed into the conference room and showed everyone how great you were. It wasn't a very nice thing to do, Sherlock."

"No, you're right. It wasn't. I can only say that I honestly wasn't thinking about it." It was true. She hadn't known Savich would put her on the spot in front of the whole Unit, but he had. There'd been no time then to say anything to Ollie. No, there'd been time. She hadn't thought about it. "Listen, Ollie, what happened was this. When I was on the plane going to Boston, I was pushed into this old woman coming out of the gangway. She turned on me and blasted me with the foulest language I'd ever heard. She looked mean. She looked at me as if she wanted to kill me. She's the one who should get all the credit if this works out."

"How did Savich know that you'd come up with something?"

"I can't tell you that, Ollie. I'd like to, but I can't. I'm sorry. Please. I might not be around much longer. I don't know."

"What's going on?" Even though Ollie was a fatalist, he forgot anger very quickly. He laid his hand on her shoulder. "It's something heavy, isn't it?"

"Yes. Very heavy."

"Sherlock. In my office. Now."

Ollie spun around at Savich's voice. "Would you like to tell me what's wrong?"

"No, this is between the two of us, Ollie. Stop looking like a rottweiler. I'm not going to pound her into the floor—at least not yet, not here. Come along, Sherlock."

But they didn't go to his office. He led her out of the Hoover Building to a small park that was catty-corner to it. "Sit." She sat on the narrow bench. Fortunately, she didn't have to wake up a homeless person and ask him to leave. It was a beautiful day, the sky clear, just a light, cool breeze. The sidewalks were crowded with fall tourists. There were two families with small kids eating picnic lunches on blankets. It was utterly foreign to her, this family thing. It hadn't been, a long time ago. That was before her mother had become ill. At least before Sherlock had realized how very ill she was.

"I've given this a lot of thought."

"You found me out so quickly, I'm sure you've had plenty of time to figure out everything."

"Look at me, Sherlock."

She looked. Then suddenly she began to laugh. "You look like Heathcliff: brooding, piercing eyes, and dangerous, like you could kill easily now. I remember thinking once that you had a pirate's eyes."

He wanted to smile, but he didn't. A pirate's eyes? That was nuts. He said, "I've reviewed the seven murders this guy did seven years ago. I called Ralph Budnack in Boston and asked if he'd heard of any murders committed with this same M.O. other than the one they'd had the other day. He said they hadn't heard about other murders, but that they had realized they had a serial killer on their hands, a guy who'd struck in San Francisco seven years ago." He paused a moment, turning at the unearthly cooing of a pigeon.

"I finally managed to get in to see Detective Budnack," Sherlock said. "He wouldn't even talk to me. He said I was a sicko and they didn't need any help."

"I know. I spoke to him right after he kicked you out of his office."

She wanted to hit him. "That was Tuesday afternoon. You didn't say a thing about it when I called you that night!"

"That's right. Why should I?"

"Well, so you really didn't have to, but you knew. You knew all the time what I was trying to do."

"Oh yes. Tell me, Sherlock, what did you do for the other two days?"

"Nothing that got me anywhere. The medical examiner wouldn't talk to me even when I managed to lie my way in. With my background, it wasn't that hard. But he was close-mouthed, said he didn't like outsiders poking their noses in his business. I spoke to the main reporter at the *Boston Globe*. His name's Jeb Stuart, of all things. He didn't know much more than what was in the paper. I bought him dinner and he spilled his guts, but there wasn't much I could use. Then I came home. To you. To get the ax for being a fool."

Savich looked out over the park. He leaned back, stretching out his arms on the bench back. Horns sounded in the background, the sun slivered through the thick canopy of oak leaves, a father was shouting at his kid. "The Boston police have asked for our help. Why didn't you tell Lieutenant Budnack that you were FBI? Chances are good he would have cooperated."

"I knew that if I did, you'd hear about it and aim your computer toward Boston and you'd find out everything. Of course you did that anyway. I should have shown my shield. Maybe I would have gotten something before Budnack tossed me out on my ear. I was stupid. I didn't think it through. I thought if I pretended to be a member of the Ramsgate family, it would be my best shot at getting information." A pigeon darted close to her feet, then away again. "They're used to being fed," she said, watching the pigeon begin to pace in front of her. "I hope the person who feeds them isn't dead."

"Old Sal usually sits here. She isn't here this afternoon because she's picking up her Social Security check. Her health is better than yours. She has names for all the pigeons. Now, what are you planning to do?"

She stood abruptly and looked down at him, hands on hips. "What do you want from me? I already told you I'd resign."

"Then I suppose you'll hightail it up to Boston and go on a one-woman hunt for the String Killer?"

"Yes. I have to. I've prepared myself. I've waited a very long time for him to strike again."

"Very well. I don't seem to have any choice." He stood up abruptly. He was very big. Inadvertently, she took a step back.

He looked impatient. "You afraid I'll throw you here in the park?"

No, she'd been afraid that he'd kill her. Like that man had killed Belinda. She tried to shrug it off. "I guess I'm a bit nervous. Sorry. What don't you have a choice about? You have a choice about everything."

"If you only knew," he said, and plowed his fingers through his hair. "I had you call me every night from Boston because I was afraid you'd get yourself into trouble."

"I'm a trained FBI agent. What trouble? Even if I couldn't get to my gun, I sure know how to fall."

He grinned down at her, raised his hand, then lowered it. "Okay, here's what's going to happen. You know more about this guy than any other living person. Would you say that's accurate?"

"Yes." Her heart began to beat in a slow cadence. "I guess you know I printed out all the police and autopsy reports from the seven murders in San Francisco?"

He nodded, looking toward an old woman who was pulling a grocery cart loaded with bags filled with old clothes, cardboard, empty cola bottles. "It's Old Sal. I'll introduce you, then we need to get back."

Old Sal looked her over with very worldly, bloodshot eyes. She could have been any age from fifty to ninety.

"Get your check, Sal?"

"Yeah, Dillon, I got it. You feed my little birdies?"

"No, Sherlock here wanted to, but I wouldn't let her."

The old eyes turned to her. "You Sherlock?"

"Yes, ma'am. Nice to meet you."

"You be good to my boy here, you get me, young lady?"

"I'm not a young lady, ma'am, I'm an FBI agent."

Savich laughed. "She's right, Sal. I rather think I'll be the one taking care of her."

"You get your problems solved, dear, then you can play with my boy here. He's a good lad."

"I will, ma'am."

"I don't like this ma'am stuff."

"It's okay, Sal. She calls me sir, right to my face, as if I were her father or something even worse."

"How old are you, Sherlock?"

"I'm twenty-seven."

"That's a good age. Dillon is thirty-two. Turned thirty-two three and a half weeks ago. We had a little party for him here. Me and my birdies. Is Sherlock your first or last name?"

"It's my last name, Sal. My first name's Lacey."

"Huh. I like Sherlock better. It gives you distinction."

"I agree."

"You need anything, Sal?"

"No, Dillon. I want to sit in this lovely sun, rest my bones, and feed my birdies. I got them a pound of unsalted peanuts. I don't want to harden their little arteries."

Sherlock was still smiling when they went back into the Hoover Building.

She wasn't smiling ten minutes later.

11

"SO HE'S GOING TO TAKE YOU to Boston. How'd you manage that, Sherlock?"

Hannah Paisley was leaning over her, her voice low and furious in her ear.

"You shouldn't be going. You're new, you don't know anything. You don't deserve to go. It's because you're sleeping with him, isn't it?"

Sherlock slowly turned in her chair, looking up. "No, Hannah. Stop this. This is all business, nothing else. Why don't you believe me?"

"You're lying. I can see right through you. I've seen women look at him. They all want him."

"Ollie told me Savich doesn't believe in becoming involved with anyone in his unit. That includes all of us, Hannah. If you want him, I suggest you transfer out. Listen, I only want to catch this monster in Boston. Actually I did lie. I do want Savich's brain and his expertise. Does that count? Is that brain lust?"

Finally Hannah had left.

Now Sherlock leaned her head back against her new sofa and grabbed one of the fat pillows to hug. She closed her eyes and thought of the woman who had just about everything and wanted more. She was sorry if Hannah loved Savich, but there was nothing either of them could do about it. Hannah had to get a grip. Sherlock was the last woman on earth who was a threat to her. No matter now. She wouldn't worry about it anymore. It was Savich's problem. She leaned over and stared at the phone. She picked up the receiver, stared at it some more, then took a deep breath. She dialed the number very slowly.

It rang once, twice, then "Judge Sherlock."

"Hello, Dad."

"Lacey?"

"Yes, Dad."

"This is a surprise. You usually only write. Is something wrong?"

"No. I didn't have time to write. How are you? How is Mom?"

"Your mother is the same as ever, as am I. So Douglas tells me you're in this special unit in the FBI and then I read about you and this genius guy catching that murderer in Chicago. You happy now?"

She ignored the hint of sarcasm in his voice. "Dad, he's struck again."

"What? Who's struck whom?"

"The monster who murdered Belinda. He's struck again in Boston. He killed a woman exactly the same way he killed the seven women in San Francisco. It's been exactly seven years since he stopped. It's a cycle. He's on a seven-year cycle."

There was no sound, no breathing, nothing.

"Dad? He's begun again. Didn't you understand me?"

"Yes, Lacey, I understand you."

"I'm going to Boston tomorrow morning with my boss, Dillon Savich, who's the chief of the Criminal Apprehension Unit. I'm going to catch this monster, Dad. Finally, I'm going to get him."

She was breathing hard. There was nothing but silence on the other end of the line. She drew a deep breath. She had to calm down. She didn't want to sound like some sort of obsessed nut.

But she was. That monster had taken everything from her and left her with a fear she'd managed to control, but it was there still, deep inside of her. No, it wasn't only for her. She wanted to get this scum off the streets. She wanted to shoot him herself.

"Lacey? What do you mean, you're going to catch him? You're not involved. Leave it to the professionals."

"That's what I am, Dad."

"No," he said, voice sharp, "no, I don't think so. Listen to me, Lacey. I think you should come home now. Your sister's been dead seven years. Seven years, Lacey. Douglas told me what you were doing, but I didn't want to believe it. We all know you've given up the last seven years of your life. It's way beyond time to let go of it. Forget it. Come home. You can play the piano again. You enjoyed that, and it sure won't get you killed. I won't say a word about law school. Come home."

Forget it? Forget what that butcher had done to Belinda, to her? She drew a deep breath. "How is Mom?"

"What? Oh, your mother. She had a quiet day. Her nurse, Miss Heinz, told me at dinner that she ate well and she watched television, *The Price Is Right*, I believe it was, with seeming understanding."

"I'm not like my mother."

"No, certainly you're not. But this has got to stop, Lacey."

"Why?"

"Let the police catch that madman."

"I am the police. The highest police in the land."

He was silent for a very long time, then he said quietly, "Your mother began this way, after Belinda died."

"I have to go, Dad. I'd hoped you'd be pleased that I have a shot at catching this monster."

Her father said nothing at all.

To her shock, a soft whispery voice came on the line. "Is that you, Lacey?"

"Hello, Mom. You sound great. How do you feel?"

"I'm hungry, but Nurse Heinz won't get me anything from the kitchen. I'd like some chocolate chip cookies. You always liked chocolate chip cookies when you were small, I remember."

"I remember too, Mom."

"Don't try to catch the man who murdered Belinda. He's too dangerous. He's insane, he'll kill you and I couldn't bear that. He's—"

The line went dead, then the familiar dial tone.

The phone rang again immediately. It was her father. "I'm sorry, Lacey. I was so agitated that I dropped the phone. Listen, I'm scared. I don't want anything to happen to you."

"I understand, but I must try to catch him. I must."

She heard him sigh. "I know. Be careful."

"I will." She looked at the receiver a moment, then gently laid it back in its cradle. She looked at the lovely Bentrell paintings on the stretch of white wall. Landscapes—rolling hills, some grazing cows, a small boy with a bucket on either end of a pole, carried across his back and balanced over his shoulders. She slowly lowered her face into her hands and cried. She saw her father's face from seven years ago, silent and still, no expression at all, the silence of the grave, and he'd leaned down and whispered very softly in her ear, right after Belinda's funeral, when she'd been so blank, so hollow, but not quite yet utterly terrified, "It's over, thank the good Lord. You'll survive, Lacey. She was only your half sister, try to remember that."

And she'd stared at him as if he were crazier than her mother. *Only* her half sister? That was supposed to mean something? It had only been three days later when the first nightmare had come in the deep of the night and her grief had become terror.

When the doorbell rang, she nearly shrieked, memories from the past overlaying the present. It was the doorbell, that was all, only the doorbell. Still, where was her gun? She looked frantically around the living room. There was her purse. She always carried her Lady Colt in her purse, in addition to the belt holster with her SIG.

She grabbed it, feeling its cold smoothness caress her hand like a lover even as the doorbell sounded again. She moved to stand beside the door.

"Sherlock? You there? Come on, I see the lights. Open the door!"

She nearly shuddered with relief as she shucked off the two chains, clicked back the dead bolt, and unlocked the door.

He was standing there in a short-sleeved shirt, jeans, and running shoes. A pale blue sweater was tied in a knot around his neck. She'd seen male models in magazines dressed like that—with the knotted sweater—and thought it looked ridiculous. It didn't on him. He was frowning at her.

He stepped inside, still frowning. "That's quite a display of gadgets you've got on that door. A strong guy, though, could kick it in."

She hadn't thought of that. She lowered the gun to her side, still saying nothing. She would have to reinforce the door. No, she was being absurd.

He closed the door behind him. "I wanted to see if you were furnished yet," he said, and walked into the living room. He looked around at the very expensive furnishings, then whistled. "The FBI must pay you too much. When did you get all this stuff, Sherlock?"

He was acting as though nothing was wrong. He was acting as though she was normal. She was normal. She gently laid her Lady Colt on the lamp table beside the sofa. "I'm not much of a shopper, and Sally Quinlan had to cancel out on me. I called an interior designer in Georgetown and told him what I wanted and needed in place before my boss found out. He took care of it. Really fast."

He turned slowly to look at her. "As I said, we must pay you too much."

"No, I have a trust fund. Normally I don't ever dip into it. I don't need to, but I wanted this place furnished and I didn't want to take the time to do the shopping myself. I knew you'd keep after me until I at least got a sofa."

"The trust is from your grandmother, right? If I remember correctly, she died four years ago and left you a bundle."

"Yes." She wasn't at all surprised. "Please tell me you have better things to do with your time than look up my personal history."

"Yeah, I'll tell you about my better things if you tell me why you've been crying."

Her hands went to her face. She'd forgotten. She stared at him, straight in the eye, and said, "I have an allergy."

"Yeah, right. Look at all the pollen floating around in the air in here. Come on, who upset you?"

"It's nothing, sir, nothing at all. Now, would you like a cup of coffee? Some tea?"

"Tea would be great."

"Equal in it?"

"Nah, only women use Equal. Make mine plain."

"No chemicals for you?"

He grinned at her as he followed her to the kitchen. A whole row of shiny new appliances, from a blender to a Cuisinart, were lined up on the pale yellow tiles. "No," he said, more to himself than to her, "not all of them are unused. I see you've pushed buttons on the microwave, but nothing else."

"That's right," she said coolly, as she put the teapot spout beneath the water spigot. "However, I've always believed that woman can indeed live by microwave alone," she added, trying to smile at him, which really wasn't all that difficult. She turned on the electric burner. "As for the toaster, that needs bread and I haven't bought any yet."

She said over her shoulder as she set the kettle on the stove, "I'm not packed yet, sir, but I will be ready in time and at the airport tomorrow morning."

"I know," he said, staring at the bread maker that looked like a lonely white block at the end of the counter. "You know how to use that thing?"

"No, but a recipe book came with it. The designer said that every modern kitchen needs one."

"Why were you crying, Sherlock?"

She shook her head, went to the cabinet, and got down two teacups and saucers.

"You got any cheap mugs? I don't want to get my pinky fingers near those. They look like they cost more than I make in a week."

"I guess they do. The guy went overboard on some of the things."

"I thought women liked to pick out their own dishes."

"Actually, I thought everyone did, guys included. But I didn't want to take the time. There's too much happening that's so much more important. I told you."

"Come to think of it, I did pick out my own dishes. They're microwavable."

"So are mine. That was the only criterion on my list, that and not too much fancy stuff."

"Why were you crying?"

"I would appreciate it if you would leave that alone, sir."

"Call me Savich and I might."

"All right, Savich. Old Sal calls you Dillon. I think I like that better."

"What's the guy's name?"

"What guy?"

"The one who made you cry."

She shook her head at him. "Men. You think a woman's world has to revolve around you. When I was young I used to watch the soaps occasionally. A woman couldn't seem to exist by herself, make decisions for herself, simply enjoy being herself. Nope, she was always circling a man. I wonder if they've changed any."

"I hadn't thought of it quite like that before, but yeah, I guess that's about right. What's his name, Sherlock?"

"No man. How about I pour some milk in your tea? Is that manly?"

"Sometimes, but not in tea. Keep it straight. You call Chico yet?"

"Things have been happening a bit fast. I haven't had the time."

"If you don't, I'll have to take you back to the gym and throw you around."

"The first dozen or so falls weren't that bad."

"I went easy on you."

"Ollie told me you nearly tromped him into the floor."

"At least Ollie's a guy, so he didn't whine."

She grinned at him. "This cup is too expensive to waste throwing at you."

"Good. Do you have plain old Lipton's tea bags?"

"Yes."

He watched her pour the hot water over the tea bags. "If it wasn't a guy who made you cry, then what did?"

"I could throw a tea bag at you."

"All right, I'll back off, but I don't like to see my agents upset—well, upset by something else other than me and my big mouth. Now, let's talk about our game plan in Boston. That's why I busted in on you this evening. There's a lot we need to get settled before we descend on the Boston PD."

"You're really not going to fire me?"

"Not yet. I want to get everything out of you, then if I'm still pissed off that you lied to me, that's when I'll boot you out."

"I'm sorry."

"You got what you wanted. How sorry can you be?"

He was right about that. She was a hypocrite. She gave him a big smile. "I'm not sorry at all. I'm so relieved, so grateful, that I'll let you say anything sexist you want, at least for to-night."

"You won't whine about getting up early tomorrow, will you? The flight's at seven-thirty A.M."

She groaned, then toasted him with her teacup. "Thank you, sir . . . Dillon. I won't make you sorry."

"Somehow I can't imagine that you won't."

Savich left at ten o'clock, singing to himself as he left. It had to be a line from a country-and-western song, but of course she'd never heard it before. She grinned as she heard his deep voice drawl, *"A good ole boy Redneck is what I aim to be, nothing more, nothing less will ever do for me. All rigged out in my boots and jeans, my belt buckle wide, my belly lean . . ."*

She closed the door, refastened the chains and clicked the dead bolt into place. That was the third or fourth time she thought she'd heard him singing country-western words. Oddly, her classical leanings weren't offended. What could be wrong with music that made you smile?

They hadn't spoken much about the case after all. No, he'd checked out her digs and told her she needed a CD player. It was clear what kind of music he preferred.

She packed methodically. She prayed he would help her find the man who had killed her sister.

12

~

SAVICH SAID TO SHERLOCK, "As I told you last night, Detective Budnack will be meeting us at the station. It's District Six in South Boston. They found Hillary Ramsgate in an abandoned warehouse on Congress Street. Somebody called it in anonymously, either the killer or a homeless person, probably the latter. But they've got the guy's voice on tape so when we catch him, we can make a comparison.

"He'll have all the police reports, the autopsy, the results of any other forensic tests they've done as of today. I'd appreciate it if you'd go over all this stuff. You got all our things?"

"Yes," she said, turning in her seat to face him fully. "Also, I doubt that Detective Budnack understood the game. He knew there was a game because of the note saying Hillary Ramsgate lost and had to pay the forfeit, but he didn't understand what it meant."

"No, but it's his first hit with this guy. By the time we get there, he'll have spoken to the police in San Francisco and probably read most of the reports. Tell me your take on his game, Sherlock. I'm sure you've got one."

They accepted coffee from the flight attendant, then settled back. The coffee was dreadful, but it was at least hot. She looked hard into her cup. A lock of hair had come loose from its clamp and curled along the side of her face to her jawline. He watched her jerk it behind her ear, never looking away from that coffee of hers. What was going on here?

She said finally, "I've pictured this in my mind over the years, refined it, changed it here and there, done many profiles on him, and now I think I've got it exactly the way he did it. He knocks the woman on the head and takes her to a deserted building, the bigger the building the better. In three instances, he used abandoned and condemned houses; in one, he used a house whose owners were out of town. He's intimately familiar with the buildings and houses. He's set up all his props and arranged the sets. He's turned them into houses of horror, then, finally, into mazes.

"When the woman regains consciousness, she's alone and unharmed. She isn't in complete darkness, although it's late night outside. There's a faint light, enough so she can see about a foot or two all around her. What she does first is call out. She's afraid to have an answer and afraid when there's dead silence. Then she's hopeful that he's left her there alone. She yells again.

"Then she gets herself together and tries to find a way out of the building. But there isn't a way out. There are doors, but they're bolted. She's nearly hysterical now. She knows something is very wrong. Then she finds the string that was lying beside where she'd awakened.

"She doesn't understand the string, but she picks it up and begins to follow it. It leads her through convoluted turns, over obstacles, into mirrors he's set up to scare her when she suddenly comes upon her own image. Then the string runs out. Right at the narrow entrance to this set he's put into place.

"Then perhaps he laughs, calls out to her, tells her she's going to fail and when she fails, he's going to have to punish her and she won't like that. Yes, he will have to punish her because she will lose the game. But he doesn't tell her why he's doing it. Why should he? He's enjoying her ignorance. Maybe he even calls out to her, taunts her, before she walks into the maze. That's possible, too. The note thing. He only did that with the first woman he killed in San Francisco. It's as though he's identified what he's done and the next time and the time after that, it isn't necessary. Everyone will know who he is."

He said slowly, "You are awfully certain of what he does, Sherlock."

"I told you, I've thought and thought about it. The shrinks believe—as do the FBI profilers—that he watches every move she makes, memorizes every expression on her face, possibly even films her. I'm not so sure about that.

"But I bet he even tells her she can win the game if she runs, if she manages to reach the center of the maze. She does run, hoping, praying that he isn't lying, that she can save herself, and she runs right into this maze he's built since there's nowhere else for her to go. There are dead ends in the maze. Finally she finds her way to the center. She's won. She's breathing hard. She's terrified, hopeful, both at the same time. She's made it. She won't be punished.

"He's waiting for her there." She had to stop trembling. She drew a deep breath, took another drink of her now-cold coffee, then said with a shrug, "This much was obvious when everything was reconstructed by experts after the fact."

Savich said, "So then he stabs her in the chest and in the abdomen until she's dead. Is everyone you know of certain he does this when she makes it to the center of the maze?"

"Yes. Instead of winning, she loses. He's there, with a knife. He also cuts out her tongue. This fact never appeared in any publicized reports so that any confessions could be easily verified."

"Why does he do that?"

She didn't look at him. "Probably to shut her up forever. He killed only women. He hates them."

"A game," Savich said slowly, looking down at a ragged thumbnail. "A game that leads to certain death. I don't understand why she loses if she manages to find the center of the maze. As you said, usually that means you've won. But not with this guy. You have any ideas about why he kills her when she makes it to the center of the maze?"

"Not a clue."

But she did and he didn't know how she did. "Do you remember the legend of Theseus and the Minotaur?"

"Yes," she said. "I remember that at the center of the cave, Theseus came upon the Minotaur. But Theseus didn't lose. He killed the Minotaur."

"And Ariadne led him out with a string."

"You're thinking that maybe he sees himself as Theseus and that the women are the Minotaur? I don't know. It doesn't make much sense to me."

"But you know it makes perfect sense to him. How much of a study did you do of the legend?"

"Not all that much really," she said.

"Do it when we get home again."

"But even if I happen to discover more parallels between what the killer does and the Theseus legend, it won't tell us anything about the man's identity, about how to find him. Do you know he used the same abandoned building for two of his victims in San Francisco? It was down in the China Basin. The very same building. Then the police put a watch on it, but it was too late. He was surely laughing at them, at all of us, because we were helpless."

"It surprises me no one saw anything. There are usually lots of homeless around those abandoned buildings. And cops do patrol. To set up all the props, he had to carry stuff in and out of the buildings, yet no one appeared to see anything. He had to transport his props. A truck? He had to make them himself or buy them somewhere."

"Yes, but only once. He took away most of his props after he killed each woman. He left only enough so the police would know what he'd done."

"And still no one saw anything. That boggles the mind."

"Evidently one old man saw him, because he was found strangled near one of the abandoned buildings. It was the same kind of string used to get to the center of the maze. He wanted the cops to know it had been him."

"What did you mean that he was laughing at us?" She had been nineteen years old at the time her sister was murdered. How was she involved? He would find out later. She was shaking her head at him as he said, very quietly, "You're on a cycle too, Sherlock. A seven-year cycle. He's done nothing for seven years, gone about his business, probably stewing inside but not enough to make him snap. As for you, you've given the last seven years of your life to him."

She was stiff, her eyes colder than the ice frozen over her windshield the previous winter. It was what Douglas had said to her, what her father had said: "It's none of your business."

"I suppose your family has told you it isn't very healthy."

"It's none of your business."

"I imagine you couldn't bear it, you couldn't bear to let

your sister go, not the way she was removed, like the pawn in a game that she had to lose."

She swallowed. "Yes, that's close enough."

"There's more, isn't there? A whole lot more."

She was very pale, her fingers clutched around the coffee cup. "No, there's nothing more."

"You're lying. I wish you wouldn't, but you've lied for a very long time, haven't you?"

"There's nothing more. Please, stop."

"All right. Do you want to shoot this guy once we nab him? You want to put your gun to his head and pull the trigger? Do you want to tell him who you are before you kill him? Do you think killing him will free you?"

"Yes. But that's unlikely to happen. If I can't shoot him then I want him to go to the gas chamber, not be committed the way Russell Bent will be. At least that's what my brother-in-law, Douglas Madigan, told me."

"No one knows yet if Russell Bent will be judged incompetent to stand trial. Don't jump the gun. Life imprisonment without parole isn't good enough?"

"No. I want him dead. I don't want to worry about him escaping and killing more women. I don't want to worry that he might be committed to an institution, then fool the shrinks and be let loose. I don't want him still breathing after he killed seven—no, eight—people. He doesn't deserve to breathe my air. He doesn't deserve to breathe any air."

"I've heard the opinion that since killing a murderer doesn't bring back the victim, then as a society we shouldn't impose the death penalty, that it brings us down to the murderer's level, that it's nothing but institutional revenge and destructive to our values."

"No, of course it doesn't bring the victim back. It's a ridiculous argument. It makes no sense at all. It should be very straightforward: If you take another human life, you don't deserve to go on living. It's society's punishment, it's society's revenge against a person who rips apart society's rules, who tries himself to destroy who we are and what we are. What sort of values do we have if we don't value a life enough to eradicate the one who wantonly takes it?"

"We do condemn, we do imprison, we don't necessarily believe in killing the killer."

"We should. It's justice for the victim and revenge as well. Both are necessary to protect a society from predators."

"What about the argument that capital punishment isn't a deterrent at all, thus why have it?"

"It certainly wouldn't be a deterrent to me, the way the appeals process works now. The condemned murderer spends the taxpayer's money keeping himself alive for at least another minimum of eighteen years—our money, can you begin to imagine?—no, I wouldn't be deterred. That monster, Richard Allen Davis, in California who killed Polly Klaas and was sentenced to death. You can bet you and I will be spending big bucks to keep him alive for a good dozen more years while they play the appeals game. Someone could save him during any appeal in those years. Tell me, if you knew that if you were caught and convicted of killing someone you'd be put to death within say two years maximum, wouldn't it make you think about the consequences of killing? Wouldn't that be something of a deterrent?"

"Yes. And I agree that more than a decade of appeals is absurd. Our paying for all the appeals is nuts. But revenge, Sherlock, plain old revenge. Wouldn't you have to say that the committed pursuit of it is deadening?"

That's what he'd wanted to say all along. She was very still, looking out the small window down at the scattered towns in New England. "No," she said finally, "I don't think it is. Once it's over you see, once there's justice, there can be a final good-bye to the victim. Then there's life waiting, life without fear, life without guilt, life without shame. It's all those things that are deadening." She said nothing more.

He pulled a computer magazine out of his briefcase and began reading. He wondered what else had happened to her. Something had, something bad. He wondered if the something bad had happened to her around the time her sister had been killed. It made sense. What was it?

Homicide Detective Ralph Budnack was a cop's cop. He was tall, with a runner's body, a crooked nose that had seen a good half dozen fights, intelligent, a stickler for detail, and didn't ever give up. His front teeth lapped over, making him look mischievous when he smiled. He met them at the District 6 Station and took them in to see his captain, John Dougherty, a man with bags under his tired eyes, bald and overweight, a man who looked like he wanted to retire yesterday.

They reviewed all that they knew, viewed the body in the morgue, and met with the medical examiner. There had been twenty stab wounds in Hillary Ramsgate's body: seven in the chest, thirteen in the abdomen. No sexual assault. Her tongue had been cut out, really very neatly, and there was a bump on her head from the blow to render her unconscious.

"Ralph tells me the guy's on a seven-year cycle and we lucked out that he happened to be here when the seven years were up. That kind of luck can kill a person." Captain Dougherty chewed on his unlighted cigar. "The mayor called before you came. The governor is next. I sure hope you can catch this guy."

"There are many meanings and contexts to the number seven," Savich said, looking up from the autopsy report he was reviewing again. "I don't know if we'll get much out of this, but as soon as we've inputted all the information from Ms. Ramsgate's murder into the program, I'm going to correlate it to any instances of the number seven as working behavior in numerology." He looked over at Sherlock, who was staring blankly at him. "Hey, it's worth a try. There might be something, it might be that our guy buys into all that stuff, that it will give us some clues about him."

Captain Dougherty said, "Use a psychic if you think it might help. A trained cat, if you've got one."

Savich laughed, not at all insulted. "I know it sounds weird, but you know as well as I do that people can be loonier than the Mad Hatter."

"I didn't catch your name," Ralph Budnack said, staring at Sherlock, "but I've seen you before. Now I've got it. You came in here claiming to be related to the victim." He turned to Savich, his jaw working. "You want to tell me what's going on here?"

"Calm down, Ralph. It's all very understandable. Her sister was killed seven years ago in San Francisco by this guy.

That's why she realized so fast that he'd struck again. That's why she came up here. Thanks to her, we're on to him immediately. Now, you don't have to worry about her. She works for me. I'll have her under control."

Captain Dougherty was staring at her, chewing harder on the unlit cigar. "I don't want any vigilante stuff here, Agent Sherlock. You got that? You even tiptoe outside the boundaries and I'll bust you hard. I don't care if you're FBI. I wouldn't care if you were Hoover's ghost. It appears to me Savich would bust you too. I wouldn't want to go in the ring with him."

"I understand, sir." Why did Dillon have to tell them the truth? She could have lied her way out of it. She caught his eye and realized he knew exactly what she was thinking. He didn't want her to lie anymore. Well, bully for him. It hadn't been his sister who'd been butchered; it hadn't been him to have nightmares horrible enough to wake you up wheezing, knowing that you were dying, that someone was close, really close, nearly close enough to kill you. She wanted to throw him through the window, although it looked like it had been painted shut.

Now Budnack would tell the other cops who she was and what she'd done, and no one would trust her as far as the corner.

"I hope we'll find out something about this seven-year thing," Savich said. "It also occurred to me that he knows how to build sets and props. Not only build them, but he has to transport them to the buildings where he intends to commit the murders. They must be constructed to fold pretty small to fit in a car trunk or in a van. That means he has to be proficient at least at minimal construction.

"Also, surely a truck would have been remarked upon. And he must do it in the middle of the night to cut way down on the chance of being seen. It's possible the seven business will correlate to building things. Who knows?"

"Like a propman in the theater," Sherlock said slowly, hope soaring.

"Could be," Savich said. "Let's get the rest of the goodies in the program, then see what we come up with." He stood. "Gentlemen, anything else?"

"Yes," Ralph Budnack said. "I want to help you input into this magic program of yours."

"You got it," Savich said and shook his hand.

The three of them took turns until late in the afternoon. Savich said, "There, that about takes care of it. Now let me tell MAX to stretch his brain and see what he can find for us. I inputted every instance of the number seven I could find. For example, two of the murders were committed on the seventh day of the week. Another murder was committed in the seventh month of the year. Sounds pretty far-out, but we'll see. The real key is the seven-year cycle and the fact that he killed seven women. MAX has more to work with here than he's ever had before. Also I gave MAX another bone—the construction angle." His fingers moved quickly over the keys. Then he grinned up at Sherlock, and pressed ENTER.

"That computer your kid?" Ralph Budnack asked.

"You'd think so," Savich said. "But no, MAX is a partner, and by no means a silent one." He patted the keyboard very lightly. "Nope, I'll have some real kids one of these days."

"You married?"

"No. Ah, here we go. MAX's first effort. Let me print it out."

There were only two pages.

Savich grinned at them. "Take a look, guys."

T HE PLEIADES?"

Ralph Budnack looked ready to cry. "We spent four hours inputting stuff and we get the Pleiades? What are the Pleiades?"

"The seven daughters of Atlas and Pleione," Sherlock read. "They're a group of stars, put in the sky by Zeus. Orion is behind them, chasing them."

"This is nuts," Ralph said.

"Keep reading," Savich said.

Sherlock looked up, her face shining. "He's an astronomer, he's got to be. That or he's an astrologer or into numerology, with astronomy as a hobby."

Ralph Budnack said, "Maybe he's a college professor, teaching mythology. He builds furniture on the side, as a hobby."

"At least there appears to be something in the seven scenario," Savich said, laying down page two. "We've got some leads. I've got a couple of other ideas, but Ralph, you and your guys can start checking this all out. Chances are, according to the profilers, that the guy has been here at least six months, but less than a year. Enough time, in other words, for him to scout out all the places he's going to take his victims."

"Good point," Budnack said, rubbing his hands together. "My other team members are interviewing everyone they can scrape up from the Congress Street area. I'll pull them off to do this."

When Sherlock and Savich were alone, she said, "You're having a problem with all this, aren't you?"

"This whole business with the seven sisters of the Pleiades, it seems too easy, too obvious."

"Why? It took MAX to come up with it. The SFPD didn't come up with it. The profilers didn't either. Also, it's a seven-year interval between killings. He kills seven women at each cycle. Two sevens is a goodly number of sevens."

Savich stood up and stretched, scratched his stomach. "You're probably right. I'm dragged down because MAX got it and we didn't. But you know, I've got this itch in my belly. Whenever I've gotten this itch in the past, there's been something I've missed.

"I need to go to the gym. Working out clears my brain. You want to come along? I won't tromp you this time. In fact, I'll start work on your deltoids."

"I didn't bring any workout stuff. Besides, I plan to protect my deltoids with my life."

The cops tracked down four possible suspects within the next twenty-four hours—two of them astrologers who'd come to Boston during the past year, two of them numerologists. Both the numerologists had come during the past year from southern California. They didn't arrest any of them. Budnack, Savich, and Sherlock met later that day in Captain Dougherty's office.

"No big deal about that," Ralph Budnack said, frowning. "All the nuts come from southern California."

"So does Julia Roberts," Savich said.

"Point taken," Budnack said and grinned. "So what do you think, Savich? It doesn't feel right with any of these guys. Plus two of them have pretty good alibis. We found a homeless guy, Mr. Rick, he's called, who said he saw a guy going in and out of the warehouse on Congress. He said he was all bundled up and he wondered about that since it was really warm that night, said it was so warm he didn't even have to sleep in his box. Said he hadn't seen him before."

"Any more specifics about the man?" Sherlock asked. "Anything about what he looked like?"

"He looked kind of scrawny, a direct quote from Mr. Rick. Whatever that means. Mr. Rick is pretty big. Scrawny might mean anything smaller than six foot. I might add that only one of the four guys we picked up could be called scrawny, and he's got the strongest alibi."

Savich had wandered away. He was pacing, head down, seemingly staring at the linoleum floor.

"He's thinking," she said in answer to Captain Dougherty's unasked question.

"Your sister was really offed by this guy?"

"Yes. It's been seven years. But you never forget."

"Is that why you got into the FBI?"

"I didn't know what else to do. I went to school and learned a bit about all the areas in forensics, then I focused on how the criminal mind works. Actually I'd planned to be a profiler, but I couldn't live what they do every day. So here I am. Thank the powers that be for Savich's new unit."

"You even learn about blood-spattering patterns?"

"Yeah, some of the examples of that were pretty gruesome. I'm not an expert, but at least I learned enough so that I'd know what to do, where to find out more, who to contact."

Captain Dougherty said, "Everyone thinks profiling is so sexy. Remember that show on TV about a profiler?"

"Yeah, the one with ESP. Now that was something, wasn't it? Why bother with profiling? A waste of time. Tune in to the guy and you've got him."

He grinned and she distracted him with another question about one of the men they'd hauled in for questioning.

It was at midnight when Savich sat up in bed, drew a very deep breath, and said, "I've got you, you son of a bitch."

He worked at the computer until three o'clock in the morning. He called Ralph Budnack at seven A.M. and told him what he needed.

"You got something, Savich?"

"I might," he said slowly. "I just might. On the other hand, I might be off plucking daisies in that big flower market in the sky. Keep doing what you're doing." He then called Sherlock's room.

"I need you," he said. "Come to my room and we'll order room service."

The fax was humming out page after page from Budnack. "Yeah," Savich was saying, "this will help."

"You won't tell me what you're homing in on?"

"Nope, not until I know there's a slight chance I'm on the right track."

"I was thinking far into the night," she said, and although it wasn't at all cold in the room, she was rubbing her hands over her arms. She looked tired, pinched. "I couldn't get this seven business out of my mind." She drew a deep breath. "We banked everything on seven, and so we got the Pleiades and all that numerology stuff. But what if it doesn't have anything to do with seven at all? What if there was the one instance of seven and that was merely the time lag before he started killing again? What if he killed more than seven women? Eight women or even nine?" She looked nearly desperate, standing there, rubbing her arms. "Not much of a big lead there. I think you're right, it's too pat, and too confining. But if there's nothing there, then what else is there?"

"You're perfectly right. You've got a good brain, Sherlock. My brain was working in tandem with yours—"

She laughed, some of the tension easing out of her. "Which means you've got a good brain too."

"Me and MAX together have a top-drawer brain. All right, let me tell you where I'm heading and if you think I'm off the wall, then you can haul me back. I've been thinking we've gotten too fancy here, exactly what you said—it's too complicated, too out there. It assumes our killer is a really deep profound fellow with lots of esoteric literary or astrological underpinnings. That he probably builds designer furniture on the side. I woke up at midnight and thought: Give me a break. This is nothing but a headache theory. It's time to get back to basics.

"I knew then that our guy isn't any of those things. I think the answer might lie with the obvious. I've been asking MAX to come up with other alternatives or new options based on new factoring data I put in." He drew a deep breath. "Remember, Sherlock, this still might not lead anywhere."

"What's obvious?"

"A psychopath who knows how to build props, make them fold up small, and make them portable. I know they checked into this in San Francisco—they went to all the theaters, interviewed a dozen prop designers and builders. I went back in to see exactly what they did find—and where they'd looked, what kind of suspects they'd turned up.

"Not much, as it turns out. So, I'm having MAX look where they didn't look. I've inputted about everything I can think of into the program so we've got a prayer of turning up something helpful."

She didn't say anything, continued to look at him. She felt hope well up, but she was afraid to nourish it. She saw he was rubbing his neck.

"What's wrong with you?"

"I worked out too hard last night after you left and then spent too much time hunched over MAX. No big deal."

"If you're not too macho, you might consider some aspirin. On the other hand, I hesitate to say anything at all now, given that you and MAX together are such a great team and MAX has got the bit between his teeth."

"Yeah, he's got a great byte."

"That was funny, Dillon, if you spelled it right."

"Trust me. I did."

"You look like you're ready to burst out of your skin and you can still be funny."

"You're not laughing."

"I'm too scared." And it was the truth. She was terrified he would kill again, terrified that he would escape and there would never be justice.

He watched her walk away from him across to the far windows that looked down eight floors to the street below.

"You want to tell me what else happened seven years ago?"

She actually flinched as if he'd struck her. He rose slowly and walked to her. He reached out his hand, looked at it, then dropped his arm back to his side. He said only, "Sherlock."

She didn't turn, shook her head.

MAX beeped. Savich pressed the PRINT button. After a moment, he picked out one sheet of paper from the printer. He began to laugh. "MAX says our person may be in building supplies."

She whipped around so fast she nearly fell. "As in a lumberyard?"

"Yes. He says that odds are good that with all the building materials the killer left behind, the type of hardware the killer used, the type of nails, the wood, the kinds of corkboard, the brackets, et cetera, that our guy works in lumber. Of course, the cops in the SFPD looked at every prop he left behind at every murder. It turns out that the wood wasn't traceable, that all the brackets, hinges, and screws were common and sold everywhere. They came up dry. Now, they never specifically went after men who worked in lumberyards. MAX thinks we should look again."

Her eyes were sparkling. "MAX is the greatest, that's brilliant."

"We'll see. Now in addition to a guy who works in lumber, we've also got a psychopath who hates women and cuts out their tongues. Why? Because he himself has taken grief from them or seen other men take the grief?"

She didn't meet his eyes. "Maybe he cuts out their tongues because he knows they bad-mouth their husbands and curse a whole lot. Maybe he doesn't believe women should curse. Maybe that's how he picks out the women to kill."

She'd known that all along, he thought, but how? It was driving him crazy, but he let it go for now. He knew she was right on the money. It felt right to his gut—no, perfect. He said easily, "That sounds possible. Weren't there some profiles drawing that conclusion?"

"Yes, certainly there were. The guy's not in the theater or anything sexy like that?"

"Nope. I'll call Ralph. He can check to see who's arrived during the past year in Boston who works for a lumberyard." Now that he thought about it, perhaps he had seen some speculation about that in some of the reports and profiles he'd read. Still, there was a whole lot more to all this. He looked at her. She looked away. Trust was a funny thing. It took time.

Marlin Jones was the assistant manager at the Appletree Home Supplies and Mill Yard in Newton Center. He was in conversation with his manager, Dude Crosby, when a pretty young woman with thick, curly auburn hair came up to him, a piece of plywood in her hand. There was something familiar about her.

He smiled at her, his eyes on that foot-long piece of plywood. He said before she could explain, "The problem is that the plywood's too cheap. You tried to put a nail through it and it shredded the plywood. If you'll come over here, I'll show you some better pieces that won't fall apart on you. Have we met before?"

"Thank you, er, Mr. Jones," she said, looking at his name tag. "No, we haven't met before."

"I'm not very good at remembering faces, but well, you're so pretty, maybe that's why I thought I'd met you before." She followed him out into the lumberyard. "What are you doing with the plywood, ma'am?"

"I'm building props for my son's school play, and that's why I need to use plywood, not hardwood. They're doing *Oklahoma!* and I've got to put together a couple of rooms that can be easily disassembled then put back up. So I'll need some brackets and some screws too."

"Then why'd you pound a nail through it?"

"That was experimentation. My husband, that fucking son of a bitch, won't help me, drinks all the time, won't take part in raising our son, won't show me any affection at all, well, so I've got to do it all myself."

Marlin Jones stared at her, as if mesmerized. He cleared his throat. "I can help you with this, Mrs.—?"

"Marty Bramfort." She shook his hand. "I live on Commonwealth. I had to take a bus out here because that bastard husband of mine won't fix the car. Next thing I know, that damned car will be sitting on blocks in the front yard and the neighbors will call the cops."

"Mrs. Bramfort, if you could maybe draw what you need to build, then I could gather all the stuff together for you."

"I don't suppose you'll help me put it all together?"

"Well, ma'am, I'm awfully busy."

"No, never mind. That's my jerk husband's job, or it should be. It's not yours. But I would appreciate your advice. I already made some drawings. Here they are."

She laid them out on top of a large sheet of plywood. Marlin Jones leaned over to study them. "Not bad," he said after a few minutes. "You won't have much trouble doing this. I'll cut all the wood for you and show you how to use the brackets. You want to be able to break all the stuff down quickly, though. I know how to do that."

She left the Appletree Home Supplies and Mill Yard an hour later. Marlin Jones would deliver the twelve cut pieces of plywood to the grade school gymnasium, along with brackets and screws, hinges, gallons of paint, and whatever else he thought she'd need.

Before she left him, she placed her hand lightly on his forearm. "Thank you, Mr. Jones." She looked at him looking at her hand on his forearm. "I bet you're not a lazy son of a bitch like my husband is. I bet you do stuff for your wife without her begging you."

"I'm not married, Mrs. Bramfort."

"Too bad," she said, and grinned up at him. "But hey, I bet lots of ladies would like to have you around, no matter if they're married or not." When she walked away from him, she was swinging her hips outrageously. "Who knows what building props can lead to?" she called out over her shoulder, and winked at him.

She was whistling to herself as she walked from where she'd parked her car toward the Josephine Bentley Grade School gymnasium. It was Ralph Budnack's car, a 1992 Honda Accord that drove like a Sherman tank. Toby, the temporary school janitor and a black cop for the Sixth Division, opened the door for her.

His voice carried as he said, "Jest about done, Mrs. Bramfort?"

"Oh yes, very nearly done now. You going home, Toby?"

"Yep, waiting to let you in. Don't forget to lock up now, Mrs. Bramfort."

"I won't."

She was alone in the gymnasium, a vast room that resounded with her breathing, with every step she took, filling the empty air with echoes. All the nearly built props were neatly stacked in the corner. She'd been doing this a good five evenings in a row now. She unstacked all of them, laying them out side by side. Not much more to do.

She began work, her right hand turning the screwdriver again and again, digging in new holes through the plywood. Some of them were L-shaped, most flat. The brackets were to support the two pieces of plywood. She didn't have all the lights on; just the corner where she worked had lighting. It wasn't much. There were deepening shadows all around her, growing blacker as the minutes passed. Soon it would be nine o'clock. Dark outside. Darker inside.

It was the fifth night.

There wasn't much more to do now except paint. Everything he'd sent over she'd used. She rose and dusted her hands on her jeans. She'd been to see Marlin Jones several times. He was always polite, always eager to help her, seemed to like it when she flirted with him. He had dark, dark eyes, almost opaque, as if no light ever shined behind them. He had dark brows, a thin nose, and full lips. He was good-looking, built well, if a bit on the thin side. He wasn't all that tall, so perhaps then he could be called scrawny. After each time she saw him, she thought that he was only a man, one who earned his living cutting wood.

"There," she said aloud, wishing something would happen soon, praying it would happen, knowing she wasn't going to like being conked on the head, but not caring. A drop of pain behind her ear, a headache, were nothing compared to what he was going to get. "Done. Now let's see how easy it is to undo all this stuff."

"It's real easy, Marty."

It was his voice, Marlin's voice. He was right behind her. She'd never heard him come in. She wanted to leap for joy. Finally, he'd come.

Her heart pounding, she whirled about, a gasp coming out of her mouth. "Oh goodness gracious, Marlin, you scared the stuffing out of me. Oh yeah, you scared me shitless."

"Hi, Marty. I came by to see how you were doing with the props. You know, you really shouldn't curse like that. Ladies shouldn't. It doesn't sound right."

"Everyone does, Marlin, everyone. You should hear that scum bucket husband of mine cut loose. Look at this. I'm all done. I still need to paint, but I forgot which colors go on which piece so I'll have to go home and get the drawings."

"Not bad," he said after a couple of minutes. He had run his fingers over the brackets, frowning when they weren't straight, frowning even more when the screws weren't all the way in.

He turned to smile down at her. "How's your husband?"

"That asshole? I left him drinking Bud in front of the television. I'm going to leave that jerk, anytime now, I'm going to tell him to haul his saggy butt out of there and—"

It came so fast, she didn't have time to do a single thing, even be frightened, even to prepare herself for it. The lights went out. At nearly the same instant, she felt a shock of heavy pain behind her left ear. She wanted to cry out, but there wasn't any sound in her throat, nothing at all, and she simply collapsed where she stood. She realized before the blackness took over everything that she hadn't hit the floor. No, Marlin was holding her. Where was Toby? Well hidden, she hoped. Please, don't let him freak out and ruin the plan. No, he wouldn't. Everyone knew she had to take a hit.

She'd begged for it.

14

$\mathcal{S}$HE WOKE UP TO DULL,
thudding pain behind her left ear. She'd never been hit in the
head before. She'd only known what to expect in theory. The
reality of it was that it wasn't all that bad. Marlin knew what
he was doing. He didn't want her incapacitated. He wanted
her up soon, panicked, scared, and begging. He didn't want her
crawling around puking up her guts from the nausea.

She held perfectly still until the pain lifted. She knew this
time she was lying on the floor, a raw-plank floor that smelled
like old rotted wood, decades of dust and dirt embedded
deep, and ancient carcasses, withered and stale, probably rats.

It should have been pitch black, but it wasn't. She knew
what was going to happen and still she felt such terror she
doubted she could even get enough saliva in her mouth to yell.
She thought briefly of the other women—of Belinda—the
terror of waking alone, head pounding, knowing something
was desperately wrong, and it was made all that much worse
because it was unknown. She was scared to her very soul even
though she knew what would happen.

She wanted to kill Marlin Jones very badly.

It seemed there were some hidden lights giving off enough
light so she could see about a foot around her. She knew she
was in a big deserted building. She also knew she wasn't
alone. Marlin Jones was here, somewhere, watching her. With
infrared glasses? Maybe so.

She rose slowly to her feet, rubbing the back of her head.
She had a slight headache, nothing more now. Oh yes, Marlin
was good at what he did. She wondered how long he'd keep

quiet. She called out, her voice credibly shaky, rife with rising panic, "Is anyone there? Please, where am I? What do you want? Who are you?"

Hysteria bubbled up, making her voice shrill now, raw in that silent air. "Who's there? You cowardly little bastard, show yourself!"

There was no answer. There was no sound of any kind except for her hard breathing. She didn't bother checking the boundaries of the building. Let him be disappointed that she was shortening the play, shortening his fun. She looked down to see the string lying where her hand had lain. It disappeared into the distance. She leaned down and picked it up. Skinny, strong string, leading her to the maze. It was fastened to something a goodly distance away. She slowly began to follow it. As she walked the dim light behind her disappeared, and the darkness ahead of her became shadowy light. Slowly, so slowly, breathing hard, she walked.

Suddenly a light snapped on overhead, fiercely white, blinding her momentarily. Then she saw a woman staring at her, a woman whose mouth was hanging open, a wild-looking woman, pale as death, her hair tangled around her face. She screamed at her own image in the mirror staring back at her, frozen for an instant in time and terror.

Slowly she backed away from the mirror, one short step, then one more. She saw walls, props, really, some fastened together with hinges, others with brackets, not amateurish like the ones she'd made. No, Marlin's props were professional all the way.

The bright light snapped off as suddenly as it had come on, and she was left again in the narrow dim light.

It was then she heard breathing. Soft, steady breathing, to her right. She whirled to face it. "Who's there?"

Breathing, no voice, no answer. An amplifier of some kind. She whimpered, for him, then again, making it louder, hugging herself, then started following the string again. Suddenly the string ran out. She was standing in front of a narrow opening that had no door. She couldn't see beyond the opening.

"Hello, Marty. Come in, I've been waiting for you."

His voice. Marlin Jones.

"Marlin, is it really you? How did I get here? You've come to save me?"

"I don't think so, Marty. No, I'm the one who brought you here. I brought you here for me."

She felt rage pour through her. She pictured Belinda standing here, not knowing what was happening or why, so frightened she could scarcely breathe, and here that maniac was talking to her in a voice as smooth and gentle as a parish priest's.

"What do you want, you pathetic bastard?"

He was silent. She'd taken him by surprise. He was expecting tears, pleading. She yelled, "Well, you fucking slug? What do you want? You too scared to talk to me?"

She heard him actually draw in his breath. Finally he said, his voice not quite as smooth as it had been, but calm enough now, "You were fast coming here. I expected you to search around, to check for a way out of the building, but you didn't. You looked down, saw the string, and followed it."

"What the hell is the damned string for? Some sick joke? Or are you the only sick joke in this silly place, Marlin?"

His breath speeded up; she could hear it. His breath was wheezing with anger. Push him. She wanted to push him. Let Savich curse her, let all of them curse her, it didn't matter. She had to push him to the edge, she had to defeat him, then obliterate him. "Well, you fucking little pervert? What is it for? Something to excite your sick little brain?"

"Now, Marty, don't mouth off at me. I hate it when a woman has a foul mouth. I thought you were so sweet and helpless when you first came to me, but then you talked filth. You opened your pretty mouth and filth spewed out. And your poor husband. No wonder he drinks—anything to escape that horrible language. And you put him down, you tell the world how bad he is because he was unlucky enough to marry you."

"I might spew out bad words, but at least I'm not a brain-rotted psycho like you. What do you want, Marlin? What is this string bit?"

His voice was now a soft singsong, a gentle monotone, as if he were seeing himself as an omniscient god and her as a child gone astray, to be led back. Led back to hell. "I'll tell you everything when you find the center of the maze, Marty. I build props like you do only I'm better because I've done it more. I want you to come in now, Marty. You'll win when you find the center of the maze. Even though you say bad things, you'll still win if you find the center. I'll be timing you, Marty. Time's always important. You can't forget about the time. Come along, now, you've got to come in or else I'll have to punish you right now. Find the center, Marty, or you won't like what I'll do to you."

"How much time do I have to get to the center of the maze so you won't punish me?"

The gentle monotone was now tinged with impatience. "You ask too many questions, Marty."

"I'll find the center if you'll tell me why the string bit."

"How else am I supposed to get you to come here? I didn't want to paint signs. That would have been too obvious. FOLLOW THE ARROWS. That's tacky. The string is neat. It's tantalizing. Now my patience is running out, Marty. Come into the maze."

There was sudden anger now, cold and hard. "Marty? What are you doing?"

"My sneaker was untied. I was tying it. I don't want to trip over myself."

"It didn't look to me like you were tying your sneaker. Come on now or I'll have to do something you won't like at all."

"I'm coming." She walked through the narrow entrance into a narrow corridor of six-foot-high sheets of plywood, painted green to simulate yew bushes. She came to an intersection. Four choices. She took the far-left turn. It led her to a dead end.

He laughed. "Wrong choice, Marty. Maybe if you didn't curse so much, God would have let you find the right way to go. Maybe if you weren't so mean to your poor husband, God wouldn't have brought you to me. Try again. I'm getting impatient."

But he wasn't at all impatient; she realized it in that instant. He was relishing every moment. The longer it took her to get to the center, the more he enjoyed himself.

"You're slow, Marty. You'd best hurry. Don't forget about the time. I told you that time was important."

She could hear the excitement in his voice, unleashed now, feel the stirring of his excitement in the air around her. It nauseated her. She couldn't wait to see him.

She backtracked and took another turn. This one also led to a dead end. On the third try, she picked the right path. There was only a small pool of light around her, never varying, never growing brighter or dimmer. She hit another dead end off a wrong turn. She heard his breathing quicken; his excitement was peaking. She was close to the center of the maze now.

She stopped and called out, "Why a maze, Marlin? Why do you want me to find the center of a maze?"

His voice trembled, he was so excited. No one had asked him this before. He was bursting to tell her. "It's like finding your way to your own soul, Marty. There are lots of wrong turns and dead ends, but if you're good enough, if you try hard enough, you'll eventually come to the center of your soul and then you'll know the truth of who and what you are."

"That's very poetic, Marlin, for a stupid psychopath. Who let you out of the asylum?"

"I'll have to punish you for that, Marty. I'm not your husband. You've no right to insult me."

She yelled, "Why the fuck not, you puny, pathetic little slug?"

"Stop it! Yes, keep quiet, that's better. Now, I'm waiting, Marty, I'm waiting for you. You're running out of time. You'd better stop mouthing off at me and run."

She did, no wrong turns now, right to the center, no hesitation at all.

He was there, standing in the center of the maze, wearing goggles. In the next moment, he'd pressed a button and a pool of light flooded down where they stood. He was dressed in camouflage fatigues with black army boots laced up to the top. He pulled off the infrared goggles. He looked as white as a death mask in the eerie light. Now he did look scrawny. He gave her a big smile. "You made it here real fast when you tried, Marty. I scared you enough so that you knew if you didn't hurry, I'd have to hurt you really bad."

"Scare me? You stupid moron, you wouldn't scare a dead chicken. Did I beat your time limit, you worthless little shit?"

His smile dropped away. He looked more confused than

angry. "Why aren't you afraid? Why aren't you begging me to let you go now? You know it makes me crazy when you say bad words, when—"

"You're already so crazy I don't have to say anything, you stupid prick."

"Shut up! I hate to hear a woman curse, hate it, hate it, hate it! You didn't make the center in time, Marty. I've got to punish you now."

"How will you do that, you little creep?"

"Damn you, shut up!" He pulled a hunting knife out of the sheath at his waist. It was a foot long—sharp, cold silver. It gleamed in that dead white light.

"Why a maze, Marlin? Before you punish me, tell me about why you use a maze?"

"It's special for you, Marty, only for you." He was playing with the knife now, lightly running the pad of his thumb over the blade. "It's real sharp, Marty, real sharp."

"Of course it is. It's a knife, you idiot. Not only are you pathetic, you're also a liar. You didn't build this maze only for me. Your little game isn't at all special. You aren't capable of any originality at all. Nope, the same thing over and over. Every one of the women you've killed had to find her way to the center of your maze. Why the maze, Marlin? Or are you too afraid to tell me?"

He took a step closer, then stopped. "How do you know about all the other women?"

"I'm psychic, you toad. I can read that miserable little brain of yours without trying. Yeah, I'm psychic, as opposed to a psychopath, which is what you are. Why the maze, Marlin? You're afraid to tell me, aren't you? I knew it, you're nothing but a pathetic little coward."

"Damn you, shut up! I'll tell you, then I'll cut out that filthy tongue of yours and I'll make you eat it before I slice you like a stalk of celery." He was panting, he was breathing so hard, as if he'd sprinted a good hundred yards. "My father loved mazes. He said they were a work of art when done well. He taught me how to build mazes. We lived in the desert outside Yuma. There weren't any nice thick green bushes, so we had to build our own bushes, then we had so many, we made them into mazes." He shook his head, frowned at her. "You got me off track. You made me change my lines. I've never done that before. I've got to punish you for that now, Marty."

"I sure hope your father isn't alive. He sounds as sick as you. You said the other women didn't make you change your lines. Why did you punish them? What'd they do to you?"

"Damn you, shut up! Don't you dare talk about my dad! And I won't tell you anything!"

"Bad language, Marlin. You're not a very good role model. Did the women you butchered always use bad language? Or was it because they insulted their husbands?"

"Bitch! Shut up!"

She shook her head at him. "I can't believe you called me that, Marlin. I hate bad language, too. It makes me crazy, did I tell you that? I'll have to punish you as well. Who goes first?"

He yelled, running at her, jerking the knife over his head.

Savich yelled, "Down!"

At the same instant, full lights came on. Marlin stumbled, blinded by the sudden lights. So was she, but she knew what to do.

She was already rolling as she jerked her Lady Colt from her ankle holster and came up onto her elbows.

Marlin Jones was yelling, bringing the knife down, slicing it through the air again and again, yelling and yelling. Then he saw her, lying there, the gun pointed at him.

Captain Dougherty's voice came out of the darkness. "It's the police, Marlin. Throw down the knife and back away from her! Do it now or you're dead."

"NO!"

"I want to kill you, Marlin," she whispered, aimed the gun at his belly, "but I won't if you put that knife down." Her finger was stroking the trigger. She wanted to squeeze it so badly she felt nausea rise in her belly.

Marlin stopped in his tracks. He stared down at her, at that gun she was training on him. "Who are you?"

"I'll tell you that in court, Marlin, or I'll wire it to you in hell. How many times did you stab all those women, Marlin? Was it always the same number of times? Didn't you ever vary anything? No, you didn't. You stabbed them and then cut out their tongues. How many times, Marlin? The same number as Hillary Ramsgate? Twenty stabs? Keep coming to me now, Marlin, if you want a bullet through your gut. I want to kill you, but I won't, not unless you force me to."

He was shaking his head back and forth, his jaw working madly as he took one step back, then another. Suddenly, in a move so fast it blurred before her, he aimed the knife, released it.

She heard Savich yell even as she jerked to the right. She felt the knife slice through her upper arm. It didn't hit the bone. "Thanks, Marlin," she said, and fired the Lady Colt. The impact sent him staggering back, his arms clutched around his belly.

Savich yelled, "He's down! Hold your fire! Don't shoot!"

He wasn't in time. Sporadic rounds of fire burst from a dozen weapons, lighting up the warehouse with dim points of light. Savich yelled out again, "He's down! Stop!"

The guns of the dozen police officers surrounding the maze fell silent one by one. They stared at the ripped-up rotted flooring. Incredibly, they hadn't hit Marlin Jones. The closest shot had ricocheted off the side of one of his army boots.

The silence was abrupt and heavy.

"Sherlock, damn your eyes, I'm going to throw you from here to Buffalo!"

She was lying on her back, grinning up at him even as he dropped to his knees beside her, ripping the sleeve off his own shirt. The knife was sticking obscenely out of her upper arm. "Hold still now, and don't move a muscle. This might hurt a bit." He pulled out the knife.

She didn't yell until she saw it in his hand, her blood covering the blade.

"Don't whine. It barely nicked you. Hold still now." He bound her arm with his shirtsleeve. "I can't believe you did that. I'm going to kill you once you're okay again. I'm going to tromp you into the mat three dozen times before I even consider letting up on you. Then I'm going to work your deltoids so hard you won't be able to move for a week. Then I'll kill you again for doing this."

"Is he dead, Dillon?"

Savich turned to look at Ralph, who was applying pressure to Marlin's stomach. "Nope, but it will be close," Ralph said. "You got him in the belly. The ambulances should be here.

You did good, Sherlock, but I agree with Savich. You nearly got yourself killed. After Savich is done with you, I think I should take you to my boat in the harbor, go a bit out into the ocean, and drown you."

She smiled up at Savich. "I sure hope he bites the big one. If he doesn't die, he'll prove he's mad, which he is, and if he gets a liberal judge and easy shrinks then he could be pronounced cured and let out to do it all again in another seven years and then he—You pulled that knife out of me. It sort of hurts really bad now. Goodness, look at all that blood."

Her eyes simply drifted closed, her head lolling to the side.

"Damnation," Savich said, and pressed harder on the wound.

He heard two men and a woman calling out, "Let us through. Paramedics! Let us through!"

Savich took the Lady Colt from her slack fingers, stared down at the little gun that could so easily kill a human being, shook his head, and pocketed it. He didn't touch the bloody knife.

15

$\mathcal{S}$HE WOKE UP IN THE AMBU-
lance, flat on her back, an IV dripping into her arm, two blankets pulled up to her chin. A female paramedic was sitting at
her feet. Savich was sitting beside her, his face an inch from
hers.

He said the moment her eyes opened, "It's all right, Sherlock. Mrs. Jameson here redid the bandage on your arm, applied a little pressure, and the wound is only bleeding lightly.
You're going to have to be checked for any arterial damage,
then have some stitches when we get to the hospital, and anti-
biotics. I'm going to tell the doctor not to anesthetize you at
all and use a big needle. The IV in your arm is water and
some salts, nothing for you to worry about. I told you, the
knife nicked you, no big deal."

Her arm burned so hot she was vaguely surprised it didn't
burst into flame. She managed to smile. "So I'm not to whine?"

"Right."

Mrs. Jameson said, "You've got great veins. How do you
feel, Agent Sherlock?"

"Really good actually," she said and nearly groaned.

"She's lying. It hurts bad. Listen to me, Sherlock. When
Marlin threw the knife at you, if you hadn't already been
moving away, it would have gone right through your heart and
none of us would have been able to stop it. I never should
have trusted you, never. I was sure you knew what you were
doing, but you didn't. You turned those summer-sky eyes of
yours on me and that super-sincere FBI voice, and I bought

everything you told me. I knew I shouldn't have, but I did, so it's my fault too. What you did really makes me mad. You lost it with that psychopath and you didn't even care. You pushed him and pushed him. He could have forgotten all about his act. He could have killed you without following his script. That was stupid. That really pisses me off, Sherlock."

"It hurts, doesn't it?" said Mrs. Jameson, drawing Savich off. "But I can't give you any pain medication. We'll have to let the doctor decide on that. Your blood pressure's fine. Now, hang in there. We'll be at the hospital in a few minutes."

At that moment, when she thought her arm would burn off her body, she said, "I'm sorry, Dillon, but I had to."

"Why did you shoot him in the gut? Why didn't you go for his chest?"

Her eyes were vague, filled with blurred shadows, but she knew there were no more ghosts to weave in and out of her mind, tormenting her. No, everything was all right now. His voice seemed farther away than an instant before. What had Dillon wanted to know? Oh yes. She licked her lips, and whispered, "I wanted him to suffer. Through the heart would have been too easy on him."

"Finish it, Sherlock."

"All right, the truth. He hasn't told us everything. If I could have gotten all of it out of him, then I would have shot him clean. Well, maybe. Yes, we have to get him to tell us everything, then I'll shoot him in the chest, I promise."

She was utterly serious. On the other hand, she was woozy from pain and shock. He said slowly, smiling at her, "Actually, if you hadn't shot him at all, if the bullet hadn't thrown him a good three feet backward in the same instant, he would have had at least thirty rounds pumped into him. So, Sherlock, the bottom line is that you really saved his life."

"Well, damn," she said, then smiled back up at him.

"If he pulls through, you can question him and get everything you want out of him. We'll do it together. Don't worry now. Despite the fact that I'm going to throw you across the gym when you're okay again, you still got him." But it had been close, far too close, unnecessarily so. She'd totally disobeyed orders. She'd been a loose cannon. On the other hand, he doubted she'd have ever done that if it hadn't been the psycho who had killed her sister. He'd chew her up some more when she was well again. He hoped it would be soon. She could have died so easily.

She said, "Thank you, Dillon. Give me a while before we go to the gym and you tromp me into the floor. I don't feel so good right now."

She leaned up and vomited into a basin quickly put under her face by Mrs. Jameson.

"You'll do, Agent Sherlock. Hey, you're not related to Mohammad Sherlock, that famous Middle Eastern sleuth?"

She wanted to shriek at him for the ghastly pain of those six stitches in her upper arm, but she wasn't about to make a peep. He'd given her a pain shot before he'd ever touched her with that needle, but it hadn't helped all that much. Savich was sitting in a chair by the small cubicle door, his legs crossed, his hands folded across his chest, looking at her, daring her to wuss out on him. She said between gritted teeth, "That's one of the best ones I've heard yet, Dr. Ashad."

He swiftly knotted off the thread. "I pride myself on not being too trite. There, all done. Now, let's pour some stuff on this, sorry, but it'll really sting, then give you three more shots in the butt—tetanus, an antibiotic, and another pain med. Then you'll be out of here. Do go see your doctor down in Washington in a couple of days. The stitches will resorb. You can forget about them. A great detective like you, I don't suppose you want anything for the pain?"

"I still have the strength to give you a good kick, Doctor. If you don't give me a shot, I'll do it."

"I thought for sure that local would be strong enough for a big FBI agent, particularly one with such a flamboyant name."

"I'm a new agent. It'll take a while to get to full pain-absorbing capacity, like that guy over there who could have his head kicked in and still sing and crack jokes."

Savich laughed. "Yeah, go ahead and give her a shot of something to knock her out. Otherwise she's so hyped up she won't shut up until I gag her."

Dr. Ashad, thin, dark-skinned, yellowish teeth from too

much smoking, said as he prepared three needles, "Are you really a new agent, or is that a joke? Come on, you guys have worked together for a long time, haven't you?"

"No, I never saw her before in my life until a month ago. Now I'm going to kill her as soon as she's fit again, so our total acquaintance will have been very short in cosmic terms."

"You're funny, Agent Savich."

"No, I'm not."

"Drop your pants, Agent Sherlock."

"In the arm, please, Dr. Ashad."

"No can do. In the butt, Agent."

"Not until he leaves the room."

Savich stood right outside the door. He smiled grimly when he heard her yell. Then she yelled again. Two shots. Another yell. There, that was all of them. That should fix her up. She'd nearly died. He should have known that she'd lose it and do exactly what she'd probably planned to do for the last seven years. He looked up to see Ralph Budnack and Captain Dougherty walking toward him.

"How is she?"

"Fine. Back to being a pain in the butt."

"That woman likes to dance right up to the edge," Captain Dougherty said. "You need to talk to her about that, Savich." Then he smiled. "Got him," he said, and rubbed his hands together. He didn't look at all old or worn out tonight. Indeed, there was a bounce to his step. As for Ralph, he couldn't hold still, jumped from one foot to the other, his hands talking faster than his mouth moved.

There was another yelp.

"Four shots," Savich said. "She deserves all the jabs the doctor gives her. I wonder what that last one was for? Maybe part of her punishment."

A few minutes later, Sherlock came out of the small cubicle tucking in her blouse with one hand since her other arm was in a dark blue sling. "He's a sadist," she said to Savich before she saw the two cops. "He's not trite, but he is a sadist. I think I might invite him to dinner so I can poison his food."

"You look pretty fit, Agent Sherlock," Captain Dougherty

told her, and patted her good shoulder with a beefy hand. "We thought maybe you guys wanted to come upstairs to see about Marlin Jones's condition."

"As of now I'm officially discharged and I wouldn't miss it," Sherlock said, then looked up at Savich. "What about you, sir? Are you feeling better too? Not quite as violent as you were five minutes ago?"

He wanted to wrap his hands around her skinny neck and squeeze. But it would have to wait. "Allow me the courtesy of processing my violent thoughts without further comment from you, Sherlock. Trust me, it's to your benefit."

"Yes, sir."

"You're not going to collapse or anything, are you, Agent Sherlock?"

"No, Ralph, I promise. I'm fine." She lasted until they got to the OR waiting room. No one could tell them anything. Jones was still in surgery. They settled in, Savich sitting next to Sherlock. She crashed two minutes later.

"I think she's out," Savich said. "Tell you what, I'll take her back to the hotel. Call me in the morning with Jones's condition and when the doctors think we'll be able to talk to him. Sherlock would be mad to miss anything, but I doubt the dead could rouse her right now."

Ralph Budnack reached back and lightly shook her shoulder. She fell more onto Savich.

"Yeah, she's out like a light. Keep an eye on her, Savich. She scared every cop in that warehouse, but she sure got the job done. Funny thing how her shooting him saved his life. If you hadn't called a quick halt, the cops would have turned him into a pincushion. Hey, we'll call tomorrow. Oh yeah, we got a lot on film."

Savich carried her into the hotel, over one wimpy protest. At least it was late and only one old guy thought Savich was a pervert, from the way he was licking his chops. Because Savich was worried about leaving her alone, he took her to his room, pulled off her shoes, and tucked her into his bed. He turned the light on low over by the desk by the windows. He called Assistant Director Jimmy Maitland, to tell him they'd caught the String Killer. He wasn't about to tell his boss yet that Agent Sherlock had nearly gotten herself killed because she couldn't control the rage and turned into a cowboy, something the Bureau ferociously discouraged.

Sherlock slept through the night. She came abruptly awake early the next morning. Her eyes flew open, she realized her arm felt on fire, and yelped.

"Good morning. You're alive, I see."

She frowned up at him, trying to piece things together. "Oh, I'm in your room."

"Yes, you are," he said. "You look pretty bad. However, I got your clothes from your room. If you feel up to it, go bathe and change. When you come out, breakfast should be here. Lots of protein, lots of iron, lots of orange juice."

"What's the orange juice for?"

"To keep you from coming down with a cold."

He watched her swing her legs over the side of the bed. That hair of hers had come loose from the clasp and was rioting around her face—red hair that wasn't really a carrot red or an orange red or even the auburn he'd thought, but an Irish sort of red kept coming to mind. She had lots of hair, beautiful hair. She looked totally different. He backed up a step. "I put out some female stuff on the counter for you. If you need to shave your legs, forget it. I've only got one razor."

He was distracting her from the pain in her arm.

"Oh yeah, Sherlock, before you go haring off to catch another killer, hold on a second." He disappeared into the bathroom, then came out a few moments later. "Here, take two pills. Doctor's orders."

She knew the little blue one would take the wretched pain away. Then maybe she could attack that breakfast Savich was talking about.

"You're eyeing those pills the way the cannibal would the sailor in the cooking pot." He handed her the pills and a glass of water. She was fast getting them down.

"Why don't you sit there until the meds kick in. I'll call room service."

Forty-five minutes later, wrapped in a robe, bathed as well as she could with one hand, Sherlock was seated opposite Savich, a fork piled with scrambled eggs very nearly to her mouth. She sighed as she swallowed.

He let her eat for three minutes, then said, "I didn't tell Assistant Director Maitland you're an idiot, that in your first situation you didn't follow orders, you taunted the suspect until he threw the knife at you, that you nearly got yourself whacked because of this obsession you have."

"Thank you, sir."

"Cut the 'sir' stuff. He'll find out soon enough. I still might kick your butt out of the Bureau. That was the stupidest thing I've ever seen, Sherlock." He'd said it all the previous night, but she might have been too dazed to get it all. He needed to pound it in.

"I wanted to push him to the edge. I wanted him to tell me everything—the why of everything. I don't know if I believe that maze story he told me about his father."

"It's a fact easily checked. I'll bet you Ralph has already got in calls to Yuma, Arizona. Tell me, Sherlock, is the obsession gone now that you took out the monster? Was your revenge sweet?"

"Is he still alive?"

"Yes. They operated on him three straight hours. Chances are he'll make it."

"There's still a chance he'll croak after we get it all out of him. Do you think that's possible?"

"I don't plan to let you near him with a weapon."

She sat back in her chair and sighed. "The pain medicine's worked really well. The breakfast was excellent. Are you going to tell Assistant Director Maitland I should be suspended or disciplined or cut off without pay, or what?"

"I told you, I'm still chewing on that. But it occurred to me this was the only reason you came into the Bureau in the first place, wasn't it?"

She nodded, chewing on a piece of toast.

"And your undergraduate degree in Forensic Sciences and your Master's degree in Criminal Psychology, these were all for this one moment—the very slim chance that you'd get to confront this crazy?"

"Yes. I never really believed I'd get him, not deep down, but I knew if I didn't try, then I couldn't live with myself. I wouldn't have even had the chance at him if it hadn't been for you. You made it possible. I thank you, sir."

"I don't like you very much at this moment, Sherlock, so cut the 'sir' crap. If I had known what I was doing, I wouldn't have done it. What would I have done if you'd bought the farm?"

"I guess you would have had to call my dad. That wouldn't have been much fun. Thank you for—"

"If you thank me one more time for letting you play bait, I'll wrap that sling around your throat and strangle you with it."

"What's going to happen now?"

"You're going back to Washington and I'll handle things here."

She turned into a stone. "No," she said at last. "No, you wouldn't do that." She sat forward. "Please, you've got to let me see this through to the end. You've got to let me talk to Marlin Jones. I've got to know why he killed my sister, why he killed all the other women. You told me I could talk to him, really, don't you remember?"

"I'd be nuts to let you keep on with this case."

"Please, be nuts for a little while longer."

He looked at her with a good deal of dislike. Actually he had no intention of pulling her out now. He tossed his napkin on the table and pushed back his chair. "Why not? At least now he can't hurt you and you can't hurt him. You won't try to shoot him, will you, Sherlock?"

"Certainly not."

"I'm an idiot to believe you. Tell you what. I'll take you to the hospital. We'll see if you can keep yourself from ripping the guy's throat out."

"I want to know. No, I've got to know. Why did he kill Belinda?"

"Did she have a salty tongue?"

"She cursed, but nothing that would shock anybody, except my father and mother. Her husband loved her very much. Douglas will be pleased that this guy has been caught. As for my father, since he's a judge, it's one more criminal off the streets. But you know, Dad never really liked her because she wasn't his real daughter. She's my half sister, you see. My mother's daughter from her first marriage. She was twelve years older than I."

"Did she ever bad-mouth her husband?"

"No. Well, I don't think so. But I can't be sure. Twelve years make a big difference. She married her husband when I was sixteen. What difference does that make?"

"So she'd only been married three years when she was killed?"

"Yes. She'd had her thirty-first birthday."

"If she didn't curse or bad-mouth her husband in public, then Marlin wouldn't have had any reason to go after her. You remember he wouldn't have touched you if you hadn't let loose with all those curse words. You added the bad-mouthing of your mythical husband for frosting on the cake. So it only makes sense your sister did something to make him go after her. Either she really lost it and cursed up a storm within his hearing, or she put down her husband in his hearing. One or the other, Sherlock. What's the most likely?"

"I don't know. That's why I've got to talk to Marlin. He's got to tell me."

"If he refuses to talk to you at all?"

She was silent, staring down at a forkful of scrambled eggs that she'd sprinkled too much pepper on. "It's odd. All the other women, no one admitted that they'd ever cursed a word in their lives or bad-mouthed their husbands. But they must have. You saw how Marlin came after me."

"You shocked my socks off when I listened to you let loose on Marlin in that hardware store."

"Good, because I knew you'd be the toughest to convince."

"As for the other women, evidently the family and friends were trying to protect the good name of the dead. It happens all the time, and that makes it even more difficult for the cops."

"He's got to tell me."

He said very gently, "You've got to bring it to a close, Sherlock."

She hated him for his kindness. He had no idea. He couldn't begin to understand. She jerked up to look at him across the table. Her voice was as cold as Albany in January as she said, "Would you like another bagel?"

He sat back, folding his arms over his chest. "You're tough, Sherlock, but you still aren't in my league. If you put cream cheese on the bagel, I'll eat it."

16

BOTH CAPTAIN DOUGHERTY and Ralph Budnack were standing outside Room 423 when Savich and Sherlock arrived at Boston Memorial Hospital.

"You don't look too bad," Ralph said, peering down at her. "On the other hand, Savich doesn't look too good. You haven't been a pain in the butt, have you?"

She rolled her eyes. "Why do you guys always stick together? I'm the one injured here, not this tough guy here."

"Yeah, but Savich had to make sure you didn't croak it at the hotel. He deserves combat pay."

"I slept all the way through, didn't moan or whine or anything to disturb His Highness. He only had to order room service. How about Marlin Jones? Can we see him now?"

Dr. Raymond Otherton, wearing surgical scrubs dotted with blood, said from behind her, "Not more than three at a time. He still isn't all that stable. You the one who shot him?" At her nod, he said, "Well, you blew a big hole in his gut. Either you're a bad shot, or you didn't want to kill him."

"I didn't want to kill him. Not yet."

"If that's true, then go easy now, all right?"

Marlin Jones was pasty white, his lips bluish. His eyes were closed. She could see purple veins beneath the thin flesh under his eyes. There was an IV going in each arm, a tube in his nose, and he was hooked up to a monitor. A police officer sat in a chair beside his bed, and another officer sat in a chair outside the hospital room.

He was awake. Sherlock saw his eyelashes flutter—dark, thick lashes.

Captain Dougherty looked at her, frowned a moment, then said quietly, "You worked him, it's only fair you talk to him first. We've Mirandized him. He said he didn't want a lawyer yet. I really pressed him on that, even taped it. So, everything's aboveboard."

She looked at Savich. He gave her a long emotionless look, then slowly nodded.

She felt her blood pound, a delicious feeling, her arm began to throb and that made her feel even better as she leaned down, and said, "Hello, Marlin. It's me, Marty Bramfort."

He moaned.

"Come on, Marlin, don't be a coward. Open your eyes and look at me. You'll be pleased to see that my left arm is in a sling. You did punish me, don't you want to see it?"

He opened his eyes and stared at that sling. "I've thrown a knife since I was a boy. It should have gone through your heart. You moved too fast."

"Yes."

"You didn't kill me either."

"I didn't want to. I thought that a gut shot would make you feel really bad, make you suffer for a good long time. I want you to suffer until you yell with it. Are you suffering, Marlin?"

"Yeah, it hurts like bloody hell. You're not a nice woman, Marty."

"Maybe not. On the other hand, you're not at all a nice man. Tell me, would you have murdered another five women if you'd managed to kill me?"

He blinked rapidly. "I don't know what you mean."

"You killed Hillary Ramsgate. If I hadn't been a cop, then you would have killed me too. Would you have killed another five women and stopped again at seven?"

The pain seemed to bank in his eyes. He looked off into something that she couldn't see, that no one could see, or begin to fathom, his eyes tender and vague, as if he were looking at someone or something behind a veil. His voice was soft with the radiance of worship when he finally said, "Who knows? Boston has rich pickings. Lots of women here need to be punished. I knew that long before I came here. Men have let them get away with foul language, with putting them down, insulting them. I don't know if I ever would have stopped."

"But you stopped your killing in San Francisco at seven."

"Did I? I don't remember. I don't like it that you're standing up and I'm not. I like women on their knees, begging me, or on their backs, watching that knife come down and down. You should be dead." Incredibly, he tried to spit at her, but he didn't have the strength to raise his head. His eyes closed, his head lolled to the side away from them.

She felt Savich's hand on her arm. "Let him rest, Sherlock. You can see him later. Yes, I'll let you talk to him again. I'm sure Captain Dougherty will agree as well, even though I think he'd like to pin back your ears nearly as much as I did."

She didn't want to leave until she knew every single detail, but she nodded, and followed them out. The little psycho was probably faking it. She wouldn't put it past him.

Marlin Jones opened his eyes as the door closed. Who was that woman? How had she known so much? Was she really a cop? No, he didn't believe that. There was more to her than that. Bunches more. There was lots of deep wormy stuff inside her. He recognized the blackness, felt it reaching out to him. Pain burned in his gut. He wished he had a knife, wished the cop sitting next to him were dead, wished he were strong enough, then he'd gut her but good. He needed to think before he spoke to her again. He knew she'd come back. He knew.

"That wasn't bad for a first interview, Sherlock."

"Thank you, Captain Dougherty. But it wasn't enough time. He was faking it."

"I think you're right, but it doesn't matter."

"No," Savich agreed. "It doesn't. We'll come back later, Sherlock. I wanted to go back to Washington today, but I don't dare take a chance of leaving you here alone. You'd probably smile at the captain here, wink at Ralph, cajole in your FBI voice, and they'd agree to anything you wanted."

"Not true," Ralph Budnack said. "I'm the toughest cop in Boston. Nobody ever winks at me and gets away with it."

She laughed, actually laughed, enjoyed the sweetness of it for a moment, then punched him in the arm. "I won't try it, I promise. As for you, sir, I really don't think you need to stay unless you really want to."

"Stow it, Sherlock. We'll both go home tomorrow. What I want to do now is go over those reports again and have MAX correlate how many times anyone said the murdered women might have even occasionally cursed or even bad-mouthed their husbands one time."

"I told you no one did. Remember about not wanting to say bad things about the dead? But there couldn't have been any other reason to cut out their tongues."

"Yeah, you said that, didn't you? However, somebody had to have said something sometime."

"He's anal, ain't he?" Ralph said, and Sherlock laughed.

"Thank God the cursing was right on," Captain Dougherty said. "You nailed him good with that, Sherlock. My people told us that you really surprised him when you let out with the curses the first time at the lumberyard. They thought Savich was going to fall over with shock. Well, not really, but you didn't do badly."

"Thank you, I think."

"I'm sure glad we weren't wrong about the cursing being the red button for Marlin Jones. And talking back to the husbands. I guess we have to score a big one for the profilers. Of course it made sense, since old Marlin had cut out their tongues."

She knew, Savich realized, looking at that sudden brightness in her eyes. She knew without question that was what pushed Marlin Jones into violence. But how? There was something else that had happened seven years ago. It drove him nuts not to know what it was. If MAX couldn't find anything in any of the interviews of the other murdered women, it meant Sherlock had based everything on the profilers' reports, that, or, well, something else had to have happened. But how could she have possibly known something that no one else did?

It was past lunchtime in San Francisco when Sherlock got through to Douglas Madigan at his law office.

"Lacey, that really you? What's happening? Are you all right? It was all over the TV on the early news about that guy being caught. You were in on it, weren't you?"

"Yes, I was, and yes, I'm fine, Douglas. We've got him. I've already spoken to him once. I'll find out everything from him, Douglas, everything."

"But what more is there to know?"

"I want to know why he killed Belinda. You know she never cursed all that much. She worshiped you, you told me that, so she wouldn't have ever cursed you out in front of any strangers."

"That's right, but so what?"

She drew a deep breath. "The reason he picked each of the women is because he knew she cursed and bad-mouthed her husband or boyfriend. If that's not true in Belinda's case, then there has to be another reason. I want to know, Douglas. I have to know."

"Were you the police decoy?"

"Yes, but please don't publicize it. I was the best one for the job. I know him better than anyone else."

"That was nuts, Lacey." It was his turn to calm down. She heard his breathing become slower. He was an excellent lawyer.

"I'm going to call Dad."

"No, let me do it, although I bet he already knows about it and that you were involved. He'll be relieved you weren't injured."

Her arm started throbbing. She needed another pain pill. "Oh no, I'm fine. What have you done about Candice Addams?"

"I married her last weekend. Funny thing was she got her period on our wedding night."

"So she wasn't pregnant?"

"She told me she'd had a miscarriage two days before but that she loved me so much she was afraid to tell me. She believed I wouldn't have married her if I'd known there wasn't a baby involved."

"Would you have?"

"Married her? No, of course not. I don't love her, you know that."

"What a mess, Douglas." She was very thankful she was three thousand miles away at that moment. "What are you going to do?"

"I haven't decided yet."

"Do you think she really loves you?"

"She claims she does. I don't know. I wish you were here. I wish I could see you, touch you, kiss you. I miss you, Lacey.

So do your father and your sweet mother. Both of them hoped we'd marry, you know."

"No, I didn't know. No one ever said a word to me about that. You were my sister's husband, nothing could ever change that."

"No, maybe not." He sighed. "Here's my lovely wife, standing here in the open doorway of my office." She heard him say to her, "How long have you been there, Candice?"

She heard a woman's voice but couldn't make out what she said, but that voice was shrill and angry. Douglas came back on the line. "I'm sorry, Lacey. I've got to go now. Will you come home now that you've gotten rid of your nightmare?"

"I don't know, Douglas. I really don't know."

Slowly, she placed the phone back into its cradle. She looked up to see Savich standing there, a cup of tea in each hand. How long had he been there? As long as she imagined Candice Addams Madigan had been standing in Douglas's office?

He handed her the cup. "Drink your tea. Then we'll go to the hospital again. I want to get this wrapped up, Sherlock."

"Yes, sir."

"Call me by my name or I'll tell Chico to wrap your karate belt around your neck."

"Yes, Dillon."

"Here's to catching the String Killer and ridding you of all your baggage. Is your brother-in-law to be considered baggage?"

She took a long drink of the hot tea. It was wonderful. She still needed another pain pill. She said finally, shrugging, "He's just Douglas. I never really realized the way he felt, until he was here in Washington a couple of weeks ago. But he's remarried now."

"Lucky for you, I'd say. I can't see that guy giving up all that easily."

"How would you know that?"

"I know everything. I'm a Special Agent."

He probably did, she thought, and excused herself to take another pill.

Rain splattered against the hospital window. The officer in the chair was sitting forward. Sherlock leaned over the bed and said in a soft voice, "Hello, Marlin. Do you remember me? I'm the woman you bashed on the head, took to your little playhouse, and forced through your little house of horrors. But I won and you lost big-time."

"What's your name?"

"Sherlock."

"No one's named that. That's stupid. That's out of some dumb detective story. What's your real name?"

"It's Sherlock, Marlin. Didn't I track you down? Didn't I bring you in? Wouldn't you say I've earned the name?"

"I don't like you, Marty."

"It's Sherlock."

"I like you even less now than I did before."

"Do you mind if I turn on the tape recorder again, Marlin?"

"No, go ahead. Turn it on. I like to hear myself talk. I'm a real good talker. Mr. Caine, he's the guy who owns the Appletree Home Supplies and Mill Yard, he begged me to be his assistant manager. He knew I could sell anybody anything, and he knew I was an expert on everything to do with building."

"Yeah, you're really great, Marlin. But a question. Tell me why you refused to say a word to the police. Why?"

"I only want to talk to you, Marty. I'm going to kill you one of these days, and I want to get to know you better."

"If it makes you feel good, you keep holding on to that thought, Marlin. You want to talk? Tell me why you killed Hillary Ramsgate. She wasn't married. All the other women you've killed were married."

"I knew her boyfriend, well I didn't really know him, I saw him a bunch of times. He told a group of guys she was a ball buster and once he had her married, he was going to teach her a lesson."

"Where was this, Marlin?"

"At a bar, the Glad Rags, in Newton Center. He was there a whole lot. He'd sleep with her, let her tell him what a jerk he was, then come to the bar and let it all out. I told him he should punish her, that she deserved it."

"Did you go into the Glad Rags a lot?"

"Oh yeah. I wanted to see this Hillary woman. He brought her in one night. They had a big argument right there. She even threw a beer in his face. She cursed him up one side and down the other. She called him a motherfucker. Most women, even bad ones like you, they don't say that word. That's a word for bad guys. Well, all the other guys were laughing, but I wasn't. I knew she had to be punished and that he wasn't ever going to do it right. No, if anything, he'd smack her around a little bit. You know that while she was tearing him down, that guy laughed, he took it. I would have sliced her up right there."

"Maybe her boyfriend liked exactly the way things were between them. Did you ever think of that?"

"No, that's impossible. She was bad. He was weak and stupid."

"Did you go to lots of bars, Marlin?"

"Oh yes. I like bars. You can sit there in the dark and watch people. No one hassles you. I saw lots of women who needed to be punished."

"How many different bars?"

He shrugged, then winced, lightly touching his fingertips to his stomach. "About a half dozen, I guess. Lots more in San Francisco. You should have been sliced up too, Marty. But you don't cuss, do you? Not really. I'll bet you're not married either. You're a cop. You said all those bad words to trap me."

"I didn't trap you, Marlin. I gave you a woman you could relate to. Nothing more, nothing less."

"I never should have believed you. The way you fell into my lap. You're still wearing the sling. I like that."

"Yeah, but I'm not lying flat on my back with my gut burning through my back."

He tried to lurch up. The cop beside the bed was up in an instant, his hand on his gun. Sherlock smiled at him and shook her head. "Marlin doesn't have a knife now, Officer Rambling. He's like an old man without his teeth."

"I sure would like to kill you," Marlin said and fell back against the pillow, breathing hard.

"Not in this lifetime, Marlin. Now, you're so good at talking, you like to do it so much, why don't you tell me about the women you killed in San Francisco? I know each of them was married. Did you hear them all bad-mouthing their husbands?"

"Why should I tell you anything? You don't like me. You shot me in the belly. It still hurts real bad. I might want a lawyer now."

"Fine. Do you have any money or shall I call the public defender?"

"I can get the best and you know it. Those guys don't care if I have a dime or not, they want their faces in the news. Yeah, get me a phone book and let me pick out the highest-priced one of the lot."

"I could connect you to the ocean bottom, if you like."

"That was funny, Marty. Lawyers and bottom feeders, yeah, that was pretty funny."

"Thanks. It's Agent Sherlock. I'm with the FBI. You want to call a lawyer now, Marlin? Or would you like to answer a few more of my questions?"

"I'll call a lawyer later. Sure, I can answer anything you ask. I can always take it back. I read all about the Toaster. He'll get off because he's crazy, and it won't cost him a dime. I'll get off too, you'll see, and then I'll come after you, Marty."

She felt a shock of rage, but no fear. She should have killed him right there in the warehouse to ensure there'd be justice. She was a fool to want all her questions answered. Besides, he could lie to her as easily as he could tell her the truth. Her face was flushed red with her fury. She'd been a fool. At that moment, she heard Dillon singing quietly from beside the door, *"I always played it cool when I was young, always swam when I wanted to sink, always laughed when I wanted to cry, always held my cards tight when I wanted to fold . . ."*

He hadn't said a single word until now. She jerked, then turned to look at him. His expression was unreadable. He was singing those words. They weren't great lyrics, but it worked. She grinned; she couldn't help herself. Talk about finding words to fit the situation. She thought briefly of her classical music training. Mozart would have cast her out of the classical club if he knew she was smiling over some god-awful country-and-western music. Her rage fell away.

"We'll see about that," she said, turning back to Marlin, calm as anything now. "Hey, you look as if you're getting tired, Marlin. You'll want to take a nap really soon now. Why don't you tell me why you killed seven women in San

Francisco—not more, not less? Exactly seven, and then you stopped."

"Seven?" He fell silent. She watched him tick off his fingers. The psycho was counting on his fingers the number of women he'd butchered. She'd bet anything he remembered every name, every face. She wanted to kill him right that instant.

"No," Marlin said. "I didn't kill seven women in San Francisco."

So the number seven had no relevance whatsoever. Bless Savich's brain. How many more women had he butchered?

"How many then?"

"Six. They all deserved it big-time. Then I was tired. I remember I slept for three days and then I was told to go to Las Vegas."

"Told? Who told you to go to Las Vegas?"

"Why the voices, of course. The Devil, sometimes his buddies. Sometimes a black cat if I saw one."

"You're making that up. You're practicing on me so the judge will find you nuts and you won't have to stand trial."

"Yeah. I'm good, don't you think? But I am crazy, Marty, real crazy."

"Six women? You're certain? Not seven?"

"You think I'm stupid as well as crazy?" He proceeded to count them off again on his fingers, this time with their names. *Lauren O'Shay, Patricia Mullens, Danielle Potts, Ann Patrini, Donna Gabrielle, and Constance Black.*

When he finished, he looked over at her and smiled.

She felt like Lot's wife: nothing more than a pillar of salt, unmoving.

He hadn't said Belinda's name.

Why? A simple omission. He'd killed seven women. He was lying. The psycho was lying.

She stood up, wanting to strangle him. He flinched, seeing the rage in her eyes. "You're stupid, Marlin. You can't even count right. Either that or you're a liar. That's what you are, a liar. I'll bet my next paycheck on that."

He was whimpering, holding himself so stiff against the backboard of the hospital bed, he looked frozen. "You want to kill me, don't you, Marty?"

"Oh yes, Marlin. When the time comes, I'd like to throw the switch on you and watch you fry."

She heard his voice from behind her, singing softly, *"Take me back to my old fat mammy. She loves me better than she loved her apple pie."*

She felt his hand on her good arm, his blunt fingers lightly stroking her skin. "Let's go, Sherlock. I'll make you a deal, you can talk to him one last time. Tomorrow, all right?"

"Yes, all right. Thank you. See you mañana, Marlin. Don't choke on your soup, will you?"

"I'll have my big-time lawyer here tomorrow, Marty. We'll see what he has to say to a dumb cop like you. Hey, I like that guy with you. He's got a real good voice. Do you happen to know that song, 'Sing Me Home Again Before I Die'?"

17

Y ES, I'LL BE HOME FOR A FEW
days, Father, when I can get away. I want to see both you and
Mother."

"You're satisfied now, Lacey?" The sarcasm was deep and
rich in his voice. She felt the familiar churning in her stomach. She had caught the man who'd killed Belinda. Why
wasn't he pleased?

Be calm, be calm. The training academy taught you that.
"Yes. I truly never dreamed I would catch him. I've even interviewed him twice now. But there is one thing that bothers me."

"What is that?"

"He claims he only killed six women here in San Francisco."

"He's a crazy little psychopath. They're liars all the way to
their genes. I know, I've sentenced enough of them."

"Yes, I agree. I don't know why I mentioned it, really. But
it's curious—he listed the names of the women he killed. He
left out Belinda."

"So he forgot her name."

"Possibly. But why didn't he forget one of the others? You
know I'll be doing all sorts of checking now to make certain
he did kill Belinda." She realized what she'd said but had no
time to apologize. Her father said in his low, controlled voice,
"What are you saying, young lady? You think it's possible
some other man killed Belinda? Someone who copycatted
this Jones guy? Who?"

"I didn't mean that, Dad. I know Marlin Jones killed her,

that he's just playing some sort of twisted game with me. But what game? Why leave out her name specifically? Why not one of the others? It doesn't make any sense at all."

"Enough of this, Lacey. He could have left out any name. Who cares? Will you come home this weekend?"

"I'll try, but I want to speak to Marlin Jones at least one more time. But, Dad, when I come home, it will be for a few days." She drew a deep breath and closed her eyes, exhaling slowly. "I'm going to stay in the FBI. I want to keep doing what I'm doing. I can make a real difference."

There was silence. Sherlock didn't like herself for it, but she couldn't help it. She started fidgeting. Finally, her father said, "Douglas has made a stupid error."

He was letting it go, at least for now. "Well, he's married, if that's what you mean."

"Yes, that's exactly what I mean. The woman went after him, then lied about being pregnant. Douglas has always been very careful about taking precautions. I tried to tell him to have blood tests, get positive proof that the child was his, but he said there was no reason for her to lie. He was wrong, of course. She got him. He told me he wanted a kid, that it was time. She wasn't even pregnant. Douglas was a fool."

"Didn't Douglas want kids with Belinda?"

Her father gave a hoarse laugh. He didn't laugh often. It sounded strange and rusty, and a bit frightening. Her fingers tightened around the phone. "Remember who her mother is, Lacey. Naturally he wouldn't want to take the risk of any child being like Belinda's mother."

"I can't believe he told you that."

"He didn't, but I'm not stupid."

She hated this. Usually he was sly in his insults to his wife, but not now. "She's my mother as well."

"Yes, well, that's different. I am your father. There's nothing of her in you."

Hadn't he told her not two weeks before that her obsession reminded him of her mother's early illness? She shook her head, wanting to hang up, and knowing she wouldn't. "I never met Belinda's father."

Her father said coolly, "That's because we've never mentioned him to you, there was no need. Indeed, Belinda didn't even know what happened to him. Again, there was no reason to be cruel about it."

"Is he still alive? Who is he?"

"His name's Conal Francis. I can't see it matters now if you know the truth. He's in San Quentin, at least he was the last time I heard."

"He's in prison?" Sherlock couldn't believe it. Neither he nor her mother had ever said a thing about Belinda's father being in jail.

"What did he do?"

"He tried to murder me. Instead he killed a friend of mine, Lucas Bennett. It was a long time ago, Lacey, before you were born, before your mother and I married. He was a big Irish bully, a gambler, worked for the mob. He must be at least sixty by now. He's four years older than I. Which is why Belinda was cursed. Her genes ruined her. Despite the fact that I raised her, she still would have turned bad. It was already beginning even before she died. A pity, but there it is."

"But Belinda knew about him, didn't she?"

"She only knew he'd left her and her mother when she was eight or nine years old. We never told her anything different. There was no point. Look, Lacey, that was a long time ago. You've caught the man who killed her. Belinda's madness died with her. Now the man who killed her will die as well. Forget it, forget all of it."

She hoped he would prove to be right about that. No, she didn't want to forget Belinda. But at least now that Marlin Jones was in custody, that helpless feeling was gone.

Except for the fact that he'd claimed he hadn't killed Belinda.

"Come home soon, Lacey." There was a pause, then, "Do you want to speak to your mother?"

"Oh yes, please, Dad. How is she today?"

"Much the same as always. She's downstairs with me in the library. Here she is."

Her fingers tightened on the receiver. Her father had spoken about her first husband and Belinda like that in front of her? Savich had come into the room, but it was too late for her to hang up. "Mom? How are you?"

"I miss you, dearest. I'm glad you caught that bad man.

Now you can come home and stay. You always were so pretty, dear, so sweet and pretty. And how well you played the piano. Everyone told me how talented you were. Why, you could teach little children in a kindergarten, couldn't you? You're so suited to something like that. Your grandmother was a pianist, you remember?"

"Yes, Mom, I remember. I'll be home to visit you soon. Not long now and then we'll be together for a couple of days."

"No, Lacey, I want you to stay here, with me and your father. I have your piano tuned by Joshua Mueller every six months. Remember how much you admired him?"

"Look, Mom, I've got to get back to work now. I love you. Please take care."

"I always do, Lacey, since your father tried to run me down with that black BMW of his."

"What? Dad tried to run you down with his BMW?"

"Lacey? It's your father. Your mother is having one of her spells."

"What did she mean that you tried to run her down?"

"I haven't the foggiest idea." He sighed deeply. "Your mother does have good days. This is not one of them. I have never harmed your mother or tried to harm her. Forget what she said, Lacey."

But how could she? She stared at the phone as if it were a snake about to bite her. She could swear she heard her mother speaking in the background, but couldn't understand her.

Savich was looking at her. Her face was white. She looked to be in shock—yes, that was it.

When Savich took the phone from her, she didn't resist. She heard him say in his calm deep voice, "Judge Sherlock? My name is Dillon Savich. I'm also with the FBI. I'm the head of the Criminal Apprehension Unit. Your daughter works for me. I hope you don't mind, but Sherlock is a bit overwhelmed by all that's happened." He paused, listening to her father. "Yes, I understand her mother isn't well. But you must realize her mother's words shocked her deeply."

She walked across the room, rubbing her arms with her hands. She heard him say in that firm, calm voice, "Yes, I will see that she takes care of herself, sir. No, she'll be fine. Good-bye."

Savich turned to look at her. He said very slowly, "What in the name of heaven is going on with your family?"

Her laugh was on the shaky side, but it was a laugh. "I feel like Alice in Wonderland. I've fallen down the rabbit hole. No, it's always like that, but this is the first time the hole is deeper than I am tall."

He smiled. "That's good, Sherlock. You've got some color back. I'd appreciate it if you wouldn't scare me again like that."

"You shouldn't have stayed in the room."

"Actually, I brought you a message from Marlin Jones. He wants to talk to you again, with his lawyer present. He got Big John Bullock, a hotshot shark from New York who does really well with insanity pleas. I recommend you don't go. He's doubtless set this up so his lawyer can humiliate you. He won't let you get to first base with Jones anymore."

He would have wagered his next paycheck she'd still insist on seeing Marlin Jones. To his surprise, she said, "You're right. The police and the D.A. can get the rest of the pertinent information from him. There's nothing more for me to say to him. Can we go home now?"

He nodded slowly. He wondered what she was thinking.

The taxi stopped in front of her town house at ten o'clock that night. She felt more tired than she could ever remember in her life. But it wasn't the peaceful, good sort of tired she would have expected, now that Belinda's killer had been caught.

She hadn't said much to Savich on the flight from Boston or on the ride in the taxi from Dulles to Georgetown. He walked her to the door, saying, "Sleep late, Sherlock. I don't want to see you before noon tomorrow, you got that? You've had more happen to you in the past three days than in the past five years. Sleep, it's the best thing for you, all right?"

She didn't have any words. How could he know that her brain was on meltdown? "Would you sing me one more outrageous country-and-western line before you leave?"

He grinned down at her, set her suitcase down on the front step of her town house, and sang in a soft tenor whine, *"I told her I had oceanfront property in Arizona. She nodded sweetly and I told her to buy it, that I'd throw in the Golden Gate for free. She thanked me oh so sweetly so I told her that I loved her and I'd be true for all time. Sweetly, sweetly, she kissed me so sweetly and bought every word I said."*

"Thank you, Dillon. That was amazing. That was also very coldhearted and cynical."

"Anytime, Sherlock. Not until noon now. Hey, it's only a silly song, sung by a lonely man who's not going anywhere. All he can do is dream he's a winner, which he's not, and he knows it deep down. See you tomorrow, Sherlock."

She watched him until he turned the far corner. It was as it had been before, Douglas's voice coming out from behind her, low, angry. Even as he spoke, she was leaning down to pull her Lady Colt from her ankle holster. She straightened back up slowly. She was so tired of angry voices. "I wish you wouldn't keep seeing that guy, Lacey. He's such a loser. What was that nonsense he was singing to you?"

"You startled me, Douglas. Please don't wait for me like this again. I could have shot you."

"You're a musician. You play the piano brilliantly. At least you used to. You wouldn't shoot anybody. What were you doing with him?"

She almost shouted at him that she wasn't that soft, pathetic girl anymore, hadn't been for seven long years, that two days ago she'd belly-shot the psychopath who'd killed her sister. She managed to hold it back. "We got back from Boston. He brought me home, that's all. I'd hardly call him a loser, Douglas. Because of him and his computer, we got the guy who killed your wife. It would seem to me that you'd want to give him a medal. Now, what are you doing here?"

"I had to see you. I had to know what you thought about my marrying Candice. She lied to me, Lacey. What am I going to do?" It was then he noticed the sling on her arm. "What happened to you? You didn't tell your father that you'd gotten hurt. Who did this? That man you were with?"

"Come into the house and we'll talk."

She placed a snifter of brandy into his hand five minutes later. "There, that will make you feel better."

He drank slowly, looking around her living room. "This is nice. Finally, you've decorated the way you should."

"Thank you. Now, what do you want to tell me about that I don't already know?"

She sat opposite him on a pale yellow silk love seat. While she'd been in Boston, her designer had had soft recessed lights installed. It made the room very warm and cozy. Intimate. She didn't like that at all. She pressed herself against the sofa back.

"First tell me how you got hurt."

"It's only a small wound. I'll take the sling off in another couple of days. It's really no big deal, Douglas, don't worry. Now tell me about Candice."

"I'm going to divorce her."

"You've been married less than a week. What are you talking about?"

"She crossed the line, Lacey. She overheard us talking on the phone, I told you that. Well, the minute I hung up she started in on me, accused me of sleeping with you, yelled that I'd slept with both you and Belinda at the same time, that you were a slut and she'd get you. I can't take the chance she'll hurt you, Lacey."

"Douglas, calm down. She was angry. I don't blame her. You were newly married and saying things to me that shouldn't have ever been said. I would have yelled too. Forget it. Didn't you discuss everything with her?"

"What was there to say? She lied to me. Your dad thinks I should divorce her. So does your mom."

"My mother and father have nothing to do with you now. It's your life, Douglas. Do what you want to do, not what someone else wants."

"So wise, Lacey. You were always so gentle and wise. I remember sitting on the sofa in your father's house listening to you play those Chopin preludes. Your playing moved me, made me feel more than what I was."

"It's kind of you to say that, Douglas. Would you like some more brandy?"

At his nod, she returned to the kitchen. She heard him moving about the living room. Then she didn't hear his footsteps. She frowned, walking slowly out of the kitchen. He wasn't in the living room. He wasn't in the bathroom. She stood in her bedroom doorway watching him look at the framed photos on her dresser. There were three of them, two of Belinda by herself, and one with both of them smiling at the camera.

"You were seventeen when I took that picture of you and Belinda at Fisherman's Wharf. Do you remember that day? It was one of the few perfectly clear sunny days and you guys took me to Pier Thirty-nine. We bought walnut fudge and ate some horrible fast food. I believe it was Mexican."

She remembered, vaguely. His details astounded her.

"I remember everything. You were so beautiful, Lacey, so full of fun, so innocent."

"So was Belinda, only she was always far prettier than I. She could have been a supermodel, you know that. She was very close to making it when she met you. She gave it all up because you wanted her to be there only for you. Come into the living room, Douglas."

When they were seated again, she said, "I can't help you with your wife. However, I do think you and Candice should discuss things thoroughly."

"She bores me."

Sherlock sighed. She was exhausted. She wanted him to leave and go back to San Francisco. It was odd, but since they'd caught Marlin Jones, she'd felt herself withdrawing from Douglas. It was as if Belinda's murder had somehow bound them together, but not anymore. "You know one thing still disturbs me," she said slowly, lightly stroking her fingertips over the yellow silk arm of the sofa. "I suppose Dad told you Marlin Jones denied killing Belinda."

"Yes, he told me that. What do you think?"

"I agree with Father. He's a psychopath. He probably skips a woman's name every time he recites them. Why did he happen not to recite Belinda's name? I don't know. Random chance? He probably doesn't know either. It has to be coincidence. There's simply no other explanation." She sat forward, clasping her hands between her knees. "But you know me, Douglas, I'm going to have to check to make triple certain he did kill Belinda."

"Of course he killed her, Lacey. There's absolutely no other choice."

"You're right, of course, it's only—" She broke off and dredged up a smile for a very nice man she'd known for nearly twelve years. "I'm sorry. It's still so painful for you as well. How long are you staying in Washington?"

He shrugged and rose when she did. "Drop it all now, Lacey. Don't do any more searching. That kook killed all those poor women. Let him rot for what he did." He walked to her, his smile deep, his eyes intent.

She took a step back, turning quickly out of the living room into the small front hallway. He followed her.

"Will you let it all go now, Lacey?"

She took another step toward the front door. "It is all gone. It's only details now, Douglas, nothing more than details. Shall we have dinner tomorrow night? Maybe you'll have made some decisions about Candice." Were they going to perform this same act every couple of weeks? Would he leave after tomorrow night? She hoped so. She hoped he'd leave for good. She was so tired now she wanted to fall over.

He brightened at that and took her hands between his. "It's good to see you again, Lacey. I wish I could see you all the time, but—"

"Yes, 'but,'" she agreed and stepped back. "I'll see you here about seven tomorrow night."

Assistant Director Jimmy Maitland nodded to Sherlock but said to Savich, "I heard from Captain Dougherty that Sherlock here didn't do what she was told to do, that she wrote her own script. He let some of it drop, then I pried the rest of it out of him. John Dougherty and I go way back. He's a good man, fair and hard."

Savich didn't change expression, merely cocked his head to one side in question. "She got the job done, sir."

"I don't like having my agents knifed, Savich. What exactly did she do?"

"I can answer that, sir."

Both men turned to look at her.

"It better be good, Agent Sherlock," Jimmy Maitland said, and broke a pencil between two fingers. Maitland had been a Special Agent for twenty-five years. He was bald, built like a bull, and held a black belt in karate. His wife was five foot nothing, blond, and punched her husband whenever she wanted to.

They had four boys, all over six foot three. She punched them whenever she wanted to as well.

She shrugged. "Really, sir, the perpetrator took us a bit by surprise, that's all, but nothing we couldn't handle. Dillon yelled out. I shot him at practically the same instant he threw the knife. I was already down and rolling when he released it. It's a minor wound."

"That's exactly what Savich said. Did you two rehearse this?"

"No, sir, certainly not."

Maitland raised an eyebrow at Savich, then said quickly, "Fine. Okay. You're excused, Agent Sherlock. Savich, you stay a moment, there's been another murder in Florida. It wasn't a nursing home on the Star of David matrix MAX generated. As for the perp disguised as an old woman, that doesn't look good anymore. They talked to every old woman in the nursing home. All of them longtime residents. Tell MAX he's got to do better."

"Agreed," Savich said. "I'll get Sherlock back on the Radnich case with Ollie. I'll see you later."

18

SHE PRAYED HER INVOLVE-
ment in the String Killer case would be kept under wraps, and
it had been, at least so far. She knew Savich had spoken pri-
vately with Captain Dougherty and Ralph Budnack. If anyone
blew the whistle on her, it wouldn't be one of them. So far no
one in the media knew anything about her relationship to one
of the victims of the String Killer. It would be a nightmare if
anyone found out.

So far the FBI had gotten lots of good publicity: always a
welcome circumstance for the continually besieged Bureau.
Savich and his new FBI unit had brought down two killers in
weeks. Reporters wanted to interview him, but he wasn't hav-
ing any of it. No one was to speak to any reporters. Louis
Freeh held a press conference, praising the work of the new
Criminal Apprehension Unit. Savich had asked not to attend.
Freeh had wanted him there but hadn't insisted.

She avoided Hannah Paisley, working closely with Ollie to
get back into the Radnich case. She wasn't looking forward to
the evening with Douglas, but it couldn't be helped.

Sherlock dressed up that evening, wearing her hair loose,
pulled back with two small gold combs, gold hoops in her
ears her mother had given her for her twenty-fifth birthday, a
nice black dress that was classic enough to be two years old
and still pass as current style, and three-inch heels. She felt
strange in her different plumage and a bit exposed. But good.
She felt really good. She realized at the last moment that
Douglas could take it wrong. But there wasn't time to change.

The first thing Douglas said when he walked in was "The

sling looks awful with that dress" and grinned at her. "Don't you have several styles and colors to match different outfits?"

The evening was lighthearted and amusing until near dessert, when Douglas dropped his good humor and said, "You've gotten what you wanted, Lacey. I want you to quit the FBI and come home. Surely you see that it's finally over, that it's your music that's important now. You nailed the guy who killed Belinda. Come home. Do what Belinda did. Come stay with me. I'll take care of you."

She looked at him across the candlelit table, at the pure lines and angles of his face, and said simply, "No."

He drew back as if she'd punched him. "I plan to divorce Candice. It will be done quickly, perhaps I can even get an annulment. It can be you and me, Lacey, as I always wanted. Give us time together, once I'm rid of Candice."

He'd always wanted her? He'd never said a word to her until she'd joined the FBI and finished her training. Had he somehow gotten turned on because she was now a law officer? It didn't make sense to her. She was shaking her head even as she said again, "No. I'm sorry, Douglas, but no."

He said nothing more about it. When they were once again in her living room an hour later, she held out her hand to him, desperate for him to leave. "Douglas, I had a lovely time tonight. Will I see you tomorrow?"

He didn't say anything, jerked her against him. He kissed her hard, hurting her arm. She pushed at his chest but couldn't move him. "Douglas," she said against his mouth and felt his tongue push against her front teeth.

The doorbell rang. He still didn't release her, kept grinding his mouth into hers. Her knee was almost in motion when she managed to jerk her head back far enough to call out, "Who's there?"

"Let me in, Miss Sherlock."

A woman. Who could she be?

Suddenly Douglas was two feet away from her, looking bewildered, wiping his mouth with the back of his hand. "It's Candice," he said blankly, then walked to the door and opened it.

The woman standing there was no older than Sherlock, with long honey-blond hair, nearly as tall as Douglas, and endowed with very high cheekbones that had to be a cameraman's dream. But it was her eyes that riveted Sherlock. Dark, dark eyes that held fury, malice, and even more fury this instant than the moment before. She looked ready to kill.

"Candice! What are you doing here?"

"I followed you, Douglas. And you came here like a little trained pigeon. I knew you'd come to her, even though I prayed you wouldn't. I'd hoped our marriage meant something to you. But you let her kiss you. You've got her lipstick on your mouth. You smell like her."

"Why should our marriage mean anything to me? You lied to me. You weren't pregnant."

"We'll have children, Douglas. I'm not ready yet. I'm hitting my stride with my career. I could make it to one of the nationals, but not if I take off now. In another year, we can have a dozen kids if that's what you want."

"That doesn't jibe with what you told me before we got married. Then you said you'd had a miscarriage and you were so upset. Now you don't want to get pregnant. You know what? I don't think you were ever pregnant at all." Douglas turned to Sherlock, waving a languid hand toward his wife. "This is Candice Addams."

"I'm your *wife*, Douglas. I'm Candice *Madigan*. She is your dead wife's sister. No, half sister. Nothing more. What are you doing here with her?"

He changed from one moment to the next. His bewilderment, his frustration, all were gone. He was standing tall and arrogant, a stance Sherlock recognized, a stance that was second nature to him. It held power and control, and the control was of himself and of the situation. He was in a courtroom, in front of a jury, knowing he could manipulate, knowing he could convince, knowing he would win.

"Candice," he said very patiently, as if speaking to an idiot witness, "Lacey is part of my family. Because Belinda died, I didn't cut her out of my life."

"I saw you kissing her through the window, Douglas."

"Yes," he said quite calmly, "I did. She's very innocent. She doesn't kiss well and I like that."

It was another damned rabbit hole. Only this time, she wasn't going to slide in. "I didn't want you to kiss me, Douglas. I wasn't kissing you at all." Sherlock turned to Candice. "Mrs. Madigan, I think you and Douglas should go discuss your problems. I have no part in any of it. Honestly, I don't."

Candice smiled at her, stepped quickly around Douglas, and slapped her hard, whipping her head back.

A deep voice came from behind them. "This appears to be very interesting, but I really can't allow anyone to smack my agents, ma'am. Don't do it again or I'll have to arrest you for hitting an officer."

Sherlock looked up to see Savich standing in the open doorway. This was all she needed. Did he have to show up whenever her life seemed to be flying out of control? It wasn't fair. She rubbed her hand over her face, then took a step back to stop herself from hurling herself on Candice. She was sorely tempted even though she doubted she could take her down, not with her arm in a sling. But she wanted to try.

"Sir," she said, although she wanted to say "Dillon." No way was she going to use his first name in front of Douglas. It would be waving a red flag. "What are you doing here? No, don't tell me. I've been elected the recreation meeting center for the evening. Do come in and close the door, sir, before a neighbor calls the cops."

"I am the cops, ma'am."

"Very well. Would anyone care for a cup of tea? A game of bingo?"

Douglas plowed his fingers through his hair. "No, nothing, Lacey." He turned to his wife. "We have to talk, Candice. I am upset with you. I don't care at all for your behavior. Come along, now."

Sherlock and Savich watched them leave, their voices raised before they even reached the end of the driveway.

"I'll take some tea now," Savich said.

Ten minutes later, she and Savich were drinking tea in the now blessedly empty living room.

"What are you doing here?"

"I was out running when I came by here. You had a hard day. I wanted to make sure you were all right. The front door was open and I heard this woman yelling. How's your cheek?"

Lacey massaged her jaw. "She's a strong woman. Actually it's a good thing you came in or else I might have jumped her.

Then she might really have beaten me up, what with my broken wing. I'll call Chico tomorrow."

"You called me 'sir' again."

"Yes, I did. On purpose. Douglas is jealous of you. If I'd called you 'Dillon,' it might have pushed him over the edge. Then you might have had to fight him. You could have messed up all my beautiful new furniture."

That gave him pause. He grinned, toasted her with his teacup, then said finally, "This was the man who was married to Belinda?" At her nod, he said, "And this is his new wife. Tell me about this, Sherlock. I love family dramas."

"I'll say only that Douglas thinks he might like me a bit too much. As for Candice, his wife, she told him she was pregnant with his child, he married her, and then it turns out she wasn't pregnant. He's angry and wants a divorce. She blames me. That's all there is to it. At least it doesn't involve me." She sighed. "All right, when I was talking to Douglas on the phone, he said some things he shouldn't have said and she overheard them. She was upset. She probably wants to kill me more than Marlin Jones does."

"Do you realize you're speaking to me in nice full sentences? I no longer have to pry basic stuff out of you?"

"I guess maybe I was a bit on guard when I first came to you. On the other hand, you were a criminal in Hogan's Alley and kicked two guns out of my hand before I overcame overwhelming and vicious odds and killed you."

"Yes, you were wary. But it didn't take too long to break you in. You've been spilling your guts for a good long time now. As for my day as the bank robber, you didn't do too badly, Sherlock. No, not badly at all." He raised his hand and lightly stroked his fingers over her cheek. "She walloped you pretty good, but I don't think you're going to bruise too much. Makeup should take care of it."

His cheekbones flushed. He dropped his hand and stood up. He was wearing gray sweatpants and a blue sweatshirt that read ACHY BREAKY COP. He looked big, strong, and harassed. His fingers had been very warm. They'd felt good against her cheek.

"Go to bed, Sherlock. Try to avoid any more dangerous women. I can't always guarantee to drop by when you're butt-deep in trouble."

"I've really never had so many difficulties in such a short time before in my life. I'm sorry. But you know, I could have dealt with this all by myself."

He grunted in her general direction, and was gone. Just plain out of there, fast.

She touched her own fingers to her face, saw his dark eyes staring at her with antagonism and something else, and walked slowly to the front door. She fastened the chain, clicked the dead bolt in place, and turned the key in the lock. What would have happened if Savich hadn't shown up? She shuddered.

She'd caught Belinda's killer and her life seemed messier than ever. What had her mother meant, ". . . since your father tried to run me down?"

She walked out of the doctor's building the following afternoon, trying to put up her umbrella in the face of a sharp whipping wind and swirling rain—hard, heavy rain that got you wet no matter what you did. It was cold and getting colder by the minute. She got the umbrella up finally, but it was difficult because her arm was still very sore. She stepped off the curb, trying to keep herself covered, and started toward her car, parked down the block on the opposite side of Union Street.

Suddenly she heard a shout, then a scream. She whipped about, the wind nearly knocking her over, her umbrella sucked out of her hand. The car was right on her, a big black car with dark tinted windows, a congressman's car, no, probably a lobbyist's car, so many of them in Washington. What was the fool doing?

She froze in that blank instant, then hurled herself back onto the sidewalk, her sore arm slamming into a parking meter.

She felt the whoosh of hot air even as she went down half into the street, half on the sidewalk. She twisted around to see the black car accelerate and take the next corner in a screech of tires. She lay there staring blankly after the car. Why hadn't he stopped to see if she was all right? No, naturally, the driver wouldn't have stopped—he'd probably be arrested for drunk driving. Slowly, she pulled herself to her feet. Her panty hose were ruined, as were her shoes and clothes. Her hair was plastered to her head and over her face. As for her healing arm, it was throbbing big-time now. Her shoulder began to hurt, as did her left leg. At least she was alive. At least she hadn't been farther out into the street. If she had been, she wouldn't have stood a chance.

She'd gotten three letters of the license plate—PRD. Now that she thought of it, it hadn't been a government license.

People were all around her now, helping her to straighten up, holding umbrellas over her. One gray-haired woman was fussing, patting her here and there, as if she were her baby. She managed to smile at the woman. "Thank you. I'm all right."

"That driver was an idiot, a maniac. The man over there called the cops on his cell phone."

A businessman said, "Miss, do you want an ambulance? That guy could have killed you!"

She held up her hands. The rain pounded down on her. "No, no ambulance, please. I'm all right."

The cops were coming soon; she didn't have much time. She was on the phone dialing Savich's number in under two minutes. He wasn't there. Hannah answered. Where was Marcy, Savich's secretary? She didn't need Hannah, not now, but there was no choice.

"Hannah, I need to know where Savich is. Do you know? Do you have a number for him?"

"No. Even if I did, I wouldn't tell you."

"Hannah, listen to me. Someone tried to run me down. Please tell me how I can get hold of Savich."

Suddenly Ollie was on the line. "What happened, Sherlock? Marcy's down in the lunchroom. Hannah and I are covering Savich's phone. It doesn't ring all that often because everyone knows he prefers email. Someone tried to run you down? Tell me what happened."

"I'm all right, really dirty and wet. I'm right in front of Dr. Pratt's building. Savich knows the location, since that's his doctor, too. Please tell Dillon where I am. Oh dear, the police are here."

It was nearly an hour before Savich strode up and knocked on the window of her car. He was very wet. He looked very angry, which wasn't right. He didn't have any right to be angry yet.

"I'm sorry," she said immediately, as she opened the passenger door, "I didn't know who else to call. The cops left about twenty minutes ago. My car wouldn't start."

He slid into the passenger side. "Good thing this is leather or the cloth would stay wet for weeks. Now tell me what happened."

She did, saying finally, "It sounds pitiful. I think whoever was driving lost it. Maybe he was drunk. When he realized he could have killed me, he didn't want to hang around."

"I don't like it."

"Well, no, I don't either. The police are certain it was a hit-and-run. I did see the first three letters of the license plate—PRD. They said they'd check it out. They laughed when I showed them my FBI shield, laughed and laughed."

"Who knew you were going to see Dr. Pratt?"

"Everyone in the office. It wasn't a secret. I even met Assistant Director Maitland in the hall, three clerks, and two secretaries. All of them asked about it. Oh no, sir, you don't think it was on purpose, do you?"

He shrugged. "I don't know anything. I like this car. I'm glad you didn't let your little designer buy it for you. He'd have gotten you one of those dainty little Miatas. When did you buy this car?"

"I knew what I wanted. I called a car club and they got one and sent it over."

"How's your arm?"

"Fine. I banged it against a parking meter. I went back up to see Dr. Pratt and he checked it out."

"What did he say?"

"Not much, shook his head and suggested that I might consider another line of work. He said being president was a lot safer than what I did. He put the sling back on for another couple of days. Why won't my car start? It's brand-new."

"If it stops raining, I'll take a look." He crossed his arms over his chest and leaned back. "As I said, I don't know anything or think anything particular at the moment. If someone tried to kill you, then you've brought me into another mess. And don't call me 'sir' again or I'll pull off that sling and strangle you with it."

She was much calmer now, her breath steady, the deadening shock nearly gone. "All right, Dillon. No one would have any reason to hurt me. It was an accident, a drunk driving a big black car."

"What about Douglas's wife?"

"All right, so I did think about her, but that's crazy. She was angry, but surely not angry enough to kill me. If she wanted to kill somebody, she would pick Douglas, not me. The cops pushed me on it and I did give them her name, but no specific circumstances. I noticed those faint white lines on your finger pads. What are they from?"

"I whittle. Sometimes the knife slips and you cut yourself. No big deal. Now, that's really good. A jealous wife would really make them laugh. It's not raining as much. Let me see what's wrong with this very nice Taurus that's new and shouldn't have stalled."

Nothing was wrong. She'd flooded it.

"I should have thought of that," she said, annoyed and embarrassed.

"You're excused this time."

"So it was an accident. I was scared that you'd find the distributor cap missing or the oil line cut."

"It doesn't have to have been an accident. It's possible it was on purpose and if it was, you know what the guy intended, don't you?"

"Yes, to obliterate me."

Savich tapped his fingers on the dashboard. "I've always thought trying to hit someone with a car wasn't the smartest or most efficient way of whacking your enemy. On the other hand, it's a dandy way to scare someone. Yeah, that sounds about right. If, on the other hand, someone did want to kill you, then I wonder why the car came at you when you'd just stepped off the curb and into the street. Why didn't the guy wait until you were nearly to your own car? You'd have been a perfect target then. That doesn't sound too professional. All the planning was in place, but the execution was way off." He shrugged. "As of this point in time, we haven't the foggiest notion. I'll run those three letters of the license plate through MAXINE and see what she can dredge up."

"MAXINE? You got another computer?"

"No. MAXINE used to be MAX. Every six months or so there's a sex change. I've had to accept the fact that my machine is a transsexual. Pretty soon, she'll start insisting that I stop swearing when I'm working with her."

"You don't swear."

"Okay, back to the accident—"

"It was an accident, Dillon. That's what the police think."

"On the other hand, they don't know you. Now, see if this wonderful ski-hauling four-by-four will start."

She turned the key and the Ford fired right up. "Go back to the Bureau, Sherlock, and drink some of Marcy's coffee. That'll fix you up. Oh yeah—stay away from Douglas Madigan and his wife. Don't you call him, I will. Where is he staying?"

She sat propped up against pillows in bed, the TV on low, for background noise, reading the police and autopsy reports on Belinda. She didn't realize she was crying until the tears hit the back of her hand. She laid down all the pages and let herself cry. It had been so long; the tears had been clogged deep inside her, dammed up, until now.

Finally, the tears slowed. She sniffed, then returned to the reports. Tomorrow she would consult with MAXINE to see if there were any differences, no matter how slight, between Belinda's killing and all the others. She prayed with all her might there wouldn't be a smidgen of difference. Now that she'd studied the reports, she hoped to be able to see things more clearly.

On the edge of sleep, she wondered if indeed Candice had tried to run her down. As her father had tried to run down her mother? No, that was ridiculous. Her mother was ill, had been for a very long time. Or maybe her mother had said that because of what her husband had said so casually about Belinda and her father. It had come out of left field. Who knew?

Of course Douglas had called her, furious that she'd allowed Savich to call him. It took her ten minutes to talk him out of coming over to her town house. He said he'd spoken to Candice, who'd been visited by the police. He was outraged that anyone would believe she had tried to run down Lacey. It had been an accident.

"I wouldn't be leaving unless I was certain it was an accident, Lacey. I want you to be certain, though, that it wasn't Candice."

"I'm certain, Douglas." She'd have said her tongue was purple to get him off the phone. "Don't worry. I'm fine. Everything is fine. Go home."

"Yes, I am. I'm taking Candice home too."

Now that sounded interesting, but she was too tired to ask him to explain.

The next morning, Big John Bullock, Marlin Jones's lawyer, was on CNN, telling the interviewer, a drop-dead gorgeous guy who looked like a model right out of *GQ*, that the FBI and the Boston police had forced Marlin to confess, that he hadn't known what he was doing because he'd been in so much pain. He would have said anything so they'd give him more medication. Any judge would throw out a confession made under those circumstances.

Was Marlin guilty? the gorgeous young hunk asked, giving the audience a winning smile even as he said the words.

Big John shrugged and said that wasn't the point. That was for a jury to decide. The point was the police harassment of the poor man, who wasn't well either mentally or physically. Sherlock knew if the judge didn't suppress the confession, Big John would go for an insanity plea. The evidence was overwhelming. Sherlock knew that when the lawyer saw all the evidence against Marlin, he'd have no choice but to go for an insanity plea.

Sherlock stared at the TV screen, at that model interviewer whose big smile was the last thing on the screen before the program skipped to a toothpaste commercial. She'd been a fool. She should have shot Marlin straight through the heart. She would have saved the taxpayers thousands upon thousands of dollars. It would have been justice and revenge for all the women he'd butchered.

By the next afternoon, MAXINE hadn't come up with a thing. There were no differences at all in Belinda's killing versus the other women's. Only tiny variations, nothing at all significant.

She felt better. Belinda would finally find justice, if the little psycho ever made it to trial. A psychopath wasn't crazy, necessarily, even not usually. But who else knew that? Then she pictured him with Russell Bent of Chicago, both of them playing cards in the rec room of the state mental institution, both of them smiling at each other, joking about the idiot liberal judges and shrinks who believed they weren't responsible for their savagery because they'd had bad childhoods.

She had to stop it. There was nothing more she could do. Her father was right. Douglas was right. It was over. It was time to get on with her life.

19

"IT HAD TO BE MARLIN JONES."

"It seems likely, but you don't sound as if you're really satisfied."

"I'm not, but MAX—oh, I forgot, he's in drag—MAXINE didn't turn up a single variation in the way Belinda was murdered as opposed to the other women. Marlin killed them all, he had to have." She sighed. "But why did he leave out Belinda in particular? It makes no sense."

"I'm glad you're not satisfied. I'm glad you have that itch in your gut," Savich said slowly, tapping his pencil on his desktop, deliberately. "You've inputted all the physical data and run endless comparisons, but there are other aspects you need to take into account. Now you've got to finish it."

She was frowning ferociously. A long, curling piece of hair flopped into her face. She shoved it behind her ear, not even aware of what she was doing.

He smiled as he said, "MAXINE and I have been doing a little work. It's her opinion that we need to go back to the props. Okay, think now about how he killed the women. Think about what he used to kill them and where he killed them."

"A knife."

"What else?"

"He killed them in warehouses and in a couple of houses. He obviously prefers warehouses, there aren't as many people around at night."

"What did he use?"

"He built props."

"Like the way Marty Bramfort was building props for her kid's school play in Boston. Think about what you had to do to build those props."

She stared at him, then leaped to her feet, her hands splayed on his desktop, her chair nearly falling over backward. Her face was alight with excitement. "Goodness, Dillon, he had to buy lumber, but the SFPD said they couldn't trace it, it was too common. But you know a better question: Is it possible to know if the same lumber was used in all the killings, that is, was all the lumber bought in the same place? Okay. He had to screw all those boards together, right? They couldn't trace all the brackets and hinges and screws, but is there any way of knowing if someone screws in a screw differently from someone else? If the slant is different? The amount of force? Is this possible? Can you tell if some lumber matches other lumber from the same yard? The same screws?"

He grinned at her. "I don't see why not. You've got it now, Sherlock. Now we've got to pray the San Francisco police haven't thrown away the killer's props from each murder. Actually, I'd be willing to bet they've got it all.

"Say they still have everything. Unfortunately MAXINE can't help us here, not even using the most sophisticated visual scanners would work. We've got to have the human touch. I know this guy in Los Angeles who's a genius at looking at the way, for example, a person hammers in a nail. You wondered if this was possible. It is. Not too many people know how to do it, but this guy does. You could show him a half dozen different nails in boards and Wild Ralph could tell you how many different people did the hammering. Now we'll test him about not only hammering nails but screwing in the brackets and hinges. Now go find out if you've still got a match."

Three days went by. It was hard, but Savich kept his distance. He'd given her Ralph York's number—Wild Ralph— nicknamed ten years before when a suspect in a murder case had tried to kill him for testifying and Ralph had saved himself with a hammer. Unexpectedly, the suspect had survived. He was now serving life in San Quentin. Savich had heard there was still a dent in his head.

No, he'd keep his mouth shut, at least for another day. To do anything active would be undue interference, and he knew she wouldn't appreciate it. If she had questions, she'd ask, he knew her well enough to know that she didn't have a big ego. He forced himself not to call Wild Ralph to see what was going on. He knew, of course, that the SFPD hadn't done any comparisons of this sort, simply because they'd never had any doubts that all the murders had been committed by the same person. Also, this kind of evidence wasn't yet accepted in a court of law. He found himself worrying. As for Sherlock, she didn't come near him. He knew from the security logs that she had worked until after midnight for the past two nights. He was really beginning to grind his teeth when she knocked on his office door three days later at two o'clock in the afternoon. She stood in his doorway, saying nothing. He arched an eyebrow, ready to wait her out. She silently handed him a piece of paper.

It was a letter from Ralph. He read: "Agent Sherlock, the tests I ran included: 1) type of drill used, 2) drilling and hammering technique, 3) type and grade of lumber, and 4) origin of lumber.

"The drill used in all the San Francisco murders except #4 was identical. However, the drill used in murder #4 was too close in particulars for me to even try to convince the D.A. that it wasn't identical. As to the drilling and hammering technique, it is odd, but I believe some was done by the same person and others were not. They were utterly different. No explanation for that. Perhaps it's as simple as the murderer had hurt his right hand and was having to use his left, or that he was in a different mood, or even that he couldn't see as well in this particular instance. The lumber wasn't identical, and it did not come from the Bosman Lumber Mill, South San Francisco. Again, it doesn't really prove anything one way or the other, it is merely of note, although again, I wonder why only murder #4 had lumber from a different lumberyard.

"This was an interesting comparison. I've spoken to the police in San Francisco. The San Francisco D.A. is speaking with the Boston D.A. They will doubtless have comparisons made between the props used in the San Francisco murders and the props used in Boston. I don't doubt that even though the lumber can't be identical, the technique will be, and thus perhaps the presiding judge will allow it to be used as evidence in Marlin Jones's trial, if and when the man stands trial.

"So, the bottom-line results of my test are inconclusive. There are differences, aberrations. I must tell you I have seen it happen before, and for no logical reason.

"I hope this is of assistance to you, but given the reason for your request I doubt that you are overjoyed. My best to Savich."

Savich said nothing, merely took in her pallor, the stark disappointment in her eyes, the hopelessness that seemed to be draining her. He wished it could be different, but it wasn't. He said finally, "Ralph said it himself. Inconclusive. It doesn't nail down the coffin lid, Sherlock."

"I know," she said and didn't sound as though she believed it. "He didn't write this in his letter, but Mr. York said on the phone just a few minutes ago that all the same particulars with the other murder props were completely identical. It was with murder number four where there were inconsistencies."

"That's something," Savich said. "Look, Sherlock, either Marlin did it or he didn't. As to Marlin claiming he killed only six women in San Francisco, Belinda not included, then someone else did. You're not happy, are you?"

She shook her head. "I wanted to be certain once and for all and it's still not proven, either way. Can you think of anything else to do?" But she didn't look at him, stared down at her low-heeled navy pumps.

"Not at the moment, but I'll think about it some more. Now let's get back to the Radnich case." He wished he could let her mull over her sister's murder, but there were too many demands on the Unit. He needed her.

"Yes. Thank you for giving me all this time. Ollie also said there was a new murder spree, a couple of black guys killing Asian people in Alabama and Mississippi."

"Yes. We'll talk about it in the meeting this afternoon." He watched her leave his office. He tapped his pen on the desktop. She'd lost weight she couldn't afford to lose. He didn't like it. Even though he saw the results of it in the families of victims, he still couldn't begin to imagine what it must feel like to have lost someone you loved in such a horrible way. He shook himself. He turned to MAXINE and typed in a brief email to his friend James Quinlan.

Sherlock stopped outside Savich's office and leaned against the wall. It was too much and not nearly enough. She had to go to Boston again. She had to speak to Marlin Jones one more time. She had to make him tell her the truth, she had to. She looked up to see Hannah staring at her. "Why are you so pale? You look like someone's punched you. Actually, you look like you're coming down with the flu."

She shook her head. "I'm fine. It's the case I'm working on. Things are inconclusive and I hate that."

Hannah said, "Yes, that's always a bitch, isn't it? How's your arm?"

"What? Oh, my arm's fine."

"How are you feeling after that hit-and-run driver nearly slammed you the other day? That must have been pretty bad."

"It was, but not as bad as this. I think it was an accident, some drunk guy who probably was so scared he nearly hit someone that he couldn't wait to roar away from me. The cops said the three numbers I saw on the license plate didn't lead anywhere. Too many possibilities. It could have happened to anybody. I was the lucky one."

"Did you hurt your arm again?"

"Banged it up a bit more, no big deal."

"Savich isn't busy now, is he?"

"I don't know." She walked away, thinking about who had had access to all the crime details in San Francisco.

She sat at her desk and stared at the blank computer screen. She heard a sound and turned to see Hannah standing by the water cooler, frowning at her. It was more than a frown, and Sherlock felt a brief burst of cold run through her. She forced herself back to the Radnich case, but there was nothing new there. Another murder and her old-woman theory hadn't washed. The afternoon meeting was canceled because Savich had an emergency meeting with his boss, Jimmy Maitland. She was still puzzling over the newest developments in the Mississippi/Alabama cases, when she heard Savich behind her. "It's after six. It's time for you to hang it up. Let's go work out."

She stared up at him blankly. "Work out?"

"Yeah, I bet you haven't moved from that desk since this afternoon. Come along. I won't throw you around because you have this wimp excuse about your arm."

She could barely walk. Nor could she talk. She was still using all her breath to pull oxygen into her lungs. It was just as well because Hannah Paisley turned up right before they were ready to leave. She looked fit and strong, and about every guy in the gym was staring at her. She was wearing a hot-pink leotard with a black top and black thong.

Savich gave Hannah a salute as he said, "Come on, Sherlock. I told you you've got to work on your breathing. More breath or you'll collapse on me the way you're almost doing now."

She eyed him and gasped out, "I'm going to kill you."

"Good. An entire sentence. You're getting it together again. You want to go shower?"

"I'd drown. I'd fall down, plug the drain, and that would be the end of it."

"Then let's walk home. A nice walk dries all the sweat."

"I want to be carried. These legs aren't going anywhere on their own."

Hannah was standing behind Savich. She lightly touched her fingers to his bare arm. His skin glistened with sweat.

"Hello, Dillon, Sherlock."

Sherlock only nodded. She was still breathing hard.

"You're looking good, Hannah," Savich said. Sherlock realized at that moment how clear it was to her that they'd slept together. They were both magnificently made, beautiful specimens. She could imagine how they'd look together, naked, all over each other. She forced herself to smile. To look the way the two of them did, they had to sweat a lot to build those sleek muscles. Sherlock wasn't too fond of sweating. She watched Savich squeeze Hannah's biceps. "Not bad. Look at poor Sherlock here. She's threatening to collapse on me all because she got her arm hurt and we had to spend the time on her legs."

"She does look a bit on the edge. While she rests up, could you come coach me a minute on my bench presses?"

"Sorry, not tonight, Hannah. Sherlock has to get home, and I promised I'd drop her off."

Hannah nodded, smiled at both of them, and walked off, every man's eyes, except Savich's, on her butt.

"She's very beautiful," Sherlock said, pleased she could talk without wondering if she was having a heart attack.

"Yes, I guess so," Savich said. "Let's go."

They stopped for a half-veggie, half-sausage pizza at Dizzy Dan's on Clayton Street.

"You only left me two slices," Savich said, picking up one slice quickly. "You're a pig, Sherlock."

Cheese was dripping down her chin. She was so hungry, she was pleased she hadn't started chewing on the red-and-white checkered tablecloth. She quickly grabbed the last slice. It was still hot enough so that the cheese pulled loose and dripped down the sides of the slice. She couldn't wait to get it into her mouth. "Order another one," she said, her mouth full.

He did, and this garden delight pizza he ate himself. She was so full she didn't want to move, didn't even want to raise her hand from the tabletop.

"You stuffed?"

"To the gills." She sighed, sat back in her chair, and crossed her arms over her stomach. "I didn't realize I was so hungry."

"If Marlin didn't kill Belinda, then someone else did. Who was it, Sherlock?"

"I don't know, truly, I don't."

"But you've been thinking about it a whole lot, ever since Marlin told you he didn't kill her. Who had access, Sherlock? Who?"

"Why don't we talk about Florida instead? Or Mississippi?"

"Fine, but you're going to have to face up to it soon. I do have some new information from Florida for you. The latest murder wasn't on the projected map matrix, as you already know. MAXINE is trying to come up with something else. We poor humans are trying too. This time the police made an effort to question everyone in sight. They herded all the residents into the rec room. They wanted to catch your old woman in disguise. The initial word I got back, and what you heard, was that it wasn't someone disguised as an old woman. However, I found out before we left this afternoon that a new cop had had two of the old folks get sick on him because of the murder and he'd let them go. One was an old woman, one an old man. Was one of them the murderer? No one knows.

"As for the new young cop being able to identify the two old people, we can forget it. All old people look alike to him. He only remembers that one was an old man and he fainted, the other was an old lady and she puked. You can bet your life that he got his ears pinned back, probably worse.

"So, it's still unclear whether or not your theory is right. You know, the likeliest person to kill a wife is the husband."

He'd steered so smoothly back on course that the words spilled out of her mouth: "No, Dillon, Douglas loved Belinda. For argument's sake, let's say I'm wrong and he hated her. He would simply have divorced her. There's no reason he would have killed her. He's not stupid, nor, I doubt strongly, is he a murderer. There was no reason for him to kill her, none at all."

"No, not that you know of. But one thing, Sherlock, he does seem to think too much of you, his sister-in-law. How long has he been looking at you, licking his chops?"

"I'm sure that's recent. And I think he's over it now." She remembered him staring at her and Belinda's photos in her bedroom—all that he'd remembered, all that he'd said about her innocence. She felt a knot of coldness settle deep into her. She was shaking her head even as she added, "No, not Douglas."

"Your daddy's a judge, but he wasn't a judge seven years ago. He couldn't have had access to everything on the String Killer case."

She wondered only briefly how he knew that, but then wanted to laugh at herself. That was easy stuff. Actually she wouldn't be surprised if Savich knew what the president's next speech would be about. She had complete faith that MAXINE could access anything Savich wanted. "No, impossible. Don't lie to me, I'll bet you know my father did have access to everything. He came out of the D.A.'s office. He knew everyone. He could have accessed anything he wanted. But Dillon, how could a man kill his own daughter? And so brutally?"

"It's been done more times than I can remember. Your dad's not all that straightforward a guy, Sherlock, and Belinda wasn't his daughter. He appears to have this mean streak in him. He didn't much like Belinda, did he? He thought she was nuts, like his wife, who claimed that he'd tried to run her down in his BMW."

She scooted out of the booth, the tablecloth snagging on her purse strap. His two remaining slices of pizza nearly slid off the table.

"Then there's Mama. Does she have mental problems, Sherlock? What did she think of Belinda?"

He was standing in front of her, very close, and she couldn't stand it. "I'm going home. You don't have to see me there."

"Yeah, I do. You've got to do some thinking. You know very well that Ralph York has sent his findings to the SFPD. They might reopen Belinda's case or they might not. No way of telling yet. At the very least though, everything we're talking about they'll be talking about too. Douglas could be in some warm water, Sherlock, no matter how you slice it. Daddy too."

"Since everything is so inconclusive, it's very possible the San Francisco police won't do a thing. I think once they talk to Boston, they'll know it was Marlin. They won't have any doubts. They'll shake their heads at Ralph's report."

"I think they will pay some attention. We're all the law. We're all supposed to try to catch the bad guys, even if it might mean opening a can of worms."

"I've got to call Douglas, warn him. This can't be right, it can't. I never meant for this to happen."

He rolled his eyes. "Maybe I'll understand you in another thirty years, Sherlock. Do what you must. Come on. I've got things to do tonight."

"Like what?"

"My friend James Quinlan plays the sax at the Bonhomie Club on Houtton Street, owned by a Ms. Lily, a super-endowed black lady who admires his butt and his soulful eyes as much as his playing. He tries to be there at least once or twice a week. Sally, his wife, loves the place. Marvin, the bouncer, calls her Chicky. Come to think of it, he calls every female Chicky. But Sally to him is a really nice Chicky. I'll never forget Fuzz the bartender gave them a bottle of wine for a wedding present. It had a cork. A first. Amazing."

Now all this was strange. She said slowly, willing, happy to be distracted, even if only for a moment, "So you go to support him?"

He looked suddenly embarrassed. He didn't meet her eyes. He cleared his throat and said, "Yeah."

He was lying. She cocked her head to one side. "Maybe I could go with you sometime? I wouldn't mind supporting him either. Also, I've never gotten together with Sally Quinlan. I heard she's an aide to a senator."

"Yeah. Okay, sure. Maybe. We'll see."

She didn't say a word. They were nearly at her town house. There was a quarter moon showing through gothic clouds— all thin and wispy, floating past, making sinister images. It was only eight-thirty in the evening, cool with only a slight breeze. "You should keep a light on."

"The FBI doesn't pay me all that well, Dillon. It would cost a fortune." But it was a good idea. Maybe she would.

"Do you have an alarm system?"

"No. Why? All of a sudden you're worried? You were mocking all my locks a while ago."

"Yeah, and I wondered why someone who faced down Marlin like a first-class warrior would need to have more locks in her house than the president has guards."

"They're two very different things."

"I figured that. I don't suppose you'll tell me about it, will you?"

"There's nothing to tell. Now, what's all this about an alarm system?"

"Someone tried to run you down. That changes things, big-time."

They were back to that. "It was an accident."

"Possibly."

"Good night, Dillon."

20

SHERLOCK UNLOCKED THE
front door and stepped into the small foyer. She reached for
the light switch and turned it on. It flickered, and then the
light strengthened. She turned to lock the front door—the dead
bolt, the two chains. From habit, she looked into the living
room, the kitchen, before she went to her bedroom. Everything
was as it should be.

She stopped. Slowly, she lowered the gym shoe she'd pulled
off to the floor. She turned, silent as stone now, and listened.
Nothing.

She was losing it. She remembered that long-ago night in
her fourth-floor apartment when she'd awakened to hear
noises and nearly heaved up her guts with terror. She'd gotten
a grip and gone out to see what or who was there. It had been
a mouse. A silly little mouse, so scared he didn't know where
to run when he saw her. And that had been the night she'd
changed.

She took off the rest of her gym clothes and went into the
bathroom. Before she stepped into the shower, she turned the
lock on the door, laughing aloud at herself while she did it.
"You're an idiot," she said, unlocked the door, then stepped
into the shower.

Hot, hot water. It felt like heaven. Dillon had nearly killed
her, but the hot water was soaking in. She could feel her
shrieking leg muscles groan in relief. He'd told her working
out kept his stress level down. It also gave him a gorgeous
body, but she didn't tell him that. She was beginning to wonder if he didn't have something about bringing down the

stress. For the hour they'd exercised, she hadn't given a single thought to Marlin Jones or to the inconclusive report from Wild Ralph York.

She finally stepped out of the shower some ten minutes later and into the fog-heavy bathroom. She wrapped a thick Egyptian-cotton towel around her head, then used the corner of her other towel to wipe the mirror.

She stared into the masked face right behind her.

A yell clogged in her throat. She froze. She realized she wasn't breathing, couldn't breathe, until air whooshed out of her mouth.

The man said in a soft, low voice that feathered warm air on the back of her neck, "Don't move now, little girl. I expected you to come home a bit later. You seemed well ensconced at the pizza place with that big guy. What's the matter, didn't the guy push hard enough to sleep with you? I could tell he wanted to, the way he was looking at you. You told him no, didn't you? Yeah, you're here a little earlier than I expected, but no matter. I had a chance to settle in, get to know you a bit."

His mask was black. His breathing was quiet, his voice so very soft, unalarming. She felt the gun pressing lightly against the small of her back. She was naked, no weapon, nothing except a ridiculous towel wrapped around her head.

"That's right. You're holding perfectly still. Are you afraid I'll rape you?"

"I don't know. Will you?"

"I hadn't thought to, but seeing you all buck naked, well, you're good-looking, you know? It turned me on to hear you singing that country-western song in the shower. What was it?"

"'King of the Road.'"

"I like those words—but they fit me, not you. You're a little girl playing cop. The king of the road goes to Maine when he's all done, right? That's where I might go once I'm through with you."

Slowly, very slowly, she brought the towel down in front of her. "May I please wrap the towel around me?"

"No, I like looking at you. Drop it on the floor. Leave the one wrapped around your head. I like that too. It makes you look exotic. It turns me on."

She dropped the towel. She felt the gun pressing cold and hard against her spine. She'd had training, but what could she do? She was naked, without a weapon, in her bathroom. What could she possibly do? Talk to him; that was her best chance, for the moment. "What do you want?"

"I want to talk you into going back to him, all the way back to San Francisco."

"Did you try to run me down?"

He laughed, actually laughed. "Do you think I could have done something like that, little girl? Though you ain't all that little, are you?" The hand holding the gun came around and stroked the dull silver barrel over her right breast.

She flinched, leaning back, only to feel him against her back, his groin against her hips.

"Now that's nice, isn't it?" He continued to press the cold metal against her breast, then downward to her belly. She was quivering, she couldn't stop it, her flesh trying to flinch from him. Fear was full-blown now, and she didn't know if she could hold herself together. She gasped out, "Why do you want me to leave Washington?"

The gun stopped. He drew his hand away. "Your mama and daddy need you at home. It's time you went back there and took care of your responsibilities. They don't want you here, involved in conspiracies and shooting people, the way the FBI does. Yeah, they want you home. I'm here to encourage you to go."

"I'll tell you why I can't go back yet. You see, there's this murderer, his name is Marlin Jones, and he killed this woman in Boston. He's a serial killer. I can't leave yet. I'll tell you more but it could take a while. Can't I put on some clothes? We can go in the kitchen, and I'll make some coffee?"

"Hard-nosed little girl, aren't you? It doesn't bother you at all with my dick pressing against your butt."

"It bothers me."

He stepped back. He waved the gun toward the bedroom. "Go put yourself in a bathrobe. I can always take it off you if I want."

He followed at a distance, not getting close enough for her to kick out at him. She didn't look at him again until she had the terry-cloth robe belted tightly around her waist.

"Take the turban off your head and comb out your hair. I want to see it."

She pulled off the towel and began combing her fingers through her hair. Had he moved closer? Could she get him with her foot? It would require speed, and she'd have to be accurate or he'd kill her.

"Use that brush."

She shook her head, picked up the brush, and brushed her hair until he finally said, "That's enough." He reached out his hand and touched the damp hair. He grunted.

Keep calm, she had to keep herself calm, but it was hard to do, really hard. She wanted to see his face, to make him human, and real, to look hard at his eyes. The black ski mask made him a monster, faceless, terrifying. He was dressed in black too, down to the black running shoes on his feet. Big feet. He was a big man, big arms, long, but his belly was flabby. He wasn't all that young, then. His voice was low, sort of raspy, as if he'd smoked too much for a long time. Keep thinking like this, she told herself over and over as she walked into the kitchen. Keep calm.

She watched him from the corner of her eye. He was leaning against the counter, the gun—a small .22—still pointed at her, as if someone had told him she'd had some training, that he shouldn't assume because she was a woman she had no chance against him.

"Who are you?"

He laughed. "Call me Sam. You like that? Yeah, that's me— Sam. My pa was named Sam too. Hey, I'm the son of Sam."

"Someone hired you. Who?"

"Too many questions, little girl. Get that coffee on. Now start talking to me about this Marlin Jones. Tell me why you're so important to this case."

Nothing she told him about Marlin Jones would make any difference that she could see, and it would buy her time. "I was the one who was the bait to catch him in Boston. FBI agents do this sort of thing. There was nothing unusual about it. I was the bait because he'd killed my sister seven years ago in San Francisco. He was called the String Killer. I begged the cops to let me bring him down. They let me and I did bring him down, but it's not over yet. I can't go back home yet."

He pushed off the counter, walked to her, and very calmly, very slowly, pulled back his arm and brought the gun sharply against the side of her head. Not hard enough to knock her unconscious, but hard enough to knock her silly. Pain flooded through her. She cried out, grabbed her head, and lurched against the stove.

"I know a lie when I hear it," he said in that low, soft voice of his and quickly stepped back out of her reach. "This guy butcher your sister? Yeah, sure. Hey, you're bleeding. Scalp wounds bleed like stink, but you'll be okay. Tell me the truth, tell me why you really want to stay here or I'll hit you again."

She suddenly heard an accent. No, her brains were scrambled, she was imagining it. No, wait, the way he'd said "bleed like stink." It was faintly southern; yes, that was it. And wasn't that phrase southern as well?

He raised his arm. She said quickly, "I'm not lying. Belinda Madigan, the fourth victim of the San Francisco String Killer, was my sister."

He didn't say anything, but she saw the gun waver. Hadn't he known? No, if he didn't know, why else would he be here? He said finally, "Keep going."

"Marlin Jones said he didn't kill her. That's why I've got to stay. I've got to find out the truth. Then I can go home."

"But he did kill her, didn't he?"

"Yes, he did. I wondered and wondered, then I even had some tests done on the wooden props used in all the murders in San Francisco, the hammering and screwing techniques, stuff like that. There's an expert in Los Angeles who's really good at that sort of thing. But his results were inconclusive. Marlin Jones killed her. He must have realized who I was and lied to me, to torture me. Who are you? Why do you care?"

"Hey, I'm a journalist." He laughed again. He was big into laughter, this guy. She felt blood dripping off her hair onto her face. She wiped it away with the back of her hand.

"Yeah, I'm a journalist and I like to know the inside scoop. You guys are so closemouthed that none of us know what's going on. Yeah, I'm with the *Washington Post*. My name's Garfield." He laughed. He was really enjoying himself.

Then he straightened, and she knew if he weren't wearing

that mask, she'd see that his eyes had gone cold and dead. "Is that all, little girl?"

"Yes, that's all," she said now, her voice shaking with fear. No, she thought, it wasn't enough. More shaking, more show of fear. "But why do you care whether or not I go home? Or does the person who sent you want me to leave? Why? I'm no threat to anyone." Marlin Jones was in her mind. Was he somehow behind this?

The man was silent for a moment, and she knew he was studying her, weighing his options. Who was he?

He said finally, reaching out his hand to touch a clump of bloody hair, "You know what I think? I think maybe old Marlin didn't kill your sister. You're like a little terrier, yanking and jerking and pulling, but you won't find anything.

"Now I believe that's all I need to know. I'll tell you one last time. Leave Washington. Stay with the FBI if you want to, but transfer. Go home, little girl. Now, let's have us a good time."

He walked toward her, the gun aimed right at her chest. "I want you to march your little butt to the bedroom. I want you to stretch out all pretty-like on the bed. Then we'll see."

She knew pleading wouldn't gain her anything. She turned and walked out of the kitchen. He was going to rape her. Then would he kill her as well? Probably. But the rape, she wouldn't take the rape, she couldn't. He'd have to kill her before she'd let him rape her. Who had hired him?

What to do? He didn't think Marlin had killed Belinda? Why did he care? What was going on here?

"Please, who are you?"

He motioned the gun toward the bed.

She was standing now beside her bed, not wanting to lie down, hating the thought of him being over her, of him in control.

"Take off that bathrobe."

Her hands were fists at her sides. He raised the gun. She took off the bathrobe.

"Now lie down and open those legs real wide for me."

"Why don't you think Marlin killed my sister?"

"Business is over. It's party time. Lie down, little girl, or I'll have to hurt you real bad."

She couldn't do it. She couldn't.

He took a step toward her, the gun raised. He was going to hit her with the butt again, probably break her jaw this time. She had to do something.

The phone rang.

Both of them stared at it.

It rang again.

"It might be my boss," she said, praying harder than she'd ever prayed in her life. "He knows I'm home. He said he might call. There was an assignment he wanted to talk to me about."

"That big guy who brought you here? That's your boss?"

She nodded and wished again she could see his face, see his expression.

Another ring.

"Answer it. But you be careful what you say or you're dead where you stand."

She picked up the phone and said quietly, "Hello?"

"That you, Sherlock?"

"Yes, sir, it's me, sir."

He was silent a moment. She was praying, hard.

"I wanted to tell you that Sally asked to meet you. She wants you to come to the Bonhomie Club tomorrow night. Quinlan's going to be playing both nights."

"That sounds nice, sir, but you know that I never mix any business with pleasure. It's a rule I always stick to, sir."

He was mouthing at her, "Get rid of him!"

"I've got to go, sir. Tell Sally I'm sorry, sir. That assignment you wanted to talk to me about, sir, I'll be in early tomorrow. I've got to go now."

The gun was pressing at her temple. She gulped, then gently hung up the phone.

"I heard what the guy said. You're lucky you didn't blow it, little girl. Now."

He pulled some slender nylon rope from his pocket. "Put those arms up over your head."

He was going to tie her down. Then he could do anything he wanted to with her.

Slowly, slowly, she raised her arms. Why had she wanted a brass bed with a slatted brass headboard? He was coming over to her; soon now, soon, and she would have a chance.

He leaned down, the rope in one hand, the gun in the other. He seemed uncertain what to do with the gun. Put it down, she said in her mind, over and over, as she looked up at him. Put it down. I'm skinny. You can take me. Don't be afraid.

He made up his mind. He backed off. "Turn on your stomach."

She stared at him.

"Do it now or I'll make you really sorry."

She couldn't do it. She just couldn't. Without thought, without hesitation, she lurched up and rammed her head into his belly. At the same time, she flung out both fists against his forearms. She heard him cursing, heard the pain in his voice, and kept hitting him. Quickly she threw herself to the floor, rolling onto her back. He was heaving hard, over her now, the gun up, and she kicked with all her strength, her foot hitting his hand.

The gun went flying.

He threw himself down on her. His fist landed hard against her jaw, then he raised her head, grabbed fistfuls of damp hair, and slammed her head against the floor once, twice, three times. She heard a yell and a moan. The sounds were from her. She tried to bring her legs up to kick him but couldn't manage it. She felt numbness, then knifing pain shot through her head. She vaguely heard his curses from above her, and they grew more distant. She thought she heard the phone ring again. She thought she heard him breathing hard over her. Then she didn't know about anything. She fell into blackness.

Savich was scared spitless. The front door stood wide open. He forced himself to be careful, to go slowly, but what he wanted to do was roar in there. What had happened?

He drew his gun and eased inside the town house. Slowly, he reached for the light switch and flipped it on. He was in a crouch in the next instant, sweeping his SIG-Sauer around him in a wide arc.

No one.

"Sherlock?"

Nothing.

He didn't even pause now. He ran into the living room, switching on lights as he went. She wasn't there. Nor was she in the kitchen.

He was in the hallway when he heard a moan.

She was lying on the floor next to the bed, naked. Blood streaked down the side of her face.

He was on his knees beside her, his fingers pressed against the pulse in her neck. Slow and steady.

"Sherlock! Wake up!"

She moaned again, low and deep in her throat. She tried to bring up her hand to her head, but couldn't do it. Her hand fell. He caught it before it hit the floor. He laid her hand over her belly.

He leaned close, an inch from her face. "Sherlock, wake up. You're scaring the bejesus out of me. Wake up!"

She heard his voice. He sounded incredibly angry—no, not angry, but really worried. She had to open her eyes, but she knew any movement at all would hurt really bad.

"Talk to me. Come on, you can do it. Talk to me."

She managed to open her eyes. He was blurry, but his voice was low and deep and eminently sane. She was so grateful, so relieved. She whispered over the pain, "You came. I knew the multiple *sirs* would get to you."

"They did. The first time you said it, I wanted to trim your sails but good, but then you said it again. I knew something was wrong. Where'd he hit you?"

"My head, with the butt of his gun."

He didn't want to ask, but he had to. "Did he rape you?"

"He would have tried, but I couldn't let him do it. He wanted me to lie down on my stomach. When he moved in I attacked him. That's when he knocked me off the bed and started banging my head against the floor. It kind of hurts, Dillon."

"Did he hit you anywhere else?"

"A fist in the jaw."

"Let me get you up on the bed."

"He's gone? You're sure he's gone? I don't want him to sneak back and hurt you."

Hurt him? Blood was trickling down the side of her face and she was worried about him? "I'll go lock the front door in a minute." While he spoke, he slid his hands beneath her and lifted her. She didn't weigh much. He laid her on the bed, then very quickly drew a blanket over her.

"Don't move," he said, turned, and went back to the front door. He looked around outside, then came back into the house and locked the door.

When he was seated beside her again on the side of the bed, he said quietly, "No one's about now. I'm going to call the paramedics and get you to the hospital."

Her hand shot up. "No, no hospital. I'm all right. I've got a very hard head. Maybe a concussion, but there's nothing they can do for that. Please, no hospital. I hate hospitals. They'll give me more shots in the butt. That's awful."

He looked down at her, then turned to the phone. He dialed a number, then said, "It's Savich. Sorry to bother you, Ned, but could you come to this address and check out one of my agents for me? The guy who attacked her hit her pretty hard in the head. I don't know if she'll need stitches. No, no hospital. Yeah, thanks."

When he hung up the phone, she said, "A doctor who makes house calls? That's got to be rarer than the great auk."

"Ned Breaker owes me. I got his kid away from kidnappers last year. He's a good guy. We became friends. Now, enough of that. It'll take him a good thirty minutes to get here. Do you feel well enough to tell me what happened?"

"After you left, I took a shower. When I got out, he was standing behind me when I wiped the fog off the bathroom mirror. He was wearing a black ski mask and carrying a cheap .22. He wanted me to leave town. Then I talked about Marlin Jones, and he seemed interested in that. I don't know whether or not the person who sent him meant for him to rape me. Maybe, like that almost hit-and-run, he was trying to scare me, which he did.

"Really, though, the bottom line was that I should go home to my family. When I asked him if he was the one who tried to run me down, he didn't answer me. I think he could have been. He had a slight accent, from Alabama, maybe."

"What did you tell him about Marlin Jones?"

"The truth. There was no reason not to. I think somehow Marlin Jones had to have sent him. He tried not to be too interested in Marlin, but he was. He wanted me to believe Marlin was innocent."

"You sure about that?"

"Yes, but again, I think his mission was to scare me to death, scare me enough to make me run. Then he said business was over. He said he wanted to rape me."

Her eyes were vague, her voice slowing down, her words slurring. He shook her shoulders. "Sherlock, wake up. Come on, you can do it." He lightly slapped her cheek, then cupped her jaw in the palm of his hand. "Wake up."

She blinked, trying hard. She wanted to tell him his hand on her jaw hurt, but all she said was, "Probably a concussion. I'll stay awake, I promise. He was going to tie my hands above my head, to the slats of the bed, but he knew I'd attack if he dropped the gun, so he told me to lie on my stomach. I couldn't do that, Dillon, I couldn't. That's when—" Curtains, black curtains were swinging down over her eyes, over her mind. She couldn't see anything.

"Wake up, Sherlock!"

"I'm awake. Don't yell at me, it hurts. I won't pass out on you, I promise. But I can't see."

"Your eyes are closed."

"That's not it."

In the next moment, she was unconscious, her head lolling to the side. He'd never dialed 911 so fast in his life.

21

THE HEAT BURNED STRAIGHT into her head. It was hotter than anything she could have imagined. Any second now she'd go up in flames. No, it was a light, a real light, not some monster her brain had dredged up. It was too bright, too strong, too hot. It burned beneath her eyelids. She tried to turn away from the light, but it hurt too much to move her head.

"Sherlock? Can you hear me? Open your eyes."

Of course she could hear him. He was using that deep voice of his that made her nerve endings quiver, but she couldn't say anything, her mouth was too dry. She tried to form the words, but no sound came out.

A woman said, "Give her some water."

Someone raised her head. She felt cold water on her lips and opened her mouth. She choked, then slowed down. She drank and drank until finally the water was dribbling down her chin.

"Now can you talk to me?"

"The light," she whispered. "Please, the light."

The same woman's voice said, "It must be hurting her."

The light was gone in the next instant and it was now shadowy and dim. She sighed with relief. "That's better. Where's Dillon?"

"I'm right here. You scared me out of a good year at the gym. We were both doing fine until you had the nerve to pass out on me."

"I didn't mean to do that. It was weak and unnecessary. I'm

sorry. Does my health coverage pay for the paramedics and the emergency room?"

"I doubt it. I think it will come out of your pay. Now, here's Dr. Breaker. He got to your house as the paramedics were pulling out, claims he was speeding to get there. Turns out he has admitting privileges here at Washington Memorial."

"Your voice made me quiver—all dark and soft, like falling into a deep, deep well. If I were a criminal, I'd say anything you wanted to keep you talking to me like that. It's a wonderful voice. Plummy—that's how a writer would describe your voice."

She could hear the smile in his voice when he said thank you.

"Agent Sherlock. I'm Dr. Breaker."

He shined a penlight in her eyes, felt the bumps on her head, and said over his shoulder to Dillon, "She's not going to need any stitches, some of my magic tape should do it. Scalp wounds tend to really bleed."

"They bleed like stink."

"Yes, that's right. Interesting way of saying it."

"It's what the man said. And he said it in a southern way. He drawled out stink into two syllables."

She'd already told him that, but he said, "That's good, Sherlock. Anything else?"

"Not yet, Savich. Hold off a bit. Let me clean her up, then you can talk her ear off." He cleared his throat. "She wasn't raped, was she?"

"No, I wasn't. I'm not dead, Dr. Breaker. You can speak to me."

"Well, you see, Agent, I owe everything to Savich here and nothing at all to you. If he wants me to report to him, he's got it."

"I report to him. You report to him. Soon the president will report to him. Maybe that's not such a bad idea. My head hurts."

"I'll bet it does. Lie still now. When you first came in, we did a CT scan. Not to worry, it was normal. We always do a CT scan when there's a head injury, to check for evidence of bleeding. You didn't have any. What happened to your arm? What's this sling for?"

"A knife wound," Savich said. "It's nearly well now. Happened a couple of weeks ago."

"Why don't you let her heal before you send her into the arena with the monsters again?"

She laughed. There was nothing else to do.

The next time she heard anything, it was a strange man speaking.

"When you roared out of the club like a bat out of a cave, I thought Sally was going to have Marvin tackle you. You scared us, Dillon. This is Sherlock?"

"Yes, in all her glory."

"She looks like a mummy."

"Thanks," Sherlock said, not opening her eyes. She realized there was a huge bandage over the cut in her scalp. She raised her hand to touch it, but to her disgust, she didn't have the strength. Dr. Breaker was right. It wasn't fair that she had to be hurt again before she'd healed completely from the other time. Her hand fell, only again Dillon caught it and laid it gently at her side.

"You alive, Sherlock?"

"Yes, thank you. I'm tired of this, sir. At least last time in that Boston hospital I was sitting up the whole time."

"Don't whine. You'll live."

"She calls you 'sir'? Do you require that all your people call you sir?"

"No, only the women. It makes me feel powerful."

"He's lying," she said, cracking open her eyes. To her relief, the light in the room was dim. "He takes all the women to the gym and stomps them into the floor. The 'sir' stuff is my idea. I hope it makes him feel responsible, and guilty."

"I don't feel guilty. I walked you home. You want me to believe I should have taken you inside? Checked all your closets and looked under the bed? Well, maybe from now on I will. You attract trouble, Sherlock, too much of it." But he sounded guilty, really guilty. She wanted to tell him not to be ridiculous, but he said quickly, "This is Special Agent James Quinlan. We go way back together."

"You make it sound like we're nearly to retirement, Dillon. Hi, Ms. Sherlock." He took her hand in his.

"You call him Dillon too." His hand was strong, and there were calluses on his thumbs. She'd seen a web of scars on Dillon's fingers and hands: fine, pale white scars. He'd told her he whittled. Whittled what?

"Yeah, I always thought Savich sounded too tough, too macho, so to spare my manhood I never called him that. Besides, I'm tougher than he is. Hey, what's in a name?"

"He was with you at that place called the Cove?"

"Nah, he came in on the deal when most of the fun was over."

"That's a lie. I saved Sally."

"That's true, he did help. A little bit. Dillon's always there to back me up."

She said, "You're Sally's husband?"

"Yes, she's mine. I've got to tell you, Agent Sherlock, I don't like any of this. You're a target and we've got to find out why."

"None of us likes it, Quinlan," Savich said. "Don't act proprietary. She's not in your unit. I will get to the bottom of this. Hey, Sherlock, you do look like a mummy. You want some more water before I start grilling you again? I'll use my special voice. Quinlan's not bad at it either."

Neither man said anything until she'd drunk her fill. Then Quinlan laughed when Savich said, "Having you suck on a straw is better than trying to balance you on the edge of the cup. You don't drool so much."

Quinlan said, "Agent Sherlock, did you know Dillon found us the wedding date and the church?"

"Why did he do that?"

"Well, I was kind of out of it at the time and Sally was so worried about me she didn't even think about marrying me. So Dillon had to take care of it."

"What he means to say is that he had a bullet in his heart and couldn't do much but press more morphine into his vein. As for Sally, she probably only agreed to marry him because she felt sorry for him."

She smiled at that, and thankfully, it didn't hurt. "Oh goodness. Have I gotten into the wrong career?"

"You're off to a good start," Quinlan said. "Wounded twice

and you've been out of training only what? A month? Hey, don't worry. I've made it to thirty-two, same as Dillon here."

They heard voices outside. Quinlan raised an eyebrow and said, "I think my whirlwind of a wife has blown in. The guard you've got out there doesn't stand a chance, Dillon."

"No indeed," said a pretty young woman about Sherlock's own age as she came into the room. She had blond hair, clasped with barrettes behind her ears, and blue eyes that looked soft and tender, and had seen too much. She looked very small next to the two men. "Don't blame Agent Cramer. He knows me. He helped me barbecue those half a dozen corn on the cob last month, remember, James?"

"Our venture into vegetarian barbecuing," James Quinlan said with disgust and poked Savich's arm. "Just for you I had to barbecue corn on the cob. I lost more of my manhood that day."

"Your manhood seems to be a lot in question lately," Savich said. "Hey, Sally, this is Sherlock. She's the one who needed your decorating help until she had it done herself. She called up one of those expensive designers and the guy tripped all over himself to please her."

Sherlock felt a soft hand lightly stroke her forearm. "You certainly scared the sense out of Dillon here. I was watching him on the phone, and he turned white, threw the phone down, and ran out of the club. Ms. Lily thought he was so horny he couldn't hold himself back another second. As for Fuzz, the bartender, he shook his head and said Savich should have a beer occasionally, it would make him more mellow. Marvin, the bouncer, said he was glad Savich didn't drink. He never wanted to have to try to bounce him."

Sherlock said, "I'd like to meet these people. Dillon said he went there to support Mr. Quinlan."

"Oh, sure, but it's not only that, he—"

"Now, Sally," Savich interrupted her without apology, "Sherlock here is looking as though she's ready to fall through the railing. Let's leave her alone. She needs to rest. Ah, here's Dr. Breaker. Ned, your patient is looking glassy-eyed."

"Out," Dr. Breaker said, not looking at any of them. When they were alone, he said quietly as he took her pulse, "I didn't intend for you to begin partying so soon, Agent Sherlock. Hey, where'd you get that neat name?"

"My dad. He's a judge. I understand that lawyers hate to be in his courtroom. They say it scares their clients to death, being up in front of a guy named Judge Sherlock." She smiled up at him, then closed her eyes, her head falling to the side.

Dr. Breaker gently laid her hand on the bed. He checked her eyes. He stood quietly and studied her face. Then he nodded. Everything was fine. She would recover. He had only one foot out her door when Savich was in his face, saying, "Well?"

"She'll be fine. She's out now and should stay out until morning, with the medication she's had. Nasty business. The guy could have killed her pounding her head on the floor the way he did, to say nothing of hitting her head with the butt of a gun."

Savich sighed, looking down at his clasped hands. "Thanks again for coming so quickly. How long will she be in here?"

"Another day, I'd say. As I told you, the CT scan was normal. No bleeding, no abnormalities that any of the radiologists could see. I'll reevaluate her again in the morning. Now I'm home to bed."

When Dr. Breaker disappeared into the elevator, Quinlan said, "This is a strange business, Dillon. You want to tell me about it now?"

Savich looked at two of his best friends and said slowly, "I'm neck deep here."

"What does that mean?" Sally said, sitting on the bench beside him.

Savich shook his head. "Listen, you guys, thanks for coming down. I think I'll stay here. One of the nurses offered me a bed. I'd feel better with Crammer out here and me inside her room. She'd really be safe then."

"You've got no idea who's behind all this?"

"It could be someone involved with Marlin Jones, that makes the most sense. But who? He's a real loner from what we know. And why would Marlin care if she left town or not? Other than Marlin, there's no one else out there waving a flag. Well, there is someone else. We'll see. It's a mystery, all deep and winding around and around." To Savich's relief, neither Sally nor Quinlan asked him more questions.

An hour later, he was lying on his back on a very hard cot, listening to her even breathing. She moaned once, sending him to his feet in an instant and to her bedside, only to see that she was still asleep. He stood there, looking down at her, white and bandaged, an IV in her arm. She twitched, her hand clenching into a fist, then relaxing again. He didn't like any of this. Why did that guy want to hear what she knew about Marlin Jones? It made no sense. If someone else had killed Belinda, one of her family, then it would make sense that they'd want her out of the way. But then why would he or she hire that man to tell Sherlock that Marlin was innocent? Surely if he thought enough about it, examined every little detail, he would find an answer. But all he could think about now was listening carefully to her breathing. He lightly touched his fingertips to her jaw. It was a khaki green. He stepped back.

He lay back down, felt the smooth cold of his gun next to his hand, and kept listening to her until finally, after what seemed an interminable amount of time, he fell asleep.

"I want to go home."

"Now, Agent Sherlock, I think another full day would be the thing for you. The medical staff likes having FBI agents in here. It makes them feel important. Ah, and a bit on the superior side since they're still on their feet and you, an agent, aren't."

"You've got to be making that up. The nurse this morning was very sweet when she poked me with a needle. And it wasn't in the rear end. Listen, Dr. Breaker, it's already four o'clock in the afternoon. I've been counting sheep since nine o'clock this morning. I'm fine. My head hurts a bit, but nothing else, not even the cut on my head. Please, Dr. Breaker, I want to go home."

"Let's talk about it a bit more," he said, backing away from the bed. "Oh yeah, you can call me Ned."

She swung her legs over and sat up. "I need some clothes, Ned."

"Keep your socks on. I've got clothes for you, Sherlock. Ned told me you'd probably demand to take off."

She looked down at her bare foot. "I don't even have any socks, only this flimsy hospital gown that's open in the back."

Savich grinned at her. "Well, Ned, shall I take her off your hands?"

"She's yours, Savich. She'll be fine. She needs another day taking it easy and these pills for any pain." He handed Savich the bottle of pills.

"Good-bye, Agent Lacey Sherlock. That's a weird name. If I were you, I'd have it changed. How about Jane Sherlock?"

"That wasn't funny, Ned," Savich said, but Dr. Breaker was chuckling. "I've never before had the chance to say that. It's an old joke, you know."

"Yes," Sherlock said. "I know."

"Heard it, huh?"

"I've heard all of them. Thank you, Dr. Breaker. Dillon, give me my clothes and see Dr. Breaker out."

"Yes, ma'am."

Savich stayed out until she opened the door. He was talking to Agent Crammer, a ruddy-faced, barrel-chested young man who had a degree in accounting from the University of Pennsylvania.

She eyed them. When Savich looked up, he took in her outfit and grinned. "Not bad, huh? You won't be arrested by the fashion police."

He'd brought her a dark green silk blouse and a pair of blue jeans, a blue blazer and a pair of low-heeled boots that she'd only worn one time. She liked the outfit but would never have picked it out. It made her look too—

"You look real sharp, Agent Sherlock," Crammer said.

"Yeah," Savich added, "cute even."

"A Special Agent shouldn't look anything but competent and trustworthy. I'll go home and change."

"With that bandage on your head, you're not going to make it into the competence hall of fame. Best settle for cute. At least it's only a big Band-Aid now. Crammer, thanks for keeping watch."

They made her ride downstairs in a wheelchair.

"You ready?"

She stared at a sexy red Porsche. "That's yours?"

"Yes, it's mine."

"How do you fit into it?"

Whatever he'd expected her to say, evidently that wasn't it, because he chuckled. "I fit," he said only and opened the door for her.

He did fit. "This is wonderful. Douglas drives a black Porsche 911. Every time I drove that dratted car, I got a speeding ticket."

"They do that to you if you don't watch it. Now, Sherlock, you aren't going home yet."

"I have to go home. I have plants to water—"

"Quinlan will water your plants. He's magic with plants. He'll probably even sing to them. Sally says she expects those African violets of his to try to get into bed with them. Don't worry about your plants."

"Where do you want me to go? A safe house?"

"No. You're coming home with me."

22

"N O ONE FOLLOWED US, AND yes, I saw you looking too. Forget the bad guys for the moment. What do you think of my humble abode?"

"I forgot about anybody following us the moment I stepped in here. I've never seen anything quite like it." She raised her face and splayed her fingers in front of her. "It's filled with light."

It wasn't a simple two-story open town house. There were soaring pale-beamed ceilings with huge skylights, all the walls painted a soft cream. The furnishings were beige, gold, and a dozen shades of brown. The oak floors were dotted with Persian carpets, the colors soft, mellow, old. A winding oak stairway covered with a running Tabriz carpet in multiple blues went up the stairs. There was a richly carved wooden oak railing running the perimeter of the landing.

"Dillon," she said slowly, turning to look at him for the first time since she'd stepped into this magic place, "my house is to this as a stable is to Versailles. This place is incredible, I've never seen anything like it. Oh dear, I'm not feeling so good."

She wasn't nauseous, thank goodness, but she did collapse into one of his big, soft, buttery brown leather chairs, close her eyes, and swallow several times. He put her feet on a matching leather hassock.

"You need to eat. No, you need to rest. But first I'll get you some water. How about some saltine crackers? My aunt Faye always fed saltines to my pregnant female relatives. What do you think?"

She cocked open an eye. She sighed and swallowed again. "I'm not pregnant, Dillon, but you know, maybe a saltine wouldn't be a bad idea."

He covered her with a rich gold chenille afghan, tucking it around her feet on the leather hassock, and took off to the kitchen. She hadn't seen the kitchen. She wondered if its ceiling went up two stories like the rest of the house.

After she ate a saltine and drank some water, she said, "I think the FBI pays you too much money. You could open this place to the public and charge admission."

"I'm poor, Sherlock. I inherited this house and a bit on the side from my grandmother. She was an artist—watercolors and acrylics."

"Was she a professional? What was her name?"

"Sarah Elliott."

She stared at him, one eyebrow arched, chewing another saltine cracker. "You're kidding," she said finally. "You're telling me *the* Sarah Elliott was your grandmother?"

"Yes. She was my mother's mom. A great old lady. She died five years ago when she was eighty-four. I remember she told me it was time for her to go because the arthritis had gotten really bad in her hands. She couldn't hold her paintbrushes anymore. I told her her talent wasn't in her hands, it was in her mind. I told her to stop bitching and to hold the paintbrushes between her teeth." He paused a moment, smiling toward a painting of an orchid beginning to bloom. "I thought at first she'd slug me, then she started laughing. She had this really deep, full laugh. She lived for another year, holding the paintbrushes between her dentures." He would never forget the first time he'd seen her with that paintbrush sticking out of her mouth, smiling when she saw him, nearly dropping the brush. It had been one of the happiest moments of his life.

"And you were Sarah Elliott's favorite grandchild? That's why she left you this beautiful house in the middle of Georgetown?"

"Well, she was worried since I'd chosen the FBI and computers for a career."

"What exactly was she worried about?" She pulled the afghan higher up on her chest. A headache was slowly building

behind her left ear. She hated it. Even her arm ached where
Marlin Jones had knifed her weeks before.

"She was afraid my artistic side would stultify, what with the
demands of my job and with my constant computer fiddling."

"Ah, so this place is to inspire you? Get you in touch with
your artistic genes?"

"Yes. You look green, Sherlock. I think it's time you took a
nap. Do you have to vomit?"

She thought about that for a moment. "I don't think so. May
I stay here for a while? It's very comfortable. I'm a bit on the
thready side."

"No wonder," he said, and watched her head loll to the side.
She was out. The chair was oversized, so he wasn't worried
that she'd wake up stiff as a pretzel. He unfolded another afghan over her, one his mother had knitted, this one so soft it
spilled through the fingers. He stroked it as he gently tucked
it around her shoulders. She'd French-braided her hair, but it
really wasn't long enough, and so auburn curls stuck up here
and there. Several strands of hair fell about her face, curling
around a bit. The big Band-Aid looked absurd plastered over
the shaved spot on her temple, faintly pathetic really, since
she was so pale.

All she needed was a little rest. She'd be fine. He lightly
stroked his fingertips over her eyebrows.

He saw she had a spray of freckles over the bridge of her
nose.

She didn't have any freckles anywhere else. And he'd
looked. He hadn't meant to, but he had. He really liked the
freckles on her nose.

No doubt about it. He was in way deep.

She woke up to the smell of garlic, onion, and tomatoes. Her
mouth started watering even before her brain fully registered
food. Her stomach growled. She felt fine, no nausea.

"Good, you're awake."

"What are you cooking?"

"Penne pasta with sun-dried tomatoes, pesto, onions, and
garlic. And some garlic toast. You're drooling, Sherlock.
You've got an appetite, I hope."

"I could eat this afghan."

"Not that one, please. It's my favorite. The nurses told me you hadn't eaten much all day. Time to stuff yourself. First, here's a couple of pills for you to take."

She took them without asking what they were.

"No wine. How about some cider?"

He put a tray over her legs and watched her take her first bite of Savich pesto pasta. She closed her eyes as she slowly, very slowly, chewed, and chewed some more until there was nothing left in her mouth but the lingering burst of pesto and garlic. She licked her lips. Finally, she opened her eyes, stared at him for a very long time, then said, "You'll make a fantastic husband, Dillon. I've never tasted anything so delicious in my life."

"It's my mom's recipe. She taught me how to make the pasta when I was eighteen and headed off to MIT. She'd told me she'd heard that the only thing they ate up there was Boston beans. She said guys and beans didn't mix well so I needed to know how to make something else. You really like it better than the pizza you devoured a couple of nights ago?"

"Goodness, it was two nights ago, wasn't it? It seems like a decade. Actually, I like it better than anything I can ever remember eating. Do you make pizza too?"

"Sure. You want some for breakfast?"

"You cook it anytime you want, I'll consume it." They didn't say anything more for a good seven minutes. Savich's tray was on the coffee table, close enough to keep a good eye on her. She stopped halfway through and stared down at the rest of her pasta. He thought she was going to cry. "It's so good. There's no more room."

"If you get hungry later, we can heat it up."

She was fiddling with her fork, building little structures with the pasta, watching the emerging patterns with great concentration. She didn't look up as she said, "I didn't know there were men like you."

He studied his fingernails, saw a hangnail on his thumb, and frowned. He didn't look up either. "What does that mean?"

"Well, you live in a beautiful house, and I can't see a speck of mess or dust. In other words, you're not a pig. But that's extraneous stuff, important, sure, but not a deal breaker. You have a big heart, Dillon. And you're a great cook."

"Sherlock, I've lived alone for five years. Man cannot live by pizza at Dizzy Dan's alone. Also, I don't like squalor. There are lots of men like me. Quinlan, for example. Ask Sally, she'll say his heart is bigger than the Montana sky."

"What do you mean you lived alone for five years? You didn't live alone before that?"

"Your FBI training in action. Very good. I was married once upon a time."

"Somehow I can't see you married. You seem so self-sufficient. Are you divorced?"

"No, Claire didn't divorce me. She died of leukemia."

"I'm sorry, Dillon."

"It's been even more than five years now. I'm sorry Claire never got to live in this wonderful house. She died three months before my grandmother."

"How long were you together?"

"Four years. She was only twenty-seven when she died. It was strange what happened. She'd just read that old book by Erich Segal—*Love Story*. She was diagnosed with leukemia three weeks later. There was a certain irony in that, I suppose, only I didn't recognize it for a very long time. I've watched the movie several times over the years. Claire's death wasn't serene and poignantly tragic like the young wife's death in the movie or the book, believe me. She fought with everything in her. It wasn't enough. Nothing was enough."

He hadn't spoken of Claire this much since her death. It rocked him. He rose abruptly and walked over to the fireplace, leaning his shoulders against the mantel.

"I'm sorry."

"Yes."

"Do you still miss her?"

He looked toward one of his grandmother's paintings, given to him on his graduation from MIT, an acrylic of a bent old man haggling in a French market, in the small village near Cannes where his grandmother had lived for several years back in the sixties. Then he looked at Sherlock, his expression faintly puzzled. "It's odd, but you know, I can't quite picture Claire's face in my mind anymore. It's all blurry and faded, like a very old photograph. I know the pain is there, but it's soft now, far away, and I can't really grasp it. Yes, I miss her.

Sometimes I'll still look up from reading a book and start to say something to her, or expect her to yell at me when I go nuts over a football play. She was an ice skater. Very good, but she never made the cut to the Olympics."

"That's how Belinda is now to me. At first I never wanted the pain to lessen, but it did anyway, without my permission. It's almost as if Belinda wanted me to let her go. When I see a photo of her now, it seems like she was someone I knew and loved in another place, another time, maybe the person who loved her was another me as well. Sometimes when I'm in a crowd, I think I hear her call out to me. She's never there, of course."

He swallowed, feeling tears of bittersweet memory he hadn't felt in years. Maybe the tears were for both of them.

Her eyes were clear and calm as she said, "You know, I'd fight too. Never would I go quietly into that good night, sort of winking out and isn't that too bad, and wasn't she a nice person? No, I'd be kicking and yelling all the way."

He laughed, then immediately sobered. Guilt because he'd spoken about Claire, then laughed? Suddenly, he laughed again. "I would too. Thanks, Sherlock."

She smiled at him. "My head doesn't hurt anymore. One of those magic pills?"

"Yeah. Now, would you like to watch the news while I clean up the kitchen?"

"No dessert?"

"You didn't clean your plate and you're demanding dessert?"

"Dessert's for a completely different stomach compartment, and my dessert compartment is empty. I know I smelled cheesecake."

She ate his New York cheesecake while he cleaned up the dishes. She watched the national news. More trouble in China. More trouble in the Middle East. More wiping out of Kurds, only which Kurds? They were as divided a group as were all the countries surrounding them. Then, suddenly, there was Big John Bullock, Marlin Jones's lawyer, full of bluff and good nature for the reporters, flinging out answers as they pursued him from the Boston courthouse to his huge black limousine.

"Will Marlin Jones go to trial?"

"No comment."

"Is Marlin crazy?"

"You know the ruling." He rolled his eyes and shrugged his massive shoulders.

"Will you plead him not guilty?"

"No comment."

"Is it true you told everyone he had a bad childhood, a mother who beat him up, and an uncle who sexually abused him?"

"Public records are public records."

"But there's a confession."

"It won't be admissible. The cops and the FBI made him confess."

"But what about that FBI agent? Your client knocked her cold and took her to that warehouse to kill her. They've got everything on tape and on film."

Big John gave an explosive wave of his arms. "Pure and simple entrapment. There wasn't a thought of killing her in his mind."

"I heard he even knifed the agent."

Big John shook his head. "No more. Remember, it was entrapment. It was all a setup. It won't be admissible, you'll see."

And one woman newscaster said, "Oh, so you're saying if he'd killed the FBI agent then it wouldn't have been entrapment?"

Lots of laughter. And a lot of faces looking hard at Big John Bullock.

"No more questions, folks. Talk to you later."

A commercial came on for Bud Light.

She felt Savich behind her. She said quietly, "I'm going back to Boston. I've got to see Marlin Jones again."

"They won't let you see him, Sherlock."

"I've got to try." She turned slowly and looked up at him. "You see that, don't you? I've got to try. I can't sit around waiting for some maniac to come after me again. If you tell them to let me in, they will."

"He's not the maniac who's after you now. Besides, you go talk to him again, and it could all come out that Belinda was your sister."

"No, I wouldn't tell him any of that. I wouldn't tell anyone about that."

"It's still a risk. Trust me on this: You can't begin to imagine what the media would do if they found out you were the sister of one of the murdered women and finding Marlin has been your obsession for seven years. You think the way I said it sounds hard. Wait until the media got hold of it. Big John would certainly squawk about entrapment then.

"I think a more worthwhile trip would be to San Francisco. Why don't I call the San Francisco office and have a couple of agents go talk to Douglas, your father, and your mother?"

She shook her head.

"As for Marlin, maybe, after you've rested a couple of days. Look, it's Saturday. I want you to take it easy until Tuesday. You promise?"

She stroked the gold chenille afghan. "I guess I could use a good night's sleep."

"Two days, Sherlock. I want your promise that you'll lie low for two days. Then we'll talk about it."

She was silent, and he felt a good dollop of anger.

"You're an FBI agent, Sherlock. That means you do what I tell you to do. You carry out assignments I instruct you to carry out. You don't go surfing any wave that catches your fancy. You got that?"

"You're nearly yelling. How could I not get it?"

He stepped forward, then stopped. "I've got a nice guest room upstairs. I also packed you a suitcase. It's still in the trunk of the car. I'll take you up, then bring it in."

She didn't think about her underwear until she was standing in the Victorian bathroom with its highly polished walnut floor, its claw-feet tub, pedestal washbowl, and plush pale yellow Egyptian towels with small flowers on them. She'd stripped down to her bra and panties, turned and seen herself in the mirror and stared. He'd picked out the softest peach silk set she owned. What had he thought when he picked them out of the drawer? Without thinking, she ran her hand over her belly, the silk smooth and slithery against her palm. What had he thought? No, she wouldn't think about that.

They were only a bra and drawers, no matter how exquisite. How potentially sexy. He probably hadn't even thought a thing, just grabbed them up. She loved pretty underwear. This set she'd bought herself for her last birthday. So expensive. Soft and flimsy and wicked. She took off the bra and rubbed the smooth lace against her cheek. She hadn't worn it in months. Dillon had picked it out.

"Sherlock."

23

S⁣HE QUICKLY WRAPPED A towel around herself and looked around the bathroom door. He was standing in the middle of the bedroom, a suitcase in his hand.

"On the bed, please, Dillon."

He thought she looked beyond tired. He probably should have left her at the hospital, tied to the hospital bed. He looked again. He'd never before realized a towel could look so sexy wrapped around someone. "You need any help?"

That made her smile. "No, sir. I can brush my teeth without you holding my arm up."

"Then I'll see you in the morning. There's no reason for you to wake up early. Sleep in. When you wake up, holler, and I'll bring you breakfast. Don't forget, Sherlock, you promised to stay put."

She hadn't, but she nodded. "Thank you, Dillon."

"Oh, another thing. I need to run a couple of errands tomorrow morning. While I'm gone, I want you to leave the doors locked and don't open up for anybody, I don't care who anyone says they are. There's lots of food, even some pesto left over for you. You don't need to go out. You open it only for me, you got that?"

"I got that."

"Your SIG-Sauer is downstairs in my office. Your Lady Colt is in the drawer by your bed. Now, let me decide what we'll do about this mess. I'll tell you tomorrow."

"What are your errands?"

He frowned at her. "Not your business. I won't be gone more than a couple of hours."

"Would you sing me a couple of lines before you go?"

"You want something down-home?"

"Yeah, real down-home."

His rich deep baritone filled the room, sounding really twangy this time. *"She ain't Rose but she ain't bad. She ain't easy, but she can be had. So am I when she whispers in my ear. She ain't Rose, and Rose ain't here."*

"Who's Rose?"

He grinned at her, gave her a salute, then left, closing her bedroom door behind him.

It was dawn when he shot straight up in his bed. He hit the floor running when another scream rent the silence.

She was wheezing, her arms wrapped around herself. She struggled to sit up in bed.

"Sherlock. You're awake? What's wrong?"

She was still sucking air into her lungs. It was as if someone had tried to suffocate her. He sat down beside her and pulled her against him. He began rubbing her back. "It's all right now. Did you have a nightmare?"

Slowly, so very slowly, her breathing began to steady, but it still hurt to breathe, as if someone had clouted her in the ribs. She couldn't talk yet, didn't want to talk. "That's it, relax. I'm here. Nothing's going to hurt you, nothing."

Her face was buried in his shoulder, her arms limp at her sides. Then, suddenly, she put her arms around his back and held on tight.

"Yeah, I'm real and I'm solid and I'm mean. No one's going to hurt you. It's okay."

He could feel her harsh breathing against his flesh, then she said, "Yes, I know. I'm all right now."

He tried to pull away from her but she still held on tight. He could feel her shivering. "It's really okay, Sherlock," he said again. "I'm not going anywhere. You can let go now."

"I don't think I want to. Give me a few more minutes." She tightened her grip around him.

She was still shivering. "Sorry, but I seem to have packed you the wrong kind of nightgown. You must be freezing."

"You're a man. You picked it out because it's sexy and sheer, just like my underwear."

"Well, yes, I suppose you could be right. It feels really soft and nice. Sorry, but my hormones must have gotten the better of me. Listen now. Let me go, Sherlock, and lie back."

If anything, she gripped him tighter.

He laughed. "I promise you everything's okay now. Listen, you've got to let me go. Come on now."

"No."

He laughed again. He sounded like he was in pain. "Okay, tell you what. I'm cold too. Why don't we both lie back and I'll keep holding you until we both warm up."

He knew it wasn't a good idea, but he was worried about her. Truth be told, he didn't want to think about his motives. He was wearing boxer shorts, nothing else. No, this was definitely not a good idea.

He got under the covers with her, lay on his back, and pulled her against him. She settled her face on his shoulder, her hand on his bare chest. He pulled the covers as high as her ears.

She was stiff. "It's okay," he said, hugged her against him hard, then eased up. "You want to tell me about it?"

He felt her jerk, her breath fan over his skin. She was still afraid. He waited. He began to stroke her back—long, even strokes. Finally, she said, "It was a nightmare, a stupid nightmare. Talking about Belinda probably brought it on again."

"What do you mean 'again'? You've had this dream before?"

She was quiet for a very long time. At least she wasn't shuddering anymore. He was hoping she'd keep talking. Getting her to open up was turning out to be one of his toughest assignments. And he was beginning to seriously doubt his strategy for calming her down. In the silence he noticed how uneven his own breathing had become. He began breathing deeply. "Tell me about the dream, Sherlock."

It was near dark, she was cocooned in blankets against him, she was safe, her mind wasn't on alert, and so she said, her breath warm and light against his skin, "I was the one in the warehouse, or I was with Belinda, or somehow a part of her. I don't know. But in the dream it's as if I'm the one who was there, I was the one in his maze, the one he was supposed to kill, not Belinda. Then I went through the whole thing in Boston. I truly believed it would bring me full circle, but it didn't."

"I'm not understanding all of this."

"No wonder. Sometimes I think I'm mad."

"Talk to me." He kissed the top of her head. It wasn't a good move. "Talk to me," he said again, his voice lower this time, deeper, because he was aware of her woman's body against him, aware of her scent, aware of her hair on his shoulder, tickling his cheek.

"Every time I've had the dream in the past, it's gone a bit further. He hasn't yet killed me, but this time I woke up as he raised the knife."

He waited, held her, and waited. He could feel her tensing, feel her heart speeding up. "Say it, Sherlock. What is it?"

"I know, Dillon, I know that when that knife comes down I'll die."

It was no longer dark in the bedroom. It was a soft pearly gray, yet dark enough so that it was still two people sharing confidences in the night. He knew she had to tell him all of it now or she might never tell him. She was vulnerable now. He didn't know how much longer it would last. Probably not long.

"The dream began soon after Belinda was murdered?"

"Yes. I've thought about it and thought about it over the years. It's as I said before—if I'm not the one who's there, then it's as if I'm actually following her same path, feeling the terror she felt." Her fingers clutched the hair on his chest and he jerked a bit.

"Sorry, Dillon. Oh my, you're not wearing any clothes. I'm sorry. I hadn't realized before."

"It's all right. I'm wearing boxer shorts. Ignore it. How long since you've had the nightmare?"

"Well over a year. This time I went through it all the way to the center of the maze and he was there, only it was so dark I couldn't see him, but I saw the silver arc of his knife. Then I screamed and it woke me up."

"Do you think what you did in Boston brought the dream back?"

"I don't know. Probably."

He was silent for a moment, then said very quietly, "So this was why you were so sure exactly what Marlin was going to do. It wasn't the profilers' reports, it wasn't all the study you've done during the past seven years, all the thought you've given to it. You knew every step. Because of the dream, you knew each move to make, each move he would make."

"Yes. But it still doesn't make any sense, does it?"

"Not this moment, but it will sooner or later."

"I have studied him. The profilers had it right—he hated women who cursed, and that's why he cut out their tongues. What they couldn't have been certain about was that the women also bad-mouthed their husbands. But I knew it was true. That's why I had to be the bait—I knew exactly how to get him to come after me, I knew which buttons to push. He didn't have to doubt for a second that I was the best candidate for punishment around.

"But there was a difference that I realized just now. In my dream, when the murderer raised the knife, it wasn't the same way that Marlin raised his knife in the center of the maze in Boston. It wasn't so vicious in the dream. It was as if he—"

"As if what?"

"As if he wasn't really serious, but I knew he was and I was scared to death. I'm sorry. That doesn't make a lick of sense."

He thought about that a moment, then said, "But in Boston, you'd put him on the defensive. He wasn't facing a terrified, helpless woman. That could make the difference." He tightened his arm around her again. "Listen to me. Even if that dream does continue on some night in the future, even if he does stick a knife into you, you can't die. It's only a dream. You've got to believe that. As real as it seems, it still isn't. It never will be."

She shuddered, then was quiet against him. Her hand had been fisted on his chest. He'd managed to ignore it, but now her hand was lower, nearly to his belly. His breathing speeded up.

"What do you think it all means?"

He thought about that a long time. It took him longer than usual because he was hard, his heart was pounding fast and strong, and he was having a good deal of difficulty concentrating. His brain no longer had any control. He wanted to pull that beautiful soft peach nightgown over her head and—

"I don't know. It's almost as if you have some connection with Belinda. But regardless, there's got to be something there. Something that happened that you don't remember. Don't you think?"

Her hand was now a fist on his belly. "I don't know. What could have happened? Why wouldn't I remember? I was never hurt at that time. No trauma or head wound of any kind."

He laid his own hand over hers, pressing down until her fingers splayed over him, her palm soft and flat against his flesh. "Relax. Everything will be all right. I know a woman who could help take you back to what really happened. There's got to be something from seven years ago, something that triggered this, something you've blocked out that's resurfacing. If anyone can get to the bottom of this, she can. But don't worry about it anymore right now."

"You really think she'll help us?"

"I really think so. Since this all started, I knew there was something you were keeping from me. You promise this is all of it?"

"Yes." The terror was gone. She didn't even care that this woman he was talking about was probably a shrink. She could see him in the dull morning light, she could feel the strength of him, the deep smooth muscles, the texture of his flesh. She didn't feel anything remotely close to terror now. She felt something she didn't think she'd ever felt in her life. The feel of him beneath her palm, beneath her fingers, it made her so alive her body was thrumming with the power of it.

"Dillon?"

"Hmmm?" He didn't know if he had any more words available to him. His brain was all in his groin, need for her was raging through him, making him shake, and it took everything in him to keep control.

"I feel really warm, but warmer in some places than in others. My shoulders feel really cool, but not other parts of me, like my chest."

She was seducing him? No, that couldn't be right. He prayed that it was, then cursed himself. He had to get out of there. He should be back in his own bedroom, with two doors closed between them. He cleared his throat. "Talking would help, but if you can't talk, then I'll go back to my own room. That would be the smart thing to do, going back to my room this very instant would be the very smartest thing to do."

"I know." She sighed deeply, leaned her face into his shoulder, and lightly bit him. She then licked where she'd bitten. "You're probably right. But I have to tell you those warmer places have gotten even warmer. Hot nearly."

"Sherlock, stop now. This isn't good. I knew it wasn't good when I got in bed with you. Now I know it's maybe one of the stupidest things I've done in a good long while." He thought if he moved now, he was in for seven years of bad luck, because he'd crack into a billion pieces, like a mirror.

She pulled her hand away from beneath his. He sucked in his breath in disappointment. "I'm sorry. Ollie told me you didn't ever get involved with your people."

Why had Ollie told her that? He had dated Hannah before she'd joined the Unit, but then he'd called a halt when she'd come on board. Well, yeah, at least at one time Ollie had been right. Actually, until an hour ago, he would have bet the farm on it. Maybe even ten minutes ago he would have bet a second farm on it. "No, I don't get involved with any of my people. At least I haven't. It seems that's all shot now, though. And don't say you're sorry again. If you do, I'll do something unsuave."

"What?"

"Sherlock, I'm outta here. I'm not about to take advantage of a nightmare. You're vulnerable and afraid and I happen to be convenient. But you don't need me now. You're okay, right?"

She didn't say a word. He thought he'd been punched in the gut when he felt her tears against his chest.

He hauled her on top of him, and kissed her. All light, feathery kisses, and between the kisses he was saying, "Don't cry. I'm trying to be noble. It's a battle and I'm losing. You've got to help me with this. I want you a whole lot, but this isn't the way. Actually, I want you whole again, I said it wrong. Does that make any sense to you?"

Her palm smoothed over his thigh, upward. She said against his ear, "That must be what it is then."

He didn't know what she was talking about. All he was thinking about was kissing her.

"I've got to stop," he said between another round of kisses, "or if I don't, then I'm going to be on top of you and that nightgown is going to end up on the floor."

She lurched away from him, taking him completely by surprise. "Let me be plain about this," she said, smiling down at him. He wanted to weep until he realized what she was doing. "Let me be straightforward. I don't want you to have any doubts where I stand on this."

He watched her pull the gown over her head and throw it across the room. She was sitting over him, naked, staring down at him, and she looked scared to death, and defiant. Yes, that was it, defiant and determined.

Oddly enough, it calmed him. He wanted to put his hands on her, but no, not yet. "What do you want me to do, Sherlock?"

"I want to make love with you, that is, if you'll make an exception for me."

"I've made an exception for you since I kicked you into the bushes in Hogan's Alley. Why do you look scared to death if you're so certain about all this?"

"I'm not scared. It's the morning light."

"Yeah, right." But he was more than willing to believe it.

She had lovely breasts, all high and smooth and round, the right size for his hands, his mouth, any other part of him that wanted to touch her there. And he wanted to. He couldn't remember ever wanting anything so much in his life.

Then he remembered that he'd wanted more than anything to be an FBI agent. That sure put a crimp in things.

24

$\sim$

Nah. That was pure bull-
shit.

In the scheme of things, that had been very shortsighted of
him. This woman sitting naked on top of him was, he figured,
about the most important milestone in his life. She was what
was real, what was urgent, more urgent to him than anything
else in his life. He wanted her, right now, he wanted all of her.
Slowly, he lifted his right hand and lightly touched his fingertips to her breast.

She drew back, as if surprised.

He cupped her breasts in his palms. Lovely, a perfect fit.
Again, she flinched.

"What's wrong? You don't like me holding you?"

"Dillon, I should tell you something."

He couldn't take his eyes off her breasts, but he did manage
to drop his hands, for the moment, although his fingers itched
like mad. But he knew he had to pay attention. Something
wasn't quite right here. Now he was looking at her ribs, at her
stomach, at the smooth expanse of thigh.

"Dillon?"

"Yes? Keep talking, I'll try to pay attention, but I can't
help but look at you, Sherlock. You're really quite nice to
look at."

She sucked in her breath, then blurted it out. "I've only
done this once. When I was nineteen. It was in the backseat
of Bobby Wellman's yellow Jaguar. It was really cramped and
no fun at all. Actually it was messy and horrible, but I was
philosophical about it, really. After all, it was the backseat of

a car. But then, well, after Belinda's death, I couldn't stand to have any men around me."

"Only once? In your whole life? In a Jaguar? Surely not an XJ6? That would be practically impossible."

"That's the truth, but Bobby managed somehow. It wasn't at all pleasant, as I said, and I didn't realize how bony he was, all knees and elbows, even his chin was sharp. I guess if anybody was looking, they'd have laughed their heads off. Bobby loved that car. I remember that the leather was really smooth and slick because he was always oiling it. Then he'd leer and say he used his mother's extra-virgin olive oil."

"What a jerk. Now that I think back on it, I did something similar to that when I was seventeen and eighteen. But you're twenty-seven, Sherlock."

"Yes. When I was nineteen, after Belinda was murdered, I shut down. I've never even been interested in another man since that time with Bobby. Not even remotely. Until you. Do you mind?"

"I don't think so. Never Douglas, then?"

"No. Once, a couple of weeks ago, he kissed me, but that's all there was to it. No, it's only you."

"Only me." That sounded incredibly fine. Actually, he thought, as he eased her down on top of him, if he didn't suffer from sensory overload first, he would give her pleasure if it killed him.

When he'd gotten her level of interest up to at least half of his, he was so far gone, he didn't know if he'd make it. He lifted her to his mouth, felt her surprise, her shock. After not more than a minute or two, he felt every quiver in her legs, the deep clenching of her stomach muscles. And when she cried out, her back arching wildly, her fists pounding on his shoulders, jerking on his hair, he knew that he was the luckiest man on the earth.

He wanted to bring her pleasure again, but he knew he simply couldn't take it any longer. "Sherlock," he said. Looking into her eyes he came into her fast and deep, his powerful arms shaking with his effort to control himself, to keep his weight off her, as he moved deeper and deeper, feeling her flesh easing slowly to accommodate him. His head was thrown back, his eyes closed. And when he touched her again with his fingers, he knew this was the best thing that had ever happened to him in his life.

She came again when his fingers touched her, and as he watched her face, heard her whimpers of pleasure, felt her draw him close and closer still, he let himself go.

And it was fine, all of it.

"Agent Sherlock, close your eyes, that's right, and lean your head back. Let your shoulders drop. Good. No, don't stiffen up. Now, breathe very deeply. Deeper, let go. Good. Yes, that's fine."

Dr. Lauren Bowers, a conservative congresswoman from Maryland and one of the best hypnotists Savich knew, raised her head and grinned at him. "People like Agent Sherlock here," she said in her normal tone of voice, "are usually the easiest to get under. Once you get past her defenses, she's an open book, all the pages ruffling in the wind, that sharp brain of hers invites you right in. Now, Dillon, you've written down your questions."

She took the sheet of paper from him and scanned it. "Did I ever tell you that you are really quite good? Of course you know you are, you've been trained by the best."

Dr. Bowers turned back to the young woman who looked flaccid and pale, as if something had been sapping her from deep inside for far too long a time.

"Agent Sherlock—Lacey? Can you hear me?"

"Of course, Dr. Bowers. I'm not deaf."

Dr. Bowers laughed. "That's very good. Now, I want you to go back, Lacey, back to the last time you saw Belinda. Do you remember when that was?"

"It was April thirteenth, three days before Belinda was killed." Sherlock suddenly lurched forward, then flopped back. She was shaking her head frantically, back and forth. "No!"

"Lacey, it's all right. Breathe in deeply, that's right."

"I want Dillon."

Without pause, he was lightly stroking her hand. "I'm here, Sherlock. I won't leave you. Let's go back together, all right? You're going to have to do something for me. You're going to have to paint that day to me in words, so I can see it as you see it. Can you do that?"

Her expression changed, softening, and incredibly, she looked like a girl again, a teenager. She sighed, then smiled. "It was very sunny, crisp and cool, a low fog swirling in over and through the Golden Gate Bridge. I loved days like that, watching the sailboats on the Bay, seeing the Marin Headlands through open patches in the fog, all bleak and barren, but still green from all the winter rains."

Dr. Bowers nodded to Savich to keep going. He said in his low, deep voice, "What were you doing?"

"I was sitting out on the deck off the living room."

"Were you alone?"

"Yes. My mother was in her room napping. My father was at the courthouse. He was prosecuting a big drug case, and he wanted to make sure the defense was sticking to the sitting judge's gag order. He said if they weren't, he'd skin them alive."

"Where was Belinda?"

Her mouth tightened, her eyebrows drew together. She wasn't smiling anymore. She started to shake her head, back and forth.

"It's okay," Savich said easily. "Where was Douglas?"

"I thought he was at work."

"But he wasn't?"

"No, he was there, in the house. He was with Belinda, upstairs in their suite. They were out on the balcony above me."

"What were they doing?"

For an instant she looked incredibly angry, then her face smoothed out and her voice was smooth, unworried. "They were making love."

He hadn't expected that. "You understood what was happening, right? It didn't freak you out?"

"No. It was embarrassing. Douglas was saying lots of really dirty things."

"Then what happened?"

"I heard Belinda cry out."

"Was she having a climax?"

"I don't think so. I heard her roll off the chaise onto the brick balcony. I heard her crying, then she stopped."

"Why?"

"I heard Douglas tell her if she cried anymore someone

might hear her and he wouldn't like that at all. In fact, if she kept whining, he might throw her off the balcony."

"Then what happened?"

"Nothing. Belinda was quiet then. After a few minutes, I heard them making love again. I heard Douglas tell her she'd better moan because if she didn't moan, he wouldn't believe she really loved him. She moaned really loudly then and he said more really dirty things to her. He kept telling her she owed him, owed him but good."

"Do you know what he meant by that?"

She shook her head.

"What happened then?"

"I waited until Douglas went out, then I went to their bedroom and called out her name. She told me to go away but I didn't. I walked in. She was standing in the middle of the room, naked. She grabbed for her jeans and put them in front of her. I asked her if Douglas had hit her and she said no, that was ridiculous. Douglas wouldn't hit anybody. But I didn't believe her. I think I saw a bruise below her ribs when she raised her hand to wave me away. But I didn't leave her. I couldn't."

"Had this happened before, to your knowledge?"

She was shaking her head. "Oh no. I'm certain. I thought they loved each other. Douglas was always so light and caressing with her, so tender. They were always laughing and hugging, kissing when they didn't think anyone was looking. But not now. She couldn't stand up straight. I wanted to kill him. But she said no, if anyone killed him it would be her. She told me to go away, that she didn't want to see me, I was a pain in the butt. She had a miscarriage that night."

"You never told anyone about this? Not even the police after she was murdered?"

She didn't say anything. She was frowning again. "She must have had a miscarriage because Douglas hit her. I'd forgotten all about that." Suddenly, her eyes opened and she stared blankly ahead of her. She looked bewildered, then frightened. He began to massage her hand, closing his fingers over hers. "It's all right, Sherlock. I'm here. Nothing bad is going to happen."

She started to cry. She stared at him, made no sound, but tears streaked down her pale cheeks. Her lips were chapped.

Dr. Bowers wiped the tears away with a Kleenex. "Now, Lacey, that's enough. I want you to wake up now. I'm going to count to three. On three, you'll be awake, smile at Dillon, and remember everything we talked about."

On three, Sherlock, her eyes still open, came back into herself. "Why am I crying?"

She rubbed her fingers over her eyes. "Oh, I remember now. It was—"

"It's okay," Savich said, pulled her against him, and began stroking his big hands up and down her back. "You don't have to talk about it right this minute."

She grew very still in his arms. Her heart was against his. He could feel the slow, steady beat. He kissed her hair. "You okay?"

She nodded against his shoulder. "I miss Belinda so much. She was more my mother than our real mother was. Our real mother stayed in her room all the time. She loved to eat Godiva chocolates. And she was so beautiful—both Belinda and my mother. I was the plain one, but neither of them held it against me, well, maybe Belinda didn't like me so much when I was older. I don't know why.

"I know Douglas had never hit her before, she told me he hadn't. I asked her why he'd hit her this time, why he'd humiliated her."

"What'd she say?"

"She wouldn't tell me. She stood there, shaking her head. She told me I wouldn't understand. That it had nothing to do with me, that I was to forget it.

"I was confused, then angry. I told her I was nineteen, that I wasn't a kid anymore, that I could play the piano and she couldn't. She laughed at that, but it hurt her rib to laugh, so she stopped really fast. She told me to forget this, that it wasn't important. She told me to go away. I went to Napa Valley with some friends. I never saw Belinda again."

"How did you know that Belinda had a miscarriage?"

"I don't remember. Someone must have told me. But no one seemed to know about it. It isn't in the medical reports or the autopsy report. I don't remember."

"But somehow you followed her through the warehouse,

followed her to her death, saw everything she saw, felt her terror, felt her die."

Dr. Bowers looked as if she wanted to leap on Savich, but he shook his head. Sherlock was stiff now, withdrawn from him, but he didn't say anything more. He held her, rocking her slightly, back and forth.

"How could I have possibly been there? It doesn't make any sense. I was in St. Helena when my father called me. I left San Francisco that very day I'd spoken to Belinda."

"What did your father say when he called you?"

"He said that Belinda had been killed by the String Killer. He told me to come home. I went. There wasn't anything more."

"Did your father tell you about her miscarriage?"

"I don't remember."

"When did you have the first dream?"

"Six weeks later. He was stalking me, and I knew he was there, only there was nothing I could do about it. I couldn't get away from him. I yelled at him, 'Why are you here? What do you want?' He didn't say anything. He kept coming closer and closer. I knew he would hit me on the head but it didn't matter. I couldn't get away from him. I felt helpless, and I was. He was right there, over me. The dream ended."

"When did you come to realize that he picked women because they cursed and put down their husbands?"

"The dreams got longer, more detailed. Later, he told me, told me over and over. That began maybe three months later. He said in my ear, after he struck me, 'You're a filthy-mouthed little bitch, aren't you? You curse and say all those bad things you shouldn't be saying and you blame your husband and call him bad names. I've got to punish you.'

"I'll never forget that, never. The dreams continued, got more and more involved until the one last night when I woke up the instant before he killed me. I honestly don't know how much the profiling papers influenced me and all my studies. There was a lot of gruesome stuff in the courses and I thought about him all the time, read all the big-city newspapers, studied other serial killers. But I don't understand where this dream came from."

"It's there, Lacey. We'll get it all out. It will take a bit of time."

"Dr. Bowers is right. It's all there in that magnificent brain of yours, somewhere. We'll unlock all of it, but no more today." He kissed the top of her head, then said in that calm unhurried voice, "Do you remember if it was Marlin Jones speaking?"

He held his breath. She was perfectly silent, perfectly still. Finally, she said in a voice muffled by his shirt, "No, I can't be certain."

Or she couldn't bear to remember. It was enough for now, more than enough. He said aloud, "I think we should pack it in for today. What do you say, Lauren? Has she had enough of the wringer?"

"I'd say so. Go watch the Redskins play ball. Eat popcorn. Forget it, at least for today. She's still recovering. She needs rest. We'll get at the rest of it in a couple of days."

25

$\mathcal{A}$SSISTANT DIRECTOR JIMMY
Maitland chewed on an unlit cigar, wrote two words in his
small black book, then looked back at Agent Sherlock, who
was sitting on the edge of Savich's sofa, looking pale as death.
Savich was across from her in his favorite leather chair, his
legs crossed at the ankles. He was, as far as Maitland could
tell, looking at Sherlock's hands. He hadn't said a word.
Jimmy Maitland, who'd known Savich since he'd become a
special agent eight years before, said, "I don't like any of this,
Savich. I got a call from Crammer's section supervisor, telling
me that Sherlock here had been attacked and that Crammer
had stayed outside her hospital room. I'd like to know why
you didn't bother to tell me about this."

Sherlock looked up. Her eyes were very bright and very
blue. "It's Sunday, sir, and we were going to watch the
Redskins game. I'd prefer the San Francisco 49ers but you
don't show them here unless they're playing on *Monday Night
Football.*"

Before Jimmy Maitland could leap on Sherlock, Savich
said, "I wanted her to rest today, sir. I'd planned to speak to
you about it tomorrow. However, it's kind of you to have
driven all the way over here."

"Why is she here?"

"She was attacked in her town house. I didn't think it was
safe for her to remain there."

Maitland grunted at that. "So what's going on here? It's
about that little prick Marlin Jones, isn't it?"

She knew if she told him she had no idea what it was about,

he'd probably have a coronary, so she said simply, "Yes, sir. I don't think our job is quite done yet. I'm going back to Boston to talk to him again. There are some loose ends, some things that don't fit together. The last thing we want is any uncertainty. Remember Richard Jewell and the Atlanta Olympic bombing? We looked like secretive, cover-your-behind boobs in that deal. We were heavy-handed, let the media in on everything before we had anything remotely conclusive, and then we left the guy twisting in the wind. We took his reputation, his good name. Sir, we even took his Tupperware. Let me finish properly with Marlin Jones. This week, sir. That's all I need."

Reference to the Richard Jewell fiasco made Jimmy Maitland nearly chew clean through his cigar. "You mean we could get burned in this?"

"It's possible, sir. As I said, I'll be going up on Tuesday and get everything settled. Maybe stay until the end of the week. Please, sir."

"Who tried to whack you, Agent Sherlock?"

She should have known he would home in on that. Mr. Maitland was a very tenacious man. "I don't believe it was a whack job, sir, more like a threat, but it is one of the loose ends."

"I don't like my agents getting whacked, Agent Sherlock."

"No, sir." As the whackee, she hadn't liked it either, but she didn't think Mr. Maitland would laugh if she said that. She moved even closer to the edge of her seat. Her head was aching. Her shoulder throbbed. She felt mildly light-headed. She wanted Dillon to kiss her. She saw him naked over her and choked on the sip of water she'd taken.

"You okay, Sherlock?" Savich half rose in his chair, then at her look, he sat down again. What would he have done anyway? Hugged her? Yeah, that would have been a real treat for Maitland. He might have stroked out on the spot. Savich prayed Maitland wouldn't ask any more questions about her attacker. He didn't have any convincing answers made up yet. He didn't want to bring in her family, at least not yet.

She said, "Yes, sir, I'm fine."

She was red in the face; she wouldn't look at him. She was staring at the black tassels on her Bally loafers. If his boss hadn't been sitting six feet from him, he might have thrown her over his shoulder and carried her upstairs. He smiled really big at Jimmy Maitland. "I'll go with her to Boston. We'll get it all wrapped up."

"Marlin Jones is in jail. Who attacked Agent Sherlock? Why?"

"We don't know yet, sir, but we're betting the answer lies with Marlin Jones."

"You don't know that, Savich. It might be entirely unrelated." No one said a word. Jimmy Maitland sighed and pulled himself to his feet. He was tired. He'd had too much beer to drink the night before at a retirement party for Tully Hendricks, an old New York agent who'd been a terror in his day. Even the Mob had sent him a gold watch. He wanted to go home and watch the Redskins too. He said, "Go on to Boston, then. I see you don't want to tell me you really have no idea if Marlin Jones is connected with this attack on Sherlock. There is one thing though, Savich. The young cop who messed up and let two of the old people go in that Florida nursing home murder—he has no idea. We were right—all old people look the same to him. Oh yeah, there's been a spate of murders in South Dakota, right in Elk Point, then the guy went over the border into Iowa. Nasty business. The police chief in Sioux City is frantic."

"I'll deal with it tomorrow, sir." Savich rose and walked Jimmy Maitland to the front door.

"This place," Maitland said, taking one last sweeping look. "I remember one night when your grandmother came down those stairs wearing this lemon yellow chiffon gown. She must have been at least seventy-five then but she was a queen. You've done well with it, Savich. Your brother the artist still pissed that she gave you the house?"

"Nah, he got over it."

"I hate that modern stuff. Tell Ryan to go Impressionist, can't go wrong there. As for that dolphin of yours I bought, I still like it. Nice work. Oh yeah, take care of Sherlock." He paused a moment, carefully wrapped his unlit cigar in a handkerchief and slid it into his jacket pocket, then walked to the front door. He lowered his voice. "I suppose you know what you're doing." He nodded toward the living room where

Sherlock was sitting still as a stone, still staring down at her shoes.

"I sure hope so, sir."

"It's been what? Five years since Claire died?"

"Yes, five years."

"Sherlock is getting high marks in the Bureau."

"She deserves them. I'm glad I was bright enough to latch onto her right out of training. She's a plus to the Unit."

"I imagine she's also other things to you, but that's none of my business. Make sure it remains none of my business. You take care of her, all right, Savich? And yourself. And call when you need backup."

"Yes, sir, I will." Savich paused just a moment, then turned, smiled, and strolled back into the living room, whistling.

She said immediately, "What dolphin was Mr. Maitland talking about?"

"I told you I whittled. The dolphin was a piece my sister stole out of here and put on consignment in the Lampton Gallery. She was all over me to quit the FBI when the piece sold. I didn't have the heart to tell her that my boss bought it."

"I see," she said slowly. "Do you happen, by any chance, to have any more whittled pieces around here?"

"A couple."

He was clearly uncomfortable. She smiled at him. "Have you ever carved teak?"

"Oh yes, but my favorite is maple."

"You've been doing it a long time. Some of the scars on your hands look very old."

"Since I was a kid."

She said nothing more.

It was chilly in Boston, the sky a dull gray, the clouds fat with rain. The buildings looked old and tired, ready to fold in on themselves. Lacey shivered in the small interrogation room, waiting for them to bring in Marlin Jones. She would have given about anything to be in San Francisco at that moment, where everything was at least two hundred years newer and the chances were really good that it was sunny. Then she remembered what was in Boston and shook her head. Where was Marlin Jones? Naturally his lawyer, Big John Bullock, would be with him. She hoped she could talk him into leaving her alone with Marlin. Five minutes; that's all she wanted. Dillon was close by, outside, speaking with Ralph Budnack, who was in charge of Marlin Jones's case. Lots of people behind the two-way mirror would be watching and listening.

She heard leg shackles pounding hard. She looked up. Marlin stood in the doorway. He looked hard and tough, all gentle edges carved off him. He stared at her for a very long time, not moving, not saying a word. Then, finally, terrifyingly, he smiled. He lifted his shackled hands and waved his fingers at her. "Hey, Marty, how's your arm? I remember how that felt, throwing that knife at you, watching it hit you, dig right into your skin. It went in so easy. Still hurt from my knife, Marty?"

"No, Marlin, I'm fine. How's your belly? Can you stand up straight yet? You got a big scar to show for my bullet?"

He grew utterly still. The vicious light in his eyes went out, leaving them dark and opaque. "You've still got that smart mouth on you, Marty. That wasn't an act you put on for me. You need a man to teach you how to behave."

"Be quiet, Marlin," Big John said, lightly touching his fingertips to Marlin's forearm. Marlin shook him off.

Big John never stopped looking at Sherlock. "Forget it, Agent. There's no way I'll leave you alone with him." He sat down.

"You sit down now too," a sergeant said, shoving Marlin into a chair. "Don't move or I'll shackle you to the arms. I'm standing right behind you, boy. Keep your hands on the tabletop. Don't even let your hair grow, you got that?"

Marlin didn't say a word. "He's got it," said Big John. "Don't worry, Officer."

"You and I did a lot of dancing when I was last in Boston, Marlin. You remember our last tango through your little maze, don't you?"

"I thought you were so pretty, so precious, but then you started saying those bad things. But you don't even have a husband, do you?"

"Nope, no husband." She was holding her ballpoint pen, lightly tapping it on the tabletop. She said, "You never saw me before I came into the lumber store, did you, Marlin?"

"Me? See you?" He paused a moment, then smiled at her. "You think maybe that's possible?" Then he shrugged and looked down at his dirty fingernails, ignoring her.

"I don't think I ever would have dated you, Marlin. You want to know why? Even though you look pretty interesting on the outside, you look dead on the inside, really dead, like you've been dead for a very long time."

"I'll ask you that question on the witness stand, Agent Sherlock," Big John said as he laced his fingers over his stomach. "Good stuff. To think I nearly refused to let Marlin say anything to you. Do keep talking. No juror will convict this poor fellow. Talk about not responsible—"

She ignored Big John. She sat forward, laid down the pen, and clasped her hands on the table in front of her. It was Formica, scarred, stained. She wondered briefly when it had last been cleaned. "Have you ever seen me before, Marlin?"

He was staring at her. At that moment, she felt she could see his dead eyes looking through her skin down to her bones, looking at the blood pulsing through her veins. For an instant, she saw him dip his hands into her blood. She jumped, then forced herself to stillness again. He was scary with those eyes of his, but she was the one making him into more than he was. He was a monster, but she was making him into the Devil. Let him stare. There was nothing he could do to her. He'd already tried and she'd won. She had to remember that. "Did you, Marlin? Ever see me before Boston?"

Slowly, he shook his head. "Nah. Maybe, but who cares? I still don't like you even though you're pretty. You're a real bitch, Marty."

"I'd like you to tell me something, Marlin."

"If I feel like it."

"Remember when you were in the hospital I asked you to list the women you'd killed in San Francisco?"

"I remember."

"You left out a woman named Belinda Madigan. Why? Why did you leave out her name?"

"Did she curse?"

"No. I've never cursed either, Marlin. Why did you leave out Belinda Madigan's name?"

He shrugged, his eyes narrowing now, and she saw into

him, clearly. He knew he could play her along, he knew he was in control, he knew he could string her along until—until what? Had he ever seen her before? In San Francisco? Did he know who she was? Something was awfully wrong. She knew he was playing mind games with her, but she couldn't stop.

He grinned, showing all his beautiful straight white teeth. "I got trouble remembering sometimes, you know?"

"Maybe my father prosecuted you? He was an assistant D.A. in San Francisco seven years ago. His name is Corman Sherlock. Was that it, Marlin?"

"I heard about your daddy, heard he was a mean son of a bitch, heard he never cut anybody any slack, but I never met him."

"Why did you kill Belinda Madigan?"

Big John roared out of his chair, knocking it over. The sergeant grabbed his arm, his gun out. The door to the interrogation room burst open, and three armed officers rushed into the room.

Sherlock stood up slowly. "It's all right, gentlemen. Mr. Bullock got a bit riled, didn't you, sir?"

"You've got no right to ask him questions like that, Agent Sherlock. If you do it again, Marlin won't say another word, the interview will be over, and there'll never be another one. You got that?"

"I got it." She saw Dillon standing in the doorway, his expression set, his eyes hard. They'd argued about this, but in the end, he'd given in, allowing her to see Marlin alone. She knew he'd seen her desperation. He said nothing now, merely looked at her. She smiled, gave him a slight nod, then sat down again. "I'll be careful with my questions, Mr. Bullock," she said. "Please sit down, sir. If you feel like bounding around like that again, please don't. I'd as soon not get shot by accident."

"You watch yourself, little lady."

"I'm Special Agent Sherlock," she said mildly, admiring his tactic.

He wasn't stupid. He merely shrugged and sat back in his chair, crossing his arms over his chest.

She turned to Marlin, who hadn't moved or spoken throughout the ruckus. "Did I entrap you, Marlin?"

"I don't know what that means, Marty. I knew I had to pun-ish you. God sent me to punish his weak vessels, to purify them, to make them whole again."

"As in to make them dead, Marlin?"

"Don't answer that, Marlin. Watch yourself, Agent Sher-lock."

"Why did you leave out Belinda Madigan's name?"

He gave her that superior smile again, disregarding her question. "Belinda who? I don't know any Belinda. That's a pretty name, old-fashioned. What's she to you, Marty?"

"Do you think I look much like her, Marlin?"

"No, I think you're prettier, I always—"

Big John Bullock's mouth was working. He didn't know what was going on, but he soon would. He wasn't stupid.

Sherlock sat back in her chair and drew in a very deep breath.

Big John said finally, "Who's Belinda?"

"She was one of the women in San Francisco that Marlin had to purify. It was seven years ago. He purified seven women in San Francisco. It was seven, wasn't it, Marlin?"

He was shaking his head. "No, not seven. I don't do seven. My pa always told me that seven was a bad number, that it was even worse than thirteen. He'd always laugh at the hotels who didn't have a thirteenth floor, told me that the fools on the fourteenth floor were on the thirteenth really, but they were too stupid to realize it. No, I never did seven, did six, like my pa told me."

"All right. The six women you purified in San Francisco, all of them cursed and bad-mouthed their husbands?"

He nodded. Big John didn't say anything, which Sherlock considered a gift.

"Did you date any of them, Marlin? You're a good-looking guy, I bet it wouldn't have been hard for you to get a date with almost any woman, right?"

He nodded again. "Ladies like me," he said, and studied his thumbnail. "They tell me I'm a great lover."

She nearly gagged. "You date Belinda?"

"I told you, Marty, she wasn't one of the women I had to purify. Why are you so interested in her anyway?"

"I like the name. It's unusual."

"I don't like the name, but I like yours, Marty. It sounds kind of like a boy's name. It was close, you know? Once I thought God wanted me to purify little boys, to correct them if they'd gotten a bad start, put them on the right path, but then I realized it wasn't boys, it was girls. Women who'd had their chance to straighten out, but hadn't. Women who'd married good men and turned on them. I slept with them, you know, to make sure they were the ones to take out. All six of them cheated on their husbands, told me what jerks they were, so then I was sure they had to walk the walk through my maze."

"Marlin," Big John said very quietly, "shut up."

"Yeah, well, purify, then. That's it, purify. I wish I'd gone to college. I could have learned more pretty words like *purify*."

She was riveted. She imagined that all the people listening to Marlin were riveted. She wondered what Dillon was thinking.

"You didn't ask me out when I came to the hardware store."

"I know. That was weird. I slept with Hillary. She was good. She sucked me off really well. Do you know she said bad things while I banged her?"

She would push back. "Why didn't you try to bang me, Marlin?"

She watched him actually flinch. None of it was an act. "Don't, Marty. That sounds so crazy coming from you. Don't talk like that, okay?"

"Okay. But why didn't you want to be intimate with me, Marlin?"

He shrugged. "You came on so strong, talking about your poor husband like you did, and then there was your foul mouth. You said all those bad words right in front of me." He sighed. "But you know, I was in a hurry. I couldn't take the time to ask you out, to see if you'd sleep with me."

"Why the hurry, Marlin?"

"Because God wanted me to go to Toronto. I couldn't until I'd taken care of six women here in Boston. Yeah, I was in a hurry. I'm sorry, Marty. Do you wish I'd made love to you?"

"I don't think so, Marlin. I do find your claim hard to believe. No one reported seeing any of the women in San Francisco with you. No one saw you with Hillary here in Boston. Why do you think that's so?"

"I knew I had to be careful. After Denver, I was real cautious, not that I could do everything I wanted to there. Only two women and then it was too dangerous. I'd been seen with both women. I had to leave. God saved me there, but he told me I had to be smarter and so I was in San Francisco. The women all loved the mystery, the secrets I shared with them, the dark little places I took them to. They all loved how I smelled, you know, like fresh-cut wood, real fresh. They all thought I was dangerous and wonderful. With two of them I didn't even have to hit them on the head. I asked if they wanted to play the maze game with me, and they couldn't wait. They both loved it. Until the end. Until I told them what I had to do. I think they forgot I was a good lover then."

"Marlin, shut up!"

26

$\mathcal{S}$HE WONDERED WHAT WOULD
happen if she threw up on the Formica table. Would anyone
even know?

"But not Belinda? She wouldn't sleep with you, would she,
Marlin? She thought you were sick. She thought you were
disgusting. She didn't want to have anything to do with you.
She wanted her husband, nobody else, just her husband."

His hands were fists. "I don't know what you're talking
about."

The sergeant was away from the wall in an instant, his
gun up.

Sherlock shook her head. "You know what I'm talking
about. God wouldn't want you to lie. Tell the truth. Belinda
didn't want you. She probably laughed at you, told you
you were pathetic. That's why you ki—purified her, isn't it?
She didn't want you, plain and simple. She didn't curse. She
didn't bad-mouth her husband. She didn't fit the mold of all
the other women. You know she didn't. Why, Marlin, why did
you kill her?"

"This is over," said Big John, rising slowly from his chair,
one beefy hand on Marlin's shoulder. "Don't say anything,
Marlin, nothing more for these folks."

"What makes you believe I didn't have Belinda?" Marlin
said in a low whisper, leaning toward Sherlock. "You really
think a woman could laugh at me? Turn me down? No way,
Marty. Yeah, I had Belinda. I don't want you, Marty. You're
cynical. You probably hate men, you probably don't ever—"

"Marlin, let it go. Listen, you moron, I told you to shut up!"

It took only an instant of time, the barest instant, for the violence to erupt. Marlin raised his chained hands, clasped them together into fists and brought them down with all his strength on John Bullock's left temple. Big John groaned very softly in his throat and slumped back into his chair, his head falling forward to hit the Formica tabletop. He was out. A trickle of blood snaked out of his right nostril.

The sergeant was all over Marlin. The door burst open again, and three cops surged in. She wondered why they didn't shoot him. It would save the taxpayers millions of dollars. But they didn't shoot him. She wanted to yell at them that he was filth, that he'd probably go to an institution and maybe get out in twenty years and begin it all again. She managed to keep her rage to herself.

"They'd send me to jail for sure if I did," Savich said close to her ear. "Sorry but I can't, Sherlock." It was then she realized she'd whispered what she was thinking. Only Dillon had heard her. No one was paying any attention to her at all. They were all over Marlin, dragging him out of the room. She heard someone yell out, "Get an ambulance in here! The guy cracked his own lawyer's head!"

Marlin turned very slightly and smiled back at her. "She was good, Marty, really good. That punk husband of hers was a monster, not me. I cared about them, cared about their souls. But he was real bad. She wanted me, Marty, not the other way around, I swear. You know something? I miss Belinda."

And then he was gone, surrounded by cops, shuffling forward, the leg shackles clanking against the linoleum of the hallway.

"What's going on here?" Savich said, his hand tightly around her wrist.

"Nothing makes any sense, nothing." They walked out of the station. She remained silent for three blocks, then stopped and said, "He was playing with me, Dillon. The minute I said Belinda's name, he began his game. You heard all those questions I asked. I was trying to learn the truth, but now things are muddier than ever."

"That's why Big John let you go on and on with Marlin

with only a bit of his famous bluster. He wanted to muddy the
waters."

"He succeeded. Do you think Marlin had sex with Belinda?"

Savich frowned at her, shook his head.

That evening, on Newbury Street, coming out of Fien Nang
Mandarin Restaurant with its red paper lanterns swinging in
the evening breeze, Savich was speaking to Sherlock, his
hand raised to flag down a taxi. He never saw the car that
came around the corner, skidding loudly on two tires, heading
right toward them, until it was too late.

He threw her to the sidewalk just before the car struck him,
flinging him onto the hood of an old Buick Riviera.

"No doctor, Sherlock. No hospital, no paramedics. Forget it.
We can't afford the time. Imagine the police reports, the in-
vestigation, the questions, it would take too long. No doctor."

He was right, but she worried. He was holding his arm, limping slightly. She knew every step hurt him. The elevator door
opened onto their floor. He leaned on her heavily. "No, don't
say anything. I'm all right. I've had enough injuries over my
thirty-two years to know when it's serious and when I'm banged
up. You promise me you're okay? I threw you pretty hard."

"I'm a little bruised on my left side, nothing more."

She unlocked the hotel room door. "If I'd been the one
struck by the car, what would you have done?"

He stopped in the middle of the room. He had the audacity
to grin at her. "You'd be strapped to a gurney on your way to
the Emergency Room."

She shut the door very quietly and locked it. She slid the
chain home.

"I see. But you, the big he-man, can take anything anybody
dishes out."

"Yep, that's about the size of it. Now, I need to make a
phone call."

She got ice and wrapped it in a towel. He was on the phone
when she handed it to him. He lifted his shirt and pressed it
against his ribs. So, it was his ribs, not his arm.

"Quinlan? I need your help. Yeah, some ugly trouble here in Boston. Can Sherlock and I visit your parents' cabin on Louise Lynn Lake for a couple of days? No, I'm not at my best at the moment. A car got me, but I only need a few days to get myself together again. No, nothing to Maitland. He's not expecting anything in any case. That gives me a little leeway. Yeah, all right."

He hung up the phone and lay back, closing his eyes. "That feels good. Thank you."

"Take the aspirin." She handed him three pills and a glass of water. He took the pills. "What's this cabin on Louise Lynn Lake?"

"It's a nice lake in Maryland where Quinlan's parents have a small home. You and I are driving there tomorrow. Rent us a nice big comfortable car, Sherlock. I'd like to get out of here early tomorrow morning."

"The wounded animal going to his lair?"

"That's about it. Quinlan's lair. I need to get one for myself. It hurts, but it's not serious." He opened his eyes and looked at her standing beside the bed, her legs spread, her hands on her hips. She didn't look happy.

"You look pretty bad. I saw you limping. You sprain your ankle?"

He tried to grin at her, but it hurt. "Only a minor sprain. No big deal. Hey, I didn't hurt my pretty face, did I?"

"Yes, a bit. Lie there and I'll clean you up. Are all your teeth still in there?"

"Teeth are fine." He watched her walk to the bathroom. She was stiff, holding on to her control. He was grateful for that. He'd already had a strip taken off him. He didn't need her to take off another one. He heard the water running. She would bring him a cold compress for his aching head. The ice sure felt good over his ribs.

She was taking this well. He sighed with relief and closed his eyes again. After she cleaned off his face and wrapped ice in a towel around his ankle, she stood there, looking down at him. "I hope you know what you're doing. If you don't, I'm going to hurt you."

He gave her a big smile. He slept until two o'clock in the morning. She was there with three more aspirin.

At six o'clock A.M. they'd checked out of the hotel and were on the road fifteen minutes later in a good-sized Ford. Savich's seat was tilted back as far as it would go. His eyes were closed. He looked bruised, wrung out. Sherlock gave him a long look before turning off onto I-95 South. It would take them a good six to eight hours to get to Maryland. At least they had a full bottle of aspirin and blankets.

Louise Lynn Lake was in southern Maryland. It took them nine hours to get there. Lacey was so wired from all the coffee she'd drunk, she couldn't keep still. She was tapping her foot on the accelerator, drumming her fingers on the steering wheel. She was too nervous to listen to music or talk radio. "You're feeling all right, Dillon? You promise?"

"Yes. Stop worrying. You want me to drive?"

She gave him a look. He closed his eyes and leaned back against the seat. Thirty minutes later, he was tapping his own fingers and looking for landmarks. He said, "Turn here. Yes, this is it. Around this bend. We're here. You did really well, Sherlock. Nice place, huh?"

"There's someone already here," she said. "We'll have to keep going. I don't want to take any chances, not with you in such bad shape. If there's more than two of them, I might not be able to protect you."

He arched a black eyebrow at that. "I could maybe take on one, Sherlock, if he was a little guy."

"No, we'll keep going. I'll drop you off at a motel and then come back and check things out."

"No, wait, Sherlock, it's Quinlan."

She watched James Quinlan come loping toward the car. She rolled down the window, giving him a big smile.

"I am so relieved it's you. We've had enough bad guys for a while."

"Nope, I'm a hero, ask my wife. Hey, Savich looks like he lost the fight, Sherlock. Did he get fresh with you? Did you have to pound him?"

"No, he was hit by a car. I'll smash him when he's feeling better. No doctors. He's a fool. Help me get him inside."

Sally Quinlan met them at the door. Behind her was a black man dressed all in Calvin Klein. He was huge, ugly as sin, and had a Marine haircut.

"Oh, this is Marvin, the bouncer from Ms. Lily's Bonhomie Club. He didn't think James could take care of all the possible trouble and insisted on coming. Marvin, this is Lacey Sherlock."

"She a nice chicky?"

"I think so."

"She's got a weird name."

"Lacey isn't at all weird." Where had the attempt at humor come from?

"Hey, maybe you're not a bad chicky after all. Oh my, Savich. You're looking beyond ripe. Ms. Lily wondered if you and Quinlan were tough enough to do this stuff." Marvin was out the door in that moment, racing down the porch steps. Lacey saw him, a giant of a man, help Dillon into the weathered porched house.

"You do look like dirt-shit, boy," Marvin told Savich as he laid him down on the long sofa. "Don't you move now. Let Marvin check out those ribs of yours. Good thing I had nine brothers. I've bandaged some ribs in my day. But you know, I don't bandage anymore. I've stayed up with medical strides. Nope, don't do anything now except to tell you to take it easy. They're not broken, Savich, but you sure got some cracks in there. My third brother, Tomalas, now that boy had broken ribs. We used to tell him jokes to see him laugh and groan at the same time."

Savich's eyes were closed. He didn't say a word, listened quietly to Marvin's rich, low voice drawling out his words until you thought the sentence would never end. He suffered Marvin, who appeared to be surprisingly gentle, his big hands moving slowly and expertly over Savich's chest.

"Nothing's broken, Marvin. I'm bruised, that's all. I'm glad you're here. Is Ms. Lily all right?"

"Ms. Lily is always all right. She won five hundred dollars last night in a poker game off this black smart-ass goon from Cleveland. Yeah, she's real happy. You look like Ms. Lily got pissed at you and smacked you but good. She smacked me once and I was laid out like you are now. Took me near three days to pull myself together again."

"Ms. Lily owns the Bonhomie Club," Sally said to Sherlock. "I've got a painkiller for him, Marvin. What do you think?"

Savich said without opening his eyes, "Sally, give me whatever you've got and I'll kill dragons for you."

"My hero," Sally Quinlan said and disappeared into the
small kitchen.

"Don't be so loose with that," Quinlan called after her.
"I'm your main hero, remember?"

Sherlock watched Marvin's big hands move over Dillon's
body, pulling slightly here and there, kneading, pressing. Finally, he rose, crossed his arms over his chest, and said,
"You'll live, boy, but I don't like this at all. You and Quinlan,
you two shouldn't have such dangerous day jobs. You boys are
too soft, too trusting. There are lots of mean turd lumps out
there. I should know, I bounce them out of the club nearly
every night."

"It was a brown Toyota Camry, license number 429JRD, a
1996, I think."

Savich opened his eyes at that. "You sure, Sherlock? All I
got was the RD. Hey, that's really good. Why didn't you tell
me before?"

"You jerk, I was worried about you."

"I'll run it now," Quinlan said and went to the phone. Sally
returned with a pill and a glass of water.

Ten minutes later, Savich's eyes were shut. Sally covered
him with a blanket. Marvin took off his shoes.

"He's got nice feet," Sally said.

"What he's got is big feet," Marvin said. "Look at these
suckers, Chicky, they're size twelve."

Both women looked up. Marvin looked from one to the
other. "Well, ain't this a kick? I've never had this problem
before."

Sally said to Sherlock, "Marvin calls every female Chicky,
except for Ms. Lily of course. How about your mother, Marvin?"

"She's the Big Chicky. Nobody screws with the Big Chicky,
even my dad. You can go to Sally now, but she's still Chicky."

"I don't mind at all."

"Chicky Savich," Dillon said slowly, relishing the sound.
"Talk about strange. I don't know if I can deal with that. But
you know, it's not as bad as Chicky Sherlock."

"We thought you were asleep. How do you feel, Dillon?"

Sherlock leaned over him, her fingertips lightly smoothing through his dark eyebrows, lightly touching the bruise on his cheek.

"Alive."

"Yes, that's good. You're kind of out of it, aren't you, Dillon?"

"No, not at all. I hurt enough still to keep me out of the ether."

"You don't know what you said, do you?"

"Yeah, I know what I said. It does sound strange, don't you agree?"

"I think," Sherlock said very slowly, staring down at the man who'd become more important to her than anything or anyone in her life, "that I could get used to it, until Marvin gets to know me well enough to call me Sherlock."

"Good," Savich said. "I hadn't really meant to bring it up here, at this particular moment. It lacks finesse and timing. It just came out of my mouth. How about I try it again later, when three people aren't staring at us?"

"Yes, I think that would be an excellent idea."

His head fell to the side. He was out cold this time.

"Chicky Sherlock Savich," Marvin said slowly. "Yeah, that's so funny it would make Fuzz's mouth split from laughing so hard."

"I prefer Sherlock Savich," Sally said. "That's unforgettable. With a name like that maybe they'd make you director one day."

Some minutes later, Quinlan said from across the room as he placed the phone back in its cradle, "The car was rented to a Marlin Jones. Paid for in cash, but he presented them with a credit card with his name on it, and a driver's license."

"I don't like this," Sherlock said, her face washed of color. "I really don't like this at all. But wait, the picture couldn't have matched, could it?"

James Quinlan said, "The guy said the picture was real fuzzy, but since the name was the same, the guy's age was about right, what was the big deal? So who knows?"

"Jones. Marlin Jones? Hey, that's the serial killer, isn't it?" Marvin the Bouncer asked as he set an old issue of the Economist magazine back down on the coffee table. "I thought he was in the can, in Boston."

"He is," Sherlock said. "I spoke to him yesterday. He's probably in maximum security. He brought his fists down on his lawyer's temple. Knocked him out cold. Actually, as we were driving here, the news said the first thing Big John Bullock said when he regained consciousness was, 'I'm going to get that little pissant off so I can kill him.' Then he passed out again. The doctors think it's a concussion."

"The guy's a real comedian," Quinlan said.

"I don't think he was concussed," Sherlock said. "I know Big John meant every word."

"I was hoping it would be one less lawyer," Sally said from the kitchen. "James, come out and help me. Everyone needs to have some dinner. It's nearly five o'clock."

"I'll go catch us some bass," Marvin said. "Where's the rods, Quinlan?"

"Why'd the guy hit his lawyer?" Sally asked Sherlock, looking up from the carrot she was alternately cutting and eating.

"He told him to shut up because he'd admitted to me that he'd killed the women in San Francisco. Marlin went nuts. I wish the cops had shot him then and there." She sighed, her hands clasped between her knees. She rose slowly. "I guess I'd better call Jimmy Maitland. I'm afraid that he's going to be really upset about this."

Savich was mending. All he had to do was lie quietly, not breathe deeply, keep his eyes either closed or focused on Sherlock, and he'd be fine. Sherlock Savich—that had a real ring to it. He couldn't wait to get her alone and kiss her. Then he could ask her to marry him again, only this time it would be properly done.

The pain in his ribs and hip and ankle came in waves, not really big surfing kind of waves, small ones, rhythmic, steady, and relentless.

He felt her hand on his cheek. "I have another pain pill for you. Open up."

He did. Soon the pain was nothing but an annoying throbbing that didn't even touch his mind. "Good stuff," he said.

"The best," Quinlan said. "It's from our favorite doctor."

"Ah, Dr. Ned Breaker."

"He said to give him a call if you need him to drive up and check you out."

"Let's call him," Sally said. "Savich, you really don't look so hot."

"I'm feeling better by the minute," Savich said. "Really. I'm not stupid. Everything's okay."

"You ready for something to eat? Marvin caught three bass, good-size suckers. I gutted them and Sally fried them."

Savich thought he'd puke right there. The thought of anything fried went right to his belly and turned nasty.

"No, I don't think so," Sherlock said, lightly cupping his cheek in her hand. "We'll have the good stuff and Dillon here can have some soup. Got any chicken noodle, Sally?"

Sherlock didn't want to leave him alone. She slept beside the sofa on three blankets, close enough to hear him breathing.

The next morning, Sherlock came into the house to see Dillon standing at the small bar that separated the kitchen from the living room. He was drinking a cup of coffee. He needed to shave.

"You're not dead."

He grinned at her over the rim of his cup. "Nope, but I appreciate you sleeping guard beside me all night. You know what might be fun, Sherlock? We could strip naked and have a bruise-off contest. I might be catching up with you. How's your left side?"

"Hardly any bruising at all. How could Marlin Jones have rented the car, Dillon?"

"Obviously someone else did, using his name. You and I are going to California tomorrow, okay?"

"No, not until you're back to your full strength. I'm not going to take any more chances with you."

"That sounds nice."

She walked to him, lightly kissed his mouth, then pulled up his shirt. "I'll be objective. Now, I think my ribs looked more like the Italian flag than yours do." He felt her fingers on his flesh, light, so light, not hurting him at all, skimming over his flesh, and to his own blessed wonder, he got hard. He didn't mean to say it, but the words just came right out of his mouth. "Do you think you could go a bit lower?"

Her fingers stopped cold. Then, she laughed. "Dillon, I'm going to have us fly First Class, all right?"

"Yeah, that's fine. I'll be okay by day after tomorrow, I swear it. We'll have a day to make some plans with Quinlan." He sucked in his breath and stared at her.

Her fingers had gone beneath the waistband of his slacks, tangling in the hair at his groin. He didn't know about this, didn't know if he was going to start crying or shouting or moaning, and not from any pain in his ribs. Her fingers touched him, then he was enclosed against her palm. He was going to die, lose it, be premature, the whole thing. But then it was academic. Marvin came into the house, singing at the top of his lungs.

"Sorry," Sherlock said and kissed his ear.

He sighed deeply. "Do you think maybe I did something really bad in a former lifetime?"

"You're breathing awfully hard, Dillon."

"Hey, Chicky, what'd you do to our boy here?"

"I was checking him out. Like you did, Marvin."

"I doubt that, Chicky. More like you tortured the poor man but good."

27

SHERLOCK STARED AT THE doorbell for a long time before she rang it. Savich didn't say a word, just looked beyond the Art Deco three-story mansion to the incredible view of Alcatraz, the Golden Gate, and the stark Marin Headlands in the distance. The day was sharp and cool, so clear and vivid it made your eyes sting. There were dozens of sailboats on the bay. The air was crisp, with a nip.

A middle-aged black woman, plump, very pretty, her eyes bright with intelligence, opened the door, gasped, and grabbed Sherlock into her arms. "My baby, it's you, it's really you. Thank the good Lord you're home. They've been telling me for weeks that you'd come home and now you're here. But I'd begun to believe that you'd finally turned your back."

Sherlock hugged her back. Isabelle had been more her mother than the woman upstairs in her elegant bedroom had ever been. She'd been the Sherlock housekeeper and cook since before Sherlock was born. "It's good to see you, Isabelle. You all right? Your kids okay?"

Sherlock drew back and looked carefully at the fine-boned face, a beloved face that radiated warmth and humor.

"Things are fine with my family, but they aren't too good here, Lacey, no, not too good at all. Your daddy's all quiet and keeps to himself. Your mama never comes out of her room now, stays there and looks at those ridiculous talk shows, best I can tell. She says she wants to write a book and send it to Oprah so Oprah will recommend it and your mama will become really rich and leave your papa. Hey, who's this guy with you?"

"This is Dillon Savich. He's also with the FBI. Dillon, this is Isabelle Tanner. She's the one who told me how wicked boys were on my sixteenth birthday. She's the one who told me to keep out of Bobby Wellman's Jaguar."

"You should have listened to her."

"Oh, lordie. You mean you let that boy crawl all over you in that little Jaguar, Lacey? Oh goodness, I thought I'd won that one."

Savich shook her hand. "Ms. Isabelle, I promise you Sherlock here hasn't gotten into any more cars since the Jaguar. You taught her well."

"You call her Sherlock," said Isabelle, clasping her arms beneath her ample breasts. "That sounds funny, but cute too. Well, come on in. I'll get you some fine tea and some scones."

"Who is it, Isabelle?"

Isabelle's face grew very still. Slowly, she turned and called out, "It's your daughter, Mrs. Sherlock."

"No, Belinda's dead. Don't do that to me, Isabelle. You're cruel."

"It's Miss Lacey, not Belinda."

"Lacey? Oh. She said she was coming back but I didn't believe her."

Isabelle said quickly, "Don't look like that, Lacey. It's a bad day for her, that's all. Besides, you haven't been around in a long time."

"Neither has Belinda."

Isabelle waved away her words. "Come into the living room, honey." She turned to the stairs that wound up to the second-floor landing. "Mrs. Sherlock, ma'am, will you be coming down?"

"Naturally. I'll be there in just a moment. I must brush my teeth first."

The house looked like a museum, Savich thought, staring around the living room. Everything was pristine, thanks probably to Isabelle, but stiff and formal and colder than a Minnesota night. "No one ever sits in here," Sherlock said to him. "Goodness, it's uninviting, isn't it? And stultifying. I'd forgotten how bad it was. Why don't we go into my father's study instead. That's where I always used to hang out."

Judge Sherlock's study was a masculine stronghold that was also warm, lived-in, and cluttered, stacks of magazines and books, both paperback and hardcover, on every surface. The furniture was severe—heavy dark-brown leather—but the look was mitigated by warm-toned afghans thrown everywhere. There were lots of ferns in front of the wide bay window that looked out onto the bay in the distance. There was a telescope aimed toward Tiburon. This wasn't at all what he'd expected. What he had expected, he wasn't certain, but it wasn't this warm, very human room that had obviously been nurtured and loved and lived in. Savich took a deep breath. "What a wonderful room."

"Yes, it is." She pulled away and walked to the bay windows. "This is the most beautiful view from any place in San Francisco." She broke off to smile at Isabelle who was carrying a well-shined silver tray. "Oh, Isabelle, those scones smell delicious. It's been too long."

Savich had a mouthful of scone with a dab of clotted cream on top when the door opened and one of the most beautiful women he'd ever seen in his life walked in with all the grace of a born princess. She was, pure and simply, a stunner, as his father used to say about a knockout woman. She also didn't look a thing like Sherlock. Where Sherlock had lovely rich sunset hair, wildly curly, her mother had straight blond hair as soft and smooth as pale silk. Sherlock's eyes were a soft summer blue; her mother's, a stormy gray-blue. Sherlock was tall, at least five foot eight, not a pound over one-twenty. She was strong, solid, but her mother was fragile, fine-boned, not more than five foot three.

Sherlock was wearing a dark blue wool suit with a cream turtleneck sweater, all business. Her mother was wearing a soft peach silk dress, her glorious hair pulled back and held with a gold clip at the nape of her neck. There was nothing overtly expensive about her jewelry or clothing, but she looked well-bred, rich, and used to it. There were very few lines on her face. She had to be in her late fifties, but Savich would have said forty-five if he hadn't known that she'd had a daughter who'd be in her late thirties now, if she'd not been murdered.

"So you're Dillon Savich," Mrs. Sherlock said, not moving

into the room. "You're the man who spoke to her father on the phone after I told Lacey he'd tried to run me down with his BMW."

"Yes, ma'am." He walked to her and extended his hand. "I'm Dillon Savich. Like your daughter, I'm with the FBI."

Finally, after so long that Sherlock thought she'd die from not breathing, her mother took Dillon's hand.

"You're too good-looking," Mrs. Sherlock said, peering up at him for the longest time. "I've never trusted good-looking men. Her father is good-looking and look what's come of that. Also I imagine you are built splendidly. Are you sleeping with my daughter?"

Savich said in that smooth interview voice of his, "Mrs. Sherlock, won't you have a cup of tea? It's rich, Indian, I believe. As for the scones, I'm certain you'll enjoy those. They're delicious. Isabelle is a wonderful cook. You're very fortunate to have her."

"Hello, Mother."

"I wish you hadn't come, Lacey, but your father will be pleased." Her voice was plaintive, slightly reproachful, but her beautiful face was expressionless. Did she never show anger, joy? Anything to change the look of her?

"I thought you wanted me to come home."

"I changed my mind. Things aren't right here, simply not right. But now that you're here, I suppose you'll insist on remaining."

"Only a few days, Mother. Would you mind if Dillon stayed here as well?"

"He's too handsome," Mrs. Sherlock said, "but again I suppose I have no choice. There are at least four empty bedrooms upstairs. He can have one of them. I hope you're not sleeping with him, Lacey. There are so many diseases, and men carry all of them, did you know that? It's been proven now at least, but I always knew it. That's why I stopped sleeping with your father. I didn't want him to give me any of those horrible diseases."

"A cup of tea, ma'am?"

Mrs. Sherlock took the fine china saucer from Savich and sat down on the very edge of one of her husband's rich brown leather chairs. She looked around her. "I hate this room," she said, then sipped at her tea. "I always have. It's the living room I love. I decorated the living room, did Lacey tell you, Mr. Savich?"

Savich felt as though he'd fallen down the rabbit hole, but Sherlock looked tired. She looked used to this. It came to him then that Mrs. Sherlock was acting a great deal like his great-aunt Mimi—in short, outrageous. She always made it known she was fragile, whatever that meant, so she could get away with saying whatever she wanted, so she could be the center of attention. Savich didn't doubt that Mrs. Sherlock did suffer from some mental illness, but how much was real and how much was of her own creation?

"I forgot to tell him, Mother," she said. "But as rooms go, this one really isn't that bad. There are so many books."

"I dislike clutter. It's the sign of a chaotic mind. Your father is going to sell that BMW of his. I believe he's going to buy a Mercedes. What model, I don't know. If it's a big car, I'll have to be really careful not to be outside when he's driving. But, you know, if you're standing in the driveway, those tall bushes make it impossible to see if someone is coming. That's how he nearly got me last time."

"Mother, when did Dad try to run you down? Was it recently?"

"Oh no, it was some time last spring." She paused, sipped some more tea, and frowned down at the beautiful Tabriz carpet beneath her feet. It was a frown, but it wasn't obvious. There were no frown lines on that perfect forehead. She waved a smooth white hand. "Maybe it was this past summer. It's hard to remember. But once I remember things, they stay with me."

"Yes, Mother, I know."

Savich said, "Perhaps your husband will buy a little Mercedes, ma'am."

"Yes, or perhaps a Porsche," Mrs. Sherlock said, looking thoughtfully at Savich.

"I own one. They are very nice. I've never tried to run anybody down in my 911. It could hurt the car. I'd get caught. No, a Porsche is a good choice."

"Actually, I've been thinking about a Porsche."

Savich was on his feet in an instant, facing a very handsome middle-aged man who was standing in the doorway. He had a fine head of silver hair, Sherlock's soft blue eyes, beautiful wide luminous eyes, and was taller than Savich was and as lean as a runner. He was looking at his wife, and the look reflected both irritation and amusement, in about equal amounts.

"I'm Judge Sherlock. Hello, Lacey."

She was on her feet as well, walking slowly to her father. She held out her hands to him. "Hello, Dad. We just got here. Do you mind if we stay with you for a while?"

"Not at all. We've plenty of room. It will be nice to have different voices to listen to. My dear," he continued to his wife as he walked to the beautiful woman who was sitting there staring at him, her eyes large and intent. "How was your day?"

"I want to know if she's sleeping with him, Corman, but she wouldn't tell me. He's too good-looking and you know how I feel about that. Why, look at what Douglas did, because he's a man and doesn't have any sense. He married that tramp and Belinda barely in her grave."

"Belinda's been dead for seven years, Evelyn. It was time for Douglas to marry again." He shot Savich a quick look from the corner of his eye with that, a look that said, I'm really sorry about this.

"That's a good point," Evelyn Sherlock said, her beautiful expressionless face turned away from her husband. "But they shouldn't be married. Can't you get Douglas to divorce her, Corman?"

"No, I don't do that sort of thing, you know that. Or don't you remember?"

"When I remember something I never forget it. That's what I was telling Lacey and Mr. Savich before you came in. Will you buy a Porsche so I'll be safe?"

"Perhaps I will, Evelyn, perhaps I will. Mr. Savich spoke about a classic 911. I like that car. Lacey, may I have a cup of tea, please? Mr. Savich, I'm delighted to finally meet you. I understand you're my daughter's boss at the FBI."

"Yes, sir. I head up the new Criminal Apprehension Unit."

"I think your approach is a fine idea. Why not use technology to predict what psychopaths will do? Why are you here with her in San Francisco?"

"We're working on the Marlin Jones case."

"Why here? Marlin Jones is in Boston."

"That's true, but there are loose ends. We're here to check things out."

"I see." Judge Corman Sherlock sat down in the beautiful rosewood chair behind his rosewood desk. The desk was piled with books and magazines. There were at least a dozen pens scattered haphazardly over the surface. A telephone and a fax machine were on top of a rosewood filing cabinet beside the desk. It was a working place for him, Savich realized. Not just pleasure in here. The man spent hours here working.

"I heard on the news that Marlin Jones hit his own lawyer, knocked him out. It was all over the news, everyone in the courthouse was talking about it. You were there, weren't you, Lacey?"

She nodded. "Yes, we both were. I believe everyone was cheering because there would be one less lawyer—" She broke off and smiled at her father. "Forgive me, but I never think of you as a lawyer since you're a judge and a former prosecutor. You put criminals away, not defend them."

"True enough. Big John Bullock has quite a reputation. Your Marlin might escape any punishment at all when he goes to trial. Big John is magic with juries. If this Marlin character doesn't already have a pitiful, tragic childhood, then Big John will manufacture one for him and the jury might believe everything he says."

"People aren't stupid, Dad. They can look at Marlin Jones and see that he's a psychopath. He's crazy but he's not insane. He knows exactly what he's doing and he has no remorse, no conscience. He's admitted to all the killings. Besides, even if he's acquitted in Boston, he'll be sent here to be tried. He also admitted that he'd murdered two women in Denver. He'll go down. In one of those places, he has to go down."

"Ah, Lacey, people can be swayed, they can be manipulated, they can see gray when there's nothing really but black. I've seen it happen again and again. Juries will see what they want to see—if they want to free a defendant, no matter what the evidence, they'll do it—it's that simple, and many times that tragic."

"I hope Marlin Jones does come to California to stand trial. At least here we've got the death penalty."

"If he got the death penalty, I think the electric chair would be too easy and quick. I think all the families of the women he killed should be able to kill him."

"That's very unliberal of you, Lacey."

"Why? It's only right. It's justice."

"It's vengeance."

"Yes, it is. What's wrong with that?"

"Not a thing. Now, my dear child, Mr. Savich probably wonders if you and I go on and on like this. Let's take a short time out. Tell me about these loose ends you and Mr. Savich are here to tie up."

Evelyn Sherlock smiled, but again, it seemed to Savich that her face still remained without expression. It was as if she'd trained herself not to move any muscles in her face that would ruin the perfect mask. She said, "They probably think you murdered Belinda, Corman, isn't that right, Mr. Savich?"

Now that was a kicker. It was Savich's turn not to change expression. He said, bland as chicken broth, "Actually, no, ma'am."

"Well, you should. I guess you're not as smart as you are handsome. He tried to run me down. No reason why he wouldn't kill Belinda. He didn't like her, hated her, in fact, since her father is in San Quentin. He said Belinda would be as crazy as her father and me. That's an awful thing to say, isn't it, Mr. Savich?"

"It's certainly not what I'd say, Mrs. Sherlock, but everyone is different. Now," he continued, turning back to Judge Sherlock, "I wonder, sir, if you would mind telling us if you ever had Marlin Jones in your courtroom."

"No."

"You're very certain?"

"Yes, naturally. I remember every man and woman who has ever stood before my bench. Marlin Jones wasn't one of them."

"Before you became a judge, did you ever prosecute him?"

"I would have remembered, Mr. Savich. The answer is still no."

Savich opened his briefcase and pulled out a black-and-white five-by-seven photo. "You've never seen this man?"

He handed Judge Sherlock Marlin's photograph, taken the previous week.

"No, I've never seen him in my courtroom. It's Marlin Jones, of course. Lacey, you're right. He does look like a classic psychopath, which is to say, he looks perfectly normal."

Savich handed him another photo.

"It's Marlin Jones but you've doctored this photo, haven't you?"

"The FBI labs are the very best. I asked them to render me photos with various disguises a man could use effectively."

"It's only a mustache, the sideburns longer, the hair combed over as if the guy wants to cover a bald spot—it's amazing. Sorry, but I've never seen this man either."

Savich gave him a third photograph.

Judge Sherlock sucked in his breath. "I don't believe this. I prosecuted this guy years ago, but I remember him. He was a hippie sort, up on marijuana charges. Look at that bushy beard and the thick bottle-cap glasses. Hunched shoulders, but he was still tall, as tall as I am. I remember that he looked at me as if he wanted to spit on me. What was his name, anyway?"

He fell silent, staring down at the photo, tapping his fingers on the arm of the leather chair. Then he sighed and said, "I'll have to look it up. I guess I'm getting old. No, wait a minute. It was a weird name. Erasmus. That's it. His name was Erasmus something, I don't remember his last name, but it was a common name. It was ten years ago. I managed to plea-bargain him into three years even though it was his first offense. He himself was so offensive I didn't even hesitate to push the public defender. He had no respect. Yes, it was three years. This is Marlin Jones?"

Sherlock took the photo from her father. Dillon hadn't told her about this. She stared at the photo, then at her father. "It's possible, then, that because you gave him that three-year sentence, he wanted revenge. It's possible when he got out, then, that he killed Belinda, to get his revenge on you."

"There's a problem here," Savich said.

Both Judge Sherlock and his daughter looked at him, their left eyebrows arched in an identical way.

"Look again at the photo, Judge Sherlock."

"Yes, all right. What?"

"Marlin Jones would have been twenty-eight years old ten years ago. This man is older, maybe fifty-five or sixty."

"Well, yes, you're right, he is. It's hard to tell with all that hair and the glasses. Oh, I see what you mean. It isn't Marlin, is it?"

"It's his father," Sherlock said slowly. "This man, Erasmus, the man Dad prosecuted, is Marlin's father. And this is an old photo of him, isn't it?"

"Yes. The FBI in Phoenix got hold of this photo from an old driver's license. Our lab people worked on it. I didn't tell you about it, Sherlock, because I didn't really think it would lead to anything."

"Is the man still alive?"

"He is as far as we know. He hasn't been back to Yuma in years. That's where he raised Marlin. Marlin left at eighteen. Erasmus drifted in and out for a few years, then disappeared. He'd be about sixty-four now. Where is he? No one knows."

"Let me see the man," said Mrs. Sherlock.

Sherlock handed her mother the photo.

"He's scruffy. I remember his sort, they were all over San Francisco back in the sixties. But he was in your court ten years ago, Corman?"

"Yes."

"I think he would be handsome without those glasses and all that hair and beard."

"His son is handsome, Mother, very handsome. Here's his photo. But you know, he's got dead eyes."

Mrs. Sherlock looked at Marlin Jones's photo, stared toward her husband, and fainted, sliding out of the chair and onto the carpet before anyone could catch her.

28

"**W**HAT DO YOU WANT?" Douglas stared at Dillon Savich. He laid down the papers he'd been reading and rose slowly, splaying his fingers on the desktop.

"It's okay, Marge. Let him in. He's FBI. Ah, you're here too, Lacey. Why is he with you? You know I don't like him. He's corrupted you, changed you."

"He's my boss. He has to be with me."

"Madigan," Savich said, barely nodding.

Douglas said nothing. He sat back down in his chair. He crossed his hands over his stomach.

"How are you doing, Douglas?"

"I'm very angry at the moment, but you don't care about that. Why are you here with him?"

Savich said easily as he sat down in one of the plush client chairs opposite Douglas Madigan's large high-tech chrome-and-glass desk, "It appears Belinda had an affair with Marlin Jones. Did you know about it?"

"No. I don't like your jokes, Agent Savich."

"No joke, Lawyer Madigan. As far as we know it's a distinct possibility—that Belinda slept with Marlin Jones seven years ago."

Sherlock was watching his face. There was no sign of pain, of anger, of remembered betrayal. Nothing.

"So you're saying you know why he killed her?"

"No, that's not what we're saying. I'm sorry, Douglas," Sherlock said, sitting forward, extending her hand to lightly touch his forearm. "It seems that there were some things about Belinda none of us knew. Mother saw a photo of Marlin Jones. She fainted. She'd seen him, she said, seen him kissing Belinda in the driveway. At least that's what she told us. You know Mother. One can never be quite certain if the flag is going to be flying high or hanging at half-mast."

"That crazy old lady is probably right about this. Belinda was a gold-plated faithless bitch."

They all turned to see Candice Addams Madigan standing in the doorway, a flustered Marge behind her, waving her hands. Douglas smiled and said, "It's all right, Marge. Tell you what, anyone else comes, wave them on in. Hello, Candice."

Candice Addams Madigan walked into the office, head high, beautifully dressed in a pale blue wool suit and a Hermès scarf. "She was a bitch and she did cheat on you."

"But was the man Marlin Jones? I doubt it. Where could she have met him?"

Candice gave her husband a scornful look. "Belinda had low tastes. I've heard she went to dives, to real low-class places. That's where she would have met this killer. Yes, I'll bet she did sleep with him. She slept with everyone. Why don't you ask *her*?" She turned and gave Sherlock a vicious look. "Yes, ask the little princess here. She probably went with her sister. Who knows, she might have slept with him too."

Sherlock had blood in her eye. Her heart was pounding, she was ready to kill. It was Savich who grabbed her wrist and kept her in her place. "Ignore her," he said low, only for her hearing. "She's miserable she's so jealous. Let it be. Let's listen. Consider this a bad play. Let's see if we can't figure out the theme."

She tried to pull away from him. She couldn't take any more. Savich said, "Okay, then, Agent Sherlock, this is an order from your superior. Don't move and be quiet."

She tried to calm her breathing, but it was hard. "That's different, then, but I still want to pound her."

"I know, but later. Now let's listen."

"What are you two talking about?"

Savich smiled at Candice Madigan. "I was telling Sherlock that you looked pregnant to me. She insists you're not, that you look too slender. But I can tell your stomach is out there. Who's right?"

Candice immediately sucked in her stomach, taking two steps away from Savich. Then she realized what he'd done to her. She dropped her hands to her sides, straightened really tall, and shot a look toward her husband. He merely smiled at her. "Go ahead, Candice. After all, I don't have a client for another twenty minutes. Feel free to talk about whatever."

Candice Madigan walked to her husband, kissed him on the mouth, then turned to say to Sherlock, "I'm not pregnant but I will be soon. You keep away from my husband, do you hear me? You haven't seen mean until you've seen me mean."

"Yes, I hear you," Sherlock said. Then she smiled. "You and Douglas planning a baby, then?"

"We will be soon. It's none of your business. You're a little gold-digging tart, like your sister. Stay away from Douglas."

"Oh, she will," Savich said. "Now, Candice, how do you know so much about Belinda? She was killed seven years ago. You weren't even around then."

"I'm an investigative reporter. I looked up everything. I spoke to people who'd known her. She betrayed Douglas, over and over again. All the women in your crowd knew about it. With this Marlin Jones character? Why not? Again, it wouldn't have been a problem for her to run into him at any one of the low-class bars she frequented."

Savich pulled out his little black notebook and his ballpoint pen. "Could you give me some names, please?"

She turned stiller than Lot's wife. "I did this last year. I don't remember now."

"Give Mr. Savich two names, Candice. Just two."

"All right. Lancing Corruthers and Dorthea McDowell. They're both rich and idle and know everything about everyone. They live right here in the city."

Savich wrote down the names. "Thank you. Actually, I'm pleased that you could come up with even one name. I'm impressed."

"I am too," Douglas said.

"They knew all about her too," she added, nodding toward Sherlock.

"That should prove to be interesting," Savich said, again taking hold of Sherlock's wrist. "You see, I'm hoping she'll agree to marry me, once I ask her properly." He paused a moment, then looked very worried. "I sure do hope they won't tell me things that will change my mind about asking you. Were you a loose teenager, Sherlock? Will you corrupt me if I marry you?"

"I don't think that Bobby Wellman could count as loose, do you?"

"Who's Bobby Wellman?" Douglas asked.

Savich shook his head.

"No one will say anything remotely questionable about Lacey," Douglas said. "Look Candice, Lacey was only nineteen when Belinda died. She was even a bit on the backward side for her age. All she did was play the piano. I don't think she ever even saw other people. She saw her music. Now, tell me that was all a joke about you marrying him, Lacey."

"He still has to ask me right and proper."

"No!" Douglas stood now, leaning toward Sherlock, and said, his voice rough and low, "Listen to me, Lacey. I've known you for a very long time. I don't think you should marry this man. You can't. It's a very bad idea."

"Why, Douglas?"

"Yes, Douglas, why?" Candice asked.

"I know his kind. He doesn't care about you, Lacey. You'd be another notch on his belt."

Savich started whistling.

Everyone turned to stare at him. Sherlock wanted to laugh, but she held it back.

"Sherlock Savich," Savich said slowly, looking up at the ceiling, rolling the words on his tongue. "It has quite a ring to it, doesn't it?"

"No, you can't marry him, Lacey. You can't. Look at him, he's one of those stupid bodybuilder types you see at the gym who are always staring at themselves in the mirror. Their biceps and pecs are all pumped up but their brains are the size of peas. He's probably on steroids."

Sherlock said mildly, "Douglas, you need a reality check here. You need to get a grip."

"All right. So he can play with computers, that's no big deal. He's a nerd with big arms. You can't marry him."

"Well she can't marry you, Douglas, you're already married

to me." Candice took one step toward Sherlock, then pulled up when she saw the look on Savich's face.

"Congratulations," Candice said, stepping back. "I do mean that. Marry him."

"This is getting us nowhere fast," Savich said. "Now, Candice, Sherlock and I are here to speak to Douglas about Belinda. Would you like to stay or go?"

"Why? Belinda's been dead for seven years. Her killer is in jail, in Boston. I've even given you two names, women who knew her, who knew what she was like. Why are you talking to Douglas? He doesn't know anything."

"There are all sorts of loose ends, ma'am," Savich said. "Tell you what, why don't we come back, after you and your husband bond or kill each other or eat lunch or whatever else you'd like to do?" Savich rose as he spoke, his hand out to Sherlock. She looked at that big strong hand and smiled. She still wanted to belt Candice.

"No, wait," Douglas called out, but Savich shook his head and waved.

She said as they walked from Douglas's office, "What will we do now?"

"Let's duck around the corner for a minute. Douglas's door is still open, Marge isn't at her desk. Who knows? Maybe we might hear something we shouldn't."

They moved as close to the open door as they could, pressing back against the wall.

"You can't still want her, Douglas. Didn't you see what she was wearing? She even chews her thumbnail!"

Sherlock looked at her thumbs. Sure enough, one thumbnail was nearly down to the quick. How had that happened?

"That's enough, Candice," Douglas said. He sounded incredibly tired. "That's really quite enough. She shouldn't marry him. I'll have to think about this, then write down all the good sound reasons why it wouldn't work. This shouldn't be happening."

"No, what shouldn't be happening is that you still lust after her. Are you blind? What's there to lust over? Get over it, Douglas. Buy some glasses."

Douglas didn't appear to have heard her—that or he was ignoring her. He said, "They're back here because of Belinda.

There must be something going on with Marlin Jones. Savich called them loose ends, but I don't trust him. Mrs. Sherlock claimed she saw Marlin Jones kissing Belinda in the driveway. You say it's likely Marlin had slept with Belinda, but you're jealous, Candice. You didn't know Belinda. It's all nuts. I don't understand any of it, but I think they must doubt Marlin Jones killed Belinda. Maybe they think I killed her and that's why they're here."

"That's crazy, Douglas. They don't have a clue. They're here fishing around. Keep your mouth shut. Now, take me to lunch. I have to be back at the station at two o'clock."

"We're outta here," Savich said. They were in the elevator and on their way down from the twentieth floor of the Malcolm Building within a minute.

Dinner had been quiet; that is, no one had had much to say about anything, which to Savich, was a relief. Evelyn Sherlock ate delicately, gave Savich disapproving looks, and said again that he was too good-looking and not to be trusted. She said nothing at all to her husband, except over a dessert of apple pie, she finally said, not looking at him, but down at her pie, "I spoke to one of your law clerks—Danny Elbright. He said he needed to speak to you but I told him you'd gone to the gas station. I asked him if I could help him and he said no, it was something really confidential. Even your wife couldn't know."

"It was probably about a current case," Judge Sherlock said and forked down another bite of pie. He closed his eyes for a moment. "This is delicious. I need to give Isabelle another raise," he said.

"No, she makes too much already," said Evelyn Sherlock. "I think she bought the pie. She's rarely here except when she knows you'll be here. I don't like her, Corman, I never have."

"How is your companion, Mother?" Sherlock said. "Her name is Mrs. Arch, isn't it?"

"She's fine. She never says anything, only nods or shakes her head. She's very boring, but harmless. She's younger than I am and looks the way my mother would look if she were still alive. She doesn't try to seduce your father and that's a relief."

"Mrs. Arch," the judge said, "is not younger than you are,

Evelyn. She must be all of sixty-five years old. She's got blue hair and is a good size sixteen. Believe me, your mother never looked like Mrs. Arch."

"So? She's not dead yet," said Mrs. Sherlock. "You've slept with every size and age of woman. Did you think I didn't know? I remember everything once I'm reminded."

"Yes, dear."

It was an hour later in Judge Sherlock's library that Savich finally said, "Sherlock didn't realize until recently that Belinda had had a miscarriage. Why didn't this come out?"

Judge Sherlock was stuffing a pipe. The smell of this particular tobacco was wonderful—rich and dark and delicious. He didn't answer until the pipe was lit and he'd sucked in three or four times. The scent was like a forest. Savich found himself breathing in deeply. Finally, Judge Sherlock said, "I didn't want any more publicity. What difference did it make? Not a bit. What do you mean that Lacey didn't remember?"

"Evidently she'd blocked it out, for some reason neither of us can figure out. She remembered under hypnosis. Do you know why she'd block it out, sir?"

"No, no reason to as far as I can see. It was seven years ago. It no longer matters," Judge Sherlock said and sucked on his pipe. The library was filled with the delicious, rich smell. Savich took another drink of his espresso, every bit as rich and delicious as the pipe smoke.

Sherlock took a deep breath. "Do you know if Douglas was the father?"

"Look, Lacey, Mr. Savich, Belinda shouldn't have been pregnant in the first place. I told you, Lacey, that Douglas knew they shouldn't ever have children because of her defective genes. Look at her mother. Her father is even worse. Yes, I keep tabs on him. He'll be out one of these days, despite my efforts to the contrary. I don't want that crazy man coming here."

"But she was pregnant," Savich said.

"Yes, evidently, but not very far along, not more than six or seven weeks. That's what the doctor said. After the autopsy, they knew, naturally, that she'd just miscarried, but since it wasn't relevant to anything, they didn't mention it. The press never got hold of it, thank God. It would have caused more pain. Was Douglas the father? I've never had reason to suspect he wasn't."

"It would have also caused more outrage," Sherlock said.

"No, not unless they led the public to think that the miscarriage was tied to her murder, and it wasn't."

But Sherlock wasn't so certain. Actually, as she told Dillon later as she walked him to the guest room where he was staying, "There are more than loose ends here. There are ends that don't seem to have any beginning." She sighed, staring down at her navy pumps. Candice was right. She looked dowdy and uninteresting. How then could she be a slut at the same time?

Savich pulled her against him, lightly pressing her face against his shoulder. "I know what you mean. It's infuriating. Everything that comes out of your mother's mouth makes Alice's Wonderland look like MIT. How long has she been like this, Sherlock?"

"As long as I can remember. She's more so now, I think. But I don't see her all that often anymore."

"Do you think she could be doing some of this to gain your father's attention?"

"Oh yes. But how much of it is real and how much is her own playacting? I don't know."

"I don't either."

"And my father?"

"I don't know," he said slowly, leaned down and kissed her left ear. "He's slippery, hard for me to read. But you know, Sherlock, it's tough not to like him."

"I like him too, most of the time," Sherlock said and looked up at his mouth. "Do you really want to marry me now that you've met my mother and father?"

"Unfair. You haven't met my family yet. Now there's a scary bunch. Actually, they're going to be so grateful that you're taking me on they'll probably try really hard not to be weird around you, at least until after we're married. Then, no guarantees. Oh yes, Sherlock, we're all alone here in the corridor. I think now's the time. Will you marry me?"

She gave him a brilliant smile and said, no hesitation at all, "Yes, I will."

He kissed her. It was sweet and warm and he tried very hard not to overwhelm her with his need, which was growing by leaps and bounds. But then she pushed him against the wall, pressing herself up tight against him. "You feel delicious," she said into his mouth, her breath warm and dark from the espresso. "You taste even better. Dillon, are you sure you want to marry me? We haven't known each other all that long. We've been stressed-out since we met, nothing's been normal or natural."

"Sure it has. I kicked your butt in Hogan's Alley and at the gym. What's more natural than that? I've cooked my pasta for you, I've fed you pizza at Dizzy Dan's. You've slept in my house. I think we've got great experience going into this. Besides, the sex isn't bad either, except it's been so long that I'm having a tough time remembering all the details, any of the details, actually."

She kissed his chin, his jaw, lightly bit his earlobe. "I don't understand how you've managed to stay footloose for five whole years."

"I run fast and I don't chase too well. Actually, I guess I was waiting for you. Nobody else, only you. I'm more surprised that no one snapped you up."

"I was so locked in the past, locked into only one path, all of it focused on Belinda. What will we do?"

He said as he slowly traced the buttons of her blouse, "I have this inescapable feeling that everything revolves around Belinda, not Marlin, not Douglas, not anybody else, just Belinda. I don't think anyone ever really knew who she was. I'd like to see pictures of her around the time she was killed. Do you have any albums?"

"Yes. I hope Mother didn't throw them away. Would you like to see them now?"

"Nope. We're still on East Coast time, so it feels like three hours later than it is. I want to get some sleep. Actually I want to sleep with you, but that wouldn't be right, not in your parents' house. Besides, your mother is so worried that we're shacking up, she might go on patrol tonight to make certain we're separated."

She laughed. "Mother is a hoot, isn't she? You never know what will come out of her mouth. But it seems she's gone even more around the bend lately. Lots of it might be an act, who knows? She's not going to change. But it still scares me because some of what she says might be true. Did my father really try to kill her? Run her down in his BMW?"

"If he did do it on purpose, at least he knows she's told us about it. Your father isn't stupid. If he did do it deliberately, it won't happen again."

"I don't want my mother to die, Dillon."

He brought her close. "She won't. Everything will be all right. I'll even have a chat with your father, make sure he understands completely."

Much later, when Sherlock was on the edge of sleep, she thought, *Who were you, Belinda?*

29

It was dawn, the bedroom a soft, vague gray, and chilly. She woke up slowly. Someone was shaking her arm, someone speaking to her. "Sherlock, we've got a problem. Come on, wake up."

He was lightly caressing her upper arms, then lightly tapped her face. She blinked up at him. "Dillon? I'm so glad it's you. I thought it was someone else, another nightmare. What's wrong? Did Mother try to run you off the property?"

He sat down beside her and she reached for him. He took her hands in his and held them tightly. "No, that I could have handled. Listen to me, Sherlock. It's Marlin Jones. Brace yourself—he's escaped."

She stared up at him, slowly shaking her head on the pillow. "No, that's impossible. A prisoner doesn't escape nowadays, except in the movies. There's no way Marlin could have gotten away. There were cops all over him. He even went to the bathroom with a cop on either side of him. Besides, he was wearing more shackles than an Alabama chain gang. This has to be an early-morning joke, right, Dillon?"

"I'm sorry, Sherlock, he's gone. The court had ordered him taken to the Massachusetts State Institute for more psychological testing. The doctors there blew fits when they saw the guards and all the restraints—he had full leg shackles. They complained that they'd never get anything meaningful out of him, that they'd never gain any true and accurate testing results unless Marlin could trust them, the doctors. The cops refused, naturally. The doctors then called the judge who'd dictated more testing. The judge then ordered the cops to remove the shackles, even the handcuffs. The cops were even ordered to wait outside the room. The long and the short of it—Marlin hit two doctors over the head, smashed an orderly's jaw, knocked him unconscious, and got out through a bathroom window that was right off the office. They haven't recaptured him yet. They didn't know he'd escaped until the orderly regained consciousness and staggered out to tell them."

She was fully awake now, sitting up, rubbing her arms with her hands. "How did you find out?"

"Jimmy Maitland called me about thirty minutes ago. He said the cops called him, but it had been on TV even before they bothered to telephone. He got hold of the FBI in Boston and put them in on it big-time. He made it sound like everything was in complete disarray."

"What do you think will happen to that judge who ordered Marlin Jones released?"

"There'll be big-time fallout. Hopefully that nitwit judge will either swear he's seen the light or he'll go down, which is what he deserves. Get on your robe and let's get downstairs. Isabelle's made us some coffee and warmed up some rolls."

Ten minutes later they were downstairs in Judge Sherlock's lair watching TV. They'd turned on the big set when a news bulletin flashed on. A big black-and-white photo of Marlin Jones filled the screen. A newswoman's voice said, ". . . The manhunt has extended in all directions now. The FBI, state and local police are all trying to find the alleged killer of more than eight women." The picture then flashed to the newsroom. A beautiful blond woman, not more than twenty-eight, was beaming at the camera, saying in her happy, perfect voice, "It's been learned that the FBI agent, Lacey Sherlock, who was instrumental in catching Marlin Jones in Boston, is the sister of one of the women he allegedly murdered in San Francisco seven years ago. What this means isn't exactly clear, but John Bullock, Marlin Jones's lawyer, has said his client was entrapped all along by the FBI."

"It's out," Savich said, and sighed. "I wonder who told them."

"Oh no." A photo of Sherlock appeared on the TV screen. The newswoman was saying, "Ms. Sherlock has been with the

FBI for only five months now. It's said the reason she joined was to catch her sister's killer." The newswoman gave a dazzling smile to the people watching her. "It appears she succeeded, but now, no one can say what will happen once Marlin Jones is recaptured. Let's switch to Ned Bramlock, our affiliate in Boston. Ned?"

They watched in silence as the cops in the Boston PD stood in stiff and angry silence. The local FBI representative stood behind the small group, saying nothing.

Ned Bramlock, who wore Italian tasseled loafers and had a full head of beautiful chestnut hair, said as he managed to furrow his brow in concern, "We've tried to speak to Judge Sedgewick who issued the order to the police officers to release Marlin Jones, but he's refusing comment at this time." They switched to an ACLU lawyer, who claimed that what the judge did was exactly correct, since to have forced the alleged killer to undergo the humiliation of guards and shackles for the testing would have been a violation of his civil rights. They switched to another judge, this one retired, who said flatly that Judge Sedgewick was an idiot without a lick of judgment or sense.

Savich turned off the TV set. He stretched. "Let's go work out."

She rose. "There's a World Gym two blocks from here, down on Union Street. It's open at six A.M. It's nearly seven-thirty now."

By the time they'd finished, Sherlock was so exhausted, even her rage was dampened somewhat, at least until she could breathe normally again. They walked home, holding hands.

"It's going to be a beautiful day."

"It usually is in San Francisco," she said. "Even when the fog comes rolling through the Golden Gate, it's breathtaking. The fog makes it more lovely." She fell silent.

"They'll catch him. He's got no money, no transportation. Everyone is looking for him. His photo is all over the TV. Someone will see him and they'll call the cops. Don't worry, Sherlock."

Sherlock was thinking about Judge Sedgewick and what she'd like to do to the guy as they walked back to her parents'

home. As they turned onto Broadway, she spotted three local
TV station vans and a good dozen people equipped with cameras and microphones parked in her parents' front yard. They
heard Isabelle yelling, "Get out of here, you vultures, go!
Scat!"

"Come on, ma'am, tell Agent Sherlock we're here. We need
to talk to her for a little while."

"Yeah, the public's got a right to know."

"Hey, did you know her sister, Belinda Madigan? Is it true
she joined the FBI just to bring down Marlin Jones?"

"Is it true she entrapped Jones?"

Isabelle looked ready to kill. She raised her hands, palms
out. To Sherlock's surprise, the rowdy group quieted down
instantly. She said in a voice that carried to the end of the
block, "Go talk to that moronic judge who made the police
remove Marlin Jones's restraints. Maybe he can take that killer's place until he's caught again."

"Good for her," Savich said.

Sherlock called her parents' house from a public phone a
block and a half away.

"Sherlock residence."

"Isabelle? It's Lacey. We saw them all in time. You did
great, told the reporters the truth. Is Dad there?"

"Yes, just a moment, Lacey. I'm glad you're out of here.
The reporters are planning to camp out here, I think. How did
they know you were here?"

Hannah, Lacey thought with sudden insight. Hannah hated
her guts. She'd do anything to hurt her. "We'll find out, Isabelle. Get Dad for me."

Twenty minutes later they were picked up by Danny Elbright, one of Judge Sherlock's clerks. He had their luggage in
the trunk. "Isabelle carried everything out the back and I
swung around to pick up the luggage.

"Judge Sherlock called the airline and got you on a flight
leaving at ten o'clock A.M. Is this all right?"

"That's great," Savich said. He stretched out, leaned back
his head, and closed his eyes. "What a day and it's only nine
o'clock in the morning. I hope the media aren't smart enough
to call the airlines yet."

"Don't worry about me, Lacey," Danny Elbright said, looking at her in the rearview mirror. "I know that if I ever opened my mouth your daddy would send me up the big river. I won't say a word. I want you to catch this creep. Wasn't Isabelle a kick? I'll bet she'll be all over the news."

Sherlock said, "Thanks, Danny. Hey, maybe Marlin's been caught as we speak."

"Let's see." Danny turned on the radio and began station surfing.

By the time their plane left San Francisco International, Marlin Jones was still on the loose. He'd been free for five hours and twenty minutes. There were two seats left in First Class, and Judge Sherlock had snagged them. Both Dillon and Sherlock were relieved when no one recognized them at the airport.

"You'll be staying with me," Savich said as he took a glass of orange juice from a flight attendant. "We're not going to take any chances."

"All right," she said, and stared down at where Yosemite would be if only they had been sitting on the right side of the airplane instead of the left.

"I know you're scared. Don't be."

"Actually I'm furious, not scared. There's no reason why Marlin would come after me. You know he's not crazy, and he'd have to be totally off the deep end to fixate on getting back at me.

"What I can't believe is that a judge—a person who's supposed to have a tad of common sense—would even listen to those idiot shrinks and their ridiculous demands."

"Well, I'll bet you no judge is going to pull that kind of stunt again anytime soon. This was an aberration, Sherlock, an unfortunate blip. Everyone will raise hell and the ACLU will look like idiots for defending the judge's ruling.

"Also, it turns out that one of the doctors might not make it. The other doctor has a severe concussion, according to the news. As for the orderly, his jaw's broken and he has a lump over his left ear the size of a hockey puck. You can bet next week's paycheck restraints will be left on prisoners in the future."

Savich took her hand. "We'll see. I do wonder where Marlin's daddy is. I have this feeling he's still out there, still kicking around. What's he doing, I wonder? Does Marlin know where he is? Is Marlin going to see him? Could Erasmus have been the one to come after you in Washington? Could he have been the one to hit me in Boston? Have Marlin and his daddy possibly been in contact and maybe even now are in cahoots?"

She sucked in her breath. "I was thinking the same thing. But as to the father-and-son-duo idea, I don't know if it's another seemingly random piece to the puzzle or a major gluing piece."

"I think it says a lot about how well we're suited that I understand exactly what you just said." He picked up her hand and kissed her fingers. He looked deep into her eyes. He tucked a piece of hair behind her ear. His fingers lightly caressed her ear. "Hey, gorgeous, what do you want from this gourmet lunch menu?"

Marlin Jones was still free when they arrived at Savich's house at seven-thirty that evening.

There were no reporters waiting for them.

"If they're anywhere, it's at your town house. Another excellent reason for staying here with me."

"Yes," she said and followed him in. "I hope Hannah doesn't tell them where I probably am."

"I'm going to call Jimmy Maitland and let him know we're back. And Ollie. Yeah, I think I'll give Hannah a ring. Yes, I think you're right. She's probably behind the leak. I'm beginning to think this might be a good time for her to transfer to another section. She'd better keep her mouth shut from now on or she'll be out of the Bureau."

"Maybe she's not the one who talked."

"We'll see. You unpack and then relax, Sherlock. We'll have dinner in. I've got some great spinach lasagna in the freezer that I made a couple of weeks ago. You'll love it."

"I think I'd rather have Dizzy Dan's pizza. Do they deliver?"

"They will for me." He frowned at her, then strode back to her, grabbed her and pulled her tightly against him. "It's going to be all right. We'll get through this. Marlin will be in jail again by tomorrow morning, you'll see. All the FBI's in on this whole thing, big-time. I don't think I've ever seen Jimmy Maitland so angry. Marlin doesn't stand a chance."

But she didn't know if she agreed. Marlin Jones was out there. She nodded though, saying nothing, and laid her cheek against his shoulder.

Her clothes went into his closet, her shoes on the floor beside his size-twelve wing tips and gym shoes. Her underwear went in the second drawer of the dresser. And when he was kissing his way down her body, finally holding her hips, his mouth against her, she forgot everything but him and what he was making her feel. The deep, tearing pleasure roared through her and she yelled and arced upward and told him between gasping breaths, "I love you, Dillon. In case you didn't hear me the first time, I'll marry you. You're the best."

"Good. Don't forget it," he said, staring down at her, and came into her.

It was nearly morning when Savich came slowly awake, aware that something strange was happening, something that was probably better than any pesto pasta he'd ever made, better even than having won a huge bet off one of his relatives. The something strange suddenly intensified and he lurched up, gasping. She was leaning over him, her tangled hair covering his belly, her mouth on him.

All he could do was moan, clutch her hair as he moaned, and twitch and heave.

And when he kissed her mouth, she said, "If you could do that to me, surely you had to like it too. It only makes sense, doesn't it? I've never done that before. Did I do it okay?"

"It was okay," he said. "Yeah, I think maybe it was okay. Really not bad for your first time." She slid down his chest again. Then it was all over for him.

Ollie said, "Jimmy Maitland has a representative speaking to the media downstairs, sir. Sherlock, don't worry, they'll lay off, that was the deal Maitland struck with them."

"Good," Savich said.

"But there's lots of gossip, lots of innuendo," Hannah said, tapping her pen against the conference table. "Marlin Jones's lawyer is making hay with Sherlock here being one of the murdered women's sisters."

"That's true," Savich said. "Does anyone know how the media found out about that?"

No one said a word.

"Hannah?" Savich said, looking at her.

She looked right at Sherlock. "No, certainly not. But I don't think it's bad that the media found out what she did. It's possible the case against Jones could be tossed out as entrapment." She shrugged. "You knew it was going to come out anyway. At least now there's time to get the media through chewing on it by the time Marlin Jones is recaptured."

She was lying, but how could he prove it? Savich smiled at her, a smile cold enough to freeze water. He said, his voice so gentle it made the hair rise on the back of Sherlock's neck, "I wonder that it didn't occur to the one who told the press that Sherlock wasn't the one who made the decision? That both the Bureau and the local cops all discussed her as bait for Marlin and okayed it?"

"I bet you talked him into it," Hannah said to Sherlock. The other agents were squirming, looking off, wishing, Savich knew, that they were anywhere but seated here at the conference table.

Savich raised his hands. "All right, that's enough. As most of you know, Sherlock is at my place. Not a word about this to anybody outside this room. Okay, we'll have our regular status meeting tomorrow. I wanted everyone up to speed on this debacle. Hannah, I'd like to see you in my office."

The meeting broke up. Ollie collared Sherlock. "I've been working through MAXINE's protocols using a different slant with the Florida nursing home killings. Come and see where I'm at. I'd like your input. Besides, it'll get your mind off Marlin Jones. You're looking hunted."

She wanted to go after Savich and Hannah. Then Hannah turned around and looked at her. Sherlock changed her mind. She didn't want to get within spitting distance of Hannah.

In Savich's office, he waved his hand to a chair facing his desk. "Sit down, Hannah."

She sat. He said nothing at all for a very long time, looked at her, his head cocked to the left.

"You wanted to speak to me, Dillon?"

"Oh yes. I know it was you who told the media about Sherlock's connection to one of the San Francisco murders. I'd like you to tell me why you did it."

30

SHE SAID IN A LOW VOICE that was hard as nails, "I told you already I didn't do it."

"You're lying. Understand this, Hannah. It wasn't Sherlock's decision to be used as bait. Sure, she wanted to do it, very badly, but it wasn't her decision. You're the last person who should have opened your mouth. The fact of the matter is that you talked to the press to cause trouble. That's unprofessional and unacceptable behavior in a Special Agent."

"I didn't do it. You can't prove that I did. Don't forget it was a judge who ordered the removal of Marlin Jones's shackles. Why wouldn't a judge throw this out as well?"

"Because of the evidence, that's why. Look, Hannah, I don't want you in this unit. I think a transfer is in order. You're a good agent, but not here, not in my unit."

"That dowdy little prig is that good in bed?"

"Special Agents don't talk about other Special Agents that way. It's not acceptable. I won't have it."

Hannah rose slowly, bent over toward Savich, splayed her hands on his desk, and said in a low voice, "Tell me what you see in her, tell me so I'll understand. You swore to me you'd never allow yourself to become serious over anyone who worked in your unit, yet you saw little miss prim and fell all over yourself."

He rose to face her. "Listen to me, let it go. Sherlock's never done anything to you. If you want a target, I'm right here, really big, right in front of you. Take your best shot. Leave Sherlock alone. Oh yeah, I know too that you called the media in San Francisco and told them where Sherlock lived.

"You have compromised this case, Hannah, you've muddied the waters because of your stupid jealousy. Now, if you want to stay in the Bureau, you'd best be very careful from here on out. I'll call Colin Petty in Personnel. You can discuss transfer options with him right now."

"Tell me why. Why her?"

Sherlock's face was vivid in his mind's eye. He looked bemused as he said slowly, "You know, I really can't answer that. Lots of things, I guess. Good day, Agent. I'll be calling Personnel right now."

She called him a shit, but it was low enough so he could ignore it. At least he hoped he was the shit and not Sherlock. He'd never meant to hurt Hannah, never meant to do anything to encourage her. He called Colin Petty, then buzzed Hannah to go see him.

He sighed, turned on MAXINE, and was soon in another world, one that he controlled, one that answered only to his siren's song, one that never let him down. He reviewed everything on Marlin Jones.

Where was he? Hiding? On the run? Was he alone?

MAXINE brought up the driver's license photo of Marlin's father, Erasmus Jones. Were they together? Did Erasmus play any role at all in any of the murders in Denver or San Francisco or Boston? Was it actually he who rented the Ford Taurus and not his son? If he had, then they were probably together.

He reviewed the reports, completely immersed until Jimmy Maitland finally said from the open doorway, "Maitland to Savich and MAXINE. Are you two hovering anywhere close?"

Savich blinked, forcing himself to look up. He rose. "Hello, sir. What can I do for you? Have they caught Marlin Jones?"

Jimmy Maitland shook his head mournfully. "No, not yet, but it won't be much longer. All the major corridors out of Boston are covered with agents and locals. Oh yeah, Big John Bullock is hassling the Bureau office in Boston big-time. He wants to see Agent Sherlock. He wants what he's calling a predeposition. He wants to make some hay now before the cops have Marlin in custody again. What do you suggest we do?"

Savich sat back in his chair. Jimmy Maitland lowered himself into one of the chairs facing Savich's desk. "This isn't easy, is it? That opportunistic jerk, I wish Marlin had hit him harder."

"Too late. Come on, Savich, do you think Big John will make hash out of Sherlock?"

"No. Besides, we'll have Simms from Justice with us. I think Sherlock is incidental. What he wants is to have the media crawling all over her, making her look guilty, and thus exonerating Marlin Jones, which is impossible. The guy's spitting in the wind."

"And if that doctor dies, it's more than impossible. They might launch him into space. Last I heard, it's still too close to call."

"If the doctor dies, I can see Big John going for manslaughter or murder two. No premeditation, an act of passion by an insane man, a man out of control, a man terrified about what was going to happen to him." Suddenly Savich sat upright in his chair, his hands clasped in front of him. "Let's do it. I think Sherlock can handle herself. Who knows? We might get something out of it."

Jimmy Maitland said very slowly, "You think maybe Marlin will find out about her being in Boston? He'll try to get to her?"

Savich was very still. "Yeah, bottom line, that's why I think we should go."

"It's a real long shot. Next to impossible."

"Yeah, but even if there's a remote chance it'd be worth it. But it's not my decision to make. I'll speak to Sherlock. But you know something? I don't think Marlin would even find out about her going to Boston—unless we let it loose to the media. Also, even if he does find out, he'd really have to be crazy to come after her."

"Maybe, but I just don't know. Big John will leak it to the media, count on it. I will too. But you're right, it's got to be Sherlock's decision. But you already know the answer, don't you, Savich?"

"Oh yes."

"The media are out in force, thicker than fleas on a one-eared dock rat," Jimmy Maitland said, blew his nose, then stuffed the handkerchief back into his coat pocket. He drew away from the window in the twenty-third-floor office of Big John Bullock. He wasn't happy with all this, but he knew that with the leak, there was no way Marlin Jones didn't know about Sherlock being here in Boston. He wouldn't be surprised if Sherlock had called the media. She really wanted Marlin Jones, badly.

Buzz O'Farrell, the SAC of the Boston field office, was shaking his head. "It amazes me how they don't send one reporter, no, it's four dozen with eight dozen mikes, enough cameras to film World War II, and everybody screaming. I wanted to shoot that damned judge, but the media? A nice deadly virus might be the answer for them."

"They ain't got no manners, that's for sure," Savich said, grinning down at Sherlock, who looked both stoic and furious, an interesting combination he would have liked to explore with her in private. Which, unfortunately, wouldn't be an option this morning.

"Big John leaked it," Jimmy Maitland said, "we didn't. Actually, we'd decided to keep our noses clean. And yes, we know he leaked it. He's still counting on coming out smelling like a rose in all this and that's why he did it."

"If he hadn't, then I probably would have," Sherlock said. "Sorry, sir, but there it is. Anything to give us another shot at Marlin Jones."

"Well, good morning to all you good law enforcement representatives," Big John Bullock said, walking into the immense walnut-paneled conference room in his law offices. He homed in immediately on Sherlock. "Good to see you again," he said.

She smiled at him. "I must say you're looking a bit more fit than the last time I saw you. Marlin sure did a number on your head, didn't he?"

"Poor boy, he was frantic to get out of that torture chamber. Shall we get down to business now?"

"That's fine with us," Savich said, all calm and cool, in that FBI voice of his.

"Do tell us exactly what you want," Georgina Simms, the FBI attorney for the Justice Department said, sitting forward. "This is on the unusual side. But we certainly want to cooperate all we can."

"Well, I really wanted to know what Agent Sherlock has to say about all her unethical behavior in the case to date."

Savich rose. He walked slowly up to Big John and said not two inches from his face, "Agent Sherlock doesn't have anything to say. Now, if you can't come up with something worth our while, we're out of here. You heard Ms. Simms. We've got a murderer to catch. Maybe you think it's funny that at least eight women were brutally murdered and a doctor is hanging on for his life as we speak, but we don't."

Big John sobered immediately, nodding to the stenographer to begin as he sat down and opened a thick file. "All right, then. Agent Sherlock, here's the problem you've created for the state. Your sister is one of the women allegedly killed by my client. Is this true?"

"Yes."

"So the reason you became an FBI agent was to get in on the inside so you'd have a better chance of catching him?"

"Yes, initially."

"Was it your idea, your plan, that resulted in the capture of Marlin Jones?"

"It was a plan developed by the local BPD and the FBI. It was also a plan approved by the local BPD and the FBI. I was merely the bait."

"Why?"

"Because I knew his profile very well. I knew better than any other female officer or agent exactly how to play him, how to work him. I was simple bait, Mr. Bullock. All he had to do was ignore me. There was no entrapment."

"That will be up to the judge, won't it?"

Georgina Simms said, her voice easy and slow, "This is all a waste of time, Mr. Bullock. If you have a point, make it now or we're leaving."

"My point is, exactly how did you know how to 'play' Marlin Jones so well, Agent Sherlock?"

She didn't pause. She saw Dillon tense up, then consciously relax. He was worried. Well, she wasn't. She'd thought about this a whole lot. "I've studied everything about the killer for the past seven years, Mr. Bullock. I felt I knew him. He cut out the women's tongues, thus it was assumed that the women he'd picked to walk the walk through his maze needed to be punished in his mind. His first marker was curs-ing. If he heard a woman using language unbecoming to a woman—and of course he was the judge of how bad the lan-guage was—that was half of his decision. The other half was whether or not she bad-mouthed her husband. This one was more iffy, but again, I felt I knew Marlin Jones, I'd studied him so closely for seven years and through my course work in undergraduate and in graduate school. As you know, he's now claimed he slept with most of the women he murdered, though we don't have any confirmation on that. It's really very straightforward. That's all there is to it, Mr. Bullock."

"So your sister cursed and bad-mouthed her husband. Did your sister also sleep with her killer, Agent Sherlock?"

"Since she's been dead for seven years, stabbed many times, her tongue cut out, I don't think we have much hope of getting the answer."

Savich could have kissed her. It had been a question meant to inflame, meant to incite rage and thus to gain an untem-pered response. She'd held firm. He could tell Jimmy Mait-land was impressed as well.

"That sounded all rehearsed, Agent Sherlock."

She shrugged.

Big John said, "It sounds to me like you're one obsessed little lady, excuse me, one obsessed little Special Agent. I would have thought the FBI interviewers and psychologists would have spotted all this and not given you the time of day. That's scary."

"No, sir, what's scary is a judge who presents Marlin Jones, a vicious murderer, with a perfect chance to escape." She sat forward in her chair. "And you're scary, Mr. Bullock. You're doing this all to enhance your career—in other words, for fame and profit. If I am obsessed or have ever been obsessed, sir, then you are unethical. You, sir, are a disgrace."

Big John roared to his feet. "You can't talk to me like that, Agent Sherlock."

"Why not, sir?"

Georgina Simms smiled. "It's a good question, an excellent point actually, but we'll let it go. Anything else you wanted to know, Mr. Bullock?"

"No judge is going to accept that she was another well-trained agent doing a job. She taints the case. She's a self-interested participant, not an objective law officer."

"We're gone," Savich said, rose, and nodded to Sherlock. "See you in court, Mr. Bullock, if the cops can't manage to bring down Marlin when he resists arrest, which you know he will."

Sherlock smiled over her shoulder at him. "Perhaps you shouldn't be spending so much time on Marlin Jones now, Mr. Bullock. You know Agent Savich is right. Marlin will resist arrest. The chance of your getting to eviscerate the law with your tactics isn't likely to happen. Seems to me you're wasting your time, which is worth lots of money, right?"

She felt Savich's palm beneath her elbow. He said close to her ear, "We're out of here. You did well."

"We'll go out the back way," Jimmy Maitland said in the elevator. "I've already scoped it out."

"That was interesting, Agent Sherlock," Georgina Simms said. "I don't understand either how you got into the FBI in the first place."

"Actually, Ms. Simms, I was surprised too. Don't get me wrong, finding Marlin Jones was a big part of my motivation for joining, but then I realized that this was what I wanted to do with my life. You know, before Mr. Savich brought me to his new unit, I could have ended up chasing bank robbers in Los Angeles. And that was the bottom line. I would have caught as many bank robbers as I could."

"I rather think a judge might buy that," Georgina Simms said. "But as I said, however did you manage to even get accepted with this in your background?"

"I guess nobody made a big deal out of it."

Before they all parted in the underground parking lot, Jimmy Maitland said to Savich, "Simms buys it because it sounds good and it is true, for the most part. However, what she doesn't know is that you've got the hots for Sherlock. What are you going to do about that? Are you two going to get married, or what?"

"Yes, but as they say, timing is everything."

"But the point is, why did you ask for her for the Criminal Apprehension Unit in the first place?"

Savich didn't hesitate. "Because she was so good in Hogan's

Alley. No, I didn't have the hots for her then, sir. I thought she'd be one of the best I could get my hands on. I found out she'd turned down profiling because she said she couldn't stomach it, but she had all this great training and knowledge in forensics. No, sir, at that time, there was no lust scrambling my brains."

Jimmy Maitland grunted. "Timing," he said. "You're right. All of this will have to be controlled very tightly. You took care of the leak out of your unit?"

"All gone," Savich said.

"I don't suppose you're going to tell me about it?"

"I would appreciate your not asking, sir, since there's no solid proof."

31

T HEY SPENT THE REST OF THE
day with the local Bureau and police, seeing exactly what was
going on with the manhunt. "It looks like everything's being
done right," Savich said to one of the cops on the newly
formed task force. "And there's zero hint or word that Marlin
Jones could have met up with someone?"

"Not an echo of a word," Officer Clintock said. "I think
I've walked from one end of the zone to the other a good
dozen times. I've spoken to every informant who's ever mi-
grated to Boston or was born here. My feet hurt."

By eight o'clock that evening, Marlin Jones was still at
large.

They decided to eat again at the Chinese restaurant on
Newbury, and walked there.

"I doubt he'll show, Sherlock."

"At least we're giving him every opportunity to make a
move."

"Okay. We'll keep walking everywhere and when the media catches up to us, we'll wave to our mothers and smile
really big. Speaking of mothers, do you think your mother
really saw Marlin kissing Belinda in the driveway?"

"Actually, I have no idea what she saw or if she even saw
anything. I think you're right about the attention bids. My father was there and she wanted him to focus on her. It was an
excellent way to go about it."

"So you don't believe your father would ever try to run her
down?"

"I don't know. But I think she loves him. I could be wrong.

It's nuts, isn't it? Maybe she did see someone perhaps speak to Belinda in the driveway, but Marlin?"

"Do you think your father prosecuted Erasmus Jones ten years ago?"

"Oh yes. My father's firmly planted in the here-and-now, no matter how unpleasant it can get. He doesn't make stuff up. If he said Erasmus Jones was in his courtroom, then he was. The question is—Is it possible that Erasmus Jones has anything to do with this?"

Savich said slowly, "There's a tremendous resemblance between father and son. Is it possible that maybe your mother saw Erasmus with Belinda, not Marlin?"

"I have no idea. But she didn't have any reaction at all to Erasmus Jones's photograph."

"No, she didn't."

Over egg rolls and fried wonton, half with meat and half vegetarian, Savich said, releasing her hand, "Your fingers are cold."

"All of me is cold."

"Next summer we'll go to Louise Lynn Lake with Quinlan and Sally. I want to see you in a bikini. A blue one. I want to buy it for you. I want to put it on you and take it off."

Next summer, she thought: a lifetime away from a Chinese restaurant in Boston where, she prayed, Marlin Jones was lurking somewhere, waiting for her to come out. Cops were stationed at short intervals all around the restaurant.

She gave him a huge smile. "Thank you," she said, stood on her tiptoes, and kissed his mouth. Then she sat down again, took a huge forkful of garlic pork, and chewed while Savich sat there, staring at her, bemused.

Princess prawns and garlic eggplant arrived. While Savich was spooning rice onto his plate, he said, "What do you think about Douglas?"

"I really don't want to think about him right now. I want to eat." She sighed, as she speared a princess prawn on her fork. "Everyone is accusing everyone else of killing Belinda. We go down one passageway, then another." She waved her fork, flinging rice onto the table. "The only thing I am sure about is that Isabelle didn't do it. My money would be on Candice if she'd only been around seven years ago."

"I find myself still going back and back yet again to your nightmare, to your experiencing exactly what happened to Belinda."

"I try not to anymore. It's too scary. It makes me sweat. Do you think we could go work out after dinner?"

He grinned at her over a forkful of garlic eggplant, which had been nicely prepared. "My soul mate," he said. "Your delts still need work. Your thighs are really nice, though. Those triceps of yours make me hard."

"I love it when you talk gym to me."

They didn't fly back to Washington until the next afternoon. Not a single sign of Marlin Jones. He was still at large.

They stopped off to see Captain Dougherty at the station on their way to Logan International. "It seems to me someone has to be helping him," Savich said.

"Yeah," said Captain Dougherty. "Everyone is coming to that conclusion now. There haven't been any murders or robberies that haven't checked out. Since Marlin didn't have any money, he would have to get some if he remained alone. He didn't so far as we know. So, someone must be helping him. Someone's hiding him, a someone who has enough money to keep him out of sight. But who? We've checked with the people at the lumberyard where he worked. He didn't have any close friends that they knew of, at least no one close enough to go out on this long a limb for him."

Sherlock handed Captain Dougherty the eight-by-ten photo of Erasmus Jones. "This is his father. You might want to distribute this photo."

"They sure do look alike. You think his old man might really be in on this thing? Do you think he's the one helping Marlin?"

"We have no idea. We don't even know if he's dead or alive. It's an idea, something we can sink our teeth into." They rose. "We're going back home, Captain. Keep us informed and good luck."

"Douglas told me he's being followed. Damn you, this has got to stop."

Candice Madigan spoke angrily from behind them as Savich was unlocking his front door.

Sherlock's hand was already on her Lady Colt, Savich already in a crouch. He took a deep breath. "I suggest you never do anything like that again, ma'am. Sherlock could have shot you and I could have broken your neck. May I inquire what you're doing here?"

"Waiting for you."

"How did you know I'd be here?" Sherlock asked, stepping directly under the porch light.

Savich unlocked the door and shoved it open. "Everyone might as well come inside. You first, Mrs. Madigan. I'd as soon keep you in front of me." He said over his shoulder, "I hope you have frequent flier miles. What is this? Your second or third trip to Washington?"

"Of course I have frequent flier miles," she said. "Do you think I'm a fool?"

If Candice was blown away by the inside of Savich's house, she didn't show it. Her eyes never left Sherlock. "Did you hear me? I know it's not the San Francisco cops. Judge Sherlock called in and found that out for me. So it has to be the FBI following him. It's your doing, isn't it? No, you don't have that kind of authority." She turned on Savich. "You'd do anything for little miss sweetness, wouldn't you? Even have my husband followed. Are you trying to blame Douglas for Belinda's murder? Stop it, he's going nuts. I won't have it."

"You know," Savich said easily, waving Candice into the living room, "when you pause to think a bit, Douglas had a very good motive for killing Belinda. He wanted out of the marriage but she wouldn't give him a divorce. He knew if he tried to get one Judge Sherlock would have ruined him. He was trapped. So he used the String Killer's M.O. and killed her. What do you think? Sound good?"

Candice lunged at him.

He caught her wrists and held her away from him. She kicked at him. He quickly turned to the side. Then he began shaking her, saying in his low calm voice, "Stop it, Mrs. Madigan. For a woman of some sophistication, you're not playing the part."

"Give her to me," Sherlock said. "I'm sick of you, Candice. You want to fight, then come here. I'd love to take you down."

"You'd wreck my living room," Savich said, looking at a red-faced Sherlock, and smiled. "Will you try to keep some control, Mrs. Madigan? I'll protect you from Sherlock if you'll mind your manners. Will you?" Slowly, she nodded. Savich let her go. She stood there, rubbing her wrists. Then, slowly, she turned to face Sherlock, but she said over her shoulder to Savich, "Did it ever occur to you that she killed Belinda? Talk about crazy, look at her family. Every gene coursing through her is nuts."

There was dead silence except for Candice's heavy breathing.

"Well? What do you have to say to that?"

Sherlock smiled, an awesome feat she told Savich later, but she managed it. "Candice, why are you really here?"

"I told you, someone's following Douglas. It's got to be the FBI. I want it stopped. So I came to make you do it."

Sherlock said, "Why didn't you call? It sure would have been cheaper. No answer to that? Maybe you wanted to hire that guy again to terrorize me? Maybe you wanted to try to run me down again?"

"I don't know what you're talking about. As for you," she continued, looking at Savich, "you're blind. Douglas was too, but only for a little while. Now he realizes what she is." Candice gave them a triumphant smile and sat down on the beautiful sofa. "Well?"

"Well what, Mrs. Madigan?"

"Will you have the FBI stop following my husband?"

Savich sighed. "Sure, Mrs. Madigan. The thing is, though, we have an agent following him in order to keep him safe. Marlin Jones is still on the loose. It's possible he plans to go back to California. It's possible that he would want to see Douglas, maybe even kill him. That's why we have an agent on him, ma'am, to protect him."

Candice said slowly, "There's no reason in the world why Douglas would be in any danger from Marlin Jones."

"Oh? Are you really so sure about that? Didn't Douglas tell you about Mrs. Sherlock seeing Marlin kissing Belinda in front of the house? Who knows what's going on in Marlin Jones's mind these days? But who cares, when all's said and done? Sure, I'll call off the FBI. Douglas can be on his own, no problem." Savich calmly picked up the phone and dialed a number.

"Do you really think he could be in danger?"

Savich ignored her, waiting. Then he said, "This is Dillon Savich. Please connect me with James Maitland. Thank you."

"What if this creep is after him? What if he does manage to get to San Francisco? Douglas needs help. You can't leave him alone like this. It's inhuman."

"Sir, Savich here. We need to call off the protection on Douglas Madigan in San Francisco. Yes, I'm sure. There's no more need."

"No, don't call it off! What if this Marlin Jones goes after Douglas? No, don't!"

"Yes, that's right. No need any longer. Thank you."

Savich hung up the phone in time to block Candice Madigan from shoving him into the fireplace.

"That's it," Sherlock said. She jumped at Candice, grabbed her arm and jerked her around. She sent her fist into Candice's jaw.

"Ow! That hurts, you mean little bitch!"

Sherlock hit her again, then groaned herself at the pain in her knuckles.

Candice looked at her, astonishment written clearly on her face, and slumped to the floor.

"Are you all right, Dillon?"

She was standing there rubbing her knuckles, asking him if he was all right. He could only shake his head. "Thank you for protecting me." She'd rushed in to protect him. Life with Sherlock would never be boring. He hoped she hadn't hurt her hand.

"Could you come and kiss me, Sherlock? I'm feeling a little shaky."

"Sure," she said, smiling sweetly at him. She kissed his chin, ran her fingertips over his eyebrows, kissed his nose. "You're better now?"

"Getting there," he said, and kept kissing her.

They stopped only when they heard Candice say from the floor, "If the two of you make out in front of me, I'm going to call the police. Then you'll both be arrested."

Sherlock began to laugh; she couldn't help it. Savich said, "Would you like a cup of coffee before you leave, Mrs. Madigan?"

"What I want is for the FBI to protect my husband."

"But you flew all the way here to get us off him."

"Look, I know I haven't been really nice to either of you, but Douglas, he's different. He needs me. Please, if you truly believe he's in danger, protect him."

Savich walked to the phone, dialed, then said, "Reinstate the surveillance on Douglas Madigan. Yes, that's right. Thank you." He hung up, then turned to Candice. "It's done."

"Thank you," she said. "Really, thank you very much." She turned to Sherlock. "As for you, you're nothing but trouble. You're going to bring trouble to this very nice man who doesn't know you at all. Stay away from Douglas."

With that, she was gone.

Savich stood there, looking toward the front door. "I guess she didn't want coffee."

"Did you really have surveillance on Douglas?"

"Oh yes."

"Did you take it off then put it back on?"

"Nope. Douglas is a suspect. I want an eye kept on him. Hey, if it protects him as well, so be it."

"She loves him," Sherlock said. "She really truly loves him."

"The two of them deserve each other. I hope they live happily ever after. Now, if you're ready for bed, I'll race you."

She'd been so depressed, then she'd wanted to shoot Candice, but now, looking at Dillon Savich, she felt relief pouring through her. "Let's go."

32

M ARLIN JONES WAS STILL FREE
on Thursday at noon. His photo was shown on TV special
bulletins throughout the day and evening. Hundreds of sight-
ings from Boca Raton to Anchorage had flooded in.

Savich tried to work, tried to concentrate on the killings in
South Dakota and Iowa, but it was tough. He called everyone
together Thursday afternoon to announce that Hannah Paisley had been reassigned. He would let everyone know where
she would be going when it was decided. No one was particularly sorry to see her go.

As for Sherlock, she felt as if a hundred-pound weight had
been lifted off her back.

An hour later, there was a resolution to the nursing home
murders in Florida. Savich, Ollie, and Sherlock were all hooting when they walked into the conference, giving everyone
high fives.

Savich, grinning from ear to ear, rubbing his hands, said,
"Good news. Great news. It turns out our murderer is an old
man—Benjamin Potter from Cincinnati who's been a magi-
cian for thirty years—he's a master of disguise, which all of
you know. Also, he's never done a bad thing in his life. He
easily entered the nursing homes as another old person
in need of round-the-clock attention. Sometimes he passed
himself off as an old woman, other times, an old man. Because he was in basic good health, no nurse ever saw him
without his clothes on, important since he could have been
playacting an old woman. He never had difficulty escaping

after each murder, because he didn't. Nope, he always stayed on until a 'relative' came to take him home to his family. He paid the 'relative' fifty bucks for this service." Savich turned to Ollie.

Ollie said, "The cops found the 'relative' in Atlanta. He denied knowing anything about the murders. He said only that the old man was a kick and it was easy money." He nodded to Sherlock.

"Benjamin Potter wouldn't have been caught after the sixth murder except that he happened to trip on a used syringe on his way out of the victim's room and suffered a heart attack. He died before he could tell anyone why he'd killed six old women."

Ollie picked it up. "Yep, the relative is my part. He said he had no clue. The old man always seemed happy and well adjusted to him. So go figure."

They all tried to figure it out, but no one could come up with anything that sounded like the perfect fit. Although Savich said MAXINE thought the old man had always wanted to be an old woman and he was killing off his competition.

"A real big one down," Savich said. "Everybody to the gym for celebrations."

There was groaning from around the table.

Sherlock was still on a high when she went to the women's room in the middle of the afternoon, a redone men's room that looked it. When workmen had removed the urinals, they hadn't patched the wall tile very well. The big room was always dank and smelled like Pine Sol.

Sherlock was washing her hands when she looked up to see Hannah in the mirror, standing behind her. She didn't say anything, just looked at her reflection.

"Your lover didn't want to take the chance I'd slap him with a sexual harassment complaint so he couldn't fire me."

"I thought you denied leaking my relationship to a murder victim to the press."

"I did deny it."

"Then how could Savich have fired you without proof? Oh enough, Hannah. Say what you have to say and go about your business."

"You're really cute, you know that? Tell me, Sherlock, did you set your sights on Savich while you were still at Quantico?"

"No."

"He'll screw your eyes out but he won't marry you. Has he made love to you in the shower? He loves that."

"Hannah, it's none of your business what either of us does. Please, let it go. Forget him. You know I'm irrelevant in all this. Even if I weren't here, Savich still wouldn't be going out with you."

"Maybe, maybe not."

"Good-bye, Hannah."

Ollie was waiting outside for her. He said only, "I didn't want her to shoot you."

"So you were waiting out here to see if a gun went off?"

"Something like that."

"I'm fine, Ollie. Any word yet on Marlin Jones?"

"Nope, nothing. Oh yeah, your father called, asked that you phone him back. He said it was really important."

She didn't want to pick up that phone. She didn't want to, but she did. She felt an urgency that she'd never felt before. Even as she was dialing her parents' home number, she was terrified.

"Isabelle? It's Sherlock—ah, Lacey."

"Oh God, Lacey, it's your mama. Let me get your daddy on the phone. You caught him in time. He's leaving now for the hospital."

"The hospital? What happened to Mother?" But Isabelle had already hit the hold button. "Father?"

"Lacey? Come home, my dear, it's your mother. There was an accident. She's in the hospital. It doesn't look good, Lacey. Can you get some time off?"

"What kind of accident? What is her exact condition?"

"I was backing out of the driveway. She darted out from the bushes that line the street. I hit her. It was an accident. I swear it was an accident. There was even a passerby who saw the whole thing. She's not dead, Lacey, but her spleen is ruptured and they're taking it out as we speak. I feel terrible. I don't know what's going to happen. I think you should come home now."

Before she could say anything, he hung up. She stared down

at the receiver, hearing the loud dial tone. What more could happen?

At nine o'clock the next morning she was on a nonstop flight to San Francisco. Savich took the Dulles shuttle with her to the terminal to catch her United flight, using his FBI identification to get through the gate. "You'll call me," he said, kissing her hair, holding her against him, his hands stroking down her back. "It will be all right. We'll get through it. Remember in the Bible how God kept testing Job? Well, these are our tests. Call me, okay?" And he kissed her again. He watched at the huge windows until her plane took off.

He didn't like her to go alone but he couldn't pick up and leave, not now. Everything was coming to a head, he knew it. More important, she knew it. It was only a matter of time. Actually he was rather relieved that she'd be three thousand miles away, although he'd never tell her that. She'd blow a fuse because he wanted to protect her and she was a professional and could take care of herself.

He stepped back onto the shuttle, realizing, as he stared blankly at a businessman with a very packed briefcase, that she would be justified smacking him but good if he'd said that to her. He had to remember she was well trained. She was a professional. Even if his guts twisted whenever he thought of her going into the field, he'd have to get used to it.

He shook his head as he walked to his Porsche. Could her father have deliberately hit her mother?

For the first time that Sherlock could remember, her mother looked all sixty-one of her years. Her flesh seemed loose, her cheeks sunken in. And so white and waxy, tubes everywhere. Mrs. Arch, her mother's ten-year companion, was there, as was Sherlock's father, both standing beside her bed.

"Don't worry," her father said. "The operation went well. They took out her spleen and stopped the internal bleeding. There's lots of bruising and she'll have some sore ribs, but she'll be all right, Lacey."

She looked over at her father. "I know. I spoke to the nurse outside. Where were you, Mrs. Arch, when this happened?"

"Your mother got by me, Lacey. One minute she was there

watching a game show on TV, the next minute she was gone. I'd gone down to the kitchen for a cup of tea."

She looked at her father. He seemed remote, watching the woman who had been his wife for nearly thirty years. What was he thinking? Did he expect her to say something against him when she regained consciousness? "Father, tell me what happened."

"I was backing out of the driveway to go to the courthouse. I heard this loud bump. I'd hit your mother. I never saw her. The first thing was to get her to the hospital, then I called the police. It was a Sergeant Dollan who found a witness to the whole thing. His name's Murdock."

"What did he tell them?"

"That she ran out into the driveway. He said he couldn't figure out why she'd do such a stupid thing."

She had to go talk to this Mr. Murdock herself.

"You don't believe your mother's crazy tale that I tried to run her down, do you?"

"No. You're not stupid."

He'd been tense before but now he relaxed. He even smiled. "No, I'm not stupid. Why did she do that?"

"Probably to get your attention."

"Now that's nuts, Lacey."

"Maybe more of your attention would be a good thing."

She looked down at her mother. She was so still. Here she was lying in a hospital bed with a squirrelly brain and no spleen.

"I'll think about what you said. Where are you going?"

"To talk to Mr. Murdock. No, Dad, I don't doubt you. I want to hear him tell it. Maybe it will help us both understand her a bit better."

Sherlock left her mother's hospital room and stopped again at the nurse's station.

"Mrs. Sherlock will be fine," Nurse Blackburn said. "Really. She'll be asleep for another three or four hours. Come back to see her later, about dinnertime."

Sherlock called the precinct station. Ten minutes later, she was driving to Mr. Murdock's house, three doors down from her parents' home. It was a fog-laden afternoon, and very chilly. She felt cold to her bones.

It wasn't nearly dark yet, but a light was shining in the front windows of his house. A desiccated old man, stooped nearly double, answered the door when she was ready to give up. Standing next to him was a huge bulldog. Mr. Murdock nodded to the dog. "I walk him at least six times a day," he said first thing. "Bad bladder," Mr. Murdock added, patting the dog's head. "He needs more potty time than I do." He didn't invite her in, not that she wanted to step into that dark hallway behind him that smelled too much like dog and dirty socks.

"You saw an accident, Mr. Murdock? A man in a car struck a woman?"

"Eh? Oh that. Yes, I did see the whole thing. It happened yesterday afternoon. This real pretty woman I've known by sight for years is standing kind of bent over in the thick oleanders. I start to call out to her, you know, I thought she must have some kind of problem, when she suddenly steps out into the driveway. I hear a car hit her. It was weird. The whole thing was weird. That's what my nephew said too when I called him about it. What do you want, Butchie? You got bladder needs again? All right. Go get your rope. Sorry, little lady, but that's all I know. Either the woman ran out into the car's path on purpose or she didn't, and that makes it an accident, plain and simple."

Sherlock walked slowly back to her rental car. Why had her mother done such a ridiculous thing? Was it really that she wanted more attention from her husband? Maybe that was too simple, but it was a place to start. She hadn't understood her mother for nearly all her life. Why should she begin understanding her now?

Her father came back to the hospital at seven o'clock that evening.

"She's the same," Sherlock said.

He walked to the bed and looked down at his wife.

He said, "Did that old man tell you I didn't try to kill your mother?"

"Yeah, he did. Look, Dad, you know I had to go talk to him, hear everything in his own words."

"You're my kid. I can understand that. I called a new psychiatrist to come talk to your mother tomorrow. I told her what had happened, what you thought. We'll see. I'm glad you didn't think I was stupid enough to try something like that."

"Oh no."

"I've found myself wondering if I could have done it. Maybe, if it had been dark and we'd been in the Andes with no possible witnesses who spoke English."

"You're joking."

"Yes, I'm joking." He looked at his watch. "I've got to be in court early tomorrow. I'll see you at lunchtime, Lacey." He paused in the doorway. "You know, it's easy to fall into certain ways of thinking, of behaving. You know your mother could irritate a saint. We'll see."

She spent the night in her mother's hospital room on a cot an orderly brought in for her. She lay there, listening to her mother breathing, thinking about Dillon, and wondering, always wondering where Marlin was.

She got a call from Dillon at nearly eleven o'clock, which made it two o'clock A.M. his time. She'd called him earlier and gotten his answering machine.

"I was going to leave you be, at least for tonight, but I couldn't. How's your mom?"

"She'll make it. I personally interviewed a witness who told me my mother appeared to be hiding in some bushes, then dashed out when my father was backing out of the driveway. I had a good talk with my dad. He's bringing in a new psychiatrist to see her tomorrow. I mentioned that maybe she was trying to get his attention. Should I have opened my mouth? What do you think?"

"I agree. It sounds like your mother really wants something she's not getting from your father. You're the daughter. Of course you should say what you think. You know, she might really be mentally unstable."

"As my dad said, 'we'll see.'"

"You hanging in there?"

"Yes, don't worry about me. Any word on Marlin Jones?"

"No. It's as though he's disappeared off the face of the earth. Oh yeah, Hannah called me about an hour ago. She wanted to come over and talk. When I said no, she told me how you'd attacked her in the women's room this afternoon. She told me you'd accused her of blackmailing me so I wouldn't fire her. She said you were furious that we'd slept together."

The last thing she needed in this crazy mix was Hannah. "I don't think so, Dillon. But that's a thought. Let me consider it. I don't know, she's pretty strong. It's possible she could take me down."

He grunted. "Yeah, she probably could. Call me at the Bureau tomorrow with an update. Sherlock?"

"Yes?"

"I miss you really bad. I had to go to the gym by myself. It used to be fine—in fact, I used to like going by myself—but now all I could do was one lat pulldown before I was looking around for you."

At least she was smiling when she gently laid the phone in its cradle.

When a shaft of light from the hospital corridor flashed across her face, Sherlock was awake in an instant, not moving, frozen, readying herself. It had to be a nurse, but she knew it wasn't. She smelled Douglas's distinctive cologne, a deep musky scent that was very sexy. She remembered that scent from the age of fifteen when he'd first come into their lives.

She lay very still. She watched him walk slowly to her mother's bed. He stood there for the longest time in the dim light sent in through the window, staring down at her mother.

She saw him lean down and kiss her mother. She heard him say quietly, "Evelyn, why did you do this stupid thing? You know he's a bastard, you know, surely, that he'll always be a bastard. What did you expect to prove by running out like that behind his car?"

Her mother made no sound.

Douglas lightly caressed her face with his cupped palm. Then he straightened and turned. He froze in his tracks, staring down at Sherlock.

"My God, Lacey. What are you doing here?"

"I wanted to stay with my mother," she said, very slowly coming up onto her knees, her back against the wall. She was wearing one of her favorite Lanz flannel nightgowns that came up high on her neck and covered her feet. "Didn't my father tell you I was staying with her? No, I guess not. What are you doing here, Douglas?"

He shrugged. "I was naturally worried about her. I wanted to make sure she was all right. I wanted to see her when I knew your father wouldn't be here."

"Visiting hours were over a long time ago. How did you get in?"

"Not a problem. I know the nurse, Lorette. She let me in. Seeing you is a surprise. I didn't know you'd come. That Marlin Jones jerk is still free. I didn't think you'd ever leave the hunt."

"Why were you kissing my mother?"

"I've known your mother for many years, Lacey. She's a good woman, almost like a mother to me."

"That kiss didn't look at all filial."

He ignored that, saying, "I don't want anything to happen to her, anything more, that is."

"That's hard to believe, Douglas. You were kissing her like she was a lover."

"No, Lacey, you're way off base. Why are you looking toward the door?"

"I'm waiting for Candice to burst in here. She always seems to show up when you're with me."

"I left her sleeping. She isn't coming here." Then he laughed. "But she'll hate herself that she missed such an opportunity. Here you are in your nightgown in the same room with me. Yeah, she'd go wild."

"Well, I'm not up to anything wild tonight. Are you certain she's home asleep?"

"I hope so."

Sherlock stood up, her nightgown like a red-patterned tent around her. There was sweet lace around the wrists and the neck. "I think you should leave now, Douglas. I don't want her disturbed. I need to get some sleep. Oh yes, my father would never hurt her. She ran out behind his car on purpose."

"That makes no sense."

She had to smile at that. It seemed to be everyone's litany recently.

She closed the door after Douglas left. She took a deep breath once she was in the blessed darkness again. She heard her mother's even breathing. She burrowed under the three hospital blankets. It still took her a long time to get warm.

Why had Douglas spoken to her unconscious mother as if she were his lover? Or had she imagined it?

Her head began to pound. She wanted nothing more at the moment than to go home, to Dillon.

33

"I DIDN'T RUN INTO THE driveway. Your father saw me pruning some oleander bushes. He called out to me, told me he wanted to talk to me about something. When I walked onto the driveway, he gunned his car and deliberately ran into me."

Sherlock said very quietly, "Mother, there was a witness. He's an old man who lives down the block from you. He claims you were hiding, then ran out so that Father could run into you."

"Old man Murdock," her mother said, her voice deep with anger. Then she winced at the pain. "That old liar. He wanted me to have an affair with him, years ago, after his poor wife died of breast cancer. I told him where to shove it. So this is his revenge. The malicious old moron."

"It's all right, Mom. Relax. That's better. Breathe deeply. You can push that button if you want pain medication."

"How do you know what to do?"

"When I was hurt, that's what they told me. It helped. Please, Mom, help me understand what this is all about. Why would Dad want to kill you?"

"To get my money, of course, so he can marry that bimbo lawyer clerk of his."

"What money? What clerk? Danny Elbright is his law clerk."

"I don't know her name. She's new, works with Danny. I don't really care."

Judge Sherlock came into the room. "Ah," he said from across the room, "you're awake, Evelyn. How are you feeling?"

In a querulous old-woman's voice, Evelyn Sherlock said,

"What are you doing here? You're always at the courthouse this time of the morning. What do you want, Corman?"

"This isn't exactly a day to have business as usual. I'm here to see how you're doing, naturally."

"I'll live, no thanks to you. I'll be pressing charges, you can count on that. Oh my, my head feels all soft. What's on TV, Lacey? I always watch *Oprah*. Is she on yet?"

"*Oprah* is on in the afternoon," Judge Sherlock said. "Get a grip, Evelyn."

"Oh, then it's *The Price Is Right*. That's a great show. I can guess the amounts of money better than those stupid contestants. Do turn it on, Lacey."

It was down the rabbit hole, Sherlock thought as she switched on the TV, then handed her mother the remote.

"You can leave now, Lacey, I'm not going to die. Your father didn't hit me hard enough. I guess he couldn't build up enough speed to get it done once and for all."

"All right," Sherlock said. She leaned down and kissed her mother's white cheek. "You take it easy, okay?"

"What? Oh yes, certainly. I'll bet that powerboat with all that stuff on it costs exactly thirty-three thousand five hundred dollars."

As Sherlock walked from the room, she heard Bob Barker call out, "It's thirty-four thousand!"

She wasn't aware her father was there until he stepped into the elevator with her.

"I'll see she's well taken care of. I've decided Mrs. Arch isn't keeping good enough control. She never should have let her get away like that. Also, after the new shrink sees her this afternoon, I'll call and let you know what she says. I'll tell you one thing, though. Right now she certainly doesn't sound as if she wants any attention from me. She sounds as if she wants me hung."

"As you said, we'll see." She looked up at her handsome father, at the uncertainty and confusion in his eyes, at that stern set of his jaw. She lightly laid her hand on his forearm. "Take care, Dad. You don't really think she'll try to press charges?"

"Probably not. She'll forget all about it by this afternoon. If she doesn't, the cops will treat her gently and ask me to see that she has better care."

"Dad, does Mother have money of her own?"

"Yes, something in the neighborhood of four hundred thousand. It's safely invested, has been for years. She's never had to touch it. Why do you ask? Oh, I see. Your mother's been claiming I married her for her money again. Not likely, Lacey."

On a hunch, she called San Quentin from the airport. Belinda's father, her mother's first husband, Conal Francis, had been out of jail since the previous Monday. She pressed her forehead against the public phone booth. Where was Belinda's father? Was he as crazy as her father had said he was?

She called Dillon from the plane and got his answering machine. He was probably at the gym. She'd surprise him. She could see him walking through the front door all sweaty and so beautiful she'd have to try to touch all of him at once, which was great fun but impossible. Suddenly, in her mind's eye she saw him and Hannah in the shower. The jealous rage surprised her. She was breathing hard, wanting to yell, but the person seated next to her on the plane probably wouldn't understand. It was in the past. Every woman he'd ever had sex with was in the past, as Bobby Wellman and his yellow Jaguar were in her past. That made her smile.

It was raining hard in Washington, cold, creeping down into the forties, and utterly miserable. She couldn't wait to get home. Home, she thought. It wasn't her own town house, it was Dillon's wonderful house, with the skylights that gave onto heaven. She got into the taxi at the head of the line and gave the black middle-aged driver directions.

"Bad night," the driver said, giving her a huge white-toothed smile in the rearview mirror.

"I'm hoping the night is going to be a lot better than the day was," she said.

"Pretty little gal like you, I hope it's a hot date?"

"Yes, it is," she said, grinning back. "In fact, I'm going to marry him."

"This guy get lucky or what?"

"Oh yes." She leaned back and closed her eyes. When the taxi pulled up in front of Dillon's red brick house, she was asleep. The driver got out of the cab and walked to the front door. When Savich answered, the driver gave him a big grin.

"I've got a nice little present for you, but she's all asleep in the back of my cab. I guess you're her hot date, huh? And the guy who's going to marry her?"

"She told you that, did she? That's a really good sign."

"Women always tell me everything," the driver said, walking back to the taxi.

Savich couldn't wait to get her inside the house.

"Dillon?"

"Yes, it's me. Go back to sleep, Sherlock. You're home now. But I'm not going to let you sleep very long. That all right with you?" He leaned down and kissed her nose.

"Okay," she said, and bit his earlobe.

She giggled. He thought it was the sweetest sound he'd ever heard in his life.

The phone rang as he laid her on the bed.

He sighed and and answered it. She lay on her back, looking over at him, listening to his deep voice, his very short answers. When he hung up the phone, she said, "Have they caught him?"

Savich shook his head. "No, but it might be really soon. That was Jimmy Maitland. A call came through from this woman in southern Ohio claiming to have seen both Marlin and Erasmus in a restaurant off the turnpike. It sounds like it's for real. They're going to check. They'll get back to us when they know one way or the other. Nothing to do now but wait."

"Is this the first time both Erasmus and Marlin have been reported being seen together?"

He nodded as he pulled his navy blue sweater over his head. He smiled at her as he unfastened his jeans.

Sometime later, she whispered in his mouth, "Please sing to me."

His rich baritone filled the air. *"You're my gateway to heaven, all tied up in a bow. Let me at your hinges and I'll oil them really slow."*

The phone rang again. He held her close as he rolled to his side. "Savich here."

"We think it's Erasmus and Marlin," said Jimmy Maitland, more excitement in his voice than Savich had heard in three months. "So it looks like they're in Ohio. I'll get back to you when I hear any more."

"That's a relief," Savich said and slowly hung up the phone. He turned back to her, saw that the sated vague look was long gone now, and there was fear there, haunting fear. "No, no, Sherlock, Maitland thinks it was Erasmus and Marlin. They're way off in Ohio someplace, far away from us. It's okay. They'll catch them." Still, the fear didn't leave her eyes. He said nothing more, just came over her again. He shuddered with the feel of her moving beneath him.

He didn't ease his hold on her until he was certain she was asleep. He kissed her temple. He wondered what had happened in San Francisco. Then he wondered if they'd caught Marlin yet and if they'd dispatched him to hell.

Sherlock was feeling mellow as she sipped Dillon's famous darkly rich coffee. Morning sunlight poured through the kitchen windows. She was leaning against the refrigerator.

Dillon took her cup and kissed her until she was ready to jump on him. Then he gave it back to her. It took another three long drinks of coffee and a distance of three feet from him before she could function again. He grinned at her.

When she had her wits together, finally, she told him about her parents, about Douglas. "Douglas was treating my mother like she was his lover. He kissed her, caressed her face, called her by her first name. I'm not wrong about this even though he denied it, denied it quite believably."

He nearly dropped his spoon. "You're kidding me. No? Well, I guess I shouldn't be surprised. When it comes to your family, I'm willing to believe about anything. Do you think it's possible Douglas was sleeping not only with his wife but also with his wife's mother?"

She took a bite of toast, added another dollop of strawberry spread. "I have no idea. Maybe he wanted all the Sherlock women. After all, he wanted to sleep with me too." She sighed, rubbed her stomach, knew she was going to have to relax or she'd get an ulcer. "It's as if I know them but they're strangers to me in the most basic ways. I found out that Belinda's father, my mother's first husband—his name is Conal Francis—was released from San Quentin a short time ago."

"Interesting. He's the one your father told you tried to kill him? That he was crazy?"

"Yes. My father told me that was why Belinda shouldn't have kids. She had too many crazy genes in her. My father also told me Belinda was already well on her way to being as crazy as her father. I think I'll call the shrinks at San Quentin and see what they have to say about it."

He rose. "Go ahead and call San Quentin, that's a good idea. You want to ride downtown with me?"

Ollie greeted her with a hug and began talking immediately about a string of kidnappings and murders in Missouri. "It's the same perps, that's pretty well established. They kidnap a rich couple's child, get a huge ransom, then kill the kid. Actually, it's likely they kill the kid immediately, then string the parents along. There have been three of them, the most recent one in Hannibal, you know, the birthplace of Mark Twain. These folk are real monsters, Sherlock. They drown the kids in bathtubs, then after they have the ransom, they call the parents and tell them where to get their child."

She felt rage deep inside her. She took a deep breath. After all, monsters were their business. She understood that, she accepted it, and wanted to get them put away, that or get them on death row. But children. That was more than monstrous. Once they had Marlin and Erasmus, she wanted to concentrate on the kidnappers. No, they were murderers, the kidnapping really didn't count.

She went back to her desk and booted up her computer. Dillon had put a lion on her screen, and he roared at her out of the small speakers on either side of the console. She heard two agents shouting at each other. She heard a woman laugh, saw a Dr Pepper can go flying past her desk, heard the agent shout his thanks. She heard the hum of the Xerox, someone cursing the fax machine, heard an agent speak in that deep, rich FBI voice on the phone. Everything was back to normal chaos. Only it wasn't, not for her, at least not yet.

Marlin Jones was still free. Belinda's killer, whoever that was, was still out there. She prayed both Marlin and Erasmus were in Ohio, with the state police getting really close. She hoped the police would take both of them out.

She looked up to see Ollie stretching. "Anything new on Missouri?"

Ollie shook his head. "Nothing, *nada*, zippo. But you know, I got this funny feeling in my gut. I know that we're going to get the perps. Despite MAXINE being really stumped on this one, I know it's going to come to an end soon now."

She sighed. "I hope so." But what she was thinking about was smoke and mirrors. Her life seemed filled with smoke and mirrors. Everyone looked back at her, but their faces weren't real, and she wondered if they were looking at her or at someone they thought was she. No one seemed as he really was. Except for Dillon.

"You haven't called Chico for a karate lesson," Dillon said as he revved up the engine of his 911 after six o'clock that evening in the parking garage.

"Tomorrow. I swear I'll call this madman of yours tomorrow."

"You'll like Chico. He's skinny as a lizard and can take out guys twice his size. It will be good training for you."

"Hey, can he take you out?"

"Are you crazy? Naturally not." He gave her a fat smile. "Chico and I respect each other."

"You going to tromp me into the ground tonight?"

"Sure. Be my pleasure. Let's swing by your place and pack up some more things for you." Actually, he wanted all of her things at his house. He never wanted her to move back to her town house, but he held his tongue. It was too soon.

But it was Sherlock who swung by her own town house, Dillon having gotten a call on his car phone. He dropped her off at home for her car, then headed back to headquarters. "An hour, no longer. There's this senator who wants to stick his nose into the kidnappings in Missouri. I've got to give an update."

"What about Ollie?"

"Mr. Maitland couldn't get hold of him. It's okay. I'll see you at the gym in an hour and a half, tops. You be careful." He kissed her, patted her cheek, and watched her walk to her own car. He watched her lock the car doors, then wave at him.

The night was seamless black, no stars showing, only a sliver of moon. It was cold. Lacey turned on the car heater and the radio to a country-western station. She found herself humming to "Mama, Don't Let Your Babies Grow Up to Be Cowboys."

She'd have to ask Dillon to sing that one to her. Her town house was dark. She frowned. She was certain she'd left on the foyer light that lit up the front-door area. Well, maybe not. It seemed as though she'd been gone for much longer than a week. She supposed she might as well rent the place out, furnished. She'd have to call some Realtors to see how much to ask. Why had Douglas been leaning over her mother, kissing her, talking to her as if she were his lover?

She knew this was one question she'd never be able to ask her mother. And Douglas had denied it was true. She wondered if all families were as odd as hers. No, that wasn't possible. Not all families had had a child murdered.

She wasn't humming anymore when she slid the key into the dead bolt and turned it. She was wishing she were at the gym. She wished he were throwing her to the mat when she turned the lock and pushed the front door open. She felt for the foyer light, flipped it on. Nothing happened.

No wonder. The miserable lightbulb had burned out. It had been one of those suckers guaranteed for seven years. She had replacement lightbulbs in the kitchen. She walked through the arch into the living room and found the light switch.

Nothing happened.

Her breathing hitched. No, that was ridiculous. It had to be the circuit breaker and that was in the utility closet off the kitchen, with more of those seven-year-guaranteed lightbulbs. She walked slowly toward the kitchen, past the dining area, bumping into a chair she'd forgotten about, then felt the cool kitchen tile beneath her feet. She reached automatically for the light switch.

Nothing happened. Of course.

Little light slipped in through the large kitchen window. A black night; that's what it was. Seldom was it so black.

"Technology," she said, making her way across the kitchen. "Miserable, unreliable technology."

"Yeah, ain't it a bitch?"

She froze with terror for a fraction of a second until she realized that she'd been trained not to freeze, that freezing could get you killed, and she whipped around, her fist aimed at the man's throat. But he was shorter than she was used to. Her fist glanced off his cheek. He grunted, then backhanded her, sending her against the kitchen counter. She felt pain surge through her chest. She was reaching for her SIG even as she was falling.

"Don't even think about doing something that stupid," the man said. "It's real dark in here for you but not for me. I've been used to the dark for a real long time. You slide on down to the floor and don't move or else I'll have to blow off that head of yours and all that pretty red hair will get soaked with brains."

He kicked the SIG out of her hand. A sharp kick, a well-aimed kick, a trained kick. She still had her Lady Colt strapped to her ankle. She eased down, slowly, very slowly. A thief, a robber, maybe a rapist. At least he hadn't killed her yet.

"Boy, turn on the lights."

In the next moment the house was flooded with light. She stared at the old man who stood a good three feet away from her, a carving knife held in his right hand. He was well dressed, shaved, clean. He was short and thin, like the knife he was holding.

He was Erasmus Jones.

The boy came into her vision. It was Marlin.

They weren't in Ohio. They were both right there, in her kitchen.

34

"**H**I, MARTY. HOW'S TRICKS?"

Dillon would miss her in another forty minutes, maybe thirty-five minutes. He'd be worried. It would be an unspecified worry, but worry he would. He might wait another five minutes, then he'd come here. She looked from father to son. She smiled, praying that only she realized it was a smile filled with unspoken terror. "Hey, tricks is fine, Marlin. How long have you and your dad been squatters in my house?"

Erasmus Jones answered as he hunkered down to be at her eye level. "Three days now. That's how long it took us to get from Boston to here. We had to be real careful, you know?"

"I would imagine so. Lucky I wasn't here."

"Oh no," Marlin said. "I wanted you to be here. I wanted you, Marty, but you'd gone. Were you with that cop? Savich is his name, right? You sleeping with him?" He said to his father, "He's a big fella, real big, lots of muscles, and he fights mean."

"I bet he ain't as mean as your mama were," Erasmus said and poked the tip of the knife into the sole of Sherlock's shoe. It was so sharp that it sliced through the sole and nicked her foot. She winced, but kept quiet.

"Mama was a bitch, Pa. She was always cussing and back-talking you, always had a bottle in her hand, swigging it even while she was hitting me in the face."

"Yep, Lucile was a mean one. She's dead now, did I tell you that?"

Another rabbit hole, Sherlock thought. Forty minutes, max. Dillon would come over here in no more than forty minutes now. Then what? He wouldn't be expecting trouble; there was no reason for him to. Erasmus and Marlin were supposed to be in Ohio. So he'd think she needed help moving stuff. He'd be vulnerable. She wouldn't let them hurt him. No, she had her Lady Colt. She'd do something. She wouldn't, couldn't, let anything happen to Dillon.

"Ma's dead?" Marlin asked as he sat down on one of Sherlock's kitchen chairs.

"Yeah."

His father was telling him this now?

Marlin said, "No, you didn't tell me that, Pa. What happened?"

"Nothin' much. I carved her up like that Thanksgiving turkey she didn't make me."

"Oh, well, that's all right, then. She deserved it. She never was a good wife or mother."

"Yeah, she was like all those women who walked the walk for you, Marlin. That maze of yours, I sure do like that. You got that from that game we used to play in the desert."

"Yes, Pa."

"Well, we got this gal here now. Let's off her and then get out of here. There's no more food anyways."

"No," Marlin said, and his voice was suddenly different— strong and determined, not like the deferential tone he'd used with his father since she'd been here. "Marty's going to walk the walk. She's got to be punished. She shot me in the belly. It hurt real bad. It still hurts. I got this ugly scar that's all puckered and red. It's her turn now."

Erasmus said, "I want to kill her here, now. It ain't smart to hang around here."

"I know, but I got my maze all fixed up for her. She'll like it. She already knows the drill. Only this time when she hits the center, she'll have a big surprise."

Thirty minutes, no more.

"You fix up another warehouse, Marlin?"

"Hey, Marty, I fixed it up real good. You'll like it. I had lots of time so it's really prime."

"Why would I walk the walk when you get me there, Marlin? I know you'll be at the center waiting to kill me. I'd be a fool to go into the maze."

"Well, you see, Marty, you'll do anything I ask you to. I got myself a little leverage here."

Dillon. No, not Dillon. Who?

"Let me go get my little sweet chops," Erasmus said and rose slowly. He stretched that skinny body of his. His legs were slightly bowed. He was wearing cowboy boots. Without boots he'd be no more than five foot six inches. "You keep a good eye on her, boy. She's tricky. Look at her eyes—lots of tricks buried in there. I bet you the FBI taught her all sorts of things to do to a man."

Marlin calmly pulled a .44 Magnum out of his belt. "I like this better than your FBI gun, Marty, although I'll take it with me, as a souvenir. This baby will blow a foot-wide hole out of your back if I shoot you in the chest. I don't think you would survive that, Marty." He assumed a serious pose, rubbing his chin with his hand. "You're real tough, but you couldn't live through this, could you?"

"No," she said, studying his face, his eyes, trying to figure out what to do. "No one could." Should she try to disarm him now?

It was academic. There was Erasmus in the door. He was grinning. "She gave me a mite of trouble so I had to smash her head." He dragged in Hannah Paisley by the hair. She was wearing a charcoal gray running suit, running shoes on her feet. She was unconscious.

"You know her, don't you, gal? Don't lie to me, I can see it writ all over your face."

"Yes, she's a Special Agent. How did you get her?"

"Easy as skinnin' a skunk. She was out running. I stole her fanny pack, saw she was with the FBI, and took her down. Nary a whimper from her. I'm real pleased you know her, personal like. That's gotta make a difference. You don't want me to kill her, now do you?"

"How did you know that I knew her?" Out of ten thousand FBI agents he had to get Hannah Paisley? No, it was too much of a coincidence.

"Oh, I was watching you come out of that huge ugly Hoover Building. There was this one, standing there, waving at you, but you didn't see her, you kept walking. I knew I had the one I needed right then. Yep, she knew you."

Hannah groaned. Sherlock saw that her hands were lashed together behind her back and her ankles were tied tightly together.

"Don't hurt her. She didn't do anything to you."

Marlin laughed. "No, but I knew you wouldn't cooperate unless we got someone. Pa followed her. He figured she was FBI and he was right. Now, Marty, you ready to come to the warehouse with me and walk the walk?"

Twenty minutes, no more than twenty minutes. There would be no way Dillon would find her if they left, no way at all. She looked around then. They had trashed the kitchen, the living room. He would come in and he would know that she was taken, but he wouldn't know where. For the first time she smelled spoiled food, saw the dishes strewn over the counters and the table. There were a good dozen empty beer cans, some of them on the floor.

"Where is this warehouse, Marlin?"

"Why do you care, Marty? It won't make any difference to you where you croak it."

"Sure it will. Tell me. Oh yes, my name's Sherlock, not Marty. Belinda Madigan was my sister. You having trouble with your memory, Marlin?"

His breathing hitched, his hand jerked up. She didn't drop her eyes from his face.

"Don't piss me off, Marty. You want to know where we're going? Off to that real bad-ass part of Washington between Calvert and Williams Streets. When I was going in and out down there no one even looked at me. They were all dope dealers, addicts, and drunks. Nope, no one cared what I was doing. And you know something else? When they find you, no one will care about that either.

"Every night I got there, I had to kick out the druggies. I'll have to do it one more time. I wonder if they'll report finding you or wait until a cop comes along. Yeah, I'll flush out all the druggies. They're piled high around there, filthy slugs."

"My boy never did drugs," Erasmus said, looking over at Sherlock. She nearly vomited when she saw that he was stroking his gnarled hand over Hannah's breasts, the other hand still tangled in her hair. "Marlin ain't stupid. He only likes gals, too, knows how to use 'em real good. I taught him. Whenever he found his way to the center of the maze I built, why I took him off to Yuma and bought him a whore."

Fifteen minutes.

"I've got to go to the bathroom, Marlin."

"You really gotta pee, gal? You're not shittin' Marlin?"

"I really do. Can I get up? Real slow?"

Marlin nodded. He'd straightened, the gun pointed right at her chest. "I'll go with you, Marty. No, I won't watch you pee, but I'll be right outside the door. You do anything stupid and I'll let my pa cut up that pretty face of yours."

"No, Marlin, I'll cut up this gal's pretty face. First I'll cut off all her hair, scrape my knife over her scalp so she looks like a billiard ball. Then I'll do a picture on her face. You got that, gal?"

"I got it." Ten minutes. Calvert and Williams Streets. She wasn't familiar with them, but Dillon would be.

Her downstairs bathroom was disgusting. It stank of urine, of dirty towels, of dirty underwear, and there were spots on the mirror. "Did anyone ever tell you you were a pig, Marlin?"

She wished she'd kept her mouth closed. He punched her hard in the kidney. The pain sent her to her knees.

"I might be a pig, Marty, but you'll be dead. Not long now and you'll be dead and rotting and my pa and I will be driving into Virginia. There's some real pretty mountains there and lots of places to hide out. Do your business now, Marty. We've got to get out of here. Hey, you gotta pee because you're so scared, right?"

"That's right, Marlin." She closed the door on his grinning face, heard him lean against it, knew he was listening. She knew she didn't have much time.

He banged on the door as she flushed the toilet. "That's long enough, Marty."

When she walked out, he shoved her back in. He looked around. "I'm not the pig. It's my pa. He never learned how to do things 'cause his ma never taught him anything, left him lying in his own puke when he was just a little tyke, made him lie in his own shit when he was older, to punish him. She wasn't nice, my grandma."

"She doesn't sound nice," Sherlock said. "Why'd you come here, Marlin? Why do you want to kill me? It's a really big risk you're taking. Why?"

He looked thoughtful for a long moment, but the gun never wavered from the center of her back. "I knew I had to take you out," he said finally. "No one can beat me and get away with it. I thought and thought about how I could get out of the cage in Boston and then that judge handed me a golden key. Those idiot shrinks were a piece of cake. I acted scared, even cried a little bit. Yes, it was all so easy. There was my pa, sent me a message in prison, and I knew where he was waiting. All I had to do was get to Brainerd, go to the Glover Motel at the western edge of town. There he was, had clothes for me, everything, a car with a full tank of gas. I knew then that I could get you, take you out, and then I'd be free. Actually, it was Pa who hit that FBI guy in Boston, nearly sent him off to hell where he belongs."

"I know. Your pa used your driver's license. We got the license plate."

Marlin wasn't expecting that. "Well, I told Pa to be careful. He was sure he'd knocked the FBI guy from here to next Sunday, but he didn't. He really got the plate, huh? No matter. Everything's back on track now. I wish that the FBI guy had gotten his."

Hannah moaned from the kitchen.

"Now, let me see if you tried to leave any message for that muscle boy you're sleeping with."

She didn't move, barely breathed. And waited. He poked around a bit, then straightened. "You're smart, Marty. You didn't try anything. That's good."

Hannah moaned again. They heard Erasmus say something to her. They heard a sharp cry. He'd hit her again.

"You'll come, won't you, Marty? You'll come to me at the center of the maze? My pa will kill her slow if you refuse. It sounds like he's already got started. You got the picture now, don't you?"

To die for Hannah Paisley, perhaps there was a dose of irony there. No, she'd die anyway. Sherlock seriously doubted that Hannah would survive this either. But Sherlock had no choice, none at all. "I'll come."

Ten minutes.

"Let me see if Hannah's all right."

"A real buddy, is she? That's excellent. No shit from you then, Marty, or Pa will make her real sorry. Then it'll be my turn to make you even sorrier."

"No shit from me, Marlin."

"Ladies shouldn't say that word, Marty."

She wanted to laugh, realized it was hysteria bubbling in her throat, and kept her mouth shut. When she walked into the kitchen, Hannah was sitting on the floor, her back against the wall.

"I'm sorry, Hannah. Are you all right?"

Hannah's eyes weren't focused, but she was trying. She probably had a concussion. "Sherlock, is that you?"

"Yes."

"Where is this place? Who are these animals?"

Erasmus kicked her.

Hannah didn't make a sound, but her body seemed to ripple with the shock of the pain.

"This is my place. These men are Marlin Jones and his father, Erasmus."

She saw that Hannah realized the consequences in that single instant. She also knew she was going to die. Both of them would die. Sherlock saw her trying to loosen the knots on her wrists.

"Gentlemen," Hannah said, looking from one to the other. "Can I have a glass of water?"

"Then you'll probably have to go pee, like Marty here," Marlin said.

"Marty? Her name is Sherlock."

Marlin kicked Hannah, the way his father had. "Shut your mouth. I hate women who haven't got the brains to keep their lips sewn together. I might do that someday. Get myself a little sewing kit. I could use different colored thread for each woman. No water. Let's get out of here. Who knows who's going to show up?"

Five minutes, but it didn't matter now. Sherlock was bound and gagged, lying on her side in the backseat of her own car, a blanket thrown over her. Hannah was behind her in the storage space.

One of them was driving a stolen car she'd seen briefly, a gray Honda Civic. Then she heard her Ford revved up but didn't know which one of them was driving. She guessed they'd leave her Taurus at the warehouse. And why not?

Sherlock closed her eyes and prayed harder than she'd ever prayed in her life. If Marlin left her hands tied behind her, there would be no way she could get to the Lady Colt strapped around her ankle.

Savich stretched his back, then his hamstrings. He heard a woman's voice from the front of the gym and started to call out.

But it wasn't Sherlock.

It had been an hour and twenty minutes. In that instant he knew something was very wrong. He called her house. No answer. He and Quinlan both had this gut thing. Neither of them ever ignored it. He immediately called Jimmy Maitland from his cell phone.

"It's dinnertime, Savich. This better be good."

"There's no word about Marlin Jones, is there?"

"No, none yet. Why?"

"I haven't seen Sherlock in over an hour. She was supposed to meet me at the gym. She hasn't shown. I called her house. No answer. I know that Marlin and his father are here. I know it. I know they've got Sherlock."

"How do you know that? What's going on, Savich?"

"My gut. You've never before mistrusted my gut, sir. Don't mistrust it now. I'm out of here and on my way to her house. She was going there to get more stuff. We made a firm time date. She isn't here. Sherlock's always on time. Something's happened and I know it's Marlin and Erasmus. Put out an APB on her car, Ford Taurus, license SHER 123. Can you get a call out to everyone to look for her?"

"You got it."

Savich was at her house within ten minutes. It was dark. Her car wasn't in the driveway. He prayed he'd been wrong. Maybe she was at his place, maybe she wanted to unpack her stuff before she came to the gym. No, she wouldn't do that. He went to the front door and tried the doorknob.

It opened.

He had his SIG out as he poked the door fully open.

He turned on the light switch. He saw the trashed living room. Furniture overturned, lamps hurled against the wall, her lovely prints slashed, beer cans and empty Chinese cartons and pizza boxes on the floor. One piece of molding cheese pizza lay halfway out of the box onto a lovely Tabriz carpet.

The kitchen was a disaster area. It was weird, but he could smell Sherlock's scent over the stench of rotted food. She'd been here. Recently. Then he saw a fanny pack on the floor under the table. He opened it but saw it wasn't Sherlock's. It was Hannah Paisley's. They had both women. How did they get Hannah? How did they know to get Hannah?

And why had they taken her?

Of course he knew the answer to that. Marlin knew he'd have to have some leverage, something to make Sherlock do what he told her to do. And that would be? To walk the maze, to get to the center, where he'd kill her, to pay her back for scamming him, for shooting him, for beating him.

So he and his father would have taken the women to some warehouse nearby. But where? There were lots of likely places in Washington, D.C. He knew Sherlock would know that he'd realize what had happened. She had to have left him something, if she'd had the chance. He looked around the kitchen but didn't see anything.

He was on her wireless to the cops when he walked into the small bathroom off the downstairs hallway. He nearly gagged at the stench. He pulled open the linen drawers below the sink. Nothing. He pulled aside the shower curtain. There was Sherlock's purse on the floor of the shower stall, open.

"Give me Lieutenant Jacobs, please. I imagine he's gone home. What's his phone number? Listen, this is Dillon Savich, FBI. We've got a real problem here and I need help fast."

Savich was dialing Jacobs's number even as he was bending down to pick up Sherlock's purse. It was a big black leather shoulder bag. He'd kidded her about carrying a full week's change of clothes and running shoes in there.

"Is Lieutenant Jacobs there, please?"

He carefully pulled out each item. It was when he got to her small cosmetic bag that he went slowly. He unzipped it a little bit at a time, holding it upright.

"Is this you, Lewis? Savich here. I've got a huge problem. You know all about Marlin and Erasmus Jones? Well, they're here in Washington and they've got two of my agents—Agent Sherlock and Agent Paisley. Hold a second." Slowly Savich turned the cosmetic bag inside out. There written in eyebrow pencil was: *Calvert & Williams, wareh—*.

She was good. "Lewis, she managed to leave me a message. There's a warehouse at Calvert and Williams. Marlin and his dad have both Agent Sherlock and Agent Paisley. He's going to make her go through a maze, Lewis, and Marlin will be at the center. He'll kill her. Do a silent approach, all right? I'll see you there in ten minutes."

He couldn't believe it. His Porsche wouldn't start. He tried again, then raised the hood. Nothing obvious, not that he was a genius with cars. He cursed, then kicked the right front tire. Then he ran into the street. A motorist nearly ran him down, slammed down on his brakes, and weaved around him. Savich cursed, then stood there, right in the middle, waving his arms.

A taxi pulled up. A grinning black face peered out at him. "Well, if it isn't the lucky man who's going to marry that pretty little gal."

35

T HERE WAS NO TIME. NO TIME
at all.

She didn't want to die, didn't want to lose her life to this
madman who was grinning at her. No, he wasn't mad, he
knew exactly what he was doing, and he knew it was wrong.
He enjoyed it. Remorse was alien to him. Being really human,
in all its complexity and simplicity, was alien to him.

She looked at Hannah, who was standing with her back
against one of Marlin's props, her head down. At first Sherlock thought she was numb with fear, but then she realized
she wasn't terrified senseless, which Marlin and Erasmus
probably thought. No, it was an act. Hannah was getting her
bearings, thinking, figuring odds.

Good. Let them think she was broken. Sherlock called out,
her voice filled with false concern she was sure Hannah would
see right through, "Hannah, are you all right?"

"Yes, but for how long?" Hannah didn't look at her, kept
breathing deeply, staring at the filthy wooden floor. "I don't
suppose there's a chance Savich will get here?"

"I don't know."

"Shut up, both of you bitches!"

"Really nice language from your daddy, Marlin."

"He can say whatever he wants, Marty. You know that.
He's a man."

"Him? A man?" It was Hannah, her voice hoarse because
Erasmus had choked her when she'd tried to get away from
him. "He's a worm, a cowardly worm who raised you to be a
rabid murderer."

Hannah didn't even have time to ready herself before Erasmus hit her hard on the head with the butt of Sherlock's SIG. Sherlock knew she'd lost it. Otherwise she would have forced herself to be silent.

"I'll enjoy cutting her throat," Erasmus said, standing over an unconscious Hannah. She was drawn up in the fetal position. There was a trickle of blood from her nose.

"So you will kill her," Sherlock said, and smiled at Marlin. "I'm not going into your maze. There's no reason to. She isn't leverage. You're going to kill her too. You heard your sweet daddy."

Erasmus raised his hand to strike her, but Marlin grabbed his wrist. "Marty's mine. I'll handle her. Look here, Pa, a little druggie. You want to take care of her?"

A young black girl, dressed in ragged, filthy jeans and an old Washington Redskins jersey, with holes in the elbows, was crouched by the door of the warehouse, her eyes huge, knowing she was in the wrong place and knowing too there was nothing she could do about it. Erasmus walked to the girl, took her by the neck, and shook her like a chicken. Sherlock heard the girl's neck snap. It was unbearable. She closed her eyes but not before she saw Erasmus toss the girl aside like so much garbage.

"I'll see if there are any more scum inside," Erasmus said and slid through the narrow opening into the huge derelict building. The area was godforsaken, bleak, an air of complete hopelessness about it. All the buildings had been abandoned by people who had given up. All were in various stages of dilapidation. There were old tires lying about, cardboard boxes stacked carefully together to cover a homeless person. It was the nation's capital and it looked like the remains of Bosnian cities Sherlock had seen on TV a while back.

Marlin took her chin in his palm and forced her face up. "Guess what, Marty?"

"My name's Sherlock."

"No, you're Marty to me. That was how you came on to me in Boston. That's how you'll go out. Guess what I found?"

She stared at him, mute.

He pulled her Lady Colt out of his pocket. "I remembered this little number. This is the gun you shot me with in Boston.

You were hoping I'd forget, weren't you? You wanted to blast me again, didn't you? Well you aren't going to do anything now. I win, Marty. I win everything."

"You won't win a thing, you slug. I'm not going to walk into your maze."

"What if I promise you I'll let her go?"

She laughed. "Your daddy's the one who's going to kill her, Marlin, not you."

"All right, then. I have another idea." Marlin twisted her chin, then slapped her. "Come on, Marty. Showtime."

Erasmus came out of the warehouse, dragging a ragged old man by his filthy jacket collar. "Just one, Marlin—this poor old coot. He's gone to his reward. I bet he'd thank me for releasing him if he had any breath left."

Erasmus lowered the old man to the rotted wooden planks, then kicked him next to a stack of tires. "Take your girlie, Marlin, and have her walk the walk. I want to get out of this damned city. It's unfriendly, you know? Look around you. People ain't got no pride here. Ain't nothing but devastation. Don't our government have any pride in their capital?"

Marlin smiled down at Sherlock, raised the .44 Magnum, and brought it down on the side of her head. She was hurled into blackness before she hit the ground.

"Now, I've got to do this just so," Marlin said to his father as he leaned down over Hannah. "I can't wait to see her face when she finally comes to the center of the maze, when she finally comes to me."

Four local police cars cruised in silently, all of them parked a good block from the warehouse. Men and women quietly emerged from the cars, Lewis Jacobs bringing them to where Savich had arrived in a taxi, a tall middle-aged black man next to him.

"Jimmy Maitland will be here soon, along with about fifteen Special Agents," Savich said quietly. "Now, here's what we're going to do."

Sherlock awoke slowly, nausea thick in the back of her throat, her head pounding. She tried to raise her head, but the dizziness brought her down. She closed her eyes. Marlin had struck her with a gun over her left ear. Harder this time than in Boston. He'd probably laughed when she was unconscious at his feet. She lay there silently, waiting, swallowing convulsively, praying Dillon had found her message, but knowing in her gut that she had to depend on herself, not on some rescue. Where was Hannah?

It was deathly silent in the huge gloomy warehouse, except for the sound of an occasional scurrying rat. The air was thick and smelled faintly rotten, as if things had died here and been left where they'd fallen. Her nausea increased. She swallowed, willing herself not to vomit. There was a small pool of light in front of her, thanks to Marlin.

There was also a ball of string.

Think, think. He had her gun, both her guns. She looked around very slowly, wondering if he or Erasmus could see her. There was nothing she could see to use as a weapon, nothing at all.

Except the string. She came up slowly onto her knees. She still felt light-headed, but the dizziness was better. A few more moments. At least he'd removed the ropes from her hands and feet. At least she was free.

She heard Marlin's eerie voice coming from out of the darkness. "Hey, you're awake. Good. It took you long enough, but my daddy said I was too excited to be patient. Marty, listen to this."

Hannah's scream ripped through the silence.

"I've got her here, Marty, at the center of the maze. This was a little demonstration. Don't panic on me. I only hurt her a little bit. She must have a real low threshold of pain to scream when I jerked her arm up. Now, if you don't get here, she won't be quite whole really soon. You start moving now or I'll start cutting off her fingers, then her nose, then her toes. Hey, that rhymes. I'm good. Now, I'll work up from there, Marty, and you'll get to hear her scream every time I take my knife to her. I won't cut her tongue out until last. You'll hear everything I do to her. Too, if she only gargles when I cut her, that wouldn't be any fun."

She stood up, the string in her hand. "I'm coming, Marlin. Don't hurt her. You promise?"

There was silence. She knew he was talking to Erasmus.

Good, they were together. She didn't have to worry about Erasmus watching her from a different vantage point.

"She'll be fine as long as I know you're on your way. Move, Marty. That's right. I can see you now."

But he couldn't, at least not all of the time, only at those intervals where he'd managed to place mirrors. She began wrapping the string around her hand. No, this wouldn't do it. She had to double the string and knot it every couple of inches. She redid it as she walked, clumsy at first, gaining in proficiency and speed as she tied it again and again. She was nearly to the beginning of the maze and the string would run out. She prayed she'd have enough.

"I'm coming, Marlin. Don't touch Hannah."

"I'm not hurting her now, Marty, keep walking toward my voice. That's right. You using the string, Marty? That's part of the game, you've got to use the string."

"I'm using the string."

"Good. You're a smart little bitch, aren't you?"

She drew a deep breath, then called out, "Oh yes, Marlin, you fucking little bastard, I'm so smart I'm going to kill you. Count on it. And no one will miss you. Everyone will be glad you're in hell where you belong." She stepped into the maze.

"Don't you talk to my boy like that, gal, or I'll take a whack at you myself after he's through."

She heard them talking but couldn't make out any words.

Marlin said, "I told my daddy I was right. Yes, I was right all along. You have a dirty mouth. He heard that bad word you said. You deserve my kind of punishment." He laughed, a full, deep laugh, but there was something in it, something that sounded vaguely like fear. Was that really fear she heard? She'd hurt him once, surely he hadn't forgotten that, but she couldn't imagine why he'd be even faintly afraid now. She was alone. She didn't have a weapon. Still, she had no other options. She decided to push. "Remember how it felt to have a bullet in your gut, Marlin? Remember all those tubes and needles they stuck into you at the hospital? You even had one in your cock. You remember that? Remember how you lay there whimpering, all gray in the face? You looked so pathetic. You looked like a beat-up little boy. I looked at you and I was really glad I'd shot you. I hoped you'd die, but you didn't. You'll die this time, Marlin. You're a crazy fucker, you know that?"

"I'll pay you back for that, Marty."

"You little bastard, you couldn't pay back anything. You're a coward, Marlin, and you're afraid of me, aren't you? I can hear it in your voice. It's shaking. You're worthless, Marlin, you're nothing but a loser."

"No!" He was heaving now, she could hear him, heaving from rage. "I'll kill you, Marty, and I'll enjoy every minute of it. You deserve to die, more than any of the others."

"Let me take her out, boy."

"No! She's mine, and this one too. I want both of them. You know this other one cusses all the time. Yes, I want both of them. You wait and see how well I slice them up. You'll be proud of me, Pa."

He was screaming and pleading with his father, both at the same time. He was really close to the edge. "I'm the best slicer in the world, not you! I'm the best!"

Sherlock walked very quietly, the knotted string wrapped around her hand. He'd built the maze very well. She hit two dead ends and had to retrace her steps.

She called out, "Marlin, it looks like you finally learned how to build a proper maze. I hit the second dead end. Too bad you're so fucking stupid that your daddy didn't teach you how to build a really good maze way back when you were young. It took you long enough to learn, didn't it, you pathetic little shit?"

"Damn you, bitch, shut up! Don't you talk like that! I know you're doing it on purpose to make me mad, to try to make me lose control, but I won't. I know you don't talk like that all the time. Do you? Damn you, bitch, answer me."

"That's right, you little jerk. It's all for you, Marlin, you miserable stupid fuck."

"Damn you, shut up!"

His voice was trembling. She could imagine him nearly frothing at the mouth with rage. Good.

Her voice rang out cold and calm. "Why the fuck should I?"

"I'll kill you now, Marty. I've got my Magnum right here, all ready to go. You walk faster or Hannah's going to lose her pinky finger."

"I'm coming, Marlin. I told you I would. Unlike you, I keep my word. Only a coward would hurt her and you've been swearing to me you aren't a coward, right?"

He was breathing really hard now. She was close enough to hear his rage, nearly taste it. It smelled sweet, coppery, like blood. "No, I won't hurt her. Not yet anyway. You're first, Marty, you. I want you, then I might be satisfied."

She walked into a narrow pool of light. She carefully held the string at her side. "Where's your daddy, Marlin? Is he lurking around one of the corners of the maze? He's a coward too. You got it all from that precious father of yours, didn't you?"

"I ain't lurking no place, girlie," Erasmus shouted out. "I'm letting my boy do what will make him happy. You do what he wants, and I won't skin you."

"Did you skin your wife, Erasmus? After you slit her throat or before?"

"Ain't none of your business, girlie. You come along now, you hear me? I want to get out of this place, it ain't comfortable. It makes my skin crawl."

"Yes, I hear you." He was on her left, some thirty feet away. Marlin was only about ten to twelve feet away, at about ten o'clock. Imagine anything making Erasmus's skin crawl.

She'd wrapped about six lengths of string around her hand. String, she thought. All she had was a handful of string to take out two killers with three guns. She loosened the string, making it into a large enough circle so she could loop it over Marlin's head. No, it had to be even bigger. It took time.

She felt the bile of terror in her throat and swallowed. She couldn't, wouldn't give up until he killed her. She thought of Dillon. He'd go nuts if Marlin killed her.

He'd already had one woman he loved leave him.

She wasn't about to let Marlin kill her.

36

THE LIGHT WAS STEADY NOW, becoming brighter with each step she took. It was from a narrow beam of light that he'd strung some eight feet overhead. She was nearly to the center of the maze now. She heard Hannah moan. She heard Marlin's breathing. Hannah moaned louder. The moans weren't from pain. Hannah was giving her directions. Both she and Marlin were at about ten o'clock. She could picture him standing there over Hannah, the Magnum in his hand, a big smile on his face. Waiting for her. He couldn't wait. Where was Erasmus? Had he moved at all?

"Hannah? Can you hear me? Are you all right?"

"I'm all right, Sherlock." Then she moaned again, a nice lusty moan. "The bastard kicked me."

"Hang in there, please, hang in there."

And she knew Hannah was thinking frantically. She knew whatever she tried, Hannah would help her if she could.

There was no sound now except for Marlin's jerky deep breathing.

Had Dillon found her message? Had he even gone to her house yet? Of course he had. She swallowed. Nearly there. Nearly to Marlin.

She walked into bright light, two spotlights shining directly into her face. She shaded her eyes with her right hand. In her left hand was the string, ready now, if only he didn't see it, if only she had time and opportunity.

"Hello, Marty," he said, nearly gasping with pleasure. "You're here."

He was standing beside Hannah, his chest puffed out, looking very proud of himself. He looked happy. His eyes were dead, and glittered. He was grinning at her.

She grinned back at him. "Hi, you little pathetic fucker. Have you killed any more women since you escaped from that madhouse in Boston?"

He lurched, as if she'd gut-punched him. "It wasn't a madhouse!"

"Sure it was. It was the state madhouse."

"I was there to talk to some shrinks, nothing else. I was visiting for a little while."

"If that judge hadn't been such an idiot, they'd have you right now in a padded cell. You know what else? They'd shackle your legs together and walk you right out of your padded cell to the electric chair. Then they'd fry you. It will still happen, Marlin. Can you imagine the pain, Marlin?"

"Damn you, shut up! Be quiet! Show some respect for me. I won, damn you, I won! Not you. You're standing there, nothing going for you this time. I'm the big winner. You're nothing, Marty, nothing at all."

"That's right, Marlin, you've won. Even though you haven't had any women walk to the center of your maze since your escape, you've still managed to kill very dangerous and very heavily armed homeless people and teenagers. That's real big of you, Marlin. Real manly. You make me puke, you gutless fuck."

"No, that was my Pa!"

"Same difference. You're his very image."

He was panting now, trying to hold himself back, and she pushed harder. "You know what, Marlin? I once thought you were pretty good-looking. You know what you look like now? You look like you're ready to drip saliva from your mouth. Is that true? Are you ready to froth at the mouth, Marlin? I've never seen a sorrier excuse for a man in my life."

He snapped. He ran at her, the knife raised. Hannah jerked from her left to her right side, whipped up her bound legs and tripped him. He went sprawling, sliding on his stomach almost to Sherlock's feet. She was on him in an instant, looping the thick knotted string around his throat. She had her knee in the small of his back, pulling back on the string, bringing his face off the wooden floor. She knew it was cutting deep into his neck.

"Hannah, where's his gun?"

"Hannah can't get it, Marty."

She turned slowly to see Erasmus holding Hannah's head back at an impossible angle. He had her hair wrapped around his left hand. His right hand held a twelve-inch hunting knife to her throat. "Let my boy go, Marty."

"I will if you release Hannah. Now, Erasmus."

He shook his head slowly. The knife point punched into Hannah's skin. A drop of blood welled up and trickled down to disappear into her running top. Sherlock saw no fear on her face, what she saw was some kind of message in her eyes. What?

"You release him real slow, Marty, or the knife goes all the way in."

"The knife goes all the way in, Erasmus, and your sweet boy here is dead." She twisted the string. Marlin gurgled. His face was darkening. She jerked back his head so his daddy could see him. He thrashed with his arms and legs, but he couldn't dislodge her.

Erasmus screamed, "You bitch! Loosen the knot! You're choking him, he's turning blue!"

Suddenly, Hannah sent her elbow back with all her strength into Erasmus's stomach.

He yelled, loosened his grip just a bit, enough so Hannah could roll away from him and that hunting knife.

There was a single shot, loud and hot in the heavy silent air. Erasmus took the bullet in the middle of his forehead. He stared toward Sherlock, surprise widening his eyes even in his own death. Slowly, so very slowly, he fell forward. Hannah rolled out of his way. He landed on his face. They heard his nose break, loud and obscene in the silence.

"Pa! Damn you, you killed my pa!"

Marlin jerked back, grabbed Sherlock's wrists and pulled her over his head. She landed on her back, winded. Marlin was on her, sitting on her chest, leaning into her face, his knife right under her nose.

"I've got you now, bitch. You killed my pa and now I'll kill you and then that other bitch."

"No, you won't, Marlin. It's too late. The cops are here. One of them shot your pa."

Marlin jerked up and brought down the knife.

"Sherlock, flatten!"

She pressed as hard as she could into the floor even as she heard the gun crack, loud in her ears. It was a very hard shot to make without hitting her in the process. Marlin had been so close to her, they'd had to hold off until they got a better angle. She felt Marlin jerk over her. She knocked him off her, sending him onto his back. The bullet had hit him in the back of the neck.

She rolled and came up on her elbows next to him. He was looking up at her. "Tell me how you did it."

"I left him a message. In my purse, in the floor of the shower. I wrote it in eyebrow pencil on the inside of my makeup bag." She looked up. "Dillon, keep everyone away. I've got to talk to him. Just for a moment."

She leaned right into Marlin's face. "Did you kill Belinda?"

He grinned up at her. Blood flowed from his nose and mouth. But he didn't look to be in any pain.

"Did you, Marlin? Did you kill Belinda?"

"Why should I tell you anything?"

"So I can judge which of you is the better man, Marlin, you or your daddy. I can't really know until you tell me about Belinda. Did you kill her?"

He looked away from her, upward, but the ceiling was dark, impenetrable. What was he looking at? "You want to know what she did, Marty?"

"What did she do?"

"She killed my kid. Oh yeah, she tried to tell me it was a miscarriage, but I know she killed the kid because she was scared it would be crazy even before it was born. She told me about her pa being a loony. That's why she killed my kid. She told me she wanted the kid, she didn't care if it was crazy, but then she went and she killed it."

His eyes were vague and wide. She leaned close. "Listen to me, Marlin. Belinda didn't abort your baby. Her husband hit her and she miscarried. It wasn't her fault. It was Douglas's fault. He probably found out the baby wasn't his and he hit her."

"Oh God, I knew I should have killed that jerk. He couldn't

father a kid, at least he hadn't been able to with her. Belinda told me he had this real low sperm count."

"You knew I was Belinda's sister, didn't you, Marlin?"

"Not at first. I recognized you when you came to the hospital. Then I knew who you were."

"But how?"

"You were a teenager then, but we did have fun with you. I took Belinda to see my maze, made her promise she'd scream and groan and carry on, all for your benefit, to punish you for hiding in the trunk, for spying on us. You really pissed Belinda off."

He closed his eyes and sucked in air. Blood trickled out of his mouth as he whispered, "We drove to the warehouse and Belinda pulled you out of the trunk, told you that you'd been captured and you'd have to walk the walk with her. She told you she was going to die, die because of you, but she prayed that you'd survive. You were sobbing and pleading with me, but Belinda pulled you into the warehouse and kept you with her. She screamed real good for you, then she even let me pretend to knife her when you got to the center of the maze, and you saw it all. You collapsed then. Nobody touched you. You fell over. Belinda got scared but I told her you were a nosy teenager and you'd get over it. When we got back to Belinda's house, you were still unconscious.

"Belinda told me later you never remembered a thing. She felt guilty about doing that to you. Even though you were a sneak, she loved you. She realized you admired Douglas and were afraid she'd leave him for me. But then she killed my kid. Then I had to kill her. I had no choice at all. She had to die. She betrayed me."

"It was a miscarriage. You killed her and she didn't deserve it. You made a big mistake, Marlin."

"I believed she'd betrayed me. I had to kill her but I didn't really want to."

"She didn't betray you."

He opened his mouth again and a fountain of blood spurted out. Blood flowed from his nose.

Sherlock positioned his head back, then leaned really close to his face. "It's over now, Marlin. You've destroyed quite enough. Yes, Marlin, die now."

He tried to raise his hand, but couldn't. He whispered, his voice liquid with his blood, "You sure are pretty, Marty. Not as pretty as Belinda, but still pretty."

His head fell to the side, his eyes still open, a small smile on his mouth.

She looked up to see Dillon standing there, not two feet away from them. There were at least twenty other police officers and special agents in a circle around the center of the maze. No one was moving. No one said a word.

She smiled up at him. "No more questions. No more mysteries. He killed Belinda. He told me so and he told me why." All this time—seven long years—she'd driven herself, felt consumed with guilt. All this time she hadn't remembered that Belinda had forced her into Marlin's maze.

She couldn't dredge up a single memory of that night, even after being told what had happened. She wondered if she'd ever remember, even under hypnosis. Well, it didn't matter. Belinda had been dead for seven years. Her murderer was dead. Sherlock's life was her own again. And she had Dillon. She had a future.

"Yes," Dillon said. "We all heard him confess. It's over, Sherlock."

"Who shot Marlin?"

A grizzled old cop raised his hand. "I'm sorry I had to wait so long but I couldn't get a clean shot."

"You did perfectly." She looked at Hannah. "Are you all right?"

"I'm fine now." She was standing beside Dillon, leaning against him.

Sherlock looked at her. "Thanks for tripping Marlin. That was really well done. I wasn't quite sure how to get him low enough to loop him. I knew you'd be ready. You'd best stand up straight now, Hannah. I don't want you leaning against Dillon ever again. You got me?"

Hannah laughed, a raw ugly sound that was quite beautiful. "I hear you, Sherlock. I hear you really well. I thought you might be mean once it occurred to you. Good going."

Sherlock slowly stood up. Marlin's blood was all over her. She looked around at the circle of faces.

She was alive.

She gave them all a huge smile. "Thank you all for saving our lives. Mr. Maitland, sir, we finally got him."

"No shit, Sherlock," Jimmy Maitland said, then punched Lewis Jacobs and laughed. Soon everyone was laughing, even as they held their weapons in their hands, their relief, their triumph, made them shout with laughter.

Jimmy Maitland said, "I wanted to say that since I first saw your name among the new trainees. I love it. Does anyone know where that line's from?"

37

D R. LAUREN BOWERS SAID
very quietly, "Lacey, do you remember getting into the trunk
of Marlin's car?"

Sherlock moaned, her head turning from side to side.

"It's all right. I'm here. Dillon is here. You're safe. This was
a long time ago. Marlin's dead. He can't hurt you. You're remembering this for you, Lacey. Now, open your mind. Relax.
Did you get into the trunk?"

"Yes. I wanted to be sure that Belinda was betraying Douglas. I'd overheard her talking to him an hour before. I heard
them make a date. I followed her and this guy. I didn't know
she knew I was there. I heard her talking to Marlin but I
couldn't make out what they were saying. When we got to the
warehouse and they dragged me out of the trunk, I'd never
been so terrified in my life. Then Marlin made me walk to the
center of the maze with Belinda.

"I believed she was as terrified as I was, but she wasn't, at
least she wasn't that night. But I believed she was. I walked
every step beside her. Once she even handed me the string.
Every few feet Marlin would call out to us, tell Belinda how
he'd have to punish her if she didn't get to the center of the
maze. I remember being so afraid, feeling so helpless."

"Yes, that's all right, Lacey. You were only nineteen. What
happened next?"

"When we finally got to the center of the maze, Marlin was
there and he was smiling. He smiled even when I thought he
knifed Belinda. I thought he'd kill me next. I can remember

screaming, running to where Belinda was lying. The horror of it just shut me down. That's all I remember."

"And you refused to remember it later," Dr. Lauren Bowers said to Savich. "Anything else?"

"Did Marlin tell Belinda he had to punish her because she cursed too much? Because she bad-mouthed her husband?"

"I think so. Wait, yes, he did."

"I think we know everything she needs to let go of the past." Dillon was silent a moment, then he said quietly, "Before you bring her back, ask her what she wanted to do with her life before Belinda's murder. Oh yes, tell her not to remember your question or her answer."

When Sherlock awoke she looked at Dillon and said, "It was there all the time, locked in my brain. I guess that's why I had the horrible nightmares for months and months after Belinda's murder, why I was terrified that someone would get to me and murder me. That's why I had the nightmare at your house, Dillon. It was coming too close. The dream helped me keep it under wraps."

Savich asked her later as they walked to the car, "Will you tell Douglas Belinda did have an affair with Marlin, that it was his child she carried?"

"I think he already knew. I don't think he knew it was Marlin, but he sure had to know that it wasn't his kid.

"Belinda wouldn't have ever had an abortion. She wanted that baby. Yes, Douglas must have known he had a low sperm count, even then he must have known. And that's why he hit her, he was furious."

"Yet he married Candice when she told him she was pregnant. Guess he wanted to believe that despite a low sperm count, he'd scored. Who knows? Now maybe he and Candice have a good shot at making it. If he can't sire a kid and she doesn't want one, well, then, all problems are solved."

"Now that I can remember, I can see that Belinda's life was out of control. I don't think she was difficult, like our mother, which is what my father told me, but she was over the edge. And I was a bratty teenager, bugging her, spying on her."

"Yes, you're probably right. And that's the answer to the differences Wild Ralph York found in all the physical comparisons he did of the murders. Marlin killed Belinda for different reasons and the differences show up in how he built the props. You know something else, Sherlock?"

She cocked her head to the side in that unique way she had. He patted her cheek. "It's all over now. Every shred of it, every scintilla. There'll be the media, but you can handle that. Jimmy Maitland will try to protect you from the vultures as much as he can. Oh yeah, there's one other detail." He paused a moment, frowning down at his shoes. "Hannah hired a hood, one of her informants, to go after you in that car, and the same guy broke into your house. She claims he didn't follow orders. She never told him to rape you, only scare you. She says she's really sorry, Sherlock, claims she never meant to hurt you. She's been asked to leave the Bureau. It's up to you if you want her prosecuted."

"Did she tell you why she did it?"

"She claims she lost it. She was crazy jealous. She thought she could scare you off, make you pack up and go back to California."

"If we get the guy she hired, then she'd have to take a fall too, wouldn't she?"

He nodded, then said, "Yes. If they catch the guy, she'd be prosecuted."

"Let me think about it."

He helped her into his Porsche, then walked around to the driver's side. He gave the left front tire a good kick. "I can't believe it wouldn't start that night. If Luke hadn't come along, we might have been in deep trouble."

"Luke's coming to the wedding?"

"Oh yes." He leaned over and kissed her. "Fasten your seat belt. I'm feeling like a wild and crazy guy."

"I'm feeling kind of wild and crazy too. Tell you what. Why don't we go home and watch old movies and eat popcorn?"

"Why don't we go home and make our own movies? Popcorn is optional."

"But you don't have a movie camera, do you?"

"Let's call this a dress rehearsal."

She gave him a slow, sweet smile. "You promise to make me a star?"

EPILOGUE

"I DON'T BELIEVE THIS," SHERlock said as she took a glass of chardonnay from Fuzz, the bartender.

"He never told you, never let on?" Sally Quinlan asked, saluting her with her own glass of chardonnay.

"Never a word. Sure, he would sing me country-and-western songs. But this? I had no idea. Doesn't he look beautiful up there, wearing those boots and that belt with the silver buckle?"

The two women sat back as Ms. Lily, draped in a white silk dress that made her look as epic as Cleopatra, said from the small square stage, "Now listen up, brothers and sisters, even you yahoos we've got here tonight. I've got a special treat for you. We finally got our Savich back. He and Quinlan are going to play for us. Take it away, boys."

"This ought to be great," said Marvin, the bouncer, at Sherlock's shoulder. "You sit back and enjoy, Chicky."

Dillon's beautiful baritone filled the smoky bar, his guitar a mellow background, Quinlan's sax running a harmony with the melody. His voice was deep and rich and sexy, carrying clearly to every darkened corner of the club.

What's a man without love?
What's his night without passion?
What's his morning without her smile?
What's his day without her in his mind?

Bring her love to my nights.
Bring her smile to my mornings.

Bring her mind to fill my days.
Just bring her back to me.

What's a man without his mate?
What's his life without her laughter?
What's his soul without her joy?
What's a man without his mate?

Bring her love to my nights.
Bring her smile to my mornings.
Bring her joy to my days.
Just bring her back to me.

Sherlock was crying. She hadn't meant to, didn't even realize she was doing it. She didn't make a sound, let the tears
gather and trickle down her cheeks. When the sax and guitar
faded out, there was absolute silence in the Bonhomie Club.
A woman sighed. A man said, "Ah, shit."

Then the applause came on, really soft and light at first,
then gathering momentum. The women were clapping louder
than the men.

"It's his cute butt," Ms. Lily said, leaning over to pat Sherlock. "Well, actually, it's both their cute butts. Now, little gal,
when are you and my Savich going to get married? I don't allow any gal shacking up with him. He's innocent. I don't want
him taken advantage of, you got me?"

"You'll get the invitation next week, Ms. Lily."

"Good. Maybe Fuzz will bring another bottle of chardonnay that has a real live cork, like he did for Sally and Quinlan. Your Dillon's real talented, honey. You let him sing
to you and bring him down here once a week. It's good for
my soul to hear him wail out his songs. Also, no crooks dare
come near the club when the two supercops are playing
here.

"Now he's looking at you and he's got that wicked smile on
his face. Imagine an FBI agent who could smile at a woman
like that. Goes to show you, doesn't it?

"Well, I'm off to win myself some money in a little poker
game. Don't tell my boys about it, will you? Their cop genes

might get scrambled and we don't want them to feel like they're in any moral dilemma."

Quinlan said from the stage, "Savich is going to get himself married, like I did. It's about time. Now, we have this song for you that celebrates his short number of bachelor days left. It's called 'Love Surfin'.'"

> Moved myself to the bright blue sea.
> Knew the change would be good for me.
> Made enough money in the old rat race,
> Sure to die if I kept my pace.
> Now I'm lying in the warm, soft sand.
> Checking all the girls showing lots of tan.
> All these girls—what's a guy to do?
> I want them all, think I'll surf right through.

> Going love surfin',
> Gonna love them all.
> Love surfin',
> Heading for a fall.
> Love surfin',
> Such a greedy man.
> Love surfin',
> Getting all I can.

Sherlock laughed so hard that when she threw her purse at him, it bounced off Quinlan instead.

Ms. Lily was standing outside of her open office door. She yelled out, "You taking your life in your hands, Savich, what with your chicky being an FBI agent."

Savich beamed at Sherlock. He said into the mike, "My sister wrote that one. I just came up with the music."

"I'll be speaking to your sister," Sherlock called out.

"I heard you got an offer on your town house."

"Yes. A very good offer. It's a done deal. I'm here to stay now, Dillon."

"Good. Let's get married on Friday."

"That would be nice but I don't think we've got the time to

pull it off. How about next month? I promised Ms. Lily that she'd get an invitation. Actually I told her she'd get one next week. Also, my friend MacDougal from the Academy is back from the desert. I want him to come."

"You mean a big wedding? All my family? Your family? Even Douglas and Candice? Even your mother and father and the BMW? A ton of people? All with fistfuls of rice?"

"I guess we have to. You once told me that family was family and there was nothing you could do about it. You made the best of it and went about your business. Hopefully Mom and Dad will try to act normal for the day; hopefully Douglas won't start screaming at Candice and then go slaver over my mother. Oh yeah, there's Conal Francis, Belinda's father, my mother's first husband. He's called my mother. My father is livid."

"Families are grand. Any idea what's going to happen there?"

"Not a clue, but it should be fun to see it played out. I don't think I'll invite him, though. My shot at trying to keep the peace. You know, Sally Quinlan said a big wedding was great sport. You don't want to?"

"Let's do it." He kissed her nose, then her chin.

"We don't have to worry about the BMW. Dad bought a Jaguar, fire-engine red. He said even Mom on her worst days couldn't possibly think he'd want to hit her driving that beauty. He laughed then. He said her new shrink is making progress. He's even had sessions with her. Also, Mom's on some new medication."

She kissed his shoulder.

"Oh yeah, I've got another piece of good news for you. They caught the guys who were murdering those abducted kids in Missouri. Ollie's gut was right. It happened really fast. Turns out that it was three young males, all twenty-one, who were reported to a local FBI agent by one of the girlfriends who was angry because her boyfriend kicked her out for another babe." He laughed. "I heard that they caught up with the girlfriend. She'd skipped bail and took off for Mexico City with all the money."

She laughed with him. "I'll bet Ollie is pleased."

"Yep, but he wanted to be the one to make the arrest. Oh yeah," he added, raising his face above hers, "your wedding present from me is arriving tomorrow. You took the day off to see your doc so I set up the delivery."

She grabbed his arms, hugged him, then shook him. "What is it? Tell me, Dillon, what did you get me?"

"I ain't talkin', honey. But I sure want to hear something out of you when I come in tomorrow night."

"You won't give me a hint?"

"Not a single one. I want you to wallow in anticipation, Sherlock."

She sighed, punched his arm. "All right, but I'll probably be too excited with all this anticipation to sleep. Would you sing me one line?"

He blinked, then raised his head and sang, *"I don't know nothin' better than a spur that's got its boot."*

"Not enough. More."

He kissed her ear, then her throat. *"I don't know nothin' better than a barb that's got its wire."*

She laughed and snuggled closer. "And the last line?"

"No, I don't know nothin' better than a man who's got his mate." He kissed her mouth. "No, my sister didn't write that one, I did. You like that? You're not putting me on, are you? You appreciate the finer points of my music?"

"Oh yes," she said. "Oh yes."

"I wrote it for you."

She gave him a radiant smile. "I thought of another verse."

An eyebrow went up.

She sang in an easy western twang, *"I don't know nothin' better than a poke that's got his cow."*

"A team," he said. "We make a great team."

He stroked his fingers over her soft skin. He began kissing her and didn't stop for a very long time. When he was finally on the edge of sleep, he wondered what she'd play for him first on the new Steinway grand piano that was being delivered tomorrow.

Turn the page for a glimpse of
Catherine Coulter's novel . . .

DOUBLE TAKE

Now available from Jove Books

San Francisco
Thursday Night

J ULIA WAS WHISTLING. SHE
was happy, she realized, actually happy, for the first time in
what seemed like forever. The cops had finally given up, the
media had gone on to new, more titillating stories to keep
their ratings up. And the soulless paparazzi who lurked behind bushes, cars, and trees, one of them even crouched down
behind a garbage can, trying to catch her—what?—meeting a
lover so they could make a buck selling a photo to the *National Enquirer*? Or maybe writing a murder confession on a
tree trunk? They'd moved on after six endless months, focusing their stalking cameras back on movie stars and entertain-
ers who were a lot more interesting than she was. Fact was, it
was her husband, Dr. August Ransom, who'd been the magnet
for the media, not she. She'd been only a temporary diversion,
just the black widow who'd probably gotten away with murdering a very famous man and medium, a man who spoke to
dead people.

Free, at last I'm free.

She didn't know how far she'd walked from her home in
Pacific Heights, but now she found herself strolling down
Pier 39 on the bay, that purest of tourist attractions, with its
shops and clever white-faced mimes and resident seals, all
just spitting distance from Fisherman's Wharf. She'd stopped
at the to-die-for fudge store, and now stood by the railing at
the western side of Pier 39, chewing slowly on her precious
piece of walnut fudge, watching the dozens of obese seals

stretched out on flat wooden barges beside the pier. She heard the sounds of people talking around her, laughing, joking around, arguing, parents threatening or bribing their kids, all of it sounding so normal—it felt wonderful. In April, in San Francisco, it wasn't the April showers that brought the May flowers, it was the lovely webby fog that rolled through the Golden Gate Bridge. The amazing thing was the air even had a special April fog smell—fresh and new and tangy, a bit damp, with a bit of a bite.

She wandered to the end of the pier and looked across the water toward Alcatraz, which was not that far away, really, but the swim could kill you, either the vicious currents or the icy water.

She turned and leaned her elbows on the railing, watching the people hungrily. There weren't that many who wandered down to the very end of the pier. She watched the lights begin to come on. It was cooling down fast, but she didn't feel cold in her funky leather jacket. She'd found the jacket at a garage sale in Boston when she was in college, and it was still her favorite. August had looked both sour and amused when she'd worn that jacket. Because she didn't want to hurt his feelings, she never told him that wearing the jacket made her feel like the young Julia again—buoyant, in both her heart and spirit. But August wasn't here now, and she felt so lighthearted and young in that moment, it was as if she'd float right off the thick wooden planks.

She was unaware of how much time passed, but suddenly there was more silence than sound around her, and all the lights were on. The few tourists who hadn't returned to their hotels for the night had entered one of the half-dozen nearby restaurants for dinner. She looked down at her watch—nearly seven-thirty. She remembered she had a dinner date at eight at the Fountain Club with Wallace Tammerlane, a name she knew he'd made up when he'd decided to go into the psychic business thirty years before. He'd been a longtime friend of August's, had told her countless times since her husband's death that August had been welcomed into *The Bliss*, that August actually didn't know who'd murdered him, nor did he particularly care. He was now happy, and he would always look out for her.

Julia had accepted his words. After all, Wallace was August's friend, as legitimate as her husband. But she knew August had scoffed at many of those so-called psychic mediums, shaken his head in disgust at their antics, even as he praised their showmanship. What did she believe? Like many people, Julia wanted to believe there were certain special people who could speak to the dead. She believed to her soul that August was one of them, but there were very few like him. She'd seen and met so many of the fakes during her years with August. Even though she'd said nothing, it seemed to her that, according to them, any loved ones who died, no matter the circumstances of their passing, were always blissfully happy in the afterlife, always content and at peace, even reunited with their long-dead pets. But she couldn't help but wonder if August really was happy in *The Bliss,* wonder if he didn't want the person who'd murdered him to pay. Who wouldn't? She did. She'd asked his friends and colleagues in the psychic medium world if they could discover who had killed him, but evidently none of them was possessed of that special gift. This lack of vision was unfortunate, especially for Julia, since the police had fastened their eyes on her and looked nowhere else, at least as far as she could tell.

She didn't know if August had been blessed with that particular gift. TV shows had psychics who could picture murderers, even feel them, see how they killed and who they killed, and who could help track them down. And there were even mediums who, in addition to being psychic, could also speak with the dead. Were any of these people for real? She didn't know.

Who killed you, August, who? And why? That was still the question always in her mind—why?

There was August's lawyer, Zion Leftwitz, who'd called her after her husband's death. August's estate, he'd said on her machine, it was very important, as were her responsibilities to that estate, an estate she knew now, that wasn't all that substantial.

Obligations, she thought, always there, at least eighty percent of life.

She really didn't want to have dinner with Wallace, didn't want to hear his comforting words, hear yet again that August was at peace. Then she'd inevitably hear about Wallace's latest triumph, perhaps how he'd contacted the mayor's long-dead grandfather. She knew all the way to her boot heels he'd seriously dent her euphoria. And it also meant taking a taxi back home. She had to leave this magic place, she had to hurry.

"Excuse me, ma'am. That's Alcatraz out there, isn't it?"

She turned to see a tall black man, firm-jawed, wearing glasses, a long belted coat, standing close, smiling down at her.

She smiled up at him. "Yes, it is."

"I'm going to visit tomorrow. But tonight—do you know when the next ferry leaves for Sausalito?"

"No, but it's never long between runs. The schedule is on the side of the building over there, not five minutes from Pier 39—" As she turned slightly to point, he smashed his fist into her jaw. The force of the blow knocked her back against the wooden railing. She saw a bright burst of lights before her eyes, then she saw the flash of something silver in his hand, something sharp—dear God, a knife. Why? But words froze in her throat in a thick veil of terror. All her focus was on that silver knifepoint.

She heard a man shout, then heard, "FBI! Stop now, back away from her, or I'll shoot!"

The man with the knife froze an instant, then cursed. He hefted her up and threw her over the railing into the bay. She splashed into the icy water and rolled over the mess of black rocks that stabbed her like stiletto blades. She tried to struggle, but knew in a flicker of consciousness that she wasn't going to escape this, that she was going to fall and fall—was that a seal honking? Was that someone shouting? It didn't matter because everything was going black as her body settled into the jumbled rocks at the bottom of the bay, the water smoothing over her. Her last thought, really more an echo, was that she wouldn't ever get to be happy again.

Connect with Berkley Publishing Online!

For sneak peeks into the newest releases, news on all your favorite authors, book giveaways, and a central place to connect with fellow fans—

"Like" and follow Berkley Publishing!

facebook.com/BerkleyPub
twitter.com/BerkleyPub
instagram.com/BerkleyPub

Penguin
Random
House